Addiction

A Novel by Lennard Carless

Published by Blackbarn Books

First published 2015 by Blackbarn Books, Usk, Monmouthshire, UK.

Website: http://www.blackbarnbooks.co.uk
Email: blackbarnbooks@aol.com

ISBN 978-1-910244-01-2

One

As he closed his front door he walked straight into the sleety rain. He could see his car windows were already iced up, not white, but round beads like little gobs of glass. Another cold night in a house he found hard to keep warm.

It was eight a.m. and barely daylight this January morning. At least it was Friday and a great weekend in prospect especially if his neighbour had done what he'd asked of her. Or rather paid her for.

There were three houses in this rural terrace. He was at one end, she at the other and the Smiths in between on holiday, skiing. You could ski here, he'd thought more than once. He had a clear view of the snow on the mountains to the west and to the north. Monmouthshire in the grip of another arctic winter.

He skidded to the front of her house and then edged past her car and up the slippery slope to her front door. He banged on it. She was up. He could see a light.

'I'm not bloody dressed yet,' she moaned at him as she just about appeared in the doorway, pulling her dressing gown with 'Dad' on the breast pocket more tightly to her bosom. He was not at all stirred by her state of undress.

'Have you got it?'

She looked particularly peeved at his question, as if it really disappointed her. She turned, leaving the door ajar enough for him to get in.

Her house was as cold as his and smelled of dog.

'Here.'

She'd retrieved a single sheet of A4 and thrust it into his hand as he entered the lounge room behind her.

Eagerly he took it from her and scanned the list of names it contained. Two names were ringed in black.

'Sister Eve and Sister Ella,' he read. 'Is that their nom d'amour this weekend?' Now he smiled, followed by a deep-throated chuckle. 'It's going to be a great time for all concerned, starting tomorrow. Are you going?'

'I work at Cottel Court, what do you think.'

Sad cow! He'd make her day. He leaned forward and planted his lips on each cheek.

Her hands dropped and the unbelted gown flopped open. He was excited, not by her, by the prospect of the coming weekend.

'It's going to be one big shagathon.' He was hyper. 'You should try it.'

He was thinking that judging by the state of her she wouldn't even get the attention of a blind man with no sense of smell unless she could pin the geriatric in his wheelchair. He smiled though. He may need her services again. 'Thanks for this.'

She watched him go, the poor bastard. He thought he was going to surprise those two girls but they were going to surprise him. He'd paid to see their names; they'd paid her to make sure that he did.

Shame he was such an arsehole. She could quite fancy him. She felt sorry for him.

Two

Seventy year old Jared Edwards and his sixty-nine year old wife Margaret took up their positions on the town side of the bridge over the River Usk in the small town of Usk in the heart of Monmouthshire. They had been out all afternoon, well wrapped up against a freshening wind coming down the Usk valley from the north, bringing with it the rawness of the Brecon Beacons. The overnight rain that had fallen as snow on the mountains had cleared throughout this last Friday in January, turning brighter but colder. Gloves were an essential part of their protection but Jared found they didn't lend themselves to easy operation of the camera.

It had been quiet, hardly any overweight lorries going through the town. They'd taken two photographs all shift and one of those lorries turned out to be legal, making a delivery to the steel-buildings fabricator behind the petrol station. Jared had photographed its progress down Bridge Street and then Margaret had followed it over the bridge to see where it was going. It turned left but she reported back to her husband that the big articulated vehicle had clipped the wall of the 18th century bridge. The far left-hand corner had a history of repeated hits, dislodging stones, sometimes within days of the last repair work.

Jared barked out an order for her to record all of it so she dragged off her right glove with vice-like teeth and pulled out her notebook with pencil attached. 'Ja wohl, mein obersturmerbannführer,' she mouthed behind her husband's back. His black leather jacket and trilby hat gave him a well-fitting Gestapo appearance.

The other lorry had been Slovakian and had gone right at the junction on the other side of the bridge heading for Pontypool or Cwmbran. Illegal, but she'd already logged that one.

Jared and Margaret were lead vigilantes of the No Lorries Through Usk campaign, set up to gather facts to prove that vehicles over 7.5 tonnes were using the town as an illegal shortcut. The committee had decided to have people on the streets every day to take photographs and had set up a website to publish them to either shame the individuals and their companies or shame the authorities into doing something more positive to stop the abuse of the law. Anyway, it was evidence.

Jared was getting chilled, probably Margaret too if he'd cared to consider her. He stamped his feet and Margaret shook as she looked over the parapet of the bridge and down at the cold waters of the river, shivering in unnecessary sympathy for the ducks and two swans swimming there. The promised warmth of a cup of coffee and toasted teacakes in café La Cantina was becoming hard to ignore.

A car, a Peugeot estate, jerked to a halt, almost level with Jared. It was indicating to turn right, down New Market Street. Another vehicle, a blue Saab convertible, was waiting to turn right out of the same street. The male at the wheel was fretfully eying the driver of the Peugeot, wanting to be allowed out first.

Jared took in the scene and his mouth dropped open in disbelief.

He saw a woman driver in the Peugeot, a teenage child in the passenger seat and two more children in the back. The car was waiting for two vans and a bus to go by in the opposite direction.

He couldn't believe it. The woman had one hand on the steering wheel and the other one clamped to her ear where she held a mobile phone into which she was talking and laughing.

He called to his wife. 'Margaret, can you see this?'

She turned to ask what but Jared was raising the camera and aiming. It was purely coincidental that he got a clean sight of the Saab and its driver. He snapped off several shots. The teenager in the front was startled by the flash and looked at Jared, saying something to the woman who heard nothing except the voice on the other end of her mobile. The man in the Saab saw the first flash of the camera too and ducked his head down, unnecessarily as it happened because two vans and a bus shielded him from Jared's successive shots.

The traffic cleared and the Peugeot drove off. The Saab waited momentarily before exiting with a squeal of tyres.

'What was it?' asked Margaret, composing herself after the shock of noise from the Saab.

'That driver, woman! ' Jared gesticulated impatiently with his camera, at the same time checking the images. 'Didn't you see it, for God's sake? An idiot woman, car full of children and she was driving with one-hand. She was on the bloody phone.'

'O,' uttered Margaret, none the wiser. 'How was I supposed to see that from there?'

'Bloody obvious!'

He nodded contentedly, happy with the images. They illustrated a selfish stupidity that he could not fathom. Such people! Such people deserved all they got by way of retribution.

Thus came to Jared Edwards the germ of a new campaign. Why had it not come to him before? Every day of the week there were ample miscreants who, unlike the juggernaut drivers taking short cuts, posed a much more real threat to life and limb. And surely the police and the courts would deal with such law breakers with more fervour than they had showed so far with illegal HGVs.

What he didn't know and couldn't know was that the most significant photo he would take of mobile phone usage in a vehicle was that very first one.

George Medlyn knew he was driving too fast through Usk but he wanted to get out of the town as fast as possible. Dumb really but that flash of the camera back there at the junction had got to him. It was only when the traffic had cleared and he got a good look across the road that he realised that the old guy with the camera was actually interested in the car with the woman in it.

Nerves; that's all it was.

Usk was soon left behind him. He had tried to memorise the route. The map was in the brown reinforced envelope in which it had come. He glanced down to the passenger seat. It was there, lying address side up, the Recorded Delivery label prominent underneath the logo 'Co♀Co' on a rural landscape background.

He turned left. The road bent left then right opening onto a smooth-tarmacked straight stretch that invited the foot on the throttle to go down to the floor. Ahead he saw a crossroads and the map in his mind went blank. He slowed and pulled left into a deep gateway in front of a large metal gate that bore the words 'Usk Showground'.

He picked up the envelope and the contents slid out: the letter of welcome, the ticket for entry; euphemistic confirmation of the activities he had selected; a copy of the mutual confidentiality and copyright agreement; a glossy leaflet detailing future event dates; some third party flyers of delights that might appeal to his particular likes; the map to Cottel Court, which he remembered was described as the "ideal secluded and atmospheric venue for a fantastic fantasy weekend".

He read the map and directions then he scanned the other literature. His nerves ebbed away, replaced by a flood of excited anticipation. He had waited all of his forty-five years and the twenty years of a disappointing marriage for this, the first of many visits he hoped.

Three

'Good afternoon, Mr. Redland,' came the loud greeting from the surgery receptionist.

'Good afternoon....Megan.' He knew her name but deliberately read the tag on her left breast, which identified her as Meg.

'How are you today?' came the old redundant question. Meg Ryan - he liked to call her Megan to avoid any possible confusion with her famous much slimmer namesake - continued without expecting a reply.

He watched her over-active mouth as she spoke without listening. He would have preferred one of her colleagues, Linda or Emma, to attend to him. They were marginally more agreeable although Linda, regardless of the weather outside, always strutted around in a dress like something out of Jane Austin; bosoms alarmingly to the fore. Not good, he thought, for elderly male patients with heart conditions. Lives could be put at risk by this display of flesh. A sudden rush of blood anywhere could prove fatal. Could they be classed as a weapon?

'Who are you seeing today?'

'Blood test,' he replied, not knowing who the female vampire would be.

'Fasting, is it?'

'Hardly.'

'Good. Right.' She located him on her computer screen. 'Nurse is running a little late.' Nurse hadn't caught up since her extra-long lunch. 'Just take a seat. She won't be long. Bitter today, isn't it? Cold for the last Friday in January, don't you think? Ice on my car this morning. Took ages to clear. Roll on Spring, eh.'

He retreated to a seat as far away from the reception desk as possible, which wasn't easy in the tiny waiting room. Usually there were never many patients waiting, such was the well-organized appointment system, but today there was quite a crowd caused, Redland surmised, by the late-running nurse. Redland sat between an elderly woman and another young woman with a child.

He ignored the rack of tatty magazines.

The seating was arranged so that everyone could have a sight of the electronic strip over the reception desk. It flashed the patient's name when their turn came round and the room to which they had to make their way.

There had been a tannoy system once but there were so many complaints that names called were drowned out by the voluble receptionists that a new visual method had been introduced. It constantly displayed messages while waiting to summon the next patient. *Well Woman Clinic Wednesdays. Book now.*

Christ, he hated this place. He hated being seen in this place. It was only a blood test today, to which he had submitted to keep the doctors sweet. There had been none too thinly veiled threats to expel him from the list if he continued to rebel against their unsolicited advice; Dr. Carys's especially.

'Alan, you're diabetic and your cholesterol is raised,' she stated. He was only just diabetic. Marginal. His cholesterol reading was also within bounds 'but that would be for a non-diabetic person,' said Dr. Carys. 'Look!' and she would retrieve a book that flopped open on well-thumbed pages with graphs. She would point at one that he couldn't read without his glasses on. 'Diabetes plus raised cholesterol plus you're nearly sixty and you're a man' she emphasized this with a wicked smile 'puts you in the danger zone.'

Statistics, that's all! Tell me I'll definitely have a heart attack or kidney failure and I'll listen.

'It's all about likely outcomes,' she would insist, 'based on known facts.'

How many times in his career had "known facts" led an investigation completely in the wrong direction?

His final argument was, to him, a strong one.

'You say I have issues that may, may cause problems but which right now do not manifest themselves in any adverse way. But you want to give me medication that may, may prevent something that is never going to happen and offers the promise of all kinds of undesirable side-effects. I'd rather have quality of life than miserable quantity of years!'

'You're also overweight,' she'd added.

He was; he had to agree. He was twelve stone or more and only five foot nine. But he was working on it. He'd promised himself a bike as a present when he kind of semi-retired in a few weeks' time. Then, six months, six summer months, of bike riding and excavating medieval ruins.

The Force called it job sharing. The budget cuts had given rise to a unique solution: six months on, six months off. Trouble was, when he was due to come back to duty in the autumn, they threatened him with a move to the Complaints section: take charge of public gripes against officers; liaise with Professional Standards, who he couldn't stand. All the shit-shoveling jobs. He knew he wouldn't like it, nobody did. He'd miss the action. He'd miss his DS, Melanie Challis, her more than the rest of the team put together.

'Good afternoon, Mr. Jenkins.' Megan's voice jerked Redland awake and he couldn't help but look at the new arrival.

'How are you today, Mr. Jenkins? Here for your LFT?' Megan enjoyed throwing around medical acronyms. 'Nurse is running a bit behind today.'

'What? Again!' he barked, making Megan jump. 'This is always happening. Do you know how much time I waste hanging around in here? I've got jobs to get to!'

Megan was flustered. 'Just take a seat. Please.' But Jenkins wanted to know how long he'd have to wait. She couldn't say.

At last, he looked for a seat. Jenkins, younger looking than Redland, exchanged grimaces with him as he walked away from the desk where, from the rear, squeals of laughter over some joke had just broken out. He turned round and scowled.

'No idea how to run a business, have they? If they had a real one to run...' Jenkins, still mumbling, took one of the two seats that were at right angles to the row Redland was in.

Jenkins' face was familiar. He'd seen him around Usk.

He noted how inappropriately dressed the man was for such a cold afternoon. Blue overalls with a hint of some sort of jumper underneath. He himself was well wrapped up. He liked a hat - his thinning auburn hair provided scant covering - and this morning it was a black homburg type – on his lap now - which complemented his black overcoat and red scarf.

'Hello.' It was Megan again, flustered this time by the arrival of a woman she did not recognize. Redland saw that Jenkins' attention was being drawn to the woman so he too chanced a glance.

She was tall, dwarfing Megan. She was wearing a woolen hat pulled down and a scarf pulled up. Her coat looked thick and warm but was short; her jeans disappeared into knee-length boots. A wisp of light blonde hair came down and flicked her face. Her profile was partly visible but she looked striking. Hard to say but she seemed to be in her late twenties or early thirties.

Redland logged her look in his mind. He had this ability to mentally photograph a face that he would retain and recall, seeing clearly in his mind's eye, for months, sometimes years. It had been invaluable at times over the years.

She spoke quietly but Redland picked up enough to get the gist and in any case Megan soon filled in the blanks.

The woman was visiting the area but needed a prescription for an inhaler as she'd left hers at home. Redland deduced that as it was not the hay fever season she must be staying in a house with animals. Megan told her she would need to see a doctor and that there was a form to fill out.

Jenkins seemed to be staring at the woman.

'You haven't put your date of birth,' Megan shouted from her keyboard as she entered the details.

'O, sorry,' said the woman in her loudest voice so far, with a faint London accent. 'It's 29, 9, 81.'

Jenkins stiffened and grunted, so much so that Redland looked to see if he was okay. Jenkins glared at him, eventually half-smiling self-consciously. 'Coincidence!' he said.

Redland smiled back and nodded but had no idea what that meant.

'Take a seat,' said Megan. 'Your name will come up in lights.' The woman was confused but Megan pointed upwards at the sign, currently advising that *Men get breast cancer. Check yours regularly.*

The woman sat behind Redland who was aware that Jenkins was still having a good look at the woman as, by the sound of things, she was opening and then removing some of the warm clothing.

I was right, he thought smugly. She's thirty; nearly.

Slowly, the nurse worked her way through the backlog. Redland looked up at the clock; twenty minutes he'd been sitting there. At least it was warm. His heating at home would have turned on by now, wasting money.

The electronic sign had flashed several names, Jenkins twitching each time. The women either side of Redland went when summoned.

Then came 'Angela Plumitis to Room 1' and Redland heard the woman behind him get to her feet.

He also heard a very audible gasp from Jenkins. Redland looked at him but Jenkins' gaze was fixed firmly on the woman as she quietly asked Megan where Room 1 was. Redland looked from Jenkins to the woman, whose face he could now see clearly, and back again but he could have been invisible to Jenkins who only had eyes for Angela Plumitis.

For the next five minutes Jenkins displayed extreme agitation. His legs crossed and uncrossed. He fidgeted constantly. Redland became more concerned. He looked across the room to see if anyone behind the desk was noticing.

Then Angela Plumitis came back to the reception desk where she asked Megan where she could find the chemist shop. She then turned and left, halting briefly at the door to reposition her hat and scarf.

Jenkins was on his feet but stood stock still for a long second. His face was contorted as if in pain. Redland got to his feet, convinced that Jenkins was about to have an apoplectic seizure. He didn't. He hurtled towards Redland, his eyes fixed on Angela Plumitis's back as she left the building. He made no move to avoid Redland who tried to get out of his way but backed into his chair, struggling to remain on his feet. He tottered as if for an age, Jenkins oblivious. He was gone, banging his way out through the door, leaving an open-mouthed Megan completely dumb-struck. She looked towards Redland with a look of "what do you think about that?" on her face but saw him, arms flailing, his body falling, chairs scattering.

He hit the floor and lay still. 'O, Mr. Redland,' cried Megan, feeling with her hands along the edge of the desk as if searching for the first time for the flap in it as her eyes remained locked on the fallen Redland who was not moving. 'Linda! Quick!'

She found the flap, lifted it and skipped through. Redland stirred as Megan began to move chairs out of the way to get to him. He pushed his way up into a sitting position. An intense pain in his chest made him catch his breath.

The chemist shop window was steamy and damp and, from the pavement, Jim Jenkins, jobbing builder, could see very little of Angela Plumitis as she waited for her prescription to be filled. He had followed her. He had had to. The revelation of first the date of birth and then the name had reawakened a long lost memory or rather a "what-if" from thirty years ago. Flesh put on an old skeleton. The possibility of its meaning became a probability. It felt right; it felt true; it felt real. He had to follow her. He had to find out more.

Angela Plumitis was passing the time looking around at various shelves. She had removed her headgear and loosened her scarf. Her blond hair was tied back tightly so her facial features were clear to see, except that she kept her head moving, looking this way and that.

He peered at her through the misted glass. The hair was right; the profile too and the shape of the lips. He could not make out the eyes but they should be blue. It could be Greta standing there.

Greta Plumitis, a daughterl of Latvian parents, post-war refugees. Greta Plumitis who, in the late 1970s, had worked in the payroll office of the same Newport building firm where the young Jim Jenkins had just finished his apprenticeship.

December 1979. He was leaving the firm that very month to take his newly-acquired skills to a better paid job in Chepstow and then, in early January, to marry his girl-friend, Beryl.

As always, the drink flowed on the last day, his last day, before the Christmas break. Office girls, married, partnered or otherwise, found their way to the site huts where music, drink and men could be found. He and Greta had been an encounter waiting to happen; all year their eyes had met across the canteen and fingers had touched for long seconds when the pay-packet was handed over.

Not much alcohol needed to be consumed before they found themselves with all the other ad-hoc couples kissing and petting.

Guided by him the two of them found themselves in a quiet stock-room behind a locked door and Jim had been amazed how up for it this amazing girl had become or perhaps had always been. She guided his hands, put them on her breasts and no girl had ever done that with him before, certainly not Beryl. She told him in no uncertain terms where else she wanted them placed. She raised her dress to give him access and now his naïve mind understood why on this festive day at work she had discarded her usual blue jeans. She was naked from the waist down. After several moments of hot gasps into his mouth, she unzipped him, got him more ready and then lay back across a cold rusting metal desk, urging him on. He hurried forward to oblige.

Then, he failed her. Very quickly. He didn't fail himself but he knew he was disappointing her. This girl with the face of an angel kept telling him not to stop; pleading. Beryl had never done that but that was because, as they both realized pretty soon into their married life, she had no idea what she was missing, what this act was capable of giving her. Greta knew what she could achieve but she had fallen well short with him. The long stoked-up desire had not lived up to the fantasy. Graciously, or desperately, she suggested perhaps there could be more of him later, they could meet up somewhere.

This wasn't the ethereal girl he had idolized from afar. She lay on the desk on a raised elbow, offering him unabashed a view of her at which he couldn't look. He was hastily covering himself up, she was lingering, fingering. Her face looked lost, begging "you stopped; why?".

He was empty of passion and full of confusion. His eyes looked everywhere except at her. She was brazen. His Beryl was a shy girl who, if ever there was a risk she was exposing too much, would yell at him 'don't look!' Greta didn't care. He glanced but couldn't take it in.

He left that room, in a rush, in case they were discovered he said; she would follow him and find him. But he didn't stop when he reached where the other merrymakers were getting more entwined. He was embarrassed by his lack of control and his obvious ignorance of how to keep up with the gorgeous girl.

And there was guilt when he thought of Beryl.

He ran out of the building, out of the place for the last time.

Some ten months later he had met up with some of the lads from the firm who came along for a night out to celebrate the birth of his and Beryl's son, a honeymoon conception, the confirmation of his manhood. Drunk, he bragged to them of his Christmas conquest of Miss Plumitis. 'A ripe Plum,' he swaggered as he swayed. The lads remembered her.

'That explains it,' one of them said. 'I thought she'd got a bit fat, before she left!' They all laughed. He laughed. It was a joke, wasn't it?

Every now and again over the years the joke came back to him and, mulling it over, he couldn't laugh at it but he could never seriously consider it either. Worse still, he was plagued with regret. Later in his life he had learned how to satisfy a woman and many times he had wanted to turn the clock back and properly enjoy that girl on the desk who had been so clearly ahead of his time.

Now, the face in the shop was turned fully towards him. It was her! Just as beautiful but was she also the same kind of woman underneath the beauty? Momentarily, that thought made him desperately sad.

Angela Plumitis. Plumitis…didn't your mother ever marry?

Four

George Medlyn stepped outside the front door of 135 Old Windsor Road in Datchet to intercept the postman at the front gate. He had done that each morning of that first week of February, sometimes he had not had time to put shoes on, having to step out in his slippers; and one morning he hadn't even been dressed, spotting the earlier-than-usual postman from the landing window and having to brave the cold easterly winds in his thin dressing gown.

He cursed the inconsistency of the delivery man's daily schedule. He seemed to turn up any time it suited him between eight and eight-thirty. Good job that his wife enjoyed to linger in the warmth of her bed in her over-heated bedroom on these cold mornings. By eight-thirty she was usually demanding her first cup of tea of the day.

This morning the postman asked him to sign for a recorded delivery, a thin square package that had arrived, at last. He'd had to wait for this, how long? Nearly a week but it seemed longer.

George Medlyn took the small hand-held delivery recording device from the fingerless gloved hand and with the plastic stick provided scrawled an unrecognizable signature where the man pointed. He thanked the postman who thought he was being more effusive than other mornings but said nothing and moved on to continue his round, musing as he had done every morning that week that the bloke's gone nuts, running out to meet him in all weathers. He would be even more confused from now on because George would not repeat the exercise.

Waiting until the postman had crossed the front of his drive and gone on to number 137 he pocketed the package and then slipped the two remaining run-of-the-mill items of correspondence into the letter box set in the right-hand brick gate pillar. He had done this all week. It allowed his wife when conscious, warmed internally by copious tea and stylistically attired against the arctic elements to bravely step outside and "do her bit", retrieving the mail. He never knew when leaving for work if his wife would deign to go the extra mile and head for Windsor, later, much later, to lord it in her shop.

It was almost the time she would be demanding tea in bed, which she did habitually regardless of her secret plans for the day. So George put the kettle on and then took out the package. He was trembling with anticipation, with excitement. He looked at it, staring at his name and address.

Stupid.

He'd been childlike, rushing outside every morning but no way did he want this package to fall into his wife's hand. But long term this was ridiculous. He would have to get a post office box or some such. Unlike his usual purchases direct from shops in London, he couldn't have this material coming to the house. No way. He'd gone up a level or two now. This was a brand new scenario and it needed better planning for future excursions.

And there would be future excursions. Cottel Court had been exactly what he wanted, what he needed. Next time though he'd be less nervous, more controlled, less urgent, more like those other guys. And that girl! Was she in charge or what? Even though the scene put her on the receiving end she was in charge.

It was all coming back to him, now that he had this plainly wrapped package in his shaking hands. His fingers curled as if to start clawing the paper but down the stairs came the far-from-plaintive cry of she who loved her bed, as long as he's not in it. He hated that fucking voice. It went right through him. One of these mornings he'd take her cup of tea, throw it in her face and then wipe it off with a pillow pressed down hard to soak up everything, especially all the life out of her, if you could call what she had a life.

The package went inside his cardigan pocket. Thank God he had this lifeline but it would have to wait, until tonight probably. She'd be abed early so he could go to his study, lock the door and plug the dvd into his laptop. Fuck. He'd have to wait all day thanks to her.

'Okay,' he yelled back. 'The kettle's on…dear.'

*

'I hate you. I hate you!' George's wife screamed through the tears of rage. 'You're nothing but an animal.'

She rubbed her neck vigorously with one hand while trying to pull down her nightdress to cover her naked lower body. Her fingers fell into the mess down there.

'You pig!'

She eased herself off the bed. God, she was sore. Her brain bruised. What was it? It was a nightmare, a living nightmare.

George was already off the bed, standing naked between her and the door. His body looked disgusting. It was old and fleshless, yet his member, now semi-flaccid, had been penetratingly large and angry. She'd forgotten, if she'd ever known.

Words failed her. She couldn't look at him and yet she could feel him staring as she staggered around the bed clutching her nightdress tight between her legs. Still she guarded her neck with one hand as, with some fear, she skirted him, half wanting to strike him dead but terrified of him re-applying those horrible constrictions on her body.

She had thought those days of painful, demeaning, humiliating physicality were long behind her. She thought she had made it clear. Yet like a demented madman he had entered her room, completely naked and already erect, and with cruel deliberation thrown the bed-clothes off her and then, as she protested, battered her with the words 'you will do as I say; you will do what I want'.

It took several moments for her to realize that he would not be verbally dissuaded from his intent so she had beat at his body. She could not get off the bed. It was then that the horror of the situation really hit home. He hurt her. His hands gripped her arms and burned into the skin. He pinned both wrists with one hand and wrenched her nightdress up and over her face and then the hand crushed her neck so she could hardly breathe.

The shame of her nakedness with all the glaring bedroom lights still on was made worse as he pushed her legs apart with his hard, bony knees that excruciatingly dug into the soft cellulite. She knew she was totally exposed and that was the moment she realized he was degrading her. Deliberately. He knew only too well, had known only too well, her beliefs on the sacred privacy of her body. She had made all that very clear to him all of the last twenty years.

He just went on with it, stronger than her, even in his spindliness. Like a demon, possessed, he raped her with such savagery. Through the smog of it all, she was convinced he would go all the way and kill her. Blindly, he was in her; he was out of her; he was in her again, each penetration tearing her dry skin and bringing scream after scream from her bitten lips. His breath was hot on her face, even through the thick material of the nightdress, assailing her with primeval grunts of the forest. She, unprepared, was ripped, repeatedly, screamingly.

Mercifully, it didn't last long. He sank onto her, the bones of his elbows and torso piercing her loose flesh.

Her arms were freed. She managed to get her numb, tingling fingers on her nightdress and tug it from her face, afraid of what she would see above her. Through wet eyes what she saw briefly was that this husband of hers for too long had, she was sure, a look of disappointment on his face. Hate was there too, she saw that, and she feared for her life.

He had finished, she knew, but he prolonged the agony, thrusting every last drop into her. He shakily eased off, leaving a snail trail across her belly.

She had made her escape to the bathroom and locked the door firmly and he heard shrieks and wailing from her. There were words mixed in, names of the farmyard variety and the only expletives she could, even now, bring herself to let fly.

'Pig! Swine! Bastard! Animal!'
It went on and he switched off.
He felt dirty. He felt guilt. He had betrayed his new found freedom. He had desecrated a memorable fullness with the emptiness that was his wife. It had to be that way. It had to be with a woman.
He had done as he had promised. She had gone to bed and he had gone to his study with his new dvd. He played it and he was immersed in it. He had become naked. He played it over and over again, addicted. His spirits were up, elated, drunk with it. He touched himself but he could not sully in that way the magnificence of what he was watching. He had to use a woman. He had to use a woman in the same way. It had to be his wife because she was there.

Five

Detective Sergeant Melanie Challis shivered as she stood in the field of frosted grass near the tree where the frozen body of Timothy Bush had been found hanging. Until satisfied that it was not a scene of an actual crime, police tape had been strung around the area.
She was trying to be unaffected by the cold. She was much more warmly dressed than she had been the previous day. That would impress the boss.
It was early, not yet nine and even if the mid-February sun had chosen to put in an appearance it would not have warmed up this particular spot. East where the sun would eventually rise was the far side of a tall stand of trees.
She was keen to examine the site again and talk to Mrs. Guster, the woman who had found Timothy Bush. She wanted to be able to put some answers on Redland's desk before his second cup of coffee.
She looked up at the branch where the previous day she had seen the body dangling, unmoving in the still winter air. The branch had been cut and the extremity removed. She knew enough forensics to work out that for the knot of rope on the branch to be kept intact it would have to be slid off the branch. Forensics would want to examine the knot in its tied state.
She'd been told that the tree was an oak. She was impressed that the uniformed officer who had informed her of this was able to make this identification. Okay, there were one or two brown shriveled leaves on various twigs but he'd known straight off. She looked beyond this tree and wondered if all the others in this, what, copse, spinney, whatever, were oak too. This one had a wide trunk, must be hundreds of years old he'd said, and the branch on which the rope was fixed was as thick as her

thigh near the trunk and then it reached out, looping downwards in the centre before heading up again towards the tip.

'Good for building ships,' he'd said, 'to fight the Frogs.' It never ceased to amaze what trivia people had stored in their brains.

The grass she was standing in this morning was long, white and wet and her footwear was nowhere near good enough for the job. She could feel a damp chill penetrating the lower part of her black trousers so she looked for a grassless spot to go stand in.

*

She needed a good second look at this site.

It had been mid-afternoon yesterday when she and her boss Detective Inspector Alan Redland had got the call. Handy. They both lived in the Usk area and the body was found two miles north of the town of Usk itself. So, a visit to the site before dark and then home early for a change. The boss looked as if he could do with an early finish. He hadn't been good for a few weeks.

Two uniformed officers were there. They had sent their position via smartphone, which was just as well as the site was off the main Usk to Raglan road, down a narrow lane.

The patrol car was parked at a metal gate just beyond a set of three terraced ex-council houses on a wider stretch. The two officers were in the field beyond the gate, cordoning off. A woman and a dog were sat in the back of the patrol car. Redland noticed her with a casual glance; Challis stooped and paused to get a better look. The woman looked up and saw her peering in. Challis gave what she thought was a warm smile but the woman did not respond. Without saying anything to each other Redland and Challis knew the woman was a witness, probably the discoverer.

Redland was already clambering over the padlocked gate and Challis straddled it to join him. The icy metal bit into her bare hands and as soon as she landed the other side she fished her gloves out of her jacket pocket and donned them. Redland gave her a disparaging look.

There was still sufficient light to get a good view of the scene but dusk was fast approaching. It was a clear winter afternoon, temperature dropping, but the sun had not yet dipped below the mountains to the south-west. They saw the two constables about two hundred metres away near some trees, responded to a wave from one of them and headed in their direction. They watched where they were placing their feet, the grassy tussocks were ideal for sliding ankles into a sprained state or waiting to trip the careless stride. It wasn't until they were halfway across that they looked up and got their first sight of the body hanging on a length of blue nylon rope.

They both recoiled. The body was virtually naked, the white underpants initially giving the impression of total nakedness. Their eyes were transfixed on the corpse.

Redland knew one of the two uniformed officers and immediately began a conversation starting with a question about the woman in the car. Her name was Meredith Guster. She lived in the house at the other end of the three-house terrace. She was walking her dog, in this field, as she often did apparently. The man she found hanging was her neighbour Timothy Bush. He lived in the house this end of the terrace. He lived alone. That had been all she could manage to tell them. She'd been shaking so much she'd been put in the patrol car.

Challis heard the beginning of this conversation but not all of it. She walked on towards the hanging man, stopping and staring some three metres away from him, unable to take her eyes off the face that was swollen and dark red. She took a deep breath and called to the other uniformed officer, asking his name.

'Bell...' He hesitated, not knowing this woman or her rank. She read his mind.

'Sergeant,' she prompted him, her voice indifferent but her eyes fixed straight at him. He nodded. He was young, which made her feel old even at thirty. He was tall but no taller than she was.

'Well, Constable Bell,' she smiled, wishing she was as well-wrapped up as he was in his bright yellow windproof top coat. 'Has anybody been nearer than this to the body?'

He looked towards the hanging man trying to gauge the distance. 'No, Sarge.'

She didn't mind the abbreviation; on the contrary she always enjoyed it when it was said with real deference. 'You or your buddy check the body?'

'No.'

'How d'you know he's dead?'

The young officer struggled to find the words. 'Sarge...just look at him.'

'Seen a lot of them, have you? Cos I haven't.'

He was silent. She let him off the hook. The bloke was dead all right.

'What about the woman?'

'She...she lives over there.'

Challis sighed. 'How close did she get?'

He didn't know.

Challis left him dangling as she ran her eyes slowly across the ground towards the tree. The grass petered out after a metre or so, the ground under the tree bare with tiny ruts. A long round log lay on its side, not right under the body but off to the right, at least a metre. The area under the tree and where she was standing would not have seen any sun all day and the air had stayed cold. White frost lay unbroken on the grassy parts, no feet had disturbed it today. She squatted down to get a grass-top view that confirmed it. The guy had been hanging there for at least a day. She came to that conclusion but stayed in the squat position. It didn't look right. Something didn't look right. She dropped her head even lower and could see that the ground sloped up gradually and away from the hanging branch. The log was up that slope, its length across the contour.

'What was the weather like yesterday?' she asked Bell just as Redland came up behind her.

'It wasn't this bloody cold,' said the DI.

She smiled to herself, getting upright. How could her boss possibly feel the cold dressed as he was? Thick overcoat, scarf, hat – he was a one-man 'bring back the homburg' campaign - gloves, probably thermal long-johns and definitely a vest underneath his shirt. Every autumn he boasted that his vest was now on and every spring he announced it would not come off until the may was out.

'Was it frosty?' she asked.

'No,' he replied.

'Then he's been up there since yesterday, or last night.' She waved her hand over the white grass to illustrate where that deduction came from.

'Possibly,' he allowed. 'The ground behind him's quite bare.'

They heard the noise of someone clambering over the metal gate. Dave Sayer, senior scene of crime officer, made his way towards them, large bag in hand, two male accomplices behind him.

Redland greeted him enthusiastically. 'Dave, the very man.'

Sayer, also so warmly clad that Challis imagined she was even chillier, ambled up, cheerlessly. 'What have we got then?'

Redland had heard this opener too many times. It sounded like people who said to you as you waited to see your doctor 'well, how are you?' He simply nodded towards the hanging man.

'Timothy Bush lives...' he turned to point 'over there. Best get some good photos before the light fades too much.'

'Billy took some earlier, sir.' This was the uniformed officer that Redland had quizzed on arrival and he was pointing to his younger colleague. 'On his phone.'

'Good, good,' said Redland, then to PC Bell. 'Get them sent in asap. And Dave, I want you to tell me how he did it.'

Sayer frowned. 'Who did what?'

Redland looked at the hanging man. 'Mr. Timothy Bush. How did he hang himself? I can see that log but is that man enough for the job, for him to get up on? Did he fall from the branch with the noose around his neck? That would have ripped his head off, wouldn't it? Was it deliberate or was he trying to get a kick out of going to the brink and it went too far? Or…was he assisted, in some way, shape or form? And why is he only wearing underpants? He'll catch his death. And so will you,' he directed the comment at Challis, 'dressed like that.' She'd wondered when he'd get round to voicing that particular opinion. He had to wait until he had an audience, didn't he? But then he added. 'Still, I suppose it's up to you what you do with your own life.' She did a minor double-take. That last jibe was so out of context.

Sayer was trying to make mental notes. 'There's a woman up there in the back of the *hedley*. She wants out.'

Redland and Challis looked across to the patrol car, the hedley as Sayer called it. It was a name for the vehicle that was in common usage in the mainly English-speaking Mon police force. The blue and yellow vehicle bore the English 'Police' and the Welsh equivalent 'Heddlu', which Sayer and other anti-Welsh language 'money wasted on bi-lingual road signs' officers corrupted into the Anglicized hedley.

'Okay, leave you three to it.' Redland led Challis away back towards the gate.

'O, Billy Bell.' Challis turned to the young uniformed officer. 'I suggest you go find whoever has the key to that gate. It needs opening. There'll be an ambulance here soon. It'll need to get in here.'

PC Bell looked at his colleague who nodded, muttering something about posting the 'stiff stiff' through the gate. Redland heard it and turned on him. 'Respect!' was his only word but his look spoke volumes.

The young PC Billy Bell trotted after Redland and Challis.

When she and Redland got to the patrol car, Guster was getting out, her dog, a Springer, Redland said, pulling at the lead. Before they could even utter a word by way of introduction, Guster declared she was going home; she couldn't stand anymore of this. She was cold and upset. Redland tried to plead the need for a question or two but she turned and marched off, across the lane and back towards the terrace of three houses.

Challis chased after her. Redland saw her take a light hold of the woman's elbow. He saw Challis put her face close to the woman and he knew what she was doing. She was offering some comfort, some words of understanding. She was establishing some closeness with the woman. She was good, he thought, smiling as he told himself he'd taught her all she knew. She was putting some plus points in store for another day; tomorrow probably, if he knew her. She hated putting stuff on hold. Do it now, get it done and move on was her mantra. He hated thinking badly of her.

*

Challis took out a tape measure and marched towards the hanging branch. It had been in her mind to do some measuring of heights and distances. She looked up. The hanging branch was out of reach.

Over her porridge that morning she had accessed the case information from the HQ database and downloaded it onto her phone. Now she retrieved Sayer's initial site notes. He had recorded that Timothy Bush was 5 feet 8¾ inches tall – he was such a metric-phobe. She eyed the tree; probably enough free space to hang yourself although she hoped that Sayer would be doing that calculation properly.

She opened the photos folder and went forwards and backwards through those of the hanging man taken by both Billy Bell and Sayer. The rope length from branch to neck seemed to be the greater compared with the toes from the ground.

Looking around, she was surprised to see the log still lying where it was yesterday. She'd assumed it would have been taken back to base as material evidence. There was no mention of it in Sayer's notes, only in hers from last night and she'd only noted that it was likely to be Timothy Bush's stepping off point and was lying up-slope at a distance of about one metre. She measured that distance now.

She measured the log, noting it but unable to work out how suitable the log may have been as a suicide platform. She looked along its length. It seemed to be smooth without any bark on one muddy side but with bark still on the other side.

Something caught her eye. She squatted closer. Fibres, in the bark. She fished out a pair of evidence gloves from her pocket and a specimen bag. Carefully she eased some of the looser fibres up and into the bag. Other fibres remained stuck more firmly.

To test the weight of the log, she carefully put her hands under one end, not touching the bare end that may hold some of Timothy Bush's DNA. Too heavy for her to lift and carry any distance. But if it had been too heavy for Timothy Bush, whose naked torso, upper arms and apparent middle-age had not indicated a Mr. Universe and who, according to Sayer, weighed in at only about nine stone, he would have had to roll it into place before tipping it up into position. And would it stand steadily on its end on the gentle slope under the branch?

If it had been rolled then shouldn't the whole log show some effects of grass and mud, not just the one smooth side?

She looked at the smooth side again. Her mother had used untreated logs like this one as soil retainers in the garden and she could remember mother complaining eventually that the side on the soil would rot long before the upper dry surface. This one had been lying on the ground for some time, but where? And it had been carried to where it now lay.

Her eyes began to roam.

No, wait a minute; this was a job for Sayer or one of his minions. She could imagine the boss's comments. Thorough though he was he would undoubtedly think she was going over the top, above and beyond her required duties. He would know that was her style, give her her head, a free rein. Leave her to put on the brakes.

But that log should be covered up. Evidence could deteriorate. At least two nights had passed already.

The metal gate was unpadlocked now; her Citroen C1 just the other side. Redland would turn a blind eye to her using her own vehicle at a crime scene; other senior officers would not. They would expect her to drive to the office, pick up a pool car and drive all the way back. She opened the boot and took out some ASDA carrier bags. With her pen-knife she cut them open and draped them loosely over the log, holding them down with a few stones she found under trees a little distance off.

Back in the car she wiped her hands on antiseptic hand towels that she kept in the door compartment for use before eating takeaway food on the move. Then she updated the case folder in the HQ database and emailed Sayer, cc Redland, with a diplomatic summary of his oversight and what he had to do to redeem himself: get the log, find out where it had come from and analyze it thoroughly, fibres and all.

Notes finished, she stepped out of the cool car into the cold air. She did her coat up even though she only had to walk a short distance to Mrs. Guster's house.

It took a few knocks on Meredith Guster's door to rouse her. She was still in night clothes, topped by a man's thick claret dressing gown. The word 'Dad' was on the left breast pocket. Challis could see why it was being worn; it hung down to mid-shin and wrapped warmly around the middle with a claret cloth belt, tied with a single loop.

To Challis, Meredith Guster looked as spaced out as she had done the previous afternoon. As she looked at this woman this morning she changed her mind about her age. The previous day she'd looked forty. This morning she looked of a well-worn age where the glass was now always half empty; frowns coming so much more easily than smiles.

The inside of the house behind her was quiet, no TV or radio noise, no dog in sight. Who, what and where was 'Dad'?

The woman stared at Challis who realized from the look that the groundwork done the previous afternoon had generated no welcome recognition but she rode right over that and spoke as if they were old acquaintances.

'Hi again.' No glimmer of response. 'Detective Sergeant Challis, from yesterday.' She didn't flash her id, wanting the re-introduction to sound informal. 'I'd like to talk about yesterday.'

'I'm not dressed.' The woman looked past Challis, perhaps seeing if her male colleague was with her.

'We'd like your help to dot i's and cross t's.'

The woman gave one weary nod of the head. 'You better come in.'

She walked away from the door, down the passageway. Challis stepped inside, closing the door behind her. She wiped her feet on a flat rubber mat that was mud stained anyway.

The woman had reached the foot of the stairs and was beckoning Challis towards a room to the right. Challis followed her down the passage that was badly lit. The walls were papered, buff or beige originally, now in dire need of a change. Underfoot, a dark red patterned carpet hid the dirt. There was a distinct doggy smell coming into her nostrils.

'Where's your dog?' she asked as she entered the large downstairs room that ran from front to back. The low morning sun was streaming in through the front double-glazed window. Little heat penetrated so the gas fire was on.

'He's out the back, in his kennel. He's only allowed in evenings.'

'Springer spaniel?' She recalled Redland's description.

'Cross.'

'Loves water, I'm told.'

'Yeah,' she managed a smile.

This was like pulling teeth. 'Any water around here for him?'

'There's a brook the far side of the field.'

Challis nodded. The woman was still standing, arms folded. 'Is that where you were going yesterday, yesterday afternoon?'

Now the woman sat, in a red upholstered armchair, the only armchair in the room. There was a brown leather settee opposite that pointed at the small screen TV, which the armchair didn't. Challis eased herself towards the settee. 'May I?'

A faint nod from the woman and Challis loosened the buttons on her topcoat before lowering herself down. Her notebook somehow appeared in her hand. She opened it with a flourish. It got the woman's attention.

'How are you feeling today?' Challis asked, putting on her caring voice.

The woman nodded slowly. 'How d'you think.' She brushed away her hair from her face. Challis noticed her red hands, chapped from the cold weather probably. She had obviously been feeling the cold the previous afternoon.

'How do you feel about going over yesterday, yesterday afternoon?'

23

'Not good, but…'

'We need to get as full a picture as possible. For the coroner. I know you spoke with the constable yesterday but I'd like to go through it again. Can I have your full name?' Pen at the ready she jotted down 'Meredith Ann Guster'. She asked her next question, what the precise address was.

'1 Pontderry Lane, Llanhelog, Usk.'

'Thanks.' Challis eyed her carefully before deciding which way to go next. 'Nice up here. I live near Usk, the other side; Capelgwm.'

The woman surprised her. 'I know, I've seen you. And your mate who was with you. D'you live together?'

'Er, no.' This had more than surprised her. 'He actually lives in Usk itself.'

'Good. You're a bit young for him, I would have thought.'

Change the subject, Challis thought. Why isn't this woman doing the usual thing and trying to ply her with tea or coffee?

'What's your dog's name?'

'Malcolm.'

'Do you walk him through the field every day?'

'Which field?'

This woman was getting too smart-arsed and was trying to dictate the direction. An older woman putting a younger woman in her place.

'Mrs. Guster…'

'Miss.'

'I was told Mrs.'

'Guster's my maiden name. I've taken it up again since my divorce.'

'I see…'

'My married name was Chen. I didn't like it so I changed it.'

Challis jotted in her notebook.

'Timothy Bush. You were able to identify him yesterday.'

Guster hesitated. Challis knew that the man's identity had not yet been confirmed by anyone or anything else.

'You were able to tell the constable his name. That was extremely useful to us but you will understand we shall need to get in touch with his next of kin. There was no answer from his house. Does he live alone?'

'I don't know.'

'Wife, children?'

'No idea.'

'How old was he?'

'I don't know.'

'But you know him. Obviously. You recognized him.'

'Yes, I've seen him. He hasn't lived there long. He looks about fifty to me.'

'How many times did you see him yesterday?'

Guster's eyes glued to Challis's eyes. To Challis, the woman did not have the look of someone trying to remember but had that of someone wondering what the best answer should be. The woman was juggling, mentally.

'When I found him.'

'That was the only time?'

'Yes'

Challis slowly and deliberately made a note. She wondered why Guster had hesitated. Her thinking was that nobody could have seen Timothy Bush yesterday because the thinking was that he'd been hanging there since the day before.

'What time was that?' she asked.

'Not sure. About two, two-thirty.'

'Did you phone 999 from there, from the field?'

'I used my mobile.'

Challis knew that. 'Right, so you didn't have to come back to the house to use your landline.' She jotted. 'So, you didn't know him that well. How come you know his name?'

The woman's hair got pushed back and then she tugged the gown tighter across her chest.

'Them next door.'

'What, the people in the middle house? They know him then, do they?'

'I don't know. They know his name.'

'Don't you all get on with each other? I would have thought an isolated group of houses like this would be friendly, neighbourly.'

'They're away. On holiday, Skiing, somewhere.'

'What are their names?'

'Jack and Marcia Smith. They're away with their kids.'

'D'you know when they're back?'

'No.'

Challis punched a full-stop onto her notebook page and closed it.

'Okay, that's fine, for now. Thank you.' She stood; Guster did too. She was short. She had slippers on but she was genuinely short. 'Dad' must have been fairly short too judging by the length of the gown.

'Who's 'Dad'?' Challis asked.

'My ex.' Challis cocked an eyebrow. Guster read the question. 'I have a daughter. She lives in Bristol.'

'Do you work? Do you have a job?'

'Yes, but I couldn't face it today. I phoned in.'

'Don't blame you. Not a very nice experience but we're very grateful for your assistance.'

They both ambled towards the door to the passageway.

'I could have asked if you wanted a hot drink. You must have been cold,' Guster said.

'Ah, you saw me out in the field, eh? Yeah, frost up to my knees.' Challis knew the offer was being made too late. 'But, no, thanks, I'm fine.' She wished the offer had been made earlier. She would really have liked to scan the place. Her gut told her that the woman had been just as helpful as she needed to be and had made sure that Challis was not left alone to snoop.

Challis heard Malcolm snuffling at the back door. 'He wants his walk by the sound of him,' she said to Guster, stopping sharply to catch her close to her. 'If you take him through the field today you'll have to avoid the cordoned off area.'

'I'm not,' replied Guster, seemingly shrinking into the cocoon of the gown.

'One other thing.' Challis spoke slowly then hesitated. 'Did you walk Malcolm through the field the day before yesterday?'

'No,' Guster said without thinking.

Challis nodded. 'You have other walks, other routes you use?'

This time Guster was slower to answer. 'Sometimes.'

'Did you see Mr. Bush that day? The day before yesterday?'

'No.' Another quick response.

Challis absorbed these responses. 'Well, thank you. We'll probably need to speak again.' Definitely need to speak again, she thought. 'Ah, your phone number here, please.'

Guster rattled it off, omitting the area code. Challis was fishing out her notebook again. 'And your place of work?'

Guster did not answer. 'Is that necessary? My employers wouldn't like the police to be calling me in work.'

'It would be best. So if you don't mind...'

Guster complied, again omitting the area code.

'Local, eh?' Challis waited for Guster to tell her who her employer was. Guster weighed it up in her mind but realized that now that she had divulged the phone number there was no point in withholding the name.

'I work at Cottel Court.'

Six

When she reached HQ just after eleven, DC Harry Muench could hardly wait to tell her that the Super wanted to see her, in his office. 'Sounded real urgent.'

Muench was one of three detective constables shoe-horned into the office Challis shared with them. He and Ray Lockett had adjoining desks near the door. The more recent recruit, Kay Ruff, had a desk facing these two. Challis's desk chair had its back to Ruff and she faced the 'cosy' glass-fronted office that DI Redland occupied. They'd enjoyed this lack of spaciousness even before the cuts started to bite.

Muench was the only one in the office and he was the one Challis least wanted to see this morning, especially with this kind of greeting. In fact, he was the last person she wanted to see any day of the week. His face carried a permanent smirk as if he couldn't believe that she was his superior and was damned if he was ever going to show that he believed it. He never called her Sarge; the other two did, on occasion.

She looked at his larger than normal smug grin, briefly, soon opting to stare at the boss's office, hoping he was in. He wasn't but no way was she going to enquire of Muench what the Super wanted, although she would have liked some hint before stepping into his office two floors up.

'Didn't you tell him where I was?' she asked. Muench shrugged. He would have known where she was. All he had to do was enquire of the on-line diary that she had updated after her porridge that morning.

At her desk she powered on her laptop. She wanted to know if the boss had been in yet but wouldn't ask Muench even if her life depended on it. Three years she had worked, or rather shared an office, with Harry Muench. He was at least five years younger and had resented her from the start. They had been assigned together on a number of cases but she found that Muench usually bypassed her and reported directly to the boss.

She went into Redland's office to see if there was any sign of his having been in yet. His desk looked exactly as it had the previous afternoon when she had stood in his doorway while he donned his hat, scarf and coat, checked his gloves were in the pockets before they headed out.

As she returned to her desk to log on her laptop Muench annoyingly reminded her that the Super had come down here personally, looking for her.

'I heard you first time.' she said testily, wishing she'd ignored him.

Muench shrugged again but she had her back to him and didn't see the gesture or the next one that he flashed at her. 'It's your funeral,' he muttered.

Challis checked her emails to see if there was anything from the boss or Sayer. Nothing new. There was one from PC Bell. She couldn't remember having given him her name. Must have been Sayer after they'd gone. The email informed her that he'd got the key to the gate from a farmer who lived two miles away near the village of Pontderry. His name was John Gee. He gave Bell the key and told him that people used the field for walking dogs, picking blackberries, etc. There was no right of way but anybody could climb over the gate. Kids had once used that same tree, hanging a swing from the same branch until he removed it and warned them off. She was annoyed that Bell had obviously not asked him what he'd seen the last couple of days. Another job for her.

She took off her coat, walked over to the hangers by the door and hung it up on her peg, aware all the time that Muench's eyes were on her. She hated his eyes. They penetrated. She suppressed the sensation, reminding herself yet again that she mustn't let this insubordinate twat spoil the good feelings she otherwise had coming into work every day. As a constable she'd always prided herself on showing respect to seniors, even sergeants. Muench didn't respect her yet toadied up to senior ranks.

She loved working for Alan Redland. DC Ray Lockett was easy to get on with; no confrontations there. She felt for him that he had to sit so close to Muench. She was even sorrier for young DC Kay Ruff, who had sat facing Muench and his innuendos for the last four months. She tried to look after this younger inexperienced pair and was sure that Redland tried to do the same. He handled Muench brilliantly, never letting the constable get anywhere near trumping his play and yet he managed to quietly bolster Muench's ego with well-placed well-dones. Challis could never bring herself to congratulate Muench for anything. Not only was he deliberately uncooperative but, she believed, lacked professionalism. Sadly Challis understood that Muench only seemed to demonstrate this attitude with her.

She was now deliberately taking her time responding to the Super's alleged urgent summons, partly to annoy Muench and partly because she didn't believe his interpretation.

Back at her desk she shuffled papers, tapped a few keys. Reluctantly, she logged off. She'd better go and get it over with but she'd much rather sit down and collate her notes from her interview with Mrs. Guster.

Seven

'Sit down, Melanie.' Superintendent O'Halloran was standing at the window. He moved his cup and saucer from his left hand to his right so that he could deliberately look at his watch. 'You got the message then.'

'Yes. Sir. Sorry. I was up at the site of yesterday's suicide. Another look.'

Her excuse was ignored as with some display of urgency he lowered the crockery to a small table and moved to his chair behind the desk. She closed the door of his spacious office behind her. Big difference to Redland's pokey place.

His hand rested on a brown folder in front of him. Other files were arranged in a pristine stack, edges uniform, to the right. On the left an array of writing tools erect in their special holder: from left to right, pens

- blues, blacks, reds, greens – pencils, light brown and sharpened to a killing point - always lined up in the same sequence, always looking unused.

There was nothing particularly pleasant about his greeting. Quite the opposite but she didn't know what to read into it. It didn't sound friendly and in these times of cuts everybody was jittery and half-expected to be called into a sterile room for a dose of bad news. That's what had happened to Redland. Called in, told he was to share his job and that he was going to be posted to the equivalent of the Russian front or worse, the Complaints section! Surely they weren't going to keep the team together and send her with him.

But no; the Super was on his own. No sign of H.R. or her union rep. Just the two of them but that was like no consolation.

She always felt dowdy in his presence.

He was in a short-sleeved white shirt, immaculate, sitting erect, his arms coming forward to rest his elbows on the desk, his chin right over the brown file, his mid-forties face topped by neat but thinning grey hair. She'd never liked his dark eyes and they were on her now, burrowing in as she strode to the proffered seat. He was not someone that she had a lot to do with but recently when their paths had crossed she had found him studying her. It made her feel uncomfortable. He was a married man and she had heard no rumours about him philandering or harassing in the workplace. Nevertheless she felt targeted. Casual conversations with her female colleagues indicated no similar feelings amongst them. This only left her even more paranoid.

He wore no tie which meant his shirt was open at the neck revealing his red birth-mark that began under the right ear and ran around the back, just below his neat hairline. It was attracting her attention despite her best efforts to ignore it. You couldn't see the bottom edge of it behind the straightness of his shirt collar but the upper edge went up and down in peaks and troughs like a graph. The long-running joke was it monitored crime detection rates, more troughs than peaks.

He sat, still fixed on her.

'Mel,' he used the shortened version now. Probably thought it sounded more intimate, perhaps even matey. 'Some unfortunate news I'm afraid.'

O, shit, she thought. Why isn't it that turd Muench?

'No easy way to say this. DI Redland is in hospital. Looks like a heart attack.'

'Shit!' Challis uttered almost involuntarily. 'How serious?'

He brought up one hand in a dismissive wave. 'No idea.'

'What happened?'

'From what I gather he was scraping ice off the car this morning and he just collapsed. Simple as that. I was talking to him just yesterday. Seemed fine.' I was talking to him about you, he said to himself, observing her closely.

'O my God.' Challis pondered the trivial activity that had caused this attack, before remembering. 'He had a bit of a funny turn a few weeks ago,' almost thinking out loud.

'What?'

She immediately regretted the disclosure. 'O, nothing much. A sudden chest pain. Hardly a pain at all he said. Like indigestion. He was at the doctors at the time for one of his regular blood tests.'

'Right.' O'Halloran seemed to be filing away this bit of info. 'He never said.'

Bugger! thought Challis. 'Which hospital?'

'Abergavenny.' He nodded. 'Luckily DCs Donahoe and Cotterill were there, in Emergency, waiting to interview a couple of stab victims from last night and they happened to see Inspector Redland being wheeled in. So, we know early for a change.'

Challis was speechless, her mind engaged on the implications. The boss out of action; the team pretty stretched.

'You know the inspector was due to start his six month gap in a few weeks' time,' O'Halloran brought Challis back to reality, 'but this could be the end for him. His replacement Inspector Hubbard was due to take over but he's not just on leave, he's on holiday in Australia, for weeks yet. Family out there or something. In the meantime, Mel, someone's going to have to run the DI's team. There's no replacement available, certainly not for now.'

'Yes, sir,' she agreed breathlessly as if someone had jumped on her stomach.

He was watching her, she knew that, but she didn't know if she should get up and go or wait for some words of wisdom from him.

She was tempted to give voice to a thought that flashed through her mind. Perhaps her move to inspector would be expedited. She'd been knocked back once, the previous year. Even 'acting' DI would be good.

It seemed an age but he tore his eyes off her and opened the folder in front of him. As the front cover flipped over she recognized it as her personnel file.

There was more, obviously, but he kept her waiting.

He didn't need to read her file again; he'd done that while he was waiting for her. This was the first legitimate opportunity he'd had to get one-to-one with DS Melanie Challis, age thirty, nine years in the Force, straight from university where she had got a two-one in criminology and psychology – he was disdainful; he'd majored in Law. She was single. That made him smile. Sergeant six years, all that time with DI Redland who gave her improving annual assessments but there was some concern about her ability to delegate.

He pretended to read on but in his mind he was turning over other attributes not to be found in the file: she was not unattractive, clearly she could be less severe than she looked with the hair tied back the way it was; little makeup; tall; slim; green eyes and small breasts that barely rippled the shirt she was wearing and, just as importantly, did not drag the eyes to dwell there. Businesslike, but then, you just couldn't tell. Looks, especially her looks, were deceptive, as he knew full well.

'So,' piggy eyes on her, 'a DS in charge of the team!'

She guessed so and here was an opportunity if she grabbed it to get her ambitions on the table. She hesitated.

'You think you're up to it?'

That sounded like a challenge and she was affronted.

'Of course.' She'd done it before, covering for the boss.

He nodded but didn't appear convinced. He got to his feet.

'How d'you get on with the team? Any...personality issues?'

He was around the desk now, brushing the corner with a hand as if preparing to perch on it. This conversation was acquiring the attributes of an informal interview.

The question was loaded. He already thought he knew the answer.

'It's fine sir. We're all...different but the boss gets results.'

'So you have no qualms. No reservations.'

'None at all, sir.' There was nothing else she could say. She was ambitious and that was bound to mean abandoning sooner or later the cosy intimacy as someone's number two.

'Look at me, Sergeant.'

She had been; she was sure. He drew a little closer, too close, inside her space.

'You've been at this level for five years?'

She was slow to answer. Her smartphone was vibrating in her trouser pocket. 'Er, nearly six. Sir.'

'Passed your inspector's exams.'

'Yes. First assessment last year.'

He made a big deal out of looking thoughtful so she decided to put in a bid. 'I think I'm ready, sir.'

Her green eyes were locked onto his. She'd stolen his thunder. He'd had this idea of gaining points with her by being the one to broach the possibility, remote though he knew it was, of her moving up the ladder.

'Really?' He was nonplussed. 'Inspector?'

'Yes sir. This would be the ideal time.'

'I called you in here to tell you your boss was incapacitated and your first reaction is to bid for his job.'

'The boss would have been the first to think about the continued smooth running of his team.'

'You can do that at your present rank.'

'Yes, sir, but DI has more clout.'

He could see she was pursuing this with real aggression.

'Don't you think so sir?' she added. Sensing his confusion and perhaps his resentment of her pushiness she was trying to coax him back.

'You'd be lucky to get an acting position at the minute,' he reflected. 'And the whole idea of job sharing was to avoid elevating to higher ranks unnecessarily.'

'Temporary acting,' she put forward knowing full well that temporary acting positions tended to evolve into permanent. She left him to think.

'But I'll have a word with the Chief Super,' he confided after a brief cogitation.

If he hadn't been standing right over her she knew exactly how she would have reacted but she was unsure how he would interpret an enthusiastic response. This could be great news but he was almost whispering it in her ear.

'Thank you sir.' She had tried to keep it matter-of-fact, as if it were her due. He retreated an inch or two.

'DI Redland now, sadly, no more. So a vacancy...'

Put that way the great news was lessened momentarily. She looked duly mournful.

'You don't seem overly...' he wanted to say grateful but he knew instinctively that would cut no ice with Challis. '...pleased at the prospect.'

'Of course I am sir. Thank you. It's just a shame that in these circumstances...'

'It's not exactly filling dead man's shoes.'

His retreat now was more marked. He headed back behind his desk.

'The Chief may need to take it higher, you know that, especially in times like these.'

'Sir,' she hesitated over her choice of words. 'The argument has to be that it's, er, not easy for a DS to run a team like...well, any team. Much more efficient as DI.'

'You forget a sergeant would then be needed, to replace you. Who would that be?'

There was only one person in the team. 'It would have to be Harry Muench, sir.'

He nodded. 'I know Harry,' he mumbled. She hated the way he said that.

He wanted to end this discussion. 'We'll see. In the meantime you'll be running the team as you are, so you and I will be having heart-to-heart chats every day and I'm a busy man so I'd appreciate from you a complete breakdown of cases being worked on and their status.' He guessed she'd be thinking how come he doesn't know that already, so he went on. 'DI Redland gets on with the job and he has my trust. I don't need detail from him but I need to know where you're starting from.'

'When will you get an answer from the Chief?'

He was irritated by her now. This was the effect she'd always had on him. She was only a DS but he had always thought that she had a mind of an equal. Either she was good like Redland believed or he was past it. But it was hard to believe the other stuff he'd heard about her.

'When he decides to give one. Don't get ahead of yourself, there's a good girl.'

That style of reprimand made her hackles rise.

'The team will still be one short sir.'

He smirked. 'Tough. Just get on with it. I can't pull bodies out of a hat.'

She straightened up in her chair. 'Do I tell the others? About the DI, I mean. DI Redland.'

Derek O'Halloran just shrugged.

She checked the missed call.

'Sayer,' she said into her phone. 'You rang.'

'Yeah,' he drawled as if annoyed she'd not answered when he'd rung.

'I was with the Super,' she explained. She blurted out the news about Redland.

'I know,' he said. 'That's why I'm calling you.' My God, Donahoe and/or Cotterill must have been on the phone to everyone. 'I guess you're it on this suicide then.'

Yes, she guessed she was. 'It was suicide then.'

He hesitated. 'Ye-e-s. It's a bit early to come to any hard and fast conclusions. I've had a preliminary look at the body and other stuff...'

'O, did you...?'

'Yes, we got the log and one or two other items that you hadn't spotted. Understandable, considering how quickly it got dark yesterday.' He was excusing himself and telling her that she was just as bad. She decided to sound upbeat and positive.

'Good.'

'The body's off to the lab later for more detailed forensics, autopsy.'

'Right, so you were saying...' There was no response from Sayer. 'You were saying it was a suicide'

'Yes, well, I was calling you to say I think you should come and have a look for yourself, before we start cutting him up. There's a backlog anyway.'

'Why do I want to come and look at a suicide?'

'Difficult to explain over the phone.'

Why was it that geeks always wanted to surround their work in mystique? Forensics, I.T., doctors; they were all the same.

She didn't have time for this today, not with the way things were panning out. 'I can't get there yet. I'm up to my eyes in it now.'

'Look, this is your case. Either get here or delegate. Somebody from your end needs to see this to believe it.'

'Look just tell me what the issue is. Give us a clue for God's sake.'

There was a heavy intake of breath at the other end.

'His underpants; they weren't his.'

'What?' Is that it? she asked herself.

'They were a couple of sizes too small.'

'You wanted me to come down there and look at his pants? I think I have more urgent stuff...'

'Didn't you notice how clean they were?'

Challis hesitated. 'Hardly. Not exactly where my attention was.'

'Course it was. Would be for any women. Didn't you ever see that Mel Gibson film...Mel? 'What Women Want'. Need I say more?'

I hope you don't, she thought. Her silence urged him on. 'Anyway, they're clean, in areas where they shouldn't be but there's something on them where you wouldn't expect it to be. They're off for a closer look.'

'So what's the urgency then? Why do you want somebody down there, for my expert opinion on pants or...?'

He interrupted her loudly. 'It looks like he hung himself twice.'

Eight

Hurrying back down the two flights of stairs to her floor, Challis was trying to wipe Sayer from her mind. He knew about Redland, he knew she was 'it' for now and yet he couldn't resist piling on the wind-up, inventing a conspiracy around Timothy Bush. There was a touch of panic inside her. The last thing she wanted, on top of everything else, was a suicide that wasn't straightforward.

At the door on the last landing she stopped. Her mind was racing and her body had done the same. The Super wanted a status report, Sayer demanded she visit the morgue and Muench was waiting back in the office, licking his lips in anticipation of bad news for her.

Well, there was bad news all right. The boss, her boss, their boss, was in hospital, in intensive care, perhaps fighting for his life, perhaps dying.

She had worked with Alan Redland for six years, ever since she made sergeant. She had often thought of him as her mentor. He'd brought her on. He could be scathing and sarcastic and master of the outrageous turn of phrase. But from very early on he had trusted her. That's why

O'Halloran's comment about trusting Redland and implying that he could not award her the same had served to cut her legs from under her. Redland, her buffer, the man she could please with her work, was out of the picture. O'Halloran would make her start from scratch like some rookie and would never give her a free rein. She doubted now his sincerity about trusting Redland. When you get to be an O'Halloran you stop trusting anyone.

She could not let this get to her. If Redland came round in his hospital bed and started worrying that she couldn't swim in the deep end - because he would - then that might just finish him off. She had to do her job as she had always done it; she knew she could. And, boy, she would be acting DI this time tomorrow with a bit of luck. She'd have the clout to clout Muench.

She entered her floor and went straight to the kitchen area. She needed a coffee. Two colleagues from the Caerphilly area were coming out, steaming cups in hand. There was a cursory acknowledgement. If the grapevine about Redland had stretched to them they didn't show it.

She grabbed the kettle. It was hot but empty. She put enough water in for one cup. Waste not, want not.

She got a mug out of the cupboard. Some people had their own but she used a common one. One spoonful of Nescafe. Milk, the semi-skimmed carton, from the fridge. Sniff it then pour it on top of the grains. Spoon from the top drawer, give it a good stir. Kettle boiled, leave it a minute, then add and stir again.

She stirred it with vigour, sending a splash or two of the brown liquid over the rim and onto the work surface.

Her stirring rhythm was a physical manifestation of the internal firing up of her own resolve. Get back into the office. Get on top of things, including Muench. No, not Muench; Harry. She must call him Harry. Undermine him by bringing him closer.

And this time tomorrow Harry Muench could call her 'ma'am'.

There's work to be done, lots of it and fewer of them to do it.

As she turned to leave with her hot coffee, DC Kay Ruff came in, braking sharply with an 'O.' She backed against a door jamb to let Challis pass. She was an inch or so shorter than Challis but much more full-bodied.

'Kay!' She was surprised to see the DC but glad. Since the younger woman had joined the team Challis had seen her as an ally. Still too many men around and Redland's team had needed the balance redressed. She wasn't too sure of Redland's view of female officers. She and he had always got on but there had been a few instances of remarks he made that could be construed as less than supportive of the ambitions of woman in the police workplace. He was sarcastic about the efforts of organizations to include the minorities. He used to quote the case of an American multi-national company which was accused of not including women, ethnic minorities or the disabled at the top of the company. So what did they do to remedy this? They enrolled a new board member: a one-legged black woman. Killed off three criticisms with one cynical blow, Redland had said, with what looked like a grin of admiration.

There was an increasing number of other ethnic officers in the Force these days and Kay Ruff was one of them. She was of West Indian ancestry but, she had told Challis, from a mix of African and Indian forebears. She had once told Challis what her maiden name had been and on hearing what a tongue twister it was it was easy to see why she now used her husband's name despite its unfortunate connotations in the minds of the more unsympathetic males. 'A bit of rough' was an easy running crack but it had no legs as the girl herself was anything but. Challis envied the young DC's skin colouring; it was like a tan to die for. Her own skin was the pale side of white and didn't seem to like exposure to sunshine.

'Come in.' Challis backed up and Ruff uttered another 'O', followed by 'Morning, Melanie.' She hurried past with a breathless 'Coffee' in her local lilt that was far more Welsh-sounding than Challis.

'Where've you been, Kay? Was it that hotel job up in Raglan?'

'Yeah.'

'How's it going?'

'Waste of time I reckon. The bloke thinks someone's pinching money but he can't prove it. I don't know what he expects from us. Probably wants us to stand guard twenty-four seven.'

Her lack of inches meant she had to stretch to retrieve mugs from the remainder at the back of the cupboard. Challis noticed that she'd brought one dirty mug in with her; Muench's personalized mug, a red dragon with the words 'Wales for the Grand Slam', and now she was getting another two down.

'Ray's in, I take it.'

'Yeah, he was right behind me.'

Challis drew closer. 'Kay, what have I told you about fetching and carrying for those two.'

Ruff shrugged. 'It's okay. I was making one for myself.'

'Make sure they take their turn. You're not here to skivvy for them.'

'They're okay. Ray often makes one for me.'

Yeah, Ray does, thought Challis.

'What's Ray working on today?'

'No idea.'

No, thought Challis. Silly question. Why would Kay know? It should be up on the board anyway.

Ruff was waiting for the kettle to boil and was busying herself putting coffee in the mugs and sugaring two of them. She liked her sugar, too much Challis thought. She could lose a pound or two. She was much rounder than Challis; a shapely figure that she kept under the radar by wearing shapeless clothing. Without turning she asked 'Everything all right with the Super?'

Good old Muench. Although, surprisingly, he obviously hadn't heard about the boss.

'I'll tell you when you get back in the office.' Challis turned to leave. 'Soon as you can.'

Ruff had a known tendency to take her coffee on a walkabout.

Challis had got as far as telling the other three in the team the position with the boss. Harry Muench took the news as if she was telling him the weather forecast. Ray Lockett was more concerned and tried to hypothesize about how and why, asking Challis questions about the boss's health.

'He's always at the doctors,' Muench commented, taking his tie off. He always wore a tie. Redland insisted that the men who worked for him looked the part and that included being clean-shaven and wearing suitable clothes, including a tie. In the past, he'd threatened Muench, promising to give him all the shitty jobs if that was all he looked fit enough to cope with. Muench complied but wore his tie loose and top button undone when the boss was out of the office. Now, he had obviously seen a signal to remove the choke around his neck completely. He regarded it as outmoded, making him and Lockett the butt of jokes from other sections. Challis couldn't help but notice. Muench did it slowly as if it was the start of a full monty. He smirked at Ruff who was also watching him.

'It's the job,' Ruff said to get away from his gaze. 'Alex says it'll be the death of me.' Alex was her husband. They all knew that he was forever going on about the stress of her job. He wanted her to start a family but she thought that right now that would be just as bad as being killed by the job.

'Hey,' Muench rounded on her. 'How was the romantic Valentine dinner last night? Did it work?'

Ruff ignored him. Challis wondered if Ruff was late partly because she couldn't get out of bed this morning.

Challis had told them as much as she knew about what had happened to the boss and the current known facts about his condition.

Lockett wouldn't let the subject go. He was a large young man with a round fresh face. The slim Muench was always taunting him about his size. 'You've got bigger tits than Challis,' he told him. At other times, Muench used to tell him he was a heart-attack candidate unless he changed his ways, so it was inevitable that now he would want to extract as much info as possible out of a close coronary experience.

Challis couldn't answer his more detailed morbid points, nor did she want to. She silenced him by moving on to the white board that detailed the jobs on the go, who was on them and progress made or not.

'Right,' she proclaimed, realizing that the first thing to do was add the suicide of Timothy Bush to the list. She spoke as she wrote. 'This was the call that the boss and I followed up yesterday. Man found hanging. He was naked except for his pants. Could have been there at least one night. Found by a neighbour, Meredith Guster. PCs Bell and...' she stepped to her desk to look it up 'Richards answered the 999. PC Bell has interviewed the farmer, John Gee, who owns the field. Early forensics show some anomalies, which is a shame. Needs following up.'

'How old is he?' asked Ruff, surprising Challis.

'We don't know for sure yet. Fiftyish.'

'You want to check if he's got a son in Afghanistan. Or daughter, I suppose.'

Challis frowned. 'Why?'

'I've read reports,' Ruff explained. 'A few fathers have gone to the extreme to get their serving sons back from Afghanistan. Self-harm. Kids come back home on compassionate grounds. A couple went too far, accidentally hung themselves. It was in one of last Sunday's papers.'

Challis nodded slowly. She couldn't rubbish this if it was fact. 'It can be checked out, Kay, once we establish if he has any next of kin. He seemed to have lived alone.' She nodded again, appreciatively, at Ruff.

'Underpants are a bit strange though,' Ruff smiled.

For all her moaning about the job killing her and her occasional disappearances Ruff had always impressed Challis with her enthusiasm. And if anyone in the office new the latest on crime trends or proposed advancements in technology or procedures it was Kay Ruff: ear to the ground, finger on the pulse, eye on all the bouncing balls.

'For some, hanging is a turn on don't forget,' Muench reminded them.

'Okay. Thanks Harry,' Challis changed tack. 'Anyway, that's the latest up on the board. Let's crack on.' She looked back at the board. 'Now I need to know, the Super needs to know, where we all are with all this other stuff up here.'

'Who's replacing the boss?' asked Muench.

Challis decided to say nothing until she knew herself. 'The Super's trying to locate Inspector Hubbard,' she lied. The Super knew where he was; Australia.

'So...' Muench started.

'So, for the time being it's just us, Harry. Now then, are you still on that robbery at...' she looked at the board '...Henderson Timber? That's been going on a while, hasn't it?'

'Yeah!' Muench was defensive, even evasive. 'I'm still liaising with the owners about the full scale of it.'

'Got a suspect?' Challis demanded.

'Nearly. I've interviewed all the employees. There's a stack of stuff on the system.' This he said almost accusingly, as if Challis should read it rather than interrogate him.

'How can you *nearly* have a suspect?' challenged Ruff. 'Should have a perp by now!'

'Narrowing it down, Krufty' he retorted, knowing she would wince at the use of his special name for her. 'It's got to be the dispatch end of the business. It's either the whole crew or a couple of individuals.'

'Have you pulled anybody in yet? Given anyone a hard time?'

He almost replied 'not quite' but Ruff was still eying him. 'Probably tomorrow.'

'Okay,' Challis jumped in. 'How much time are you putting into this for the rest of this week? Will that be it tomorrow?'

He fumbled with papers on his desk. 'I don't know. Can't say for sure.'

'Well we need to know, as soon as you like, please, Harry.' Her manner was calm as she jotted a reminder on the board alongside Henderson Timber.

'Kay,' she said with deliberation, to impart to Muench that she didn't like Krufty either. She went on to quickly sort out Ruff with her hotel job.

'What makes them so sure someone's on the take?'

'Book-keeping figures,' Ruff replied, going on to explain. 'The margins are down. Mr. Giovanni the manager reckons he knows how much he should be taking in on bar takings. It's simple, he says. You know the cost of the alcohol and by applying the markup you know how much it should be earning for you. There's a shortfall, he reckons. Somebody's helping themselves to cash to the tune of £100 a week some weeks.'

'For how long?'

'Since before Christmas he says. Busy time, Christmas. Good turnover, or it should have been. He reckons he lost even more over the holiday period.'

'Got to be one of the bar staff surely.'

'If it is, he doesn't know how they're doing it.'

'Well, he needs to find out before we can do anything more.'

'Perhaps he ought to sack the lot and start again,' Lockett suggested.

'He doesn't want to do that. Some good people working for him.'

'Sounds like it,' moaned Lockett.

'What you ought to do,' said Muench almost gloatingly, 'is get uniform back on it. Just get 'em to show their faces in there a few times; that'll give whoever's on the take the shits. Pound to a penny the books'll balance in no time.'

Challis hated to admit it but it wasn't a bad suggestion.

'Try it,' she told Ruff.

'They won't like it,' she argued.

'Tough.'

Ruff also had another two cases allocated to her that seemed to be dead in the water.

Ray Lockett was working on a stabbing from the previous weekend. Three men had needed emergency treatment, all of them with stab wounds. Lockett was trying to find who did what to who first. This job had taken priority over three other minor nuisance jobs, still outstanding.

'We need to wrap up some of these,' Challis announced. 'I need you to tell me what we can take ahead.'

They engaged in a long debate on what needed to be done, at the end of which she was not much clearer on the state of things, had no idea how to present it all to O'Halloran and Muench had gone off to lunch.

Nine

After lunch that she didn't have time for, Challis phoned the Super to check his availability to go over the job list only to be told by his secretary that he was off-site until the following morning.

She sighed as she realized the games that were afoot. Redland had once said to her that Chief Superintendent Derek O'Halloran was all piss and wind. He'd confided that over a pint of London Pride in his watering hole in Usk, well, over several pints, in front of a vast roaring fire. She'd only drunk two as she had to drive the three miles to Capelgwm but he could stagger just a few streets to his bed.

It had been a similar situation that Redland had recalled; O'Halloran demanding in front of the DCC that Redland furnish him with info that was 'already late in forthcoming', so he reckoned. When Redland presented him with the report the next day it went straight into the pending tray and was still there two weeks later. She was getting the drift herself now.

Bugger him, she thought, and took her breakdown of outstanding tasks and best estimates for further activity up to his office and left it for him. She'd cribbed the format from Redland's last report that she found on the system, sitting at his desk, using his laptop, but couldn't help notice that old cases were lingering and all the time new ones were coming on board. 'This is no bloody good,' she mumbled to herself. 'Overload alert.' And she was sure that O'Halloran would think the same. How could the boss let things mount up like this?

One thing she was sure of; she wasn't going to hold a communal inquest like that again. Took too much time. Too much wriggling to get out from under the truth. She now knew the score; she'd play it differently in future.

Muench did not return from lunch. Lockett and Ruff were back from their short breaks, chewing the last crumbs, and were on their keyboards, presumably updating their case files. Challis still had to add the Guster interview notes so she sat at her desk and drew out her notebook.

Shit! Her notes put the suicide back into her mind; and Sayer as well She had to concede that maybe he hadn't been winding her up and that perhaps whatever he had discovered might shed a different light on Guster's evidence. So, what comes first? Go see Sayer, she decided.

She called him. He was sarcastic but would see her if she'd get over to the mortuary in Abergavenny by three. Is he this condescending with male colleagues, she wondered? Never witnessed it with the boss.

As soon as she got to her feet, the fact that she was in charge made her hesitate. She really wanted to go off on her own to see Sayer but if this thing escalated she'd need help.

'Kay, you busy?'

'Just updating.'

'Finish it when we get back.'

*

'Notice the two v-shaped marks.' Sayer drew the attention of Challis and Ruff to the neck of Timothy Bush. 'One is a severe inverted V bruise. The upper one. The neck above that is swollen and dark. See. Now, below that one, see a second V shape. That was where the rope was placed when we took him down. Nice and tight but it was the upper one that killed him.'

The two detectives leaned over the naked corpse to follow what Sayer was describing.

'So the rope slid down, as he struggled,' concluded Challis, knowing that even those intent on killing themselves this way would invariably struggle if death was a long time coming.

Sayer shook his head. 'Don't forget, he was hanging there, his weight pulling down on the rope. It wouldn't move downwards.'

'Okay, it started at the lower point and moved up due to his weight and the struggling.'

'There are no abrasions on the skin between the two points to indicate that.' He pointed. 'Also, there is no swelling or darkening above that lower point and crucially there is no bruising at that point itself.'

The two were taking all of this in, thinking how to offer another contradiction. Sayer beat them to it. 'Which means that the rope was placed there post-mortem.'

'After he was dead?' queried Ruff.

Sayer drew in a builders-type breath. 'That's post-mortem for you.'

'Hang on,' said Challis, standing up and back. 'Nobody could move that rope down this man's neck while he was hanging there, not without taking his weight first.'

'That's probably true,' agreed Sayer. 'But it could happen if he'd hung himself somewhere else and then been moved to where he was found.'

Challis almost laughed at the suggestion. Sayer went on.

'Look at these marks, on his chest. They're also on his back. Pressure marks, I'm pretty sure. Again post-mortem. This guy was roughly handled after he was dead. And before you say it, not by us. Feet first with us.'

Challis was absorbing all of this as Sayer carried on. 'Since I called you this morning we've started having a closer look at the rope as well.' He took them to an adjacent table where the blue rope with its noose and knot still intact lay. 'Standard blue nylon rope. Buy it in any B & Q store. Pretty new. Looks like it's never been used before. May have been bought specifically for the purpose. You might be able to trace that: credit card, receipts. Anyway, we found some black stuff embedded in it. It's being analyzed but it looks like some sort of black paint., ground right into the rope strands. There look, below the knot from the tree branch.' Challis and Ruff peered at the rope and could see ingrained black streaks.

'If you look at the inside of the knot from the branch you will see the same sort of ground-in effect but this time it's green with sap and lichen. So, to expand on my twice hung theory I could surmise that for the first hanging this rope was knotted, here, around something that was painted black.'

'Aw, come on,' said Challis. 'That rope could have been used for anything before this. That black stuff does not make your case.'

'Not on its own,' conceded Sayer. 'But we'll do more in-depth analysis – that includes DNA by the way - and I bet the ground-in effect of sap juice and black paint will be exactly the same. This poor sod has been well hung. Talking of which...' he turned back to the corpse '...you will have noticed this.' He pointed at Timothy Bush's genitals. There were bloody scabs.

Challis realized it was pointless reacting to Sayer's below-the-belt assumption. He'd beaten her up on that issue earlier in the day. She and Ruff stared down at the scarred foreskin, shaft and testicles.

'Quite old,' Sayer helped them out. 'Dried blood. Scabs about to come off.. Maybe a few weeks. Could have been self-inflicted. Perhaps a lead-up to his suicide. Self-loathing, eventually killing himself. You might need to check any medical history on the guy, you know, psychiatric treatment...'

Challis turned away; Ruff was slower to do so.

'What about the knots?' asked Challis, retreating from the suppositions surrounding the dead man's injuries back to the tangible evidence. Disappointed, Sayer followed her to the other table; Ruff also jerked back to attention.

'Er, ordinary slip knot round the neck.' He picked up the rope again. 'This knot around the tree branch looks more complex. I'll have to consult my boy-scout manual. Took us a while to slide it off the branch without undoing it.'

'Yes, I saw your woodworking handiwork.'

'Yeah, but look, the knot slides up and down the rope easily but regardless of the weight won't come undone. See?'

She nodded as he demonstrated but her eyes had caught sight of a plastic evidence bag on the table. 'What's that?'

'Ah yes.' Sayer picked up the bag. ' Nearly forgot. Well spotted.' He handed it to Challis who, with Ruff looking over her shoulder, stared through the bag before opening it for a better look. She peered inside. 'Piece of gravel, isn't it?'

'Yes, that's right. Found it between toes, right foot. Lots of other marks, small indentations, under both feet as if he'd tippy-toed over a gravel bed. No sign of mud and grass stains on his little piggies. Told you. He was moved.'

Challis sighed. 'Here.' From her pocket she fished out the evidence bag containing the fibres off the log she had collected that morning. She explained their origin.

'Yeah,' Sayer acknowledged casually. 'We got some too. They're off for analysis. But thanks. Every little helps.'

Ten

Challis had no intention of leaving the hospital without personally checking up on her boss. When she and Ruff got to the main A&E reception they were told he'd been moved to Emergency Assessment. She suggested Ruff go wait in the car.

'No way,' was the response. 'It's bloody cold out there and besides I'd like to see how he is.'

Challis wasn't going to argue.

DC Donahoe was still waiting in A&E. No sign of his colleague Cotterill who had gone outside to wait for the arrival of uniformed officers who were going to relieve the two DCs.

'He was conscious when they brought him in,' Donahoe told Challis and Ruff. 'He told us what had happened. He didn't look any worse, though, when they wheeled him out about an hour ago. They went that way.'

Challis and Ruff followed his finger. Challis had always thought Donahoe was okay; not so sure about Cotterill, another one who clearly thought female sergeants were an unnecessary luxury.

They followed the signs, through the warren until they came to yet another reception desk outside of double doors over which was the sign Emergency Assessment Unit. The diminutive receptionist was just leaving her post as they arrived; she was off through the double doors with a couple of files in her hand. Challis tried to hail her but failed to halt her progress. She checked the clock high on the wall: three-forty. A man arrived and strolled up to the desk, looking over it, left and right. He glanced timidly at the two women.

'You waiting?' he asked. 'Or have you been seen to?'

Challis nodded. 'Waiting.'

It struck her as a paradox that hundreds, thousands, of people worked in these hospitals and yet sometimes you couldn't find a single one of them.

Another couple of minutes and the woman came back, not looking at any of them. She went behind the high desk. Fortunately for her the workstation was elevated. She managed a smile at Challis, Ruff and the man, unable to determine who was next.

'We need to see Alan Redland,' said Challis.

The woman tapped on the keyboard and addressed the screen on the desk, which Ruff observed was not ergonomically positioned. She'll get neck ache.

'Are you family?' the woman asked.

'No.'

The woman gave herself some time, studying the screen. 'Well, I'm sorry but…'

Challis had her warrant card in her hand and flashed it. 'Police.'

Ruff cast a sideways glance at her. She could see Challis was trying a perk of the job but the little jobsworth wasn't complying that easily.

'I'm not sure Mr. Redland is well enough,' she said calmly.

'Please check,' Challis requested, equally calmly.

The woman got down and started to leave again.

'I'm here to see my wife,' exclaimed the man. 'I was called, told to come here. Mrs. Swift. Shirley. Shirley Swift.'

'I'll be with you now,' the little woman shouted over her shoulder as she hurried off through the double doors.

'She collapsed, they said,' he spoke to the backs of Challis and Ruff. 'Shopping she was. Waitrose.'

They both turned but only Ruff produced a smile. 'She'll be fine, I'm sure.'

'Probably the prices,' Challis murmured.

A young woman, younger than Challis and probably Ruff as well, dressed in a white coat, stethoscope protruding out of one pocket, came out of the double doors behind the little receptionist who returned to her place behind the desk and half-heartedly turned her attention to Mr. Swift, not wanting to miss any conversation between Dr. Jade Gupta and the two police-women.

'Police?' asked Dr. Gupta.

'That's right.'

Dr. Gupta nodded. 'Here to see your colleague, Inspector Redland?'

'That's right.' Challis was non-committal. 'How is he?' She eyeballed the doctor. Ruff's feet shuffled with barely disguised discomfort. The doctor averted her gaze to look down at a file she was carrying.

'He's…he's stable.'

'Nothing serious then?'

A smile now from the doctor. 'Too early to say but too early for visitors, I'm afraid. If you were family…'

'He hasn't really got any family.'

The doctor read the file again. 'He…has a nephew; his next of kin…'

Ruff spoke next. 'We're all family in a sense.'

'Ah, yes, I'm sure. In every sense except the legal one.' She looked from Ruff to Challis. Ruff couldn't help but admire the way the beautiful Dr. Gupta was handling the situation. 'Look, I can tell you that he's awake, drowsy, and being closely monitored. All being well he'll be in a ward soon, perhaps this evening.'

'Was it a heart attack?' Ruff asked.

'We'll know more, later.' She put her hand in the pocket that didn't hold the stethoscope and pulled out a small notepad. 'Is one of you Sergeant Challis?'

'Yes,' admitted Challis.

'He thought you might be here sometime. This is for you.'

Dr. Gupta handed over what Challis recognized as Redland's notepad. She took it.

'There was no need to try it on with us, you know,' was the doctor's parting shot as she turned and retraced her steps through the double doors. Challis and Ruff saw the grin on the lips of the little receptionist who was still pretending to attend to the poor man. 'Mr...?'

'That could have been embarrassing,' observed Ruff but she was secretly pleased by the clever Dr. Gupta.

Challis was about to ignore her when she stopped in her tracks. Ruff turned and looked back at her, not noticing a tall man coming towards them in a frontal attack.

'Melanie!' he called out, coming on unhesitatingly. He bypassed Ruff with a casual glance, moved up to Challis and pecked her forcibly on the cheek, his gloved hands gripping her upper arms.

'Stuart,' Challis breathed, barely loud enough for Ruff to catch it.

'I was hoping I'd see you,' he said, still holding her. She looked as if she wanted to back away from someone with bad breath. His words registered but she clearly hadn't wanted to hear them. 'How's Alan?'

She eased herself away. Her mind was racing, almost missing the question. 'Not too bad, so they say.'

Ruff had sidled forward. 'We weren't allowed to see him.' She stared at this man. He was a fine figure, immaculately dressed, well-wrapped up. This time he looked her up and down. Challis reacted, glad of the distraction that Ruff's intervention had provided.

'This is my colleague, Kay,' she introduced, then, immaturely, she babbled on. 'She works in your uncle's team too.'

Ah, uncle, thought Ruff; that explains the winter clothing.

'Kay,' Challis continued, her face reddening, much to Kay's surprise, 'this is Stuart Devlin.'

'O, hi,' greeted Ruff with enthusiasm. 'You're the nephew.'

He smiled. 'Yes, bit of a shock this. I got a call.'

'Stuart!' A female voice called to him as a woman came around the corner. She smiled broadly as she approached. 'There you are.'

He grabbed the new arrival and kissed her full if briefly on the lips. As she pulled slowly away from the embrace she smiled at Challis and Ruff, half expecting some introduction.

'Sue, these are colleagues of my uncle,' Stuart offered.

'O! Right.' She stared at both of them as if deciding a selection.

Challis said nothing. For some reason she enjoyed a slight elation that this woman obviously didn't know the boss; if she had Stuart would have used his name.

'Well, we'll go and see how the old fella is.'

'They'll let you in most probably,' added Ruff.

'Yes,' he agreed. He seemed to hesitate, wanting to say something else to Challis. 'Probably see you again, Melanie.'

'Yeah, yeah. Perhaps.' Challis agreed quietly. 'Tell him...' Tell him what, she couldn't decide.

'I'll give him your love.' Stuart eyed her mischievously.

'We'll be back.'

'I'll keep you up to speed with his progress if you like.'

Challis didn't know why she would want that from him but momentarily she couldn't think how else she would easily know about the boss's progress or lack of it. She gave half a nod. 'Fine.' Christ, she did feel as if she'd left her front door wide open.

'Nice to have met you, Kay.' His stare bored into her and then he and his female friend were gone to the reception desk.

Eleven

Seeing Stuart Devlin had taken Challis's breath away. It was so unexpected and yet it shouldn't have been. The boss's next of kin. The doctor had reminded her. Bound to be there sooner or later; just a hell of a shame that he should turn up while she was there. Ideally she would have liked some warning. And then avoided him.

She had no idea who the woman had been. She'd been all over him; in his face, literally. Not a conquest of his. Too full of herself.

'He was a bit of all right,' Ruff chuckled as they made their way out of the hospital. 'See the boss's influence i.e. the dress code, wrapped up nice and warm. Obviously hasn't got to his girl-friend yet though. How can anyone expose their cleavage in weather like this?'

Ruff could see that Challis was not responding to her attempts at humour. 'How come you know him?'

Challis shivered. Nothing to do with the weather. 'About six years ago I met him at the boss's,' she replied without looking at Ruff.

She had first met Stuart Devlin just after she'd joined the Redland team.

The boss thought there should be a celebration. He had a new sergeant who lived in the same neck of the woods as himself. Many people he worked with accused him of living with the upper crust, such was a reputation of Usk, the mid-county small town, population two thousand and something, property prices astronomical and the perception it was very much a cliquey society. All crap, Redland protested. He liked the town because it was handily placed for getting off to all points of the compass, had great pubs and you could enjoy its culture on the fringes if you chose. And the area ticked his other boxes, archaeologically speaking: Stone Age, Iron Age, Roman, medieval, all on his doorstep.

So, he'd been smugly chuffed to find that his new DS lived not quite in Usk but near enough, just three miles to the east, and had done all her life, in the house she had inherited from the parents, killed as a result of a road accident in Spain a couple of years earlier. He readily admitted that he was a newcomer having moved into his semi-detached house just nineteen years before.

He'd invited her to a meal at his house. He hadn't called it 'dinner' because he didn't think that his culinary skills could produce food that could be described thus. She had been nervous about accepting but she did because she thought he would be inviting the others from the team. It was too late to back out when she discovered that it would be just her. Redland was new to her; she knew he had no wife and the invitation certainly got her wound up by the others in the team, especially the males.

She needn't have worried. She wasn't the only one there.

Redland's nephew, Stuart Devlin, was there as well, and not just for the meal. He was living there at the time. He was a public servant and had just moved down to the area from somewhere near Windsor to work in the Office for National Statistics in Newport where he was an IT Security expert. His uncle Alan had offered him accommodation until he found a place of his own.

It transpired that, as that evening wore on, uncle Alan was no threat to her at all but his nephew was all charm.

'We're in the same line of business really,' he smoothly assured her.

'Are we like hell!' Redland objected.

Stuart refused to be beaten down and nodded conspiratorially at Melanie. 'We are,' he softly insisted while Redland's back was turned. 'Security is security no matter how you dress it up.'

He declared how much he liked this part of the world and hadn't visited it nearly enough over the years. His mother, uncle Alan's sister, had married and moved away from the ancestral home in Newport and had brought Stuart to visit only rarely. Uncle Alan, having only himself to think about, was the one who visited them.

Melanie had intended to drink little that evening, planning to eat and run. Although it took a while she eventually relaxed. The boss was straight in his approach to her, informal, no edge to him, no ulterior designs. So she had a glass of red wine or two and Stuart Devlin sidled in with a subtle flank attack. She enjoyed his intimate eye contact. Not enough men applied that technique.

Before she knew it he was inside her weakening defences. At the table, his head came close as he teased 'uncle Alan'. She liked him whispering loudly in her ear while she threw glances at Redland that said 'I don't believe what he's saying about you'. He was tactile: a squeeze on the shoulder, a hand on the knee as the three sat with coffee and liqueurs. Subtle fingertips, fleeting palm prints.

And she failed to notice how little alcohol Stuart was actually drinking.

The only music in her ears that evening was the easy words from Stuart's lips. Unusually, the boss did not possess a music system, not even a combined radio/CD player. Stuart apologized to her about this deficiency but Redland explained that nearly all music left him cold, not that he was tone deaf but he simply abhorred the cult of the iconic singer or, as he put it, the pointlessness of all those strings and wind instruments competing with each other. He admitted to liking the theme from Dr. Who and those rousing studio fanfares that used to precede old movies.

'You're not serious,' Melanie wondered.

'He is,' Stuart answered for him. 'Mind you, he does have this weird collection of 1950s comedy songs that he inherited from his father: Bob Hope, Bing Crosby and…what's his name?'

'I don't know,' Redland shrugged. 'Spike Jones?'

'Whatever.' Stuart threw up his hands in surrender. 'But he has no means of playing them.'

'Just imagine,' Redland was still on his anti-music hobby horse over the bought-in apple strudel and his umpteenth beverage, 'a spaceship landing here, having traveled billions of light miles…'

'Light years.'

'Whatever…and its occupants stumble out only to see some noisy individual or worse still a whole collection of them standing in full view of a screaming, hand-clapping crowd, completely out of their brains. They'd either think no danger here and summon all their friends to come take us over or think the planet was one vast lunatic asylum and exterminate the lot of us.'

He would not concede that any pleasure could be derived from such behaviour, from such cacophony, from such a waste of time, space and energy.

This was greeted by Melanie as a drink-induced flight of fancy and she responded in like manner. Then Stuart joined in and they ganged up on him, together creating a front for musical relaxation and uplifting experiences. They argued and quoted contradictory evidence and examples. Redland stuck to his guns and Melanie could not decide if he was just being deliberately argumentative or really meant it or was trying to justify a mean streak in not wanting to spend money on that particular pastime.

The banter quietened and Stuart assured her that his uncle was serious. He'd never known him like music.

'In his car though,' Stuart explained, 'he has a tape player.'

'O yes,' Melanie winked. 'A secret music lover.'

'No,' Stuart continued. 'Old comedies. I don't know what they're called. Used to be on the radio centuries ago.'

'Gems,' said a contented Redland. 'Pure gems. Now they are music to my ears.'

When it came time to conclude the evening Melanie did not need much persuading that she had drunk too much to drive. She readily accepted the situation and pulled out her phone to call the local taxi service.

'They'll be an age,' Stuart warned. 'It's one man and his pony and trap.'

There was some truth in that statement, not the bit about the pony and trap, but the local service was not exactly well-endowed with a fleet of limousines waiting for your call. Normally, the cars had to be pre-booked, especially on weekend evenings like this, otherwise it was pot-luck if one was available.

'I haven't drunk much. I'll drive you home,' Stuart volunteered.

'You've had some,' said the unsure but non-objecting Melanie.

'You can show me the back roads.'

She silently accepted his offer.

Redland was too far gone to think much of it but after they'd left he began to wonder if Stuart would be back before morning. He knew his nephew well enough – had actually got to know his regular night time habits since his arrival some weeks earlier – but he had no idea of his new DS's proclivities. So when he heard Stuart returning not thirty minutes later, his self-satisfaction at his choice of sergeant swelled. His nephew had met his match. Unless she was a lesbian. He had wondered. But he was too numb to think more about it and his bed was soft and warm and sleep inducing.

His powers of deduction were far from reliable and his assumption way off the mark.

Melanie had allowed, welcomed, a first kiss, a passionate kiss full of promise and expectation, from her gallant chauffeur. She had not had a man in any way shape or form for quite some time and that night she had been so lulled into a feeling of well-being and inevitable acquiescence that the kiss confirmed that she was ready for this man, this lovely man. Her softened brain had this phrase going round and round: ripe for plucking. It sounded sensuous.

She stepped from his car, a cramped two-seater sports job, roof down on that mild summer night. He jumped from the seat out onto the road, ran around to take her outstretched hand. She led him across the one-car concrete driveway to the door of Daubwthyn Cottage, once two adjoining two-up, two-down cottages that her parents had bought and knocked into one and extended. In Welsh, not their native tongue but a patriotic concession, they had named the resultant dwelling 'daubwthyn' in memory of its prior duality.

By the light of the motion-detecting outside lamps, she withdrew her key only for him to take her hand and help her slide it slowly into the lock of the front door. He was up against her as he pushed it ajar and eased her into the vestibule. Right behind her, he spun her round, pulled her to him and planted another kiss on her open mouth as he took her into a promising embrace, tightly, bringing up an unstoppable moan of delight from deep down.

'Sleep well,' he whispered into her face as he drew away. All she could do was watch him walk back to his car. Her hand gripped the door jamb to support her weak-willed knees. He vaulted back into the driving seat. 'I'll call you.' The car started, he reversed into the drive, turned it and sped off back to Usk.

He did call; the very next day, early, well, nearly ten, but a bit early for Melanie that morning-after. He sounded depressingly chirpy. She was barely conscious. Thank God it was Saturday! He was on his way but she managed to persuade him to give her half an hour for a shower at least.

She was under the water when it occurred to her that she had greeted his plans to visit her with enthusiasm, which, on reflection, she should not be displaying. Last night, her appetites, among other things, had been exceedingly whetted. Was he dense or did she not give off the right signals? Aw shit, she thought. Forget it; let's have a nice platonic fun friendship. It was a beautiful morning, he'd come and take her in his open-top sports car, the wind would be drying her hair and perhaps there would be a nice lunch at the end of it. Besides, he was the boss's nephew. It could be awkward to make more of it.

It was the third Saturday of the month and Stuart surprised her with a trip to the Farmers Market in Usk. His enthusiasm for the place was unbounded. He knew all the stalls and chatted with many of the stall holders, Melanie silent in his wake. He purchased bhajis and samosas, the spicier the better, he said. Lunch, he told her. This would put her right.

They drove back to Daubwthyn Cottage. Once inside, he took over, found plates and cutlery and served her the Indian food. He'd also brought cold Tintern beer, which he forced on her despite her protestations that the combination would give her hiccups.

She ate and drank and was whole again.

He only had to kiss her the once for her to take him by the hand and lead him up the stairs. She crossed to her bedroom window to pull the curtains shut but he was right behind her, restraining her, pulling her arms gently back.

'No,' he whispered. 'Leave the daylight. I want to see you'

Thank God for net curtains, she managed to think before complying, still nervous. She had never been particularly proud of her body.

He undressed her with slow deliberation; she him with a touch more urgency. As they both became naked she was confused why he held her hands away from his body. 'No,' he said again. 'Don't touch.'

He held her close but not skin-to-skin. He left himself enough distance between them to permit his eyes to take in her nakedness. With fingernails he drew tracks on her skin. 'You're like alabaster,' he said. 'Like a perfect figurine, almost too precious to touch.' But he did, seemingly sculpting; marveling, almost drooling, she thought.

His lovemaking was so different. His foreplay consciously avoided those body parts that inflamed men usually made a beeline for. With his tongue in her mouth he fingered her head and nape, the tingle from her scalp coursing like boiling waters down the rapids. Her upper arms were caressed with tips of fingers; he stretched them up, pinning them out of the way so that the skin was taut like a drum and her hands helpless. Her spine, ribs, belly and hips were played unmercifully and deliciously. He seemed to be on every inch of her body but those intimate areas had to wait their turn as he gradually circled on them, buttocks, thighs, behind the knees and then the calves, even her feet received some contact from him but by then she could not distinguish what it was he was using to stimulate her.

When he did assail those special places it was completion, full and satisfying.

She knew that she had a slim body, perfect skin, yes, that he found stirring, yet not the obvious curves and buttresses of some of her peers. But the effect of Stuart's expert ministrations was to make her feel wholly voluptuous.

She had never experienced anything like it before and not once had he allowed her own hands to touch any part of him. She found she was a willing accomplice; her obedient helplessness totally erotic.

She had no idea if he was using a condom. The dangers of being without did not seem to enter her head. If he hadn't thought of contraception then she certainly hadn't but she didn't care. Sheer practicalities and mechanics could not be allowed to get in the way of what she was experiencing; it could not be permitted to spoil the rise and rise of extreme pleasure. At the end of it only the broad smile on his wet lips gave any indication of his own satisfaction.

It was her best ever sex, although in the days that followed she knew that the three-letter word was just not big enough to come anywhere near describing what she was enjoying.

In the next weeks, he let her learn to work on him in exactly the same way. Erogenous zones became a new reality for her. The touch of lips, mouth and fingers on unexpected places gave her the pleasure of pleasuring someone else. He was ecstatic as her expertise grew.

She came to know his body as well as he did hers. On first seeing the long scars on his back and right-side ribcage she was shocked. He would not explain their origin. 'For Queen and country,' he said. 'I never talk about it.' She thought he joked but he never did elaborate. Later, Redland told her his nephew had served in the Iraq War of 2003, wounded by a friendly American Chinook who mistook his tank for an enemy one. She did not let slip to Stuart that she knew his secret but she let her lips linger on the pink and red stripes on his otherwise faultless body. They added a certain spice to the affair; a war hero whose wounds she was soothing.

Then it came to an end, not immediately, not even when he moved to his own place in Newport, a dozen miles away, but soon after. Whereas she was content, Stuart wanted more, to move on and expand, extend, their eroticism. He lost patience with her reluctance, shouting, condemning her, trying to persuade her by making her recognise how dull and unimaginative she was. He would leap from her in mid-session. She came to dread intimate overtures. Her body dried up and her limbs became paralytic.

Love had never got a mention. Other social excursions ceased. She came to realize that their relationship was all about getting naked; she had become a means not an end until she failed to provide the means to the ends he craved.

Who broke it off, she couldn't say. She hoped it had been her, she'd been angry enough and she told him so.

'Yeah? And?' Ruff persisted.

'And nothing.'

'Was that his wife?' Ruff persisted.

'No idea. Never seen her before.'

'Has he...?'

'Look!' Challis exploded mildly, now staring fiercely at her colleague. She was going to say more but why should she. Ruff got the message and pulled a facial apology but she didn't know why she had to.

Challis was mad with herself. She had now given the impression that there was more. Why the hell had he crossed her path? He'd ruined her. She'd been on the lookout for something like him ever since and in her fantasies she wished that she had let him take her across those other thresholds, but that was in fantasies. She had never convinced herself that, when push came to shove, she could ever have gone that extra distance with him.

Twelve

'Okay, we need to check out his next of kin,' Challis said to Ruff as she drove back to the office.

Ruff had Redland's notepad in her hands. Challis asked her to flip through it to see what the boss had to say. He had listed several bullet points under the heading 'Timothy Bush':

. *Mrs. Guster: interview*
. *Next of kin: formal id*
. *Clothes: where are they? How come no-one saw a naked man?*
. *Car: check it out*
. *House: check it out*
. *Sayer: collate findings: how did he do it?*

Challis was forcing her mind back onto the job after that unwanted detour around Stuart Devlin.

She was sure that she had thought of all of the boss's points herself, or soon would have.

'The boss is right,' she went on. 'If we were really asked we couldn't swear that the guy is Timothy Bush. We've only got Ms. Guster's word for it. See what you can do by close of play.'

'Okay,' replied Ruff, trying to get over Challis's earlier mood. She detected more urgency and authority in Challis's voice than was usual. Often, Challis would make a request, not an order, but this sounded now more like the latter. She was about to ask what to do about her current jobs but Challis pre-empted her.

'Put your other stuff on ice. I also want you to go see Farmer Gee. PC Billy Bell had a word when he went to get the key for the field gate but we need to know if he saw anything or anyone in that field yesterday, the day before, the day before that...I want to know everyone who's been in there, going back as far as he can. Names, addresses...'

Challis switched the car lights on. It was gone three and getting gloomy already. It was cold and there could be snow in the offing which would cover everything in the field as well as make it difficult for her to get into work.

'You don't really believe this twice hung theory, do you?' Ruff asked. She'd nearly said 'well hung', certain images still making shapes on her retina.

Challis said she thought it a bit far-fetched. Ruff was more explicit than that but she was reminded by her senior colleague that they relied on forensic evidence to paint them a picture, sometimes only an outline, so whatever the likes of Sayer came up with couldn't just be discarded. She was in no position to understand what to look for under the microscope.

'It's a bloody ugly suicide though, if you ask me,' said Ruff.

Sayer had reiterated that it was not strangulation. The autopsy would confirm it, he was sure. It was not murder, not in that sense, but assisted suicide, if that's what it was, was as good as. Murder by hanging wasn't unknown but Sayer had said there was no sign of restraint to subdue the man. If he was drugged unconscious then the autopsy would show it.

A conclusion on all this was essential. It would decide if the case stayed with them or transferred to homicide. Challis didn't know if she should warn the Super now or leave it until more sure. Redland would have known.

She had worked with homicide, been seconded, a number of times, first when she was a raw recruit doing house-to-house on a hit and run case. Later, as a new DC, she was part of a huge team in 2002 that investigated the brutal killing of a teenage office worker, beaten to death on the shop floor of the Newport electrical factory where she worked. Challis was involved with interviewing the work-force including contractors, delivery people, casuals, in fact anyone who had ever set foot in the place. Turned out after all that it was the girl's ex-boyfriend who didn't even work in the place but the investigation went on for months and she learned a lot, about interviewing, taking statements, getting corroborative information, as well as working in a team and maintaining a large case computer database. Her typing skills improved considerably.

'You've got to move on this, Kay,' Challis urged Ruff. 'Next of kin will get us into the dead man's house, which we have to do anyway, but I need to know if I need a warrant sooner rather than later.'

Ruff was beginning to notice use of the first person pronoun rather than Challis's normal plural pronoun. That was another change. Challis obviously wasn't feeling inclusive; keeping things formal. She was unsure how to address her. She wasn't sounding like Melanie.

'What are you going to be doing…Sarge?' Ruff managed to ask her.

Challis was tempted to tell her more of her conversation with the Super. She desperately wanted to talk to somebody. She resisted the temptation.

'I might get Ray to find out where Bush was employed, where he drank,' she answered eventually. 'Check out his vehicle. It was parked outside his house. Find out when the other neighbours are coming back from holiday.'

'You're giving this a lot of attention,' Ruff observed. Yes, she was, she realized. Better to be safe than demoted. 'What about dragging in Harry the Munch?'

Maybe I will, thought Challis.

Harry the Munch was still not in the office when they got back.

'Haven't seen him,' said Lockett, unbidden. Muench, he said, hadn't called in and he hadn't said where he might be going or what he'd be doing. As usual.

Challis had to believe that the boss would have known what Muench was up to but she didn't and now she needed to.

That would have to wait. She directed Ruff to get on with the tasks discussed in the car, telling her to delegate as much as she liked to Lockett, making sure that he knew of his inclusion in the investigation of the suicide of Timothy Bush.

*

Harry Muench was, at that moment, knocking on the door of room 212 in a motel in Pontypool. An eye checked him through the central spyhole. The door opened enough for Muench to slide through. A woman stood behind the door, in the doorway of the shower room. The room was small but big enough for their purposes. She wore nothing but a large bath towel that was secured by a fold-over knot in the front just above her large bosom. As Muench closed the door she stepped backwards slightly and raised both hands to rest at head height on each side of the doorframe. This motion caused the towel to gape below her waist. The pose offered submission.

'I've just showered,' she said; it was just something to say. He stepped closer, his firm hands overlaying hers.

'You smell delightful, Mrs. Henderson.' Her hands stayed put, *his* worked their way down her arms. He wrested the towel away from her. She closed her eyes. His coarse topcoat pressed into her skin and he kissed her with a matching roughness that set her nerves jangling.

Thirteen

There was snow the next morning. Not a lot, Challis was glad to observe, but more than a dusting. A white sprinkle was still coming down as she lifted the blinds in the kitchen of Daubwthyn Cottage and looked out at the squabble of house sparrows and tits on the bird feeders, topped up the night before as soon as she'd got home, around eight. She always liked to stand for a moment at the window first thing to see what was feeding there. As she watched, a female great spotted woodpecker landed on one of the peanut holders, scattering the smaller birds to the nearby twigs where they dislodged showers of snow-dust, watching and waiting for the larger black and white bird to finish.

Out of the lounge window Challis checked the state of the lane up to the main road. The council never gritted here so it didn't take much of the white stuff to make it a slippery climb. There were car tracks in the snow already so it was clearly passable with care. It was only just gone seven, just daylight and she had to judge if she should go earlier than normal in case the snow got heavier.

As she made coffee and put some muesli in a bowl to soften in the hot milk she switched on Radio Wales to hear what the BBC was saying about the weather and driving conditions. She joined the broadcast mid-song and a shudder hit her spine as she recognized it: 'Breakaway'; Kelly Clarkson. One of "their songs", from 2004. Her cheeks warmed, especially as the lyric reached *I'll spread my wings and I'll learn how to fly* and she remembered her own words for this line as she had lain with Stuart Devlin, here, in her lounge room, on one of her mother's settees. It hadn't been her wings she'd been spreading. Christ, it was almost as if he was back inside her again! She'd gone to bed last night and under the warm duvet had thought of him, been with him in her mind, letting him take her to those more outlandish places that he had once described to her in such detail. Back then she had turned them down. Last night, after a few years of not venturing anywhere near that fantasy, she lived it all in her mind's eye.

Her career had held her back. That was it. She had to admit she had been tempted, sorely tempted, but she was a police officer and she was bound to honour that role and accept its constraints. That's what she had thought then; now she wasn't so sure that such absolute denial to oneself was healthy.

Shit, shit, shit! She was angry.

What she had done on her own in the warmth of her bed last night was instigated by him. He had come back, just seeing him enough to set her off. So what? The result had been her private invention. But this morning she hated his renewed intrusion into her solo world, as if she could not have achieved the pleasure without him as a stimulus.

She re-tuned to Radio 2.

She was tempted to drive by the boss's house in Usk on her way through, just to check it out. Perhaps if she went to see him today she would get his key off him so she could go in and make sure the heating was timed to come on some of the day to keep the house and water pipes warm. It wouldn't be good for his dickey ticker if the place flooded.

His house was in the shadow of Usk Castle. It was a semi with concrete gardens, back and front. It did not even sport a pot anywhere. No greenery, no flowers. Despite the entreaties of the Usk In Bloom committee he would not give a home to anything that demanded precious time be spent. He once responded to them with a bunch of plastic flowers taped to his front wall.

No pets either, although he did tolerate a house martin nest under the eaves, all the while complaining about the mess they deposited on the slabs beneath.

There was plenty about Alan Redland that could get under Challis's skin but at least he was no concrete-garden bore. Whereas gardeners could weary you with diatribes about and, worst of all, photographs of their green-fingered prowess, Redland proudly had nothing in his garden to be proud of and the grey expanse surprised everyone who visited him for the first time.

'Covered it all in concrete the minute I moved in,' he would state, proud of his achievement. End of conversation.

Challis slowed down as she approached the house, gave it a casual glance and then drove on, promising herself she would look in on the way home, if he wanted her to because she was sure she would be seeing him today, one way or another.

The roads were white and crisp. It had not been totally easy getting out of Capelgwm; twice Challis's Citroen had slid across the lane. She cursed. She paid the same council tax as everyone else, more probably, than town dwellers, and got next to nothing for it; garbage collection once a fortnight, that was about all. She used to joke she never saw a bobby down her way. There was a 'Neighbourhood Watch' sign at the top but she didn't get involved.

The main road was okay, salted and swept clear by a larger volume of traffic, which was good news; she didn't want anything to delay her. She might get her acting DI this morning. Exciting stuff. She mentally mulled over what her first moves would be when the confirmation came through. Move into the boss's office? Yeah, probably. Keep on top of the team, on top of the Timothy Bush case. Couldn't let everything else slide but she couldn't work up any enthusiasm for the other stuff on the books, but that wouldn't go down well with O'Halloran. Muench, she pondered. What about Muench? Or Harry now, isn't it? She had a knot in her stomach thinking about him. He wouldn't take her elevation lightly.

The drive was fine although light snow continued to fall. Lockett was in when she got to the office but no Muench or Ruff.

'Abersychan,' said Lockett in defence of Ruff. 'Always a bugger in the snow. Doesn't take much.'

Unconsciously, Challis looked south-west out of the window at Mynydd Maen and the four hundred metre peak of Twmbarlwm beyond, both white-topped, thicker up there, as it would be in the higher reaches of the eastern valley, some eleven kilometres north of the office. The thought came to Challis that she lived further away than Kay and she was here on time.

Her smartphone sounded off. It was Ruff. She'd walked down the mountain to get a bus and was about five minutes away.

'By the way,' she added before hanging up, 'Ray's looking for the next of kin. Is he in yet?'

'Anything on the next of kin, Ray?'

Lockett looked at Challis as if collecting his thoughts; more like getting his brain into gear, she thought. 'Timothy Bush, Ray?'

'Yeah, I know.' He fumbled through papers on his desk.

'Haven't you put it all in the system yet?'

No answer from Lockett as he fished out a paper and held it up.

'And?' prompted Challis, unable to read what was on it, if that was his patience-trying intention. He pulled it down.

'Married, er, 1984 to, er, Robynne Fuller. Three kids: two daughters and a son. Divorced 1991. He lived in Newcastle then; that's where he was from, born 1964, so he's, er, forty-six. He seems to have moved down here in the late 90s, bought the house near Usk just four years ago.'

'Okay, good. Live on his own?'

'Looks like it.'

'Family then; where are they? Did he keep in touch?'

'Don't know yet.'

'Right, well, married '84, divorced '91, three small kids, did he pay maintenance, visit them, help them in any way? Actually, that's all too much info at this time but we need to get hold of one or all of them to come and id him. So keep on it.' But then she thought better of her brusque confused message and added an attempted form of endearment 'Ray', which only caused Lockett to look up expecting more directives.

She turned away, feeling she had no idea how she should be behaving. She scolded herself; pull yourself together; one at a time…

'O!' exclaimed Lockett. 'I found out where he works – worked. A software house. He was some sort of consultant. I've got the details.'

Having her attention recaptured by Lockett she took a piece of paper off him, read it and gave it straight back.

'Get over there today. Get some personality details. Why would he kill himself, that sort of thing.'

He nodded.

'But get all this stuff in the system will you, so we can all see it?'

She looked from her desk to Redland's office and moved quickly to her usual place, trying to appear busily preoccupied. As she seated herself, the door opened and Muench crept in. He quickly straightened himself, which seemed to be an effort. Lockett looked up.

'My God,' he couldn't help uttering. Muench's face conveyed a wish that Lockett had refrained from the too-loud exclamation because it drew Challis's attention. Muench refused to stand still to be inspected and sat down behind his desk but the DS rose and slowly approached him. He pulled at his jacket and shirt collars but his shirt was clearly the one he'd had on the day before and had grey areas around the neck. He was unshaven but his hair was slicked back.

'Jesus, Harry,' said Challis. 'You look bloody awful.'

Lockett was all eyes waiting to hear explanations from his fellow DC but Challis beckoned to Muench to follow her into the boss's office. Lockett watched Muench, expecting him to be reluctant to obey. To his surprise, Muench rose albeit slowly, eased himself around his desk, grinning to Lockett behind Challis's back. He was not feeling particularly light-hearted. Sleep had been hard to come by and he had woken in the motel to find the woman gone and, worse, she hadn't paid for the room as she normally did, so he had to fork out for it and no time for breakfast.

'Shut the door, Harry.'

Challis chose to sit on the corner of the boss's desk.

'What?' Muench asked quietly, dying for a bacon sandwich and a latte.

'Where were you yesterday afternoon?'

He pulled a face, derisory. 'I don't get this off Redland. He let's me get on with it.'

'Well he's not here and I need to know.'

'No you don't. I'm out there doing my job.'

'What, that timber company? All night? You haven't even been home, have you?'

'That's none of your business.'

'The way you look is my business. If the boss saw you like that he'd go nuts.'

'He's not here, is he?'

'It's not good enough. You were going to get a result on your case by today and I told the Super as much, so what's the status?'

'Look, I'm not telling you anything. I'll tell the Super. It doesn't worry me.'

'You'll tell him, looking like that.'

'The Super's not old school. He doesn't care how you look. It's the results that matter.'

'Well, from where I'm looking you fail on both counts. Go and get a shave, tidy yourself up, put a tie on.'

He scoffed.

'You've got ten minutes,' she carried on, 'then I want you back at your desk and I want to know why you're not getting anyone in here for charging. And if I don't like your answers I'll take it over.'

'You can't do that.'

'Ten minutes Harry.'

She thought he was going to continue the argument; his lips moved but no sound came out. He left and Challis breathed a sigh of satisfaction and followed him out of the boss's office.

As Muench was opening one of his desk drawers to find a razor the office door opened and a well-wrapped up Ruff came in and held the door open for Superintendent O'Halloran to come in behind her.

Lockett jumped to his feet, his swift movement catching O'Halloran's attention. His eye moved on to take in Muench and lingered, up and down on the DC. The Super, resplendent in his uniform, gave an almost imperceptible shake of the head. 'Tie,' was all he said to the hapless Muench.

He smiled at Challis who thought to herself 'that's old school for you'.

'Glad you're all here,' he said, going centre stage, his back towards Challis. 'Just a quick update on Inspector Redland. It seems it was his heart. May not be too bad but we won't be seeing him back soon, if at all. We'll have to see.' He looked at the white board. 'You have a lot of cases on the go. There are too many outstanding. Need to clear your board. DS Challis has been asked to supply an update…'

'Done, sir,' Challis interrupted, pissed off that he hadn't bothered to find that out. 'Left with your secretary yesterday.'

He was not put off his stride.

'You've got to work harder. It's even more important now. The DS will be expected to get these jobs cleared and it's up to all of you to support her in this, certainly for the time being. DI Hubbard will be back from leave and when he does he'll take over as was the original intention.'

He looked around the room to reinforce his message but not in any way inviting questions or comments.

'Carry on,' he instructed and made to leave.

'Sir,' Challis called. 'Can I have a word?'

He turned only to see her step back into Redland's office. He looked put out as he followed her, standing just inside the door which then had to remain open. Challis would have preferred it closed.

'Sir, yesterday…there was talk of an acting DI position…' She spoke as quietly as she could so her voice wouldn't carry past the Super.

'You did mention it,' he agreed, 'but it's not on. Deemed unnecessary considering the short timescales. Just carry on, Sergeant' it had been Mel yesterday 'but keep that lot smart and up to the mark. They deal with members of the public. Image. Self-esteem.'

'Yes but a DI has more clout…'

'Are you saying you can't manage them, Sergeant?'

'Not at all, sir, but a DI…'

'Crap, if I may say so. A respected sergeant can get maximum effort out of a team as I'm sure you know.'

All Challis could think of as she quietly seethed were Redland's words that described O'Halloran: "all piss and wind". She also remembered another piece of advice from the boss. "You can tell if O'Halloran has a temper brewing. His red spot burns brighter." She didn't dare try and study it.

She was deflated by this attitude. Disappointment hardly described her emotions. She saw the elevation in position as a platform from which to direct the team with authority, a vote of confidence from above that would impress those below.

More than anything else, she was ambitious. She had long since come to the conclusion that the police was a career for life for her and why shouldn't she rise to the very top. There were plenty of examples to follow. She was ready for the next step up on the ladder. What really pissed her off about this situation was that O'Halloran had not spoken to her first about this decision. As far as she could see, he tried to totally ignore it, forcing her to remind him virtually in front of the rest of the team.

O'Halloran studied Challis's reaction. He knew all about ambition; he was sympathetic, even where female colleagues were concerned.

Challis had until recently been something of an unknown quantity. She still was on a professional level. He'd double-checked her personnel record after their meeting the previous day. The assessments confirmed she was thorough; Redland had confidence in her but there seemed to be some reservations about her communication skills. Certainly she was not like some sergeants who constantly tried to raise their profile by pushing themselves forward, always finding access to ranks way above their own. With Challis, this was his first real close encounter. He liked her straight looks but he wondered if she would now whine like a disappointed child. He wasn't going to stand there as a potential target for too long. And besides, there were other images of her that he couldn't shift easily from his mind.

'Sir, this suicide case we're working on.'

This surprised him. 'What suicide case is that?'

Challis gave him a swift, concise précis of Timothy Bush's demise.

'Dave Sayer reckons it could be an assisted suicide.' She realized that she was turning Sayer's theory into semi-reality. 'In which case the case...' she winced inwardly at the thoughtless repetition of the word but ploughed on 'should be with homicide. Shall I talk to DCI Moray?'

'Spare me the 'what-ifs', Sergeant. I can't abide people who hypothesize til the cows come home. No, don't bother her with it unless you have solid evidence. You run with it.'

'I'll probably have to put the entire team on it.'

He smiled thinly. 'So long as you clear that board.' And he turned and swept out of the office with a final despairing glance at Muench.

'Coffee, Sarge?' Lockett asked as Challis walked to her desk, head up. She'd just lost the game two-nil, outgunned, but wasn't going to show it.

She nodded. He took drinks orders from the others and went out with Muench.

Fourteen

Ruff pulled into High Copse Farm. She'd phoned the farmer, John Gee, late the previous afternoon and arranged to visit him mid-morning. Her problems getting into work had made her think she might not make it. The state of the roads to the farm could also have been an issue. First and foremost was how the hell she was going to get there.

No problem. Mel had told her to keep her coat on, have her coffee and then get going.

She had been amazed how single-minded the sergeant had been after her public interview with the Super. Not everything that had been said, especially by Mel, had been audible but enough had come out of the boss's office to give the impression that something had been expected but not delivered. Mel's stumbling protests seemed to have incurred rebuke from the Super. She did hear Mel's attempt to offload this particular case but she thought she was flying kites there; no way yet was this was anything more than a suicide.

The long drive from the public road up to the farm was the first encounter with a slippery road surface. The front drive wheels of the pool car struggled to grip in places but the mini potholes in the concrete actually helped. Ruff took it easy, surprised by how well-hidden this farm was from the road below, and slowly picked her way across a yard full of what looked like junk to her. John Gee appeared from behind a pile of what looked like old batteries and rusted metal in front of an equally dilapidated stone out-building. In the back of her well-read mind she felt sure that there were regulations that applied to the storage of waste batteries and this pile in front of her did not appear to be very well secured. Perhaps she'd mention it.

John Gee was a tall, thin man, about sixty, wearing orange overalls and a woolly hat. His unshaven face was gaunt and less than welcoming. As Ruff got out of the car he halted his approach, unsure if this was in fact the expected police officer. She looked too young and, well…

'Mr. Gee,' she called as she closed the car door. 'Detective Constable Ruff.' She had trouble with her gloves, getting them off, but eventually had a bare hand that drew her warrant card out of her pocket. She waved it in front of her as she approached him. He greeted her with a grunt. He'd have preferred a bloke in a uniform.

Farmer John Gee opened the fire-door of his ancient Aga and threw in lengths of pallet wood, nails and all. Ruff briefly saw flames leap up to engulf the fuel. The kitchen of High Copse Farm in which they were standing was very warm. Next to the Aga was a rocking chair and in it was Farmer Gee's mother, at least eighty years of age Ruff estimated.

Ruff undid her coat as the overpowering heat of the room began to penetrate. The old woman probably suffered the cold and needed the heating at full blast. Once John Gee's eyes had feasted enough on the young police officer Ruff was able to get started on her questions.

She jotted not just his answers but other bits of information that he offered unbidden. It was another example to her of how the analysis of a situation could be unexpectedly influenced by the unknown – Donald Rumsfeld's "unknown unknowns": those facts that can come to life that you would not necessarily have known in advance to ask about. She believed in them.

It sometimes worried her that luck could affect outcomes and that serious crimes could be treated less so because the right questions were never asked or were never even thought of. They had drilled this into her during her training but it scared her nonetheless because such things were not boxes that could be ticked, they were intuitions bred of experience that you might not acquire for years and perhaps never. She had heard of such failures for some coppers over a lifetime in the business, those who never learned by their omissions.

She learned now who had been in his field opposite the row of three council houses that he insisted on describing as if that's what they still were. He gave her the names of kids who used the field to swing from the oak tree. He told her how "her from number one" used to walk her dog most days as far as he knew, but then he didn't go down that way every day. He'd seen her that day, though, but without her dog, in the field, about midday as he was coming back from the shops. When he said this, Ruff asked him to wait a second while she got out her smartphone and linked into the case database. Yes, she thought so; this didn't tally with what the Sarge had found out. She kept this to herself but asked John Gee to confirm what he had just said.

'Could you see what she was doing?'

'Just walking, quick like, back towards the gate.'

'What about Mr. Timothy Bush?'

'Who?'

Ruff explained he was the man whose body had been found.

'O, aye, from number three,' John Gee recalled. 'What about 'im?'

Had he ever used the field? John Gee shook his head. 'Nah. Got no dog, has he?'

Ruff examined the database on her smartphone. Anything else? she wondered.

'Would she like tea?' old Mrs. Gee asked her son, pointing to the kettle steaming on top of the Aga.

Ruff declined, barely lifting her eyes from her mobile. Think, girl, she urged herself.

'Okay, Mr. Gee, one more thing. Mr. Bush was found the day before yesterday but it may be he'd been in your field overnight from the night before, that would be Monday night or evening or late afternoon even. Did you see anything down there on Monday?'

'Monday?' he scratched himself somewhere.

'You was late Monday,' his mother reminded him. 'I 'ad to wait ages for dinner that night.'

'O yeah, that's right. My van got stuck by them council 'ouses. I 'ad to move over to get round that bloody great Range Rover thing and I slid on the ice and ended up 'alf in the ditch. I 'ad to walk up 'ere to get my tractor out to go back and pull it out and that bloody car 'ad gone by then.'

'What time?'

''bout five.'

'Where was this Range Rover?'

'Outside them 'ouses. Other end, outside number one I suppose could be.'

'Did you recognise it?'

''Course! It was a Coco the Clown.'

'Sorry?'

'Coco. You know. Co, Co.' Ruff had no idea what he was saying. John Gee delighted in her ignorance as he explained for her. 'Cottel Court. Co, Co.' It's on all their vehicles. It's their what-you-mcall.'

The penny dropped. 'Logo,' Ruff exclaimed. This was not a word that John Gee fully understood but he nodded.

'Aye. Cottel Court...Co and then another Co.'

'His bloody lordship,' cursed Mrs. Gee and Ruff thought for a moment that the old woman was going to spit to reinforce the curse. She turned on her son. 'You're always getting stuck down there. Tell her. Who was it the other week, in his bloody big lorry?'

John Gee thought. 'O aye. That was Jenkins the builder, mam. He was dawdling up the lane by there. Don't know what he was doing. He 'ad no load on but he got out the way when I 'onked.'

As soon Ruff had left the house, Mrs. Gee asked her son 'Who the bloody 'ell was that?' When he replied 'Police, Mam' she warned her son not to get involved with all this.

'Bloody queer lot down there in them 'ouses. Gawd knows what they all get up to.'

God knows orright, you old nag, thought John Gee. But it ain't my cup o' tea.

He was watching the young policewoman out of the window. She was blowing her nose into a tissue, wiping it furiously. She buttoned up her coat and bent over, looking at the wheels of the car or something. Her coat was short and her trousers fitted her awful tight. She'd said something about needing a formal statement so she'd probably be back, sometime.

*

Mid-morning, Sayer walked into the office, file in hand.

Muench had head down, updating the system with something. He had shaved and wore a tie albeit loosened and with the top shirt button undone.

Challis was on the phone but that didn't stop Sayer giving out a loud greeting. 'Gudday, inmates.' It made her look up. It made Muench grin.

Without breaking his stride he closed on Challis and slapped a buff folder onto her desk. If he expected her to react to this he was disappointed. It did make her lower her voice as Sayer stayed uncomfortably close, looking down at the back of her head. She wished she'd had the courage to go into the boss's office to use the phone there. It wasn't so much lack of courage but an attempt to keep onside with Muench, to not provide him with ammunition to shoot down what he would allege was her jumped-up presumption that she had a right to use it. She did have a right to use it, she was sure she did and next time she would clear her mind of any self-censorship and bloody well use it whenever she wanted to. She had to sort out more clearly what to do to get the job done.

She was on the phone trying to get hold of DCI Harriet Moray of Homicide. Despite the advice from the Super earlier she wanted to bounce the issue of assisted suicide off her. It could be purely hypothetical; no need to go into detail about the case itself. It was just that she felt a little exposed and ill at ease as to its implications. Strangely, the landing on her desk of this hand-delivered file made her think that Sayer with his exposure to all methods of sudden death would be a good one to ask. Unfortunately, his depth of knowledge would come, she was sure, with an equally well-rounded patronizing attitude.

DCI Moray was unavailable. Challis left no message. She hung up, lifted the file from Sayer and glanced up at him as she opened it.

'Morning,' she said with believable brightness.

'There you go,' he chirruped. 'Hot off the press.' And then began annoyingly to describe the contents as Challis tried to read for herself.

*

Timothy Bush's black Ford Escort estate car was unlocked. Ruff tried the door handle with a gloved hand and eased the driver door open. She pulled it wide and peered inside. It smelled a bit, sort of stale and a little damp and was a far from clean interior. The side pockets were stuffed with all sorts of debris, there were crumbs on the floor and stains on the dash.

On the back seat and floor clothes were strewn; they looked like a male's clothes. She opened the rear door for a closer look and there seemed to be a full enough set of male attire from underwear to top clothes. She couldn't be absolutely sure because some items lay on top of others.

She closed the back door. There was an ignition key in place ready to fire up the engine. Just one key on the fob. She wondered then if there may be more keys in one of the pockets of the clothes in the back; perhaps a key to the house; perhaps also some form of id. The temptation was to rifle through them, gently of course, to find such useful items. I mean, she thought, what was the point of stopping here on the way back from High Copse Farm if not to glean as much info as possible? The car was unlocked so there was a danger that stuff could get pinched. It was fortunate that nothing had been so far, although she could not claim that for certain. Some unknown items may have been lifted.

No, she decided, slipping the ignition key from its location in the steering column. She would lock the doors and pocket the key. Forensics could come and fetch the car.

She dictated brief notes into her smartphone strolling up the path towards the house. Could be, she mused, that the house was not locked either. Had Mel tried the door when she had visited Meredith Guster, next door but one? No record of that.

She lifted her eyes from her phone. Couldn't be sure but she could have sworn that the curtain in the front upstairs window twitched. She stared up at it waiting to see some confirmation of this impression. There it was again. It was a windless day and no windows of the house were open, so...

What to do?

She was on her own outside the house of a suicide victim, thought to live alone. She could approach the front door and then what? Push it to see if it was on the latch? Knock, thus assuming that if there is someone in there they are there legitimately? But if there is someone in there and they have no right to be there they could flee, out the back way, or resist.

At least she'd locked the car.

The decision was made. She rushed to the front door, pushed it but it didn't yield. She put her mouth to the letterbox, knocked with one fist on the door and yelled 'Police. Please open up.'

She stood back and listened, her heart thumping. Nothing. Her phone was at her lips and she was about to speak 'Control' to call the number for assistance when the front door slowly opened, just a crack. Ruff moved to get a better view, her phone still positioned near her chin. A woman's face came into view as the door opened a bit more.

'I don't know you,' said the woman.

'Miss Guster?' Ruff guessed correctly.

Fifteen

'You've got Guster downstairs?' Challis was agog.

Ruff had come in, cool as the arctic weather outside and calmly informed Challis that she had found Guster in Bush's house.

'What was she doing in there?'

'She wouldn't say, Sarge.'

'Did you go inside and check the place out?'

'Yes, I went inside. She didn't try to stop me or try to run when my back was turned.'

Well, where was she going to run to? Challis thought. 'And?'

'And what?'

'And what state was the place in? Had she turned it over, or what?'

'I didn't look. I just secured the place and grabbed her.' Make your mind up, Challis thought.

'So why d'you bring her in?'

'Well, she wouldn't say what she was doing in there.'

'How'd she get in?'

'Back door was open, unlocked I mean, so she said.'

Challis was thoughtful. 'Okay. We could stretch a point now; do a proper search without paperwork as his place has become the site of an illegal entry. A crime scene, it could be argued.'

Ruff went on to tell of Bush's car, also unlocked, and the loose pile of clothes in the back.

'Tell Sayer,' Challis ordered. 'Get it all brought in.'

Ruff left the best til last and Challis's eyes lit up when she heard that Farmer Gee reckoned he'd seen Guster, dogless, in the field earlier on the day the body had been reported by Guster herself. So why did she wait until later to report it? That was cause enough to bring her in for questioning.

'I didn't say anything to her about what the farmer said.'

'And she's refusing to speak?'

'Yeah, well, except about that dog of hers. Kept going on about needing to get back to it.'

She lifted the file that Sayer had left with her, thumbing through it.

'Did you notice her hands?' she asked Ruff.

The question took Ruff by surprise but strangely enough she had noticed Guster's hands. She had taken hold of one of them when she thought about cuffing her.

'Yeah,' she replied, curiosity mounting. 'Bit rough, raw looking. Bit like she'd had to put something on them. Why, Sarge?'

Challis passed the file over, pointing to a paragraph on the page that dealt with Sayer's analysis of the underpants, on the sides of which he'd found the residue of a cream, one commonly used for the hands.

Looking out at the darkening sky, clear now with a cold night obviously looming, Challis turned to Ruff. 'Let's leave her to stew over that dog of hers for a while then we'll see how talkative she becomes. Pop in and tell her we'll get the RSPCA to go collect her Malcolm. That'll give her plenty to think about.'

'That's a bit cruel.'

'Kay, look at me. I'm a mere sergeant; what do I know?'

*

As they went down to the interview rooms some hour and a half later Challis, more in hope than certainty, enquired of the custody sergeant if Muench had anyone in for interview or had had during the day. The reply was negative. She let that piss her off. Getting Muench to pull his finger out was like pushing a pea uphill in the snow. He wasn't in the office again either.

Meredith Guster was pacing the floor. Challis invited her to sit as Ruff took a seat next to the recording device.

'Do you know what time it is? Do you know how long I've been in here? What about my dog? It's cruelty. Cruelty to animals. To my dog. Get that in the papers and you'll have people threatening to kill you, you know that.'

Challis thought there was probably some truth in that. Guster went on. 'I'm saying nothing. Until you let me out to see to my dog I'm saying nothing.'

'Continue to say nothing, Miss Guster, and you may find you don't get out for a very long time.'

Ruff switched on the recording device and announced the names of those present and the time.

'Did you assist Timothy Bush to commit suicide?' Challis asked. Guster had ceased her agitation and had sat down, side-saddle, her eyes anywhere but on Challis and Ruff. She said nothing.

Challis continued. 'You see, we know you were in that field on Tuesday, earlier in the day than you originally told us. Is that when you helped Timothy Bush end his life?'

Nothing.

'We have a witness who will swear you were there.' Challis waited. 'Do you realize how serious this is for you? And for Malcolm?'

This made Guster twitch even more.

Challis changed tack. 'Tell me about your husband. Sorry, your ex-husband.' This time Guster looked at her and frowned. 'Small man wasn't he? Didn't take all his stuff with him when he left you. Some of it came in handy, didn't it?'

Still nothing.

'Okay,' Challis stood. 'This is getting us nowhere. We can't waste time like this. I'm going to get a search warrant to search your house because according to our forensic tests on items found on and near the body of Timothy Bush we believe you're concealing evidence. We'll get the RSPCA along to collect the dog.'

'No,' shouted Guster.

'Why not?' asked Challis. 'Why shouldn't I?'

'I'll take you to my house. I'll let you in. Can we go now?'

'That's a kind offer but no, I need something from you by way of…'

'A sign of good faith,' Ruff offered.

'Exactly,' Challis eagerly agreed.

'What?' asked Guster.

'Tell me about your husband. Small man was he? Is he?'

Guster gave half a nod.

'You put a pair of his old underpants on Mr. Bush's body, didn't you? Why was that?'

Guster went quiet and still. 'Cover him up,' she said quietly.

Challis let it sink in. 'Why?' she asked again, quietly.

Guster now shook her head more urgently. 'It wasn't nice, to see him, completely…'

She was struggling so Ruff helped her. 'Completely naked, with those nasty cuts and scabs all over his private parts. No, you're right. Not nice. Ugly to see.'

Challis was glad Ruff's opinions came to a halt. She'd thought for a minute that her colleague was going to go on and on.

'So you found Mr. Bush quite early in the day. I mean, you must have found him, gone back home for the underpants, unless you carry a pair of your ex-husband's pants around with you, gone back into the field to put them on him. Why didn't you get a pair of his own underpants, from his house?'

'I didn't know the house was unlocked, did I? Not then.'

Ruff jumped in. 'Why not get the ones out of his car? There was a pile of his clothes in there, probably the last set he'd worn.'

'How was I supposed to know there were clothes in his car?'

Challis wondered about these clothes in the car. Did Bush leave them when he stripped off or was he stripped by someone else? If it was someone else, why put them in his car? 'So, you put the pants on him and then later, much later, you decide to call the police. Why the delay?'

'I was going to call when I first found him…'

'What time was that?'

'Er, in the morning.'

'But you didn't.'

'No, wanted to cover him up first and after I did, I don't know, I was all of a shake.'

'How did you get the pants on him? Couldn't have been easy. Did you do it from behind him or in front of him?'

'From behind. I couldn't stand in front of him, up close…I had to stand on a log to pull them right up.'

'The log; where was it?'

'Nearby. I had to manhandle it. Roll it. It was heavy. I slipped and fell once.'

'What coat were you wearing?'

Guster frowned again.

'Was it one of your husband's? I've done some enquiries. Your husband, John Chen, was in the army, Royal Signals, served in the first Gulf War, in Iraq. There were coats, parkas, issued to the American soldiers.' Challis opened Sayer's file again and read. '*Night Desert Camouflage Parka with attached Hood, worn as an outer garment in areas for night desert camouflage. Fastened with drawstrings at waist, bottom, neck and around face to protect against wind and blowing sand.* Does that sound familiar? Must be quite warm and cosy in this weather we've been having. You see, British soldiers swapped our stuff for American gear like this parka. We found fibres from it on the log.'

Guster gave out a contemptuous sniff. 'So what? My husband never had one. He never got anywhere near an American let alone an Iraqi. He was... "in the rear with the gear".' She laughed 'He wouldn't get anywhere close to bullets firing and shells going off. Great little coward my Johnny.'

'What were you doing in Mr. Bush's house?' Ruff asked as Challis collected her thoughts, consulting Sayer's file.

Guster shrugged. 'Being neighbourly. Checking...checking there were no leaks.'

Challis took up this line of questioning. 'Neighbourly? For a dead neighbour? That hardly applies, does it? And you told me you scarcely knew the man; why this sudden concern, for his property of all things?'

'Seeing what you could pinch,' Ruff came in. 'I mean, you were upstairs, in the bedrooms.'

'No I wasn't.'

'I saw you, behind the curtains; that's why I approached the house. Anything good up there? Anything worth...salvaging?' Guster shuffled in her chair but didn't reply so Ruff decided to pile it on. 'Were you looking for stuff for yourself or for your friends in work?' Challis looked sideways at Ruff wondering where her colleague was going with this. 'You work at Cottel Court don't you? What was one of their vehicles doing outside your house the night before Timothy Bush's body was discovered, o, that's right, by you?'

Now Challis turned full-face towards Ruff who realized the sergeant didn't know about that. She leaned across and whispered into Challis's ear. 'Farmer Gee.'

'No idea what you're talking about,' replied Guster, thin-lipped.

'The vehicle was outside your house for some considerable time,' Ruff went on.

'I wasn't home. After work that night I went shopping. ASDA.'

'On a Monday?'

'It's quieter. I always go on a Monday.'

'And was there a vehicle outside your house when you eventually got home?'

'No, but I tell you what was there. John Gee's van, stuck in the ditch on the other side.'

*

'You might want to consider waffling for Wales,' Challis said to Ruff.

'What d'you mean?'

'You've got to learn when to be cryptic and when to drum home a point when you're interviewing. You just went on at times.'

'I don't...'

'And don't ever bring up something in an interview about which I know absolutely nothing.'

Ruff had a puzzled look on her face.

'The vehicle outside Guster's house on Monday night!' Challis declared.

'Yeah. Sorry. It was in my notes but I forgot to mention it. John Gee saw it. It made him swerve and get stuck then he had to go fetch his tractor to pull it out.'

They were on the way to give the Bush house the once-over. By now it was very late afternoon, almost dark. Another cold night looming but no snow. Guster had already been released and a lift home organized for her. The uniformed WPC who had driven her had been instructed to stay put there until Sayer and his crew arrived to take possession of the Bush car.

Actually, Challis was quite impressed with Ruff's work and her interview technique had not been that bad. She remembered what she had been like in her early days; nervous and tongue-tied. Ruff seemed to be more confident than she had been as a young detective.

'Very weird woman, Ms. Guster,' Ruff said, taking Challis's criticism on the chin, 'O, and by the way, the two front tyres on this heap could do with replacing.'

Sixteen

Detective Chief Inspector Ralph Lassman of the Berkshire Police had to park his car behind any number of patrol cars and other official vehicles outside the entrance to the drive of 135 Old Windsor Road, Datchet. He got out unseen by the uniformed officer who was just draping police tape across the driveway. He stood behind a lanky constable, stroking his greying goatee that no longer matched his dark moustache. The young officer jumped. 'Sir!'. Ignoring him completely, Lassman squeezed himself through the small remaining gap. He strode on, crunching his way across the frozen gravel towards his DS, Laurie O'Toole, who was shining a torch around the back of a car, a Saab convertible, registration number M769ZWO, he read. Forensics in their blue coveralls were there already, swarming over the car and beginning to scan the area immediately around the vehicle.

'Guv,' O'Toole saw his boss coming; heard him first from the crunch of frosted gravel. 'A shooting, guv. Victim, George Medlyn, forty-seven. In the driving seat there.'

Straining to look first up at the taller O'Toole and then beyond him towards the vehicle Lassman was already pulling gloves from his coat pocket.

'Found by?' he asked.

'Wife. Patricia Medlyn. She's in the house. She found him an hour ago when she came in from shopping.'

Lassman looked at his watch. 'Out shopping until seven-thirty?'

'Apparently. Some women shop at midnight.'

Lassman shook his head, not in disbelief but in total lack of comprehension. 'What did she buy I wonder. Shot, you say.'

'Yes. Twice. Once in the head and once, well, once through the lower stomach area. The house was then entered. Mrs. Medlyn found the door open.'

'Who's in there with the body?'

'Dr. Scott's in charge.'

'Ah, Scotty. What's she had to say?'

'Nothing yet.'

'That's not like her. Normally can't shut her up. Need some more light here.'

'They're just about to set some up. Got the outside house lights on. Gives some light on the subject.'

The car itself took Lassman's interest. 'Bit old this car if the plates are original.'

'They are. He's had it from new. A bit of Saab freak, I gather, from the neighbours.' He pointed to the detached house next door. 'They heard nothing. None of the neighbours saw or heard a thing. No houses opposite...'

Lassman turned around. Across the road a broad expanse of empty land stretched away to where the M4 could be heard and just about seen. Overhead planes headed in, one a minute, towards Heathrow. O'Toole followed his upward gaze.

'I don't think anybody up there would have seen much.'

'Any other cars in and out? Walkers?'

O'Toole shook his head. 'No, nothing. Yet. We're still doing house-to-house.'

Lassman let his mind spin. Might be we'll be looking for someone in one of these houses.

'What's he do for a living?'

'Er, something in the city.'

'Hmm,' Lassman was unimpressed. 'A lot of smells in the city.' He slowly advanced on the car. 'Scotty!'

Dr. Jill Scott, a short, stout woman in her early forties, eased herself out of the passenger side of the Saab.

'Ralph,' she acknowledged. 'No closer please. For now.'

Lassman held up his hands in submission. She was the boss right now. 'Can we speak?'

She ambled round the front of the car, her protective clothing rustling. She lowered her face mask.

'Two shots by the look of it. Not sure which one first yet. Probably the head shot. No idea what the belly shot is all about. But the head shot is facing the passenger side so I wouldn't mind betting the shooter was actually sitting there. Can't tell much in this light and even if we light it up like Blackpool we need to get it back home to do a proper job, the sooner the better too. It's getting bloody colder by the second.'

'Nobody seems to have heard anything. Silencer used?'

Scotty cogitated. 'Interesting thought. Silencer and clean head shot equals pro job. Gut shot equals something else; something personal? Can't say until we extract the bullets.'

Lassman nodded. 'Carry on with the good work, Scotty, but I think we should keep the number and unique style of the shots to ourselves for now. Right, DS O'Toole, let's go see the widow.'

'Before we do, guv...about the widow. According to the neighbours...' he pointed in the same direction again 'Mrs. Medlyn moved out a couple of weeks ago.'

'Moved out,' Lassman repeated.

'Mmm. As in *left* poor Mr. Medlyn.'

'These neighbours, seem to know an awful lot but bugger all about tonight. Need to know how they got on with the deceased. So, what's she doing back here then and with the shopping? Shall we find out? O, Scotty...' He just managed to stop Scotty getting back in the car. '...how long ago?'

'Rough guess at this time, about two hours, three. Tell you later.'

*

'I didn't say I came home with the shopping,' protested an annoyed Mrs. Medlyn. 'I told the officer I came home from my shop in Windsor.'

'You work in a shop; which shop?' O'Toole asked.

'I don't work in it, I own it.'

'Came home, Mrs. Medlyn?' queried Lassman. 'I was given to understand that this was no longer your home.'

'For Christ sake, this is my home. Has been for twenty years near as damn it until two and a half weeks ago.'

'So where are you living now?'

'Over the shop. My shop. Upmarket souvenirs.' To Lassman that sounded a bit of an oxymoron.

She gave out the name and address.

'How did you get here?' O'Toole asked.

'In my car, of course.'

'It's not outside.'

'Well, no. It's in the garage.'

Lassman scratched his head. 'So, you drove passed the Saab with your husband's dead body in it slumped over the wheel and didn't notice anything? I mean, doesn't your husband put his classy car in the garage?'

'No, not always at first. Sometimes he goes out again.'

'Where? Where does he go?'

'I have no idea.'

'Why did you leave him two and a half weeks ago?'

The blood seemed to drain out of her lips. 'It's personal.'

Lassman sighed. 'I'm sorry to tell you this but I'm afraid it's no longer personal.'

'It is to me and I'm damned if I'm going to talk about it to you. To any of you.'

'How long were you married?'

'Twenty years, nearly twenty-one.'

'And you'd never walked out on him before?'

'I didn't walk out. I ran.'

'Really? So why have you run back?'

'To collect some things.'

'But you parked in the garage you say. Has an air of permanence about it, wouldn't you say?'

'I…it was just habit.'

'Do you do that every time you come back here?'

'Yes. No.'

'So you've been back a few times. To see your husband.'

'No. I come when he's in work.'

'In the city?' Lassman turned to O'Toole. 'Do we have his employer?'

'Yes, sir.'

He turned on Mrs. Medlyn. 'So it was a real surprise when you realized you husband was here.'

'His car was here. I didn't know he was until…'

'Is there a gun in the house, Mrs. Medlyn? I mean, if there is we'll find it but it would be nice if you could point us in the right direction.'

She shook her head.

The house was alive with activity. The three of them plus a young policewoman hovering near the door were in the front lounge room, standing on a floor strewn with cds and dvds. But in every other room of the house an increasing number of uniformed and plain clothed officers were beginning a detailed search.

'Mrs. Medlyn,' Lassman continued, 'somebody killed your husband and probably used his keys…' he looked at O'Toole with a questioning eyebrow.

'They were in the front door, guv, in the lock. House keys car keys on one ring.'

Lassman went on '…used his keys to come in here and have a good old look around. What's missing?'

'Look at the mess…' she didn't know what to call him. She'd forgotten. 'How the hell do I know.'

'What time does your husband normally get home from work?'

She stuttered. 'Late, usually. Later than tonight.'

'Mrs. Medlyn. I can't help but notice that you don't seem particularly upset by the fact that your husband has been killed right outside; not only killed in cold blood but his body also mutilated…'

O'Toole frowned at his boss's disclosure of that fact.

'What d'you mean, mutilated?' Mrs. Medlyn's eyes were wide open.

'…not more than two hours ago. He was alive when he drove in here. Alive, Mrs. Medlyn, and you say you got here about seven-thirty. Are you sure about that? Are you sure it wasn't nearer six-thirty?'

'You said mutilated? I didn't see…'

'So listen please. We're going to leave you here now with this nice policewoman, WPC…?

'Olluwala,' the girl answered. Lassman had been going to repeat the name but thought better of it

'…so that you can think over the questions that we've asked that you haven't answered at all and consider what else you can tell us that will help to clear up this very serious crime. Constable…' he beckoned WPC Olluwala closer 'notebook at the ready, constable. Mrs. Medlyn may want to chat to you but you don't want to chat to her, understand?'

'I think so, sir,' replied a straight-backed WPC Olluwala.

'Guv,' DS O'Toole spoke as they left the lounge and were back in the hallway watching the team going about their work. 'The mess in there, in that room. It seemed to be just CDs scattered around. Their sound system was still there, good one too by the looks of it.'

'O'Toole, just think on a bit. Scotty said she wouldn't mind betting the shooter was sitting in the passenger seat. If that's true, when did he, or she, get in? Did he, or she, jump in when Medlyn stopped in the drive? Jump in at a set of traffic lights? Or did Medlyn know him, or her, and actually drive here accompanied? And was it just one passenger? The neighbours saw no other car. So the…person or persons unknown may have been on foot. In which case they couldn't really cart off a stereo or anything else too bulky. Could carry off a CD though.'

O'Toole had to mention something that was burning his brain. 'Guv, you told her he'd been mutilated. I thought…'

'Sir!' There was a call from upstairs.

'I didn't say how, did I, Sergeant?' Lassman smirked, smoothing his little beard. 'Besides, I don't like Mrs. Medlyn. Far too frigid if you ask me. And anyway, a little ghoulishness goes a long way.' He led the way up the stairs, the longer-legged sergeant in his wake. 'O'Toole,' he called over his shoulder, 'when you can, find out why the remorseless widow left her husband.'

A detective constable was waiting at the door of a room to the right at the top of the stairs. 'In here, sir.'

'What is Farouk?' came Lassman's rhetorical question as he simultaneously stepped across the threshold. 'Ah ha!' he gave out as he stood in the doorway and ran his eye over the scene. The room was relatively small. An ideal study size. On the right was a window, curtained. Against the opposite wall a metal desk, grey, cheap office type, Lassman thought; two drawers on one side. Wires trailed towards the wall where a 42-inch plasma screen was fixed up and towards a printer sited on a small trolley on the left.

'Looks like we're missing a computer,' O'Toole observed, peering over the boss's head.

The wall on the left was given over to shelves on which were books but one shelf was devoted to dvds or cds, most of which now lay on the carpeted floor.

Lassman held back O'Toole while he stepped carefully towards the pile. He bent and lifted one, barely concealed a snigger before holding it up for the sergeant to see, DC Farouk too. A brief look down at others confirmed they were all of a type, a type that appealed to lonely middle-aged men, to enjoy in the privacy of an isolated room. Gross some of them looked but the pictures and titles on the covers seemed to be all of consenting adults.

'We'll leave Scotty and her boys to do this room. Farouk, nobody but forensics in here, clear? And no souvenirs, except this one.'

He showed the dvd to O'Toole who read the title out loud "Naughty Asian Babes". The title's hardly necessary. The picture says it all.'

'If you say so, O'Toole. Now, do you suppose all this stuff in here was the cause of the widow's pique? Made her up and leave?'

O'Toole shook his head. 'Hardly. That's a collection years in the gathering.'

'I bow to your greater experience.'

'So, she knew he was linking his PC to the screen on the wall for maximum viewing pleasure. But what did she do with the missing computer?'

Lassman thought. 'Okay. If it wasn't her, a computer, a laptop even, easy enough to cart off. But why? If that was his porn vehicle, what's so special about that? Unless there was other stuff on it.'

'I think, sir, we need to talk to the not-so-merry widow again.'

Seventeen

Challis got a lift for Ruff back to HQ with one of Sayer's team. Once again it had been too dark for Sayer to do much with Bush's car at the scene so they carted it off for examination in a more well-lit and warmer environment.

Before departing the scene, Sayer voiced criticism of Challis's assessment of the case. Why hadn't she made up her mind yet about the 'questionable suicide', as he phrased it?

'I'm surprised you're still running with it,' he argued. 'I'd have thought homicide would have had it by now.'

She didn't confide in him that the Super had told her she had to hang on to it.

'My report shows,' he went on, emphatically 'without doubt that the man was hung t-w-i-c-e. The rope, brand new, has black metal paint engrained. The man's weight undoubtedly forced large particles of paint deep into the rope's fabric. He was hung somewhere else I tell you. I'd have a word with DCI Moray if I was you.'

She had tried to, but she didn't tell him that.

As she drove to the hospital in Abergavenny she moved all of the known details around in her mind. Sayer had identified the knot used to fix the rope to the tree. In his report he called it an Evenk Knot, a knot used by survivalists and not that hard to undo; one tug on one of the lengths frees it completely but it is constructed so as not to slip. He included a series of diagrams showing how to tie and release it. This was a new one on Challis. All Sayer had said to her as she struggled with it was that she was obviously not a fan of Ray Mears. Then he had to explain to her who Ray Mears was while he expertly tied and released the knot, showing off to her and Ruff.

Redland had been moved to a general ward. As she entered the hospital she thought perhaps she should have brought him something. She had all the case notes in her brief case. Redland could read Sayer's report if he was desperate.

Hospital wards are never the most enticing venues and Challis had a pathological hatred of them, born of the days following the accident that had killed her parents. Her father had been killed outright in Spain but her mother had survived badly injured to be repatriated and then to die a nightmarish week later. Someone had said to her then that being carried into a hospital and then walk out of it is okay; it's the reverse that's a bit of a bugger. Sadly, her mother had been carried in and out.

She felt it, or rather smelt it, as soon as she entered the mixed ward and a wave of panic swept over her. Anxiously she scanned the beds, desperate to see a familiar face, a living face. She saw him, at the far end of the room. Blinkered, she made a beeline for him.

Redland was lying flat but he raised himself up on his elbows as he saw her approaching. She noticed he was hamstrung somewhat by tubes and wires, well, one tube and one wire. In a laboured fashion, he jiggled his arms about to make sure the attachments had enough slack. Challis had started to approach his bed with a smile but she saw immediately how old he looked and the way he struggled to sit upright showed he didn't have the energy to pretend otherwise. Her smile forced its way back, perhaps exaggerated, as he leaned on his pillows and greeted her, his auburn hair, thick at the back, splayed bedraggled.

'Melanie,' he took a deep breath but said no more.

'Hi-ho, sir,' she could almost give him a hug. She pulled a chair closer to his bed. 'Christ, it's warm in here.' She began to strip off top layers.

'Good to see you're properly dressed,' he said, not smiling, but she was. 'Still cold out, eh?'

'Bloody freezing. You're in the right place here.'

'I don't think so.'

'No,' she quickly agreed. 'I know you hate this question in circumstances like this but how are you?'

He smiled half-heartedly at her appreciation of one of his foibles. 'No, I think that right now it's not a bad question, considering.'

She waited but not for long. 'And?'

'Angina, so they say. Nasty one but not a heart attack in the strict sense of the phrase.'

'That's not so bad though, is it? Not as bad as a heart attack, is it?'

He shrugged. 'The worse thing about it is that Dr. Carys at the surgery will say "I told you so". I'll be another point of proof on her graph of life's frailties. I've been laying here and that's all I can think about. My well-honed arguments down the bedpan. It's all a real pain in the arse!'

'Hmm,' she smiled. 'Unusual symptom I would have thought.'

'Aye, well, you know what they say if love's a pain in the arse, don't you?'

She did know but wished he hadn't gone down this route, so she sat straight-faced, nodding imperceptibly, and he did not pursue the joke, although he smiled long and stared hard. Not much wrong with him, she thought.

'I wondered if you'd like me to look in on your house,' Challis said, her lightness lifting them out of that dark inappropriate moment. 'Unless…I saw Stuart here yesterday…'

'Yes, he was. You were here?'

Obviously Stuart had not said so to his uncle.

'Mmm,' Challis confirmed. 'They wouldn't let me in to see you. I tried the old warrant card trick but then he turned up.'

'I can't remember much. How was he? How'd he look?'

She knew he could remember. He was fishing for something. 'Okay. The well-dressed public servant as ever.' She was dismissive. No care one way or the other in her voice. She could act as well as he could but really she didn't much care.

'Public servant? He's not one of those anymore. He's moved on. Security consultant now; runs his own company. In Cardiff I think he's based.'

'Really? You never said.'

'Didn't think you'd want to know.' Still fishing. 'Nothing to do with you, is it?'

Challis gave no indication as to what she thought about that. 'So is he keeping an eye on your house?'

'I shouldn't think so. He's off somewhere on business today he said. Don't see much of him. It was good of him to come like that; busy man.'

It was on the tip of her tongue to go on and mention the blonde, Sue, who had been with Stuart but she knew how that would appear to Redland.

'So would you like me to pop in; check the mail, the milk. Make sure no pipes are leaking?'

'Yes, thanks. But unlike you my milk is not delivered; a carton from the Spar when required. You could check the fridge, chuck stuff out, check the use-by dates' He reached for his keys from the bedside cabinet which was sadly bare of other personal items.

'Thanks for your notebook you left with the doctor. Useful. I should have brought you some things. Anything you need, want?'

'I'm hoping I won't be in here too long. My old mother had angina, for years. Killed her in the end. Who's running the team?' he asked. Challis had been undecided how much she should talk of work.

'Me, I suppose, for now.'

'Well don't sound over-enthusiastic will you?'

She sighed. 'O'Halloran mentioned the possibility of an acting DI for me.'

'But changed his mind, eh? He's a nice old bastard.' Once again she was none too sure whose side Redland was on. The tone of the phrase he'd used to describe O'Halloran was lacking real condemnation.

'He wants the board cleared asap but this suicide is sucking us all in.'

Redland looked amazed. 'You don't get dragged into long-winded investigation of a suicide!'

'Yes, well, it's not that straightforward,' Challis moaned before going on to explain the theories of Sayer.

'Give it to Moray then.'

'The Super won't let me until I have the evidence. The theory's not enough for him to park it on homicide.'

'Huh! So you're all working on it.'

'Well, Kay and me mainly.'

'Melanie, I've told you before. You can't just work with the people you can easily dominate. If you're management material you've got to able to delegate to everyone available even if they say they're not available.'

'That's all very well, but we were all running with other stuff before this cropped up. Anyway, Ray's on it and Harry will be if I can catch him in the office now and again.' She was showing more bravado with the Harry challenge while it was just a discussion point.

Redland went thoughtful. 'Is he still on that Timber yard robbery?'

'Uh-uh,' Challis confirmed. Redland pondered inwardly. He had let Harry Muench run with that case far too long. It hadn't seemed justified but selfishly he was happy to not get into a contest with him over it; he was keenly anticipating the fact that Hubbard would be back from holiday and he'd be gone for six months. Now the problem was in Challis's lap.

'You've got to use them all as you see fit.'

Challis nodded. She knew that. She knew it all, in theory.

'And I don't know if you'd ever noticed but Kay doesn't exactly lend herself to be dominated,' she reminded him.

Redland flopped back on his pillows as if the conversation was too draining both mentally and physically. Challis considered her options. She hadn't been there with him very long. Could she escape already? Looking around the ward she could see that despite the lateness of the hour and the near termination of visiting time many of the patients still had visitors by their beds. Redland would not have many come in to see him; she was sure of that.

'Sir,' she started, as much to see his reaction. His gaze, which had never actually wavered from her, concentrated on her eyes. There was interest there. She took this as a sign to continue. 'What do you know about Cottel Court?'

*

82

Challis and Ruff had entered No. 3 Pontderry Lane, scene of the suspected break-in carried out by Meredith Guster. They'd got a set of her fingerprints that she had kindly donated so Challis had Sayer's team join them to sweep the house for matching prints, purely for the record. Meanwhile, the two of them intended to begin a less specific search of the property; keen to see what might just turn up.

Ruff was eager to do the upstairs as that was where she was sure she had observed Guster behind the quivering front bedroom curtains but Challis held her back as it became immediately obvious that a search in the house had already been conducted by a person or, she conceded, persons unknown.

They and one of Sayer's team stood in the doorway of the lounge-cum-dining room, surveying the scene. At the dining end, along one wall, was a music system. Its accompanying cd/dvd storage units had been rifled and the floor was littered with plastic cases. Drawers had been ripped out of a modern dresser and contents strewn on the dining table. The dresser's cupboards had been emptied.

'You didn't mention all this,' Challis accused Ruff.

'I didn't know. I mean, that woman, Guster, was at the front door. I just grabbed her and put her in the car and took her in.'

What a pity, thought Challis.

In the lounge there was a glass-topped unit and it too had been rifled. Not content with such obvious storage receptacles whoever had done the searching had turned to the couch and two armchairs, removing cushions.

Ruff moved along the short passage to the kitchen. 'It's the same in here,' she called.

Challis cast a glance in Ruff's direction and could see the mess on the kitchen floor. Ruff turned back and headed straight upstairs. 'And up here.'

Challis followed her. As Ruff had said, it was the same devastation as downstairs. In one of the rooms there had been a computer but now there were just dangling wires, one of which went to an Epson printer, tucked into a low shelf. While Ruff looked around in there Challis went into what was the main bedroom. Everything that could be pulled out of drawers and cupboards had been and bedding torn off the bed, flung on the floor. She stood in the doorway from where she could lean to the right and look into the third room which was a shove-everything-in-and-close-the-door room. There was a bike, two bikes, one for the road, the other for indoor exercise. There were chairs, clothes baskets, clothes for washing, rolled-up rugs, a gate-leg table holding items of china and, in one corner, a stringless guitar standing up against the wall.

'Sarge,' Ruff called. Challis joined Ruff in what used to be the computer room. The DC was standing next to the printer. She had raised its cover and there, on the glass, face down, was a sheet of paper. 'I'm always doing that,' Ruff confessed. 'I photocopy or scan something and leave it in the printer. Then I'm cursing for hours because I can't remember where I put it.'

'What is it?'

Ruff's gloved hand picked up the A4 sheet by its corner and flipped it over onto her other hand. It was a list of names and addresses. Down the left-hand side were the names, in the next column addresses. Then there was a column headed "Badge Id" and the final column was headed "Requirements". The names were of men and women and halfway down Challis excitedly pointed at one: Timothy Bush, next to him the address of the property they were now in. His "Badge Id" was *IT Man* and his "Requirement", whatever that was, was *1 to plus 1F*.

Further down the page two consecutive entries under the "Badge Id" column were ringed in black ink. Entered in this column were *Sister Eve* and *Sister Ella*, respectively. Challis scanned across to the name column and saw that Sister Eve was Jennifer Wheeler and Sister Ella Elizabeth Wheeler, both from Coleshill, Warwickshire. Perhaps they were sisters, Challis thought. Their entries in the "Requirements" column were bracketed together with one phrase *2 to 1M*.

'My God, look at some of these... badge ids,' Ruff read. 'Christ, *42D*, *DaggerMan*, *Belle69*, *HolyGirl*, *XtraLarge*, *FurryCup*, *Moaner*...requirements, *GBang*, *OG*, *1 to 1F*, *1 to 1M*...'

Ruff had a pretty good idea what all of this was adding up to. Glancing at Challis she was unsure if the penny had dropped with her.

'This is a hell of a shopping list,' Ruff went on, 'and look, look at that.' She pointed to the top right-hand corner of the sheet. 'CoCo,' she remembered John Gee's extended version, 'the Clown.'

The logo "Co♀Co" was printed there. Challis frowned so Ruff had to explain. 'Cottel Court. It's their logo.'

'Really. I think you'd better go fetch Ms. Guster.'

*

'Cottel Court,' Redland repeated. 'What about it?'

Challis went over how the place seemed to keep cropping up in this investigation. 'A vehicle of theirs outside Guster's house the night that Timothy Bush may have been hung out in the field. Guster works there...'

'Those two things may be innocently connected,' Redland pointed out.

'...and we find this...list with their logo on it in Timothy Bush's house.' She pulled the A4 sheet in its protective plastic out of her brief case. Redland took it, turning it over straight away to see if anything was on the reverse side before even running his eye down the printed side.

'Is this the only sheet?' he asked.

'What?'

'Well, it seems to continue. There must be more.'

'No, just that one.'

He read the page, making no comment as he did so. He seemed to show no real interest but he hesitated when he reached the bottom, looking puzzled, thoughtful.

'So,' he spoke, slowly dragging his eyes up and away from the list, 'did you speak to Guster again?'

*

They did. Ruff had fetched her and her guardian WPC from her house at the other end of the terrace of three. Challis and Ruff stood in the lounge room doorway with Guster in between them. She was shivering. She'd come out of her house under-dressed and it was freezing cold in Bush's house. A forensic team member, Catherine Finch, otherwise known as Twink – stuck since childhood with the nickname for a chaffinch – was busying away in there. Others could be heard upstairs.

'It was like this when I got in here,' Guster claimed. 'I told you there was something odd about the place that's why I came looking.'

Challis shook her head. 'No, you said you came in to check for leaks. I'm now wondering what kind of leaks. Where's Mr. Bush's computer?'

'I didn't see one.'

'Just the wires dangling loose.'

'Yeah.'

'So,' Challis grinned, 'that confirms that you were upstairs contrary to what you told us earlier. You see the problem we're having is believing anything you say. What were you looking for?'

Guster lowered her head and stared into the room. 'I didn't do any of this. It was already like it.'

'Okay. Who did it then?'

Silence from Guster. Ruff spoke next. 'What's your job at Cottel Court? You may as well tell us because we can find out from them.'

'I work in the office,' Guster almost whispered.

'In the office,' Ruff repeated. 'Admin. An admin role. Paperwork.'

They took it that Guster's silence was affirmative. Ruff looked at Challis and Challis looked at Ruff. Challis understood the keyword "paperwork" and where Ruff was going with it. She withdrew the list found earlier in Bush's printer, now in a plastic cover, from her brief case.

'Do you recognise this?' Guster did; they could tell. 'Can you tell us what it is and what it's all about?'

'No, I...'

'Don't forget, if you've handled this paper your fingerprints will be on it,' Challis interrupted.

'I think I need a solicitor,' Guster suddenly decided.

'Actually,' Challis said in measured tones. 'I'm not sure that you do. You may be a habitual liar but I'm struggling to identify anything terribly illegal that you may have done. So far, that is. Let's look at what we've got: interfered with a dead body; failure to report the finding of a dead body; breaking and entering this house; possibly ransacking it; possibly perverting the course of justice. All could be considered fairly minor, especially if we believe your good-neighbour excuse for coming in here. However, I have to tell you that the case against you could get worse if it's proved that Mr. Bush was in fact murdered or at the very least but equally serious was assisted in his suicide. Now, this list has your employer's logo at the top. At the back of our minds we can't help suspecting that some of the information on here could be, or should be, confidential. As it's got their logo on it we could go and ask them to explain it but they may want to know how we came by it. Could this be the leak you came in here to check for? Cottel Court info leaked to your neighbour?'

'I'm cold,' said Guster, wrapping her arms around herself.

'Then the sooner you answer, the sooner you can go somewhere warm.'

Guster eyed Challis with disgust. 'You're a bit of a cow, aren't you? Is this how you get off?'

Ruff jumped in. 'Is that was this list is all about? Getting it off?'

'Why not,' Guster shouted at Ruff, 'if that's what you want to call it. You're like a bunch of frustrated lesbians, you lot!' She spat it out, making Twink Finch look up from her work with distaste.

'Why, what would you call it?' Challis asked calmly. 'Tell me about Cottel Court.'

*

'And did she tell you?' Redland asked Challis.

'Yes, kind of.'

A bell rang somewhere not too far off and nurses began to look busy in the ward. Visitors were rising to their feet, some kissing their bedridden relatives goodbye, others, like Challis perhaps venturing a handshake or a simple touch on the back of the hand. Although the ward was very warm, many started buttoning up topcoats, swirling scarves around exposed neck skin and making sure they had their gloves to hand, all this to be ready for stepping out into the freezing night.

'Goodnight, sir. I'll look in at your house on the way home.'

'No, it's late. Leave it.'

Challis smiled not wishing to argue about something like that.

'Thanks for coming,' were his parting words as she turned and headed out of the ward without a backward glance.

When she was waiting in her cold car in the frosty hospital car park for the windscreen to heat up and disperse the ice already crusting it she took out the plastic envelope containing the list and looked at the bottom entry that had seemed to hold the boss's attention.

Name: Angela Plumitis. Address: 312 Slough Street, Windsor. Badge Id: Angelick. Requirement: Vikings.

Eighteen

Ray Lockett pulled up a chair alongside Challis, at her desk.

'The name of the software house is TorfGov Software Ltd,' he told her. 'Head office in Old Town. No other offices anywhere. They sell systems into hospitals. Timothy Bush was one of their longest serving consultants. Got on with everyone okay, so they said, but his private life was very much his own. He never went out on office parties or restaurant visits. Last was in work last Friday. He had no close personal friends there and nobody knew of any outside of work. He seemed to have few personal phone-calls. He had a company mobile. Has it been found yet?'

'No,' Challis snapped, waiting impatiently for Lockett to get to something useful.

'They let me look at his emails. The secretary there took me through them. I think she was told to be careful what I looked at, commercially sensitive stuff she said. But he had a personal folder and one what she said was a personal message in his inbox. She let me print off all those. Here they are. There's one or two from his son. She was amazed, the secretary. Nobody knew he had any kids. He wasn't married, as far as they knew. Here look.'

The first one he showed her was dated 7th February. That was a Monday, nearly two weeks ago. The second one from the inbox was dated the Monday just gone, the 14th.

Challis read the first one.

'Dad, This has been amazing. I can't believe the coincidence, that we should be looking for a new system and you come along to demo one last week. I knew who you were straightaway. I was nervous coming up to you afterwards but the look on your face was really something. I told you I

think I moved from Newcastle 2 years ago when I got the job in this hospital, in IT, like you. Liz and Jen moved south too to the midlands where they're both students, so they say. Attached is a photo of the 3 of us taken last Xmas. Jen in the blonde wig, Liz in the red. We were all a bit drunk. They're real party animals and they're dying to meet you. We haven't said anything to Mum, yet. What would she say, eh? She's still with our other dad. Send me a recent photo so I can pass it on to the girls. Bye for now. James.'

Challis looked at the from-address: jw@glos.nhs.uk. At the bottom there was a global signature that showed that 'jw' was in the IT section of Gloucester Royal Hospital. There was a phone number.

'O bugger,' she sighed. 'Looks like we've found our next of kin but Jimmy W has only known his father for three weeks! That's not going to go well.'

'How come it's W and not B for Bush?' Lockett asked.

'Probably took his step-father's name. It happens.'

'Right. So the problem is they've just met for the first time probably since 1991 when Timothy Bush divorced Jimmy's mum, they've met once and Jimmy thinks he's his dad.'

'Yep. And we have no evidence, I assume, that Timothy Bush acknowledged Jimmy as his son.'

'No, no emails back to Jimmy that I could find.'

Challis cogitated. 'DNA might help. In the meantime, do I break it to him? We don't even know his surname. There's always the mother though, his ex-wife. Let's look at the second email.'

They did but that was just a brief note chasing any photo from Timothy Bush. Still no surname though.

'Okay. Let's call this number,' Challis decided, lifting the phone on her desk and dialing. The call was answered fairly quickly, announcing that Challis was through to the Gloucester NHS IT Department. It was a female on the other end.

'Hello, IT. Claire speaking. How may I help you?'

'Hello,' Challis started. 'I'm Detective Sergeant Challis of Mon CID.'

'Sorry,' came the response. 'Where?'

'Mon CID. South Wales. Monmouthshire. The county next to yours.'

'Okay.' Claire was slow. 'And your name was?'

'Challis,' she spelled it then repeated 'Detective Sergeant.'

There was a long drawn-out 'Right'.

'I'd like to speak with a colleague of yours and all we have to go on is that his email id is JW, first name James.'

'James,' the girl repeated. 'JW.'

'That's right. Could I ask what is your name?' Challis knew the girl had said it already but it hadn't registered.

'I'm Claire.'

'Good.' Challis waited for Claire to answer the first query. God preserve me from all IT people on the other end of the phone! They talked dumb or talked down; they had either user-help constipation or technical diarrhea.

'O, Jimmy,' Claire shrieked. 'That'd be Jimmy Wheeler.'

'Jimmy Wheeler! Fine. Is he there? Could I speak to him Claire?'

'Er, no. He's not in the office today.'

'When's he back?'

'Tomorrow I think. Is this a system query?'

Challis ignored the question. 'Do you have another number I could contact him on?'

'Yes but I can't tell you. It's our policy.'

'I understand. Claire, could I speak with your manager or supervisor?'

Claire put Challis through to someone called Darryl, the IT Manager, but he too wouldn't provide the information she wanted. He wanted to know how she got this number so she had to explain it was from an email that had come to light during an investigation that she couldn't talk about. His parting shot was that she could be anybody.

Challis managed to leave her number for James Wheeler to call back before the conversation was terminated. 'Jobsworth,' she complained.

Ruff was standing over her with a photocopy of the list of names found at Timothy Bush's.

'Did you say his name was Wheeler?'

As soon as Ruff said it something clicked in Challis's brain. Ruff didn't need to lower the A4 sheet in front of her eyes; she could visualize the circle of black ink drawn around the badge ids of Sister Eve and Sister Ella and the real names to which they referred: Jennifer and Elizabeth Wheeler. She looked back at the email from Jimmy to his new-found father; his sisters were Liz and Jen.

*

'You're not thinking what I'm thinking, are you?' Ruff put the question to Challis. The two of them and Lockett had retreated to Redland's office. It was Challis who had led the retreat.

The facts that had begun to unravel needed some walkabout to re-form the threads into some kind of plausible pattern. Her promenading had led her into the boss's office and the other two followed her, still clutching their pieces of evidence that ended up draped across the boss's desk.

Challis was not ready to give voice to what she was thinking so Ruff picked up what they had and began to move forward with it.

'Okay. We know what Cottel Court is all about now and Miss Guster kindly explained some of the hieroglyphics on this paper, this list. Ray, you don't know about this. Cottel Court offers adult weekends, you know what I mean. Sex games, fetishes, experiments with other like-minded people.'

'I do know that as it happens,' Lockett corrected her. 'Harry was talking about it, ages ago. Him and the boss. I overheard some of it. Adult parties and so on.' He smiled or was it a smirk.

'Has he been there then?' asked Challis, wide-eyed. 'Harry?' She paused. 'Or the boss?'

'Dunno,' Lockett replied quickly. 'I don't know,' he repeated. He looked from one to the other to check they were convinced.

Challis thought back to her visit to the hospital last night. She'd specifically asked the boss if he knew about Cottel Court and he said nothing.

How come she didn't know about all this? She was angry. Men's toilet talk again, full of 'way-hey', nice work if you can get it; nudging and winking. Do they ever grow up? But she was surprised at the boss. And yet as Ruff continued her recap she wondered if she was in the know as well and was she the only one left out of the loop? Or had she herself heard of the place but dementia had set in early...?

Ruff was in full flow. 'Clients book the weekend or whatever time span is on offer and select a preferred...a preferred method of achieving their personal nirvana. That's this column here titled "requirements". Very euphemistic. "1 to 1F" means a man is looking for a thing with one female, "1 to 1M" the same but reversing the sexes, "OG" is Orgy and so on. Against Timothy Bush is a requirement for one male looking for it with more than one female and down here we find a match, the Wheeler sisters looking to get it together with one male.'

'What was *Vikings*?' Challis asked, remembering the line on the list that seemed to attract Redland. She pointed to it at the bottom of the page at the Angela Plumitis entry.

Ruff shook her said. 'She didn't say. Why?'

'What's the badge id?' Lockett asked.

'Everyone selects a name that will identify them, that will also make them anonymous. So Timothy Bush called himself IT Man – we know why now - and the Wheeler girls called themselves sisters.'

'Did they dress up as nuns?' he wondered.

'Dunno. Not sure if they went that far.'

Challis looked grimly at Ruff. 'Kay, compared with what we think may have happened dressing up as nuns would have been child's play.'

'What is it you think happened?'

Ruff and Challis were stunned by Lockett's question but it made them stop and realize that they only had circumstantial evidence in front of them.

Challis told the other two to sit while she took Redland's chair. 'Meredith Guster was quite forthcoming, eventually,' she began, mainly directing her words towards Lockett. 'She told us that Timothy Bush had been using the Cottel Court facilities for nearly a year. She had introduced him to their offerings. Before the last weekend of activities in January he had pestered her to break a confidence and give him information on the two girls he'd spent time with previously. He rated them highly, he said, but of course all he knew were their badge ids. Guster resisted but he offered her money, more and more, and in the end she gave in and looked up Sister Eve and Sister Ella, printing off this sheet for him. Hence the ring around their ids. There's no way of knowing, yet, if he tried to contact them outside of Cottel Court. Then what happens? After nearly twenty years...'

'He bumps into his son,' Ruff inserted.

'And the son sends him a photo of his sisters...of Timothy Bush's grown up daughters. Incidentally, do we have a copy of that photo?'

'No. They have this odd email software at TorfGov Software Ltd. Attachments coming in are stripped off and kept in sort of quarantine area then copied in or printed or deleted. The girl looked for me but we found nothing.'

'Shame. Anyway, does he make the connection? I think he does. Imagine what that does to him.'

They all pondered. Each one of them had a different effect come to mind but only Ruff said the word that was on all their minds. 'Incest. It is, isn't it?'

Yes, but in the context of a sexually liberated atmosphere incest entered into by consenting adults with obviously great appetites for extreme pleasuring would have challenged even the great excesses of the court of Caligula. But could it be lived with once it was realized?

'I think it destroyed him,' Challis offered. 'He could have self-harmed himself in a way that would attack the instrument of it all. I think he could have killed himself because of it.'

'On the other hand he could have laid back and enjoyed being carved up,' Ruff observed.

'Where do we go from here?' Lockett asked. The two women looked at him questioningly. 'I mean, incest between consenting adults, especially when carried out unknowingly can't be a crime. He's dead and they don't know he's dead or who he was. Nobody knows; only us.'

'We are the police,' Ruff was flabbergasted at Lockett's naivety. 'Incest carries a maximum of 14 years. And what about the coroner's inquest? Why did he do it? That'll be the question and we have the answer. It won't be our little secret for very long will it?'

'O, fuck, this is horrendous.' Challis swearing surprised them.

'Yeah. Those poor girls,' said Ruff.

'What do you mean *poor girls*?' Lockett was incensed. 'They're just as culpable, if not more so. Two sisters getting down together with whatever they got up to is hardly normal.' His metaphors were somewhat paradoxical but they got the gist. 'What did their brother call them? Party animals? This wasn't a one-off for them. They enjoyed doing what they did to some guy, any guy; never mind what they did to each other!'

'Whoa!' Ruff protested. 'You can't lay all this on them.'

'I think you'll find you can.'

'That's enough,' Challis intervened. 'We're making a lot of assumptions here. We need to know for sure. One, are the Wheeler sisters in the photo the same Wheeler sisters on the list? Assuming they are then Two, did Timothy Bush have a session with them; and Three, do the Wheeler sisters know who Timothy Bush is? Then Four, if all this is true then a crime *was* committed but the fact that it may have been unknowingly committed – and that is another point, did either party know the true relationship before the event? – and that one party is dead would probably mean a prosecution would not be contemplated for one second.'

She looked from Lockett to Ruff both of whom thought a comment from them was expected. Words failed them.

There was a reason for Challis's pregnant pause. These two had just exhibited sufficient prejudice to rule them out of following up on these points. Their bias would affect both their questioning and recording of facts. Not only that but Lockett certainly would not be most diplomatic when broaching the subject in the first place. Skillful phrasing of questions would be necessary to actually draw the girls out about their fun weekends. And early mention of the *I* word would have to be avoided.

Challis was not convinced that either of her junior colleagues was up to it. She thought that, of the two, Ruff would be the safest bet but she could hear Redland's admonishment ringing in her ears.

'Let's sleep on it,' Challis sounded as if she was ordering a moratorium. 'None of this answers Sayer's points about him being twice hung but does that pale into insignificance now I wonder? I'll write it all up.'

'Is this a private coven or can anyone join?' Muench had come into the office, saw everyone congregated around Redland's desk and bowled right in.

'Just talking about Cottel Court,' Lockett volunteered.

'O aye,' Muench seemed interested. 'What's this for then? The next office party? Can't fault it.'

'No,' began Lockett but Challis cut him short.

'In late again, Harry, but at least you look as if you've been home to bed this time.'

Muench did a mini swagger, pretending to tighten his tie, which was well knotted enough.

'Stopped by Henderson Timber. Brought in a couple of lads. They're downstairs now, waiting for charging.'

'Hey, result,' said Lockett.

'At last,' said Ruff.

'Well done, Harry,' Challis joined in. 'The boss will be pleased. Put it up on the board.'

She stared at Muench. What about sending Harry to interview the girls and their brother, she thought. Fuck, no; don't be stupid!

*

'What's up, Kay?

They were in a car again, heading for Cottel Court. There was no ice. The sun was out and the temperature above zero for a change.

Kay Ruff had been quiet most of the ride, so, as Challis drove towards Usk, she quizzed her companion again.

'You're very quiet,' she said, trying to tempt Ruff to speak. But Ruff's lips were tight and even though her skin was brown Challis could almost swear she was red in the face. She had been silently steaming ever since they left the office.

Ruff had felt really good earlier when it looked like they'd made great inroads into the *ugly suicide*, as she kept calling it. To her mind, their latest discoveries had made the whole thing even uglier. She wasn't still narked by Lockett's comments about the Wheeler girls, was she? Challis conjectured.

*

After they had heard Muench's news, Challis had left the office for a long call of nature leaving Ruff to gather up the cups to go and make coffee, Lockett and Muench sat where they were in the boss's room. They were still in there when she had come back in with the tray, their backs to her but the door open. She could hear them talking and Muench laughing. He was in full flow, she could tell. Cottel Court was mentioned followed by more laughter from Muench. She could guess the tenor of his monologue.

She stepped closer but kept silent. Muench was enjoying himself; his voice was raised.

'Consenting adults, what's wrong with it? Everybody needs to get their rocks off one way or the other and you only got to look at some people to know how they get theirs. Yours, Ray, sticks out like a sore thumb; not married, no girlfriend, plenty of internet porn I'd bet. The big brown breasted Krufty, oooh, voluptuous or what. I bet she wraps herself around poor little Alex. I'd love to fuck her tits. Large women, large appetites. I mean, look at her full lips; you know what they're good for, don't you? Although, she's a vegetarian and I always wonder if veggies are permitted to indulge in oral sex. And Challis...she's the sort of woman who wishes her vibrator could mow the lawn as well. She doesn't like men but I don't think she likes women either...'

'You're all bullshit!' Lockett was seriously not amused but his reaction did not gain many brownie points from Ruff listening outside. 'You're the same as me,' he told Muench. 'You got nobody.'

'How do you know? Listen, my old uncle told me once to always go for the ugly women because they're most grateful. Good advice, if you fancy shagging just ugly women. But I tell you, Raymond, other men's women are just as grateful; they like the novelty, the danger, the tastier treats on offer...'

Eavesdroppers never hear any good of themselves was the old saying but Ruff did not blame herself for what she'd heard. She let the tray clatter onto her desk with some spillage of coffee and didn't wait to see the two men turn around. She was gone.

Now Melanie was asking her what was wrong? If she started to tell her she had a fear she would lose it.

'It's that fucking Munch,' she began, taking a big breath. 'He was talking to Ray, about what goes on at Cottel Court. They were having a right old laugh. Then he started talking about...about all of us, including you. You should have heard what he said he wanted to do to my tits.' Her words came spitting out of her mouth. She had to swallow her anger back but it wouldn't go. 'He's a cunt!'

Challis had a spasm of panic when she heard that word, especially coming from Kay. Never before had she heard that from her. It was a swear word that she herself would never ever use.

She didn't know how to react. She kept her eyes on the road ahead. Kay had come out with the word and then gone silent. Enough said.

Challis hated the word, always had. Hearing it again brought back the unpleasant aspects of sex with Stuart Devlin. He was very vocal during their sessions. Initially, he'd delighted in telling her she was "silent but violent" but soon he was urging her to become more verbally graphic. That particular word was high on his list of favourites and he cajoled her to plead explicitly with him to do things to that part of her body. He told her that he had worked in offices with women who habitually used the word, most often out of context, as purely an expletive. He had tried to get her to use it and its like in the context of their conjoining, as he did, but such explicit descriptiveness did nothing for her and he knew it and because he knew it he lost respect for her. She was not the kindred spirit he was obviously looking for. It became one of the fracture points in their relationship. Both were disappointed as a result of the use of such vocabulary.

Kay was actually repeating the phrase in her own mind, using it as a calmative without much success.

Challis wanted to come out with some utterances of comfort and she could easily have sided unequivocally with Kay but she was in charge of the team now and felt constrained to be constructive: objective rather than subjective.

'You've got to get used to it, Kay,' she offered, although she never had come to terms with blatant sexism directed at her, openly or covertly.

She wanted to tell Kay she was better than the men in the team. It would have been a truth but after what Redland had said the previous night about dividing her favours across all team members she thought she should hold back on that one.

Christ, this bloody job's getting difficult! 'And you mustn't let it interfere with the good work you're doing. I need you to continue being focused. Don't let me down. I need all the support I can get at the minute.'

She turned her head to look at Kay. The young DC was wiping away a tear. Challis smiled thinly and offered herself up for sacrifice. 'What did the bastard say about me, then?' Her voice was light trying to give the impression that whatever it was it was a joke.

'That you're a woman who wishes her vibrator could mow the lawn as well.' Kay laughed as she said it.

'Ha! Harry's more perceptive than I thought.' And she smiled broadly, superficially amused. 'But he's obviously insecure. Deep down he worries most women prefer the artificial to the real thing.'

Kay was smiling now. 'He also reckoned you don't like men but also you don't like women,' she added.

'Sad bastard,' Challis finally allowed herself a Muench put-down. 'Men! No wonder I love my rabbit.' Ruff had no idea how serious Challis was being.

'Aw, shit! What's this?'

They had entered the thirty mph stretch into Usk. A large articulated lorry was right across the road, its front end almost on the petrol station forecourt, its backend lying through a new gap in the listed Usk stone bridge, rubble strewn under its wheels. The driver was out of his cab, walking back to inspect the damage. As he did so, an elderly man, Jared Edwards, who Challis recognized as a neighbour of Redland's, wielded his camera, snapping away, one minute at the driver, the next at the gaping hole in the bridge wall. His equally elderly wife Margaret was gesticulated wildly at the driver, her mouth going nineteen to the dozen. Challis noticed that the lorry had Dutch plates so how much the driver was taking in was anybody's guess.

Nothing was moving into the town.

'Where's a copper when you need one?' Challis muttered.

No traffic could move so Challis did a U-turn and crossed the river downstream. This detour east of the river took them into Usk past the prison where hangings took place once upon a time.

It was lunchtime or near enough when they reached Usk; Challis said they would stop and get a bite to eat. The change of route hadn't cost them much in the way of lost time and traffic could be seen to be flowing again through the town.

She drove into the main car-park and then guided Ruff along Bridge Street. Shops were mainly on one side of the road which made the constricted pavement a busy one. Passing lorries were far too close for comfort. Ruff was led into a newly opened sandwich shop. Challis assured her fastidious companion that vegetarian options were available. Even so the DC interrogated the young female shop assistant about the content of the advertised vegetarian sandwiches and rolls.

'That one says brie, salad and dressing. What kind of dressing can I have? Do you have pesto?'

The girl made enquiries with an older assistant.

'You and your pesto,' Challis observed. 'You have it every day, don't you?'

'I love it,' Ruff explained but with a look of why-should-I-have-to.

A baguette with pesto was available so she took it. Challis had a beef sandwich with horseradish, a packet of crisps and a bottle of water.

Back in the warm car they began to eat. It took Ruff a little while to get going. She was less than comfortable eating in this pool car that showed ample evidence of past meals of one sort or another having been consumed: discarded wrappers and crumbs everywhere. Eventually she sank her teeth into the baguette. She chewed slowly, her face changing from blissful expectation to abject disappointment. She prised open the baguette and sniffed the contents.

'Smell that,' she almost ordered Challis who somewhat reluctantly complied, coming away with a blank look. 'There's no pesto, is there?'

Before waiting for an answer, Ruff had re-bagged the baguette and was getting out of the car. 'That's not what I asked for. Not what they said I was having.'

She was a known complainer. If anyone promised something that did not materialize Ruff would complain. She was gone, back to the shop. She returned several minutes later with another offering, sat and ate it quietly. Challis sat in quiet disbelief, much like the way Oliver Hardy stared with amazed bewilderment at Stan Laurel as he somehow turned a non-event into a triumph. Annoying. Ruff could be tenacious, she'd give her that; shame it didn't always apply to her work.

Challis had eaten her sandwich and crisps while Ruff had been sourcing her desired filling. She took one last swig of the water.

'Let's go and get on with this.'

The car jerked away; Ruff in mid-bite, gagging, reminding her of something else Muench had said about her. Ignorant bastard!

Challis left Usk by the old Chepstow Road and then on towards Cottel Court, some four miles north.

Nineteen

DCI Lassman had been more than a little dismayed to find no clues in and around George Medlyn's house that might help to resolve the murder of the man: no identifiable fingerprints other than those of the deceased and of the deceased's wife. The house was a mess top to bottom. The only item known to be missing was a computer. Neighbours were useless. Nothing seen or heard.

The man's widow was less than no use at all. In the cold light of the following morning she had been brought to the local Station. Even though not under caution, she brought a solicitor with her.

She was so disinterested, cold and detached that Lassman considered her for a while as the perpetrator of choice. He challenged her attitude, accusing her of being complicit in her husband's death and demanding she should reveal why she had suddenly left him after years of marriage. She remained silent at first but when Lassman told her of the finds in the upstairs study and the subject matter on dvds and, tucked away, vintage video tapes, she calmly offered him 'Well there's one good reason then isn't there?'

'Did you never go in that room?' O'Toole queried. 'It didn't seem to be locked.'

'Why would I want to go in there?'

'I dunno,' O'Toole shrugged. 'I thought perhaps he might have invited you in, to share his hobby.'

She went dead-pan.

Both Lassman and O'Toole could easily guess that she had been invited in, once, and didn't like it. She didn't like it then and that was probably in the early days of his collection, so why had she only left him now, recently?

They had separate bedrooms; that was plain to see; and smell. No cohabiting at that level. It had been WPC Olluwala who had suggested something to Lassman. She had seen Mrs. Medlyn's bedroom. It was clean and tidy: a place for everything and everything in its place. Except the bed. It was unmade, not just unmade but, as she put it, thrashed about a bit. She stopped short of admitting that her own bed sometimes looked like that after a damn good session with her boyfriend and instead pointed at areas on the bedding where there was some staining. Scotty had been asked to take charge of the sheets and make out of it what she could. She needed DNA samples from Mrs. Medlyn, for elimination, as it was her bed after all. Mrs. Medlyn refused.

The man with whom she had lived, with whom she had still been married and shared the same house until just a few weeks ago, had been brutally gunned down and she obviously couldn't care less.

'Your bedroom was a bit of a mess,' Lassman began, 'or at least the bed was. Stuck out like a sore thumb compared with the immaculate state of the rest of the room. Why did you leave in such a hurry?'

The solicitor intervened, wondering what the condition of Mrs. Medlyn's bed had to do with the death of her husband.

'Quite simple,' explained Lassman. 'Motive.'

We need a motive.

He thought that this solicitor was a little bit of a green man, someone that Mrs. Medlyn knew but was not necessarily the best person for this role. 'Who else would want your husband dead?'

'Inspector!' The solicitor sat forward. 'I really must suggest that the implication in that question is completely unfounded and slanderous.'

'I'm sorry,' Lassman's eyebrows rose as if in total surprise. 'Motive, motive! Who else has a motive?'

'Inspector…'

Patricia Medlyn put her hand on her solicitor's arm. 'Strangely, I've been wondering that myself. Who would want to kill such a non-entity? And in such a way? And then search our house, my house? What on earth could he possess that no other pervert with a computer could not find for themselves? Inspector, my husband's death was the most noteworthy part of an otherwise sad and twisted existence. A truly remarkable end to a totally shallow life that I am glad is no more. But I didn't shoot him; I mean, what with? I didn't arrange for anyone else to do it either. Do you really think I would lower myself, risk a lifetime in jail for stepping on a louse?'

Later that afternoon DC Farouk called Lassman and O'Toole over to his desk. His computer was on and a flash memory stick inserted.

'We found this in Medlyn…Mr. Medlyn's desk drawer in his office in the city. It was locked but this was all that was inside.'

Lassman grunted, partly in appreciation of Farouk's self-correction of his naming of the victim. Lassman insisted on full respect being paid, by others.

'Watch this, sir.'

Via Explorer he accessed the drive letter for the stick. There was a single file name in the list: "VKS: January 2011". He clicked on it and a video began to play, drawing the wide-eyed pair of senior officers ever closer to the action on the screen.

Twenty

Cottel Court nestled out of sight. The house could not be seen from the road, high hedges of mixed cropped trees meant that a vehicle had to be of some height for its occupants to get even the merest glimpse of the roof. It was tucked down into one of two small parallel glacial valleys. To its northern side a steep smooth scarp rose like a velvet pommel on the saddle of land with the Court on its left divided from the lake on the right by a treed ridge.

Mid-winter was the best time to get a view from the Roman ridge road. There was a single-track strip of tarmac running down some four hundred metres to the house. Challis drove slowly in case the track was iced but without incident she reached the gate into the inner graveled shorter driveway that fanned out onto a large stone area in front of the ivy-covered front with its two-pillared portico in mid-wall.

The black wrought-iron double gates with "Cottel Court" spelled out on a wrought-iron arch were closed. Odd, Challis thought, that the house should be thus advertised down here out of sight while the entrance at the top maintained an anonymity. As the car approached, a man stepped out from a small lodge-type building on the left. Challis could see there was no easy way to get into the inner courtyard, the wrought-iron was also utilized in six-foot railings that swept away left and right.

The only way to gain entrance seemed to be to get out of the car and walk up to the gates to speak to the gatekeeper through the ironwork. Challis nudged Ruff to get out and do the introductions.

Ruff stepped out of the warmth, wrapping her coat tighter about her body but keeping her hands ungloved so as to retrieve her warrant card, warm from her inside pocket. Challis saw her wave it at the man then gesticulate towards the car probably to inform him who else was with her. The gatekeeper stared at the car. He was not rushing, trained not to bow to pressure of any sort.

He disappeared inside the lodge building on the gable end of which a cctv camera stared with its Cyclops eye glaring red. Panning around Challis spotted another one on a pole the other side of the inner drive.

Still the gates didn't budge and Ruff stayed where she was, trying to indicate to Challis that she had been asked to stay put. After a minute or two, the gatekeeper reappeared, paying attention to the front door of the house. He had reported in and was waiting for someone, presumably of a higher authority, to appear.

Challis watched him and was gradually taken with the coat, the parka, that the gatekeeper was wearing. It was of a camouflage type, hooded, with draw-strings dangling either side. She turned and grabbed the case file off the back seat. Flipping pages, she came to Sayer's description of the garment from which the fibres on the log could have come. He had included a picture of the American parka whose composition of nylon and cotton and colouration of dark and light green shapes made it a prime candidate. To Challis, the gatekeeper's looked identical.

She took the opportunity presented by the delay to step out of the car to join Ruff.

'He's phoned the house,' Ruff told her.

'See the coat?' Challis said in a low voice.

Ruff was slow to understand; she had only skimmed through some parts of Sayer's report. Challis helped her out. 'The fibres on the log.'

She held her face down as she spoke so as not to appear at all interested in the man in the parka. Now she saw that the light dusting of snow allowed the underlying gravel to peak through, little grey peaks in the white. With her foot she idly swept the ground and saw that specks of black came up to the surface. She started to bend to pick a piece but thought better of it. Instead she let her eyes drift idly upwards. Metal gates and metal arch all painted black.

Meanwhile the gatekeeper had strolled away from them as he spotted another figure leaving the house and coming their way. Another male, hat-wearing, Barbour coat up to his neck. He waved at the gatekeeper in a circular motion which the latter interpreted as "open the gates", making him hasten at a slighter faster rate of slouch into the lodge. The gates slowly opened. The two policewomen turned to get back in the car.

'Wait,' came the man's voice, now close. Challis spun round, a sudden tightness in the throat at the sound's familiarity. 'Melanie! Hi!'

'It's Redland's bloody nephew again,' Ruff muttered under her breath.

Challis was less circumspect. 'What the fuck is he doing here?' was her thought.

'Kay,' he greeted the DC without hesitation, her name tripping off his tongue as if she was a long-standing friend. His smile disarmed her as he offered her his hand with full eye contact.

'Hello again.' She was glued to his face. He seemed to stamp himself on her but quickly he turned on Challis and embraced her, her hands couldn't help but come up and rest on his hips.

'Twice in two days,' he observed. She wondered if there was any harking back to earlier times between the two of them.

She disengaged.

'We're here officially.' She tried to appear officious but his gleaming smile would have none of it.

'Snap!' he beamed. She couldn't fathom that comment, which he saw in her face. 'I mean I'm here officially too.' He unbuttoned two top buttons of his Barbour and pulled a red tape hanging from around his neck. An identity tag popped out. He held it out for her to study. His photograph was on it and his name, both under the banner 'SD Security' with some curious logo that she couldn't make out. 'My company runs the security. You're lucky to find me here. Just arrived. You've met Chas.' The gatekeeper was back out from the lodge. 'My man...' he added proprietarily.

'Okay,' Challis tried to wrest back the initiative. 'Well you know who we are. Perhaps you could direct us towards someone to answer a few questions we have.'

'Can I ask what about?'

'You can ask but I need to talk to someone who controls and organizes the use of vehicles.' She pointed towards one such vehicle, a Range Rover, visible now on one side of the house.

'Move your car up to the house,' he ordered. 'I'll meet you inside.' He strode off.

There was no mistaking Ruff's close study of Challis's body language. She couldn't possibly know the full impact that the unexpected appearance of Stuart Devlin had had on the DS. The sense of purpose with which she had headed for Cottel Court had evaporated. She almost wanted to retreat. At worst his presence could actually compromise this element of the investigation; at best it could cloud all of the points to be covered. She could of course stay in the car and let Ruff do the questioning but that wouldn't create the right impression with either the DC or Stuart Devlin and the way he had immediately soft-soaped Ruff would probably render her professionalism less than effective. No, she was here and had to keep control.

'What were you saying about the coat?' Ruff asked as soon as they were settled in the car. That was good, thought Challis. Kay was focused, more than she was, and back on the job in hand. Also it brought her back to the other points of interest: the gravel, the metal arch, the black paint. Challis voiced her observations to Ruff.

'O right,' Ruff understood. 'Look. Look what's stuck to my shoe.' She took out an evidence bag and carefully scraped the bottom of her shoe. She held up the bag and with the flakes of snow were pieces of gravel and some specks of black flecks of what looked like paint. 'Hardly scientific I know but it may give us a clue. You know what this might mean?' Ruff continued importantly. 'I know you're thinking the same. Sayer's twice hung theory. Hanging number one here, especially if these black specks are metal paint and match what was on the rope.'

As she tucked the bag away she held Challis back as she was about to exit the car. 'Would you like me to run with this? The fact that the nephew is here, does that get in the way for you?'

Once again, Challis was amazed how Ruff's thought processes mirrored her own.

The first person they saw inside the house was Meredith Guster. She could be seen behind a glass partition that fronted what had once been a reception room now converted into an office with space enough for at least three desks that Challis could see. The neighbour of the former Timothy Bush caught sight of the two detectives, scanning from one to the other, fearful that she had been pursued to her place of work for more questioning. Challis and Ruff gave her no indication as to their purpose. It was not their place to give cheery waves or to even acknowledge the woman.

Stuart Devlin stood before them, peeling off his headgear and Barbour. It certainly was a lot warmer in the hallway. A central wooden staircase was immediately behind him, not overly broad but impressive as it rose up before dividing to send more shallow rises both left and right. Opposite the room where Meredith Guster was located was a heavy oak door and then further back another door on either side of the staircase. These doors were not open and neither was a double doorway that could just be seen behind and beyond the stairs.

Challis and Ruff loosened their clothing, aware that Stuart Devlin's eyes were on them, not boring in, but taking in as much as he could. Challis made sure she avoided eye contact, lifting her face to study the decorative plastered ceiling and frieze.

'Impressive place.'

Stuart Devlin said nothing but ushered them into the Meredith Guster room. They had to pass close to her desk but none of them made any display of recognition; there was little time as they were guided through the office and into a smaller room at the far end. It was sparsely furnished: a desk at one end, two chairs and a safe on the floor to one side of the desk. As the door was closed by Stuart Devlin Challis caught sight of Meredith Guster rising from her desk and heading for the door into the hallway.

'Can I get you ladies coffee?' he asked. Who's going to get it for you, Challis wondered, now that the Guster woman has disappeared.

'I'd prefer you to get the person we need to speak to.' Ladies! She hated the patronizing sound of the word. 'Who would that be...sir?' That didn't sound right to her either.

'It'll have to be me,' he replied unflinching, maintaining a light touch.

She issued a confused sigh and made a bit of a performance, he thought, of opening her bag which she had rested on the edge of a table near the door. Ruff extricated her notebook.

'Really? You don't work directly for this...organization, I gather. You are contracted to provide certain services.'

'I think you'll find it amounts to more than just that, Melanie. What is this all about? You haven't told me yet.'

Ruff knew he was trying to get under the DS's defences and was worried he'd unnerve her. O well, she had offered to take the lead...

'We're investigating the suspicious death of a man whose body was found near Llanhelog...' he was about to interrupt but Challis went on '...and the fact that one of Cottel Court's vehicle was seen parked near the spot at the time. How many vehicles are operated here?'

'Two,' he answered immediately. He knew it was the wrong answer but let it ride. There was an unsure moment that conveyed itself to both Challis and Ruff. He was given a chance to revise his reply.

'Are you sure?' Challis pushed him but gently.

'There was three. One's off the road.'

'Which one is that?' she looked down at her paperwork as she asked the question as if to ready herself to check his response. All they had by way of evidence was John Gee's half-hearted description – a bloody great Range Rover - and that wasn't what she was actually looking up right then anyway. It's a game; one of Redland's favourite expressions.

'Not sure.'

'Well, you say there are three. There's a Range Rover outside so what are the other two?'

'A Land Rover and a Volvo estate. It's the latter one I believe.'

Ruff was scribbling.

'Who drives them?'

'Well anybody who works for the company.'

'Including yourselves? You and...'

'Chas,' Ruff prompted.

'You and Chas?'

'We could do.'

'Is a log kept of who drives what and when?'

'Of course.'

'So, who was driving it on Monday last at...' she looked at Ruff.

'Five p.m.'

'We'd like to speak to the driver and have a look at the vehicle itself.'

'Melanie, slow down,' he tried to grin and extend his reach towards her but it was made brief as Challis gave him a distant look.

'Please,' she paused for effect. 'This is a serious business. We have reason to believe a perversion of the course of justice is the very least offence that may have been committed and that's serious enough, so I would please ask that you respect what it is we have to do here. Now, who was the driver that evening?'

He sniffed and sneered. 'I have no idea.'

'Really? I thought you had your finger on every pulse.' Bugger! She knew immediately it was a bad choice of words. He saw his opportunity.

'You remember then, Melanie.'

Ruff saw the innuendo flashing back and forth between the two of them and knew she had to step in.

'What was the Range Rover doing outside Miss Guster's house on Monday last?' Her question failed to register, failed to break the moment. 'Mr. Devlin,' she persisted, got his attention and repeated the question.

'She may have been the driver,' he suggested.

'Wrong. Try again.'

'Look I have no idea. Delivering something to her.'

'Kay,' Challis turned to her colleague. 'Go and find Miss Guster and put those points to her.'

Ruff was surprised to be instructed to leave Challis alone with Stuart Devlin. She questioned it with a look but she knew she had no choice but to go.

The door had hardly closed behind her when Challis turned on Stuart Devlin.

'Do you think you're being smart or clever? I have a job to do and I find you're verging on the obstructive. It matters nothing that we know each other. That was a long time ago. Now either you're going to co-operate here or I'll take you somewhere else under caution and we'll do it by the book.'

He wagged his finger slowly at her. 'You're the one who's having the problem. You're finding fault with me where there is none. I don't think you're man enough. You can't shake off the memories. You're compromised. Conflict of interests; keep leaving yourself wide open. You should hand over to someone else. Young Kay seems a good substitute.

She could be single-minded about things, like you used to be. Okay, okay!' He held his hand up in submission as he saw she objected to his references to times past. Through his mind flashed the impulse to mention his uncle Alan Redland but he held that one back. That would really rub salt in the wounds. He changed his tack. 'Have you been here before? Let me show you round. You'd like it I think.'

'I know what goes on here, Stuart.' Again, another regret: the use of his name. 'The man who died had used this place and we have reason to believe that this place caused his death. Sadly, not in a criminal way but things of a criminal nature could have happened later.'

'Rubbish!'

'A man is dead. Having been here, he died.'

'Yeah, suicide. Hardly anyone's fault.'

'I didn't mention suicide.'

'It's common knowledge. Meredith Guster's neighbour.'

'So you know her neighbour and of his connection with this place. Now that is interesting. Do you know everyone who comes here for…relaxation? Is that part of your job?'

It wasn't and he couldn't answer.

'Melanie…'

'Detective Sergeant Challis,' and she flashed her warrant card in his face.

He scoffed. 'Now you're being ridiculous.'

'You're old hat. Self-important. Probably God's gift to, what was her name, at the hospital? Sue?'

He laughed. 'Not jealous are you, Melanie? No need. Like you and me, Sue and I are just fuck buddies.'

That hit her below the belt.

'You were so close to the next level,' he went on, 'but you just wouldn't let it happen. It wasn't your nose you cut off and certainly not your face that you spited. Such a little girl. Then!' She couldn't quite work out if he was being sadistic or trying to seduce her all over again. 'But it's not too late Melanie. Come here.'

Now it was Challis who held up her hands, but not in surrender.

'Melanie, you've not had the like of it since have you?' he pleaded. 'You miss it. I can tell. This is a good place. This is the kind of place that's at that next level, even the next after that. There's no limit.'

He was right; sickeningly correct. He'd reached the next level, whatever that was, she could tell by his face. But she'd always known, it was obvious but not to him, that the next level would always be at best the penultimate level. Any fool could see that. How would anyone ever know what the ultimate might be?

But here he was; *come into my parlour said the spider to the fly.*

Into this web.

There were no limits in this place. Timothy Bush and the Wheeler sisters were evidence of that, plain to see.

Okay, maybe it hadn't been deliberate between them. It could have been a twist of twisted fate, a horrible twist. I mean, how could anyone set out to commit incest? How could a man know that the daughters with whom he'd lost complete touch would have inherited his hunger for extreme sexual adventures?

No father could imagine that.

And yet it surely was not that far-fetched. The person that Timothy Bush had become would be a stranger to his own parents, just as they may well have been to their own in turn. Because so it always is; the same old discoveries of each new generation.

But in the normal way of life it is insignificant; no parent would care to know. It only matters, she realized, in a place like this place, where the drive is to escape the normal, to achieve the unnatural. To not care if secrets are kept.

And the great destroyer is when you step way over that line so that even a devoted participant would find it ultimately totally distasteful.

That the paths of close relatives should unknowingly cross because their "requirements" ticked the right boxes was Destiny having a real sick laugh or God wielding a bloody big vengeful stick, for once.

It had killed Timothy Bush.

Challis was intrigued to know what the effect of such a mortal sin would be on the Wheeler sisters. This had been playing on her mind ever since the relationship between the threesome had become a probability. They had been happy to take on an older man, two sisters together, joining forces to do God knows what.

Challis eyed Stuart Devlin, her head tilted to the right so as not to give him her full face. She suspected, she almost knew for certain, that he would join in such perversion. It would never just happen to him by accident. Try it, once at least; that was him.

She wished she could run him in just for having abnormal desires. She had convinced herself he had them, frequently. She could believe anything of him, believe him capable of anything. She'd been there, almost; up close. What had saved her: her suppressed nature, her modest cowardice, her passive selfishness, not giving, only receiving?

'That attitude,' she said at last, 'means you will never be satisfied. You know that don't you? There's always the next level to go for, if you can find it. But I'm not getting into this with you. That's not why I'm here. I want some answers to these questions. This place is not innocent in all this and I'm far from convinced that you are. You say you're in charge here so that's where the buck stops.'

He was unmoved. 'A suicide,' he scoffed. 'It does not deserve your undivided attention, my sweet. My sweet fuck buddy,' he said again, his lips mouthing the words in an exaggerated movement.

Yes, she despairingly agreed to herself. I guess I was. I guess that's all I've been to anyone ever since.

*

Lockett hated being caught listening to the ravings of Harry Muench. It had always been in his nature to not side with a bully. He and his sister had seen enough of that at home. In school there had been a boy who was the butt of cruel jibes and although he, Lockett, might have been part of the group doing their worst he had not vocalized with them and when out of their company he often grabbed the chance to, not so much befriend the abused boy, but exchange a gentle word with him. He had been impressed with the boy's lack of self-pity, with his acceptance of his lot bearing no malice towards his antagonists who, Lockett came to understand, were actually pitied by the boy himself.

So it was in the workplace; bullying from those who rode rough-shod over others, stereotyping the whole world around them. He didn't agree with Muench and, cowardly, he paid the man the undeserved compliment of listening to his bigoted rantings.

He'd actually had enough of it and today tried to put his point across but Muench as always had the last word.

It wasn't just the last word that Ruff had heard; obviously. She had heard Muench's reduction of herself to a thing of mouth and breasts. She had grabbed her coat and hurried out.

Challis had given him some last instructions about working out a plan to get to Timothy Bush's son and daughters. Muench was told to get those guys from Henderson Timber processed.

'I wish you'd keep your mouth shut sometimes, Harry,' Lockett admonished Muench, fed up with Ruff obviously tarring him with the same brush, guilty by association.

It had been later in the morning when Muench got a phone-call that wiped the earlier gloat from his face. He was all smiles as he answered the call but this changed instantly and he rose from his desk and took his mobile into Redland's office, closing the door behind him. He'd then taken his coat and left the office, saying to Lockett he had to go out but giving no idea when he might return.

*

Henderson Timber had reported thefts from their timber yard just after Christmas. It was reported by Anne Henderson who ran the business with Jeff, her husband of fifteen years. He was managing director and Anne, a trained accountant, was Finance Director. It was she who realized from an internal audit that all was not how it should be. Harry Muench had been assigned the case by Redland. He had quickly identified one important fact. Mrs. Henderson was worth pursuing.

As she stood to greet his arrival in her office that she shared with no-one he could see that beneath her flowing cardigan was a figure of some substance. She had a body, he thought, that the slight and wrinkled Mr. Henderson did not deserve to have access to. He looked "half-soaked", as Muench's mother would have said; a cold fish, probably functioned okay as a managing director but offered no warmth for the marital bed.

Muench detected a chilly atmosphere between the couple. He'd seen it before where the pecking order of the household did not necessarily transfer easily to a business environment. Mrs. Henderson ran their personal life and very much wanted to run the business life. There was an uneasy tension about their relationship; contradictions, sometimes of a petty nature, crept into their verbal exchanges in front of Muench.

Mrs. Henderson was an attractive nearly-forty-year old but he was careful to show them equal attention when interviewing the two of them together. Cleverly though he was able to persuade Jeff Henderson that he needed to go through the books that had roused Mrs. Henderson's suspicions and that for him to get a full grasp of the magnitude he would appreciate time to go through it all with her. He used these words, key-words well tried in other similar circumstances where he hoped to lay groundwork. Very often they sparked no sign of recognition in the mind of the intended seductee but now and again he found that he was able to eventually reap what he had sown. And there was favourable reaction from Mrs. Henderson. She had a habit when in conversation of extending both arms up above and behind her head as if to help her thought process. Muench found it was a stimulating unconsciously submissive gesture.

Jeff Henderson had left them alone.

'Okay,' began Muench, 'show me your figures.'

They began the work, sitting side by side for ease. This position meant there was much leaning over each other to point at the computer screen or a printout. More cleverly, though, he quizzed her, almost critically, about her style of book-keeping, all the while maintaining a kind of false disinterested eye contact with her. She had dark green eyes with small disguised dark patches under each one. Her hair, that he made sure she saw catch his eye from time to time, was bunched back, her face free from all but a stray independent strand or two. She wore little makeup but smelled good. The criticism of her book-keeping style raised a temperature within her and she stood her corner, justifying the reasons.

Muench managed to squeeze all of this into little more than three-quarters of an hour at which point he said he had another appointment, untrue, and could they continue another time and that he was available outside working hours if she was too. She agreed his suggestion so Muench came back that evening after six and they resumed their positions but very quickly the eyes had no desire to look at screens full of general ledger double entries. Muench had generated the electricity required and, behind the locked door of her office, they had instinctive sex on the desk, in her chair and on the floor.

She had had sex like that once before since her marriage but never in the workplace. She realized later it was a very risky thing to do, so, after that, they used a hotel and she always paid. But entering her office on the days that followed brought smiles of reminiscence. The chair, the desk and even the floor made her cheeks tingle.

The Hendersons had a house on the hill that overlooked their place of business. Muench had never been here before. Anne Henderson opened the door before he even knocked. She stood back half hidden as he went in. He went to embrace her but she pushed the door closed past him.

'Anne, what's wrong with you?'

'Come in and I'll show you.' She was totally without a hint of welcome for her lover. She led him from the spacious hallway and into a small study off to the left.

'Read that.' She waved at a laptop on the antique-looking desk near the window. Muench loosened his top-coat and, made apprehensive by her obvious tension, sidled up to the computer. There was an email on the screen, an email from a Facebook user. The name of the sender meant nothing but then Facebook permitted anonymity. He read the message, carefully, then he read it again.

'You will have to release them,' she said plainly.

He spun around. 'No I can't. I've been months on this case. It's all but closed.'

'You must.' Her teeth were set firm. 'Otherwise we're both fucked. They know about us.'

'So?'

'Jeff would not be forgiving. I wouldn't have a bean. And you? Would your superiors approve you screwing around with married women and dragging out the case just so you could carry on with it. Face it. Let them go. Not enough evidence.'

'We'll both be left wide open to blackmail; don't you realize?'

She was intransigent. 'Let them go Harry.'

Twenty-One

Ruff was temporarily at a loss when she found that Meredith Guster was no longer at her desk.

She deduced that Challis had a good reason for wanting her out of the inner office. There was a bit of a head-to-head going on in there.

Clearly the boss – the first time she'd thought of her as that – must have another agenda. There was history there; sex, that was obvious. Couldn't blame Melanie, although there was something about him...

So, she decided not to return to the small office but to seek out Miss Guster.

Things did seem a little quiet at Cottel Court this particular day. Miss Guster had been the only one in this office. Ruff glanced at her desk. Pretty tidy; little piles of paperwork neatly stacked. This surprised her. Meredith Guster was a scruffy dresser. The other two desks were clear of any noticeable work. None of them displayed any personal items; no family photos. Perhaps Miss Guster was the sole occupant of this office. Be good to know the size of the workforce.

Between the two windows was a multi-functional printer, photocopier and probably fax machine. Filing cabinets, three, stood one to each desk. Each desk had a slim-line computer screen with processing units under the desks. Most interesting in the far corner were cctv screens, two of them at the moment showing images from the cameras at the gates. She could see that Chas standing outside his lodge, smoking a cigarette. He's a good boy, she thought, stepping outside to smoke when as far as she knew he was the only occupant of that building. He could have had a drag in the warm.

Wait up! He was being joined by somebody else. Miss Guster, her face visible briefly before she raised the hood on the coat to cover her head. Not just any coat either but another one of those parkas. Company issue? she wondered.

Miss Guster sidled up to Chas putting her face close to his. When she pulled back Ruff could see she too was puffing on a cigarette. She watched the two of them, moving closer to the screen for a better look. Chas's arm was now about Miss Guster's shoulder. He drew her in and, yes, there was a kiss on her cheek. Miss Guster did not so much object to the kiss but seemed more fearful of being spotted in that brief moment of intimacy. She pointed up at the cctv camera.

Ruff's notebook was still in her hand so she jotted down 'cctv-check'.

Having given the office the once-over she stepped out into the hallway to wait for Miss Guster to come back in. There was less light in there now than there had been when they had arrived. It was chillier in the semi-gloom. She moved in line with the front door and looked through its glass top to see if there was any sign of her quarry. There wasn't.

She wondered what sort of people had walked through this portal in the years of the house's history. She wasn't to know that, as a grand country house, it was fairly young; mid-19th century but built where a farmhouse of some substance had stood at least as far back as the civil war. There was a theory that a medieval manor house may have occupied the site before that.

First and foremost she thought of the people who came here now, these days. The "activities" listed under the "requirements" heading on the document found at Timothy Bush's house and partly translated by Meredith Guster would not stay out of her mind. These activities must have taken place in the various rooms of this house.

The oak door of the room directly opposite the office was slightly ajar. A pale light came through the gap, just daylight from a window. She checked she was still alone and crossed the hallway, gently pushing the heavy door fully open.

She was disappointed. The room was bare of almost all furnishings. The floor was wood, varnish worn off in long streaks and small patches. There was a desultory rug laid down near the rough fireplace as if it didn't know if it should be near to the fire or not. In the bay window which was part curtained was a chaise longue upholstered in a fading green material.

There was a curious smell; reminded her of cosmetics.

At the far end of the room was a double door off to the left, leading obviously further into the bowels of the house. There was no light emanating from the doors, one of which was wide open, but the inquisitive brown moth that was DC Ruff was drawn inexorably towards it. There had to be more to this place than she had seen so far. She almost hoped that there was.

Her eyes could see little to start with. All she was able to do was gauge the size of the room. It wasn't large by any means but at least it had a floor covering, a close-woven carpet. She supposed it may once have been a small sitting room or withdrawing room or some such; she was no expert but she been around a few National Trust properties, a hobby of her parent's.

There seemed to be more furniture like the chaise longue she'd seen in the first room. She slowly reached the nearest one and extended a hand to touch it. It was like velvet and now she could make out that it was pale blue in colour and at its head were pillows of a slightly darker hue. As she tried to step alongside the chaise her legs were obstructed by a protuberance and she noticed that there was something similar at the head end. She looked around trying to make out the layout of the others, straining her eyes which were gradually becoming accustomed to the lack of light. She could now make out other shapes on the walls.

'Some light on things would no doubt help.'

The voice from behind her, somewhere near the door, startled her. She heard a switch click and soft lights barely came on but enough for her to see a man standing there, his hand still on the wall as he slowly turned a dimmer switch to up the illumination. He didn't overdo it. The lighting now was soft and ambient, gentle on the eye. It came from overhead where small round lights were sunk into the ceiling. Not white light but from some a creamy hue, from others dark pink.

She thought the man may have been Stuart Devlin but the voice was nothing like. It was smoother.

He left the wall and came nearer to her. He was a lot more elderly than Stuart Devlin; mid-sixties she guessed. He was dressed in a dark topcoat, multi-coloured scarf still tightly curled about his neck and a trilby-type hat held in his left hand as if he had just come in from the cold. Clean-shaven yet his face had a shiny appearance similar, she thought, to one of Sayer's dead clients after he had worked on it. However, for his years, he was not an unattractive man. His eyes were lively.

'I startled you,' he said but it was nowhere near an apology and he gave Ruff no chance to respond. 'I love this room. One of my favourites.' He waved a hand.

Now Ruff could see clearly what she had been stumbling over. What she had thought was a chaise wasn't. It was flatter and wider. Across the way was a large leather chair but with what looked like foot rests splayed out at the bottom. Beyond these were two more, variations on the same theme. What she did notice was that at the top and bottom of each recliner were what appeared to be handcuffs, not the regulation sort that she was familiar with but ones that had the metal clad in coloured fur. She saw there were sundry straps of leather and lengths of rope hanging from the walls.

'It's adored by the lovely ladies,' he told her, his eye telling her she was included in that category. 'My dear, you look as if you have not the faintest idea of what it is this room could, nay, can, offer you.'

'O, I think I know what this room is about.'

'Do you?' he persisted. 'Then tell me.'

'May I ask who you are?' Ruff tried to adopt a detached tone.

'Me?' he looked shocked. 'I find you, a lost soul, wandering about my property and you want to know who I am. But the fair damsel has the right to know the identity of the man who has just discovered her in this vessel of pleasure, I suppose. I am Roger de Cottel. And you are?'

She had her warrant card at the ready in her left hand and flashed it. 'Detective Constable Ruff.'

'Ha, how beautiful. A woman of power. And with your own restraints no doubt, eh?' He reached out and held her hand steady, studied it and her ring finger. 'That photograph doesn't do you justice.' Ruff pulled her hand away. 'Stressful job I should think. We get many people in stressful occupations using our facilities to relax. This room, for instance, relieves executive stress in the new breed of top women. Gentlemen use a room opposite.' He drew closer to Ruff. 'You see, the woman who has to make important decisions all day and every day really likes to be rendered, how shall I say, not powerless but unable to influence anything, even the method and extent of her...pleasure. They find it so very invigorating and therapeutic.'

To Ruff, de Cottel, or Lord de Cottel as she now realized, was clearly a man with his expertise on the marketing side of the business. He spins a good spiel. She cast her eyes around, from one seat of pleasure to another. De Cottel read her mind. He began to promenade, approaching each of the four items, his hands sweeping demonstrably, his arms opening to illustrate how a submissive female would have limbs extended. He kinked his arms at the elbow to simulate the bending of the knees outward. His eyes constantly sought contact with Ruff as he stroked, as he would a pet, the arms and leg supports of the various recliners. His sales pitch went on, seemingly describing something absolutely normal, verging on the clinical. He explained that the bare room that she had walked through was the lubrication salon, where plastic sheets would be lain on the floorboards and copious quantities of lubricant would be available for slip sliding, as he phrased it.

That was what the smell had been, she realized. Baby oil.

'And in this room, well, many...ladies...find a group scenario very stimulating. They are helpless so they cannot prevent...spectators or...stimulators moving from one lady to another and so on.' He was cool and aloof in his objective description of the mechanics of the possible permutations. Ruff accepted it all in exactly the same way. It could have been dressed up in far more erotic terms, she knew that.

'You know what we're able to enjoy here,' de Cottel was relentless. Ruff looked up at him, afraid to hazard any kind of guess. 'The benefits of my youth. I'm sixty-five, you know. A child of the Sixties some would say but I prefer to look back fondly on the Seventies. That was when sexual freedom really found its feet and became the norm. It had evolved and has continued so to do right up to now and will continue. Where will it end? I tell you...' he looked again at her ring finger '...Mrs. Ruff, it will never end. Technology is thrilling and unstoppable. So you don't have to rush. Besides, this vessel, as I like to call it, is but one. Total painless submission in here, less painless elsewhere, or perhaps a room full of kindred spirits for you to pick and choose from, or a fantasy you have always had can suddenly be made flesh. There is something here for everybody and everybody for anything. There are no exceptions if you are honest with yourself. Now, detective, what can I do for you?'

There was a twinkle in his eye that suggested he expected her to make a selection from the menu he had just outlined for her. But he wasn't painting a picture that she could envisage modeling for, not without Alex.

'You're a wicked old man,' she admonished him mildly, 'Lord Cottel.'

'Ha, you are a detective or well-informed. Same thing I suppose. And I'm glad to see you appreciate all that is on offer. I hope you don't think I was giving you the hard sell. I wouldn't have mentioned it at all had I not detected something myself, your obvious interest, your...well, you know what I mean.'

His smile was all sincerity. Ruff for some reason felt stripped bare. If her body language were to let her down she knew he'd have her signing on the dotted line, waiving her rights to think it over, falling for the spontaneous urge to say yes to this offer of a lifetime. Sex had often been like that for her. Act now, regret tomorrow; well, sometimes she'd had regrets the same day, the next minute!

She pulled out her notebook. Having the tool of her trade in her hand dressed her back in costume.

'Do you live here?'

'What, here? Above the shop as it were? Why, no, I do not. Why do you ask?'

This man was dangerous in a harmless sort of way. He believed in what he was selling unless he was an extremely good actor. Perhaps he was; perhaps he had spent his life acting the part that he thought the world wanted to see.

'We're investigating the suspicious death of a local man who had links with Cottel Court. In fact,' she thought she'd not hold back with the smooth old bugger 'he had bought himself some extreme sessions here and the evidence suggests that he couldn't live with what he had done and he killed himself.'

His reaction surprised her. 'Ah. Yes.' His gaze went hazy as he looked at nothing at all. 'I've known it happen. A surfeit of pleasure.'

Twenty-Two

Challis had to drive Ruff all the way back to HQ. Ruff bent her ear about her encounter with his lordship.

'He's a bit of an old charmer but an odd man altogether. He's like a child with a doll's house. You could almost believe that the exotic furniture was all there was to it and that his description of what they could be used for was straight out of his imagination, a game that he may sometimes wheel in some dolls to play. We know different, though, don't we?'

Challis laughed at the DC's story. She needed to be lightened up after her conversation with Stuart Devlin who had seemed to believe that Cottel Court was like the gateway to Shangri-la.

Ruff went on to tell of his lordship's attempts to persuade her to have a full tour of the house, to inspect all the other rooms, or vessels. She refused so he tried to provide her with a brief description of each one and its delights. She switched off and eventually made a small concession to him before she was able to take her leave. She had at least learned what was the meaning of the "requirements" that Challis had asked her about. She now knew what "Vikings" was all about: it didn't do much for her, not her cup of tea that was for sure, so much so that she had pushed it to the back of her mind and didn't resurrect it for Challis's benefit. She couldn't work out why the DS would be so keen to know more about an activity like that.

Her one case-related suggestion was that the relationship between Meredith Guster and Chas should be followed up. When she had finally caught up with the woman and put to her the point about a delivery of some sort going to her house via the Cottel Court Range Rover all she got was a negative shrug of the shoulders.

'Chas Davrot,' Challis completed his name that she had gleaned from Stuart Devlin. 'He used the Range Rover and was outside Meredith Guster's.'

'Well don't we need to speak to him?'

'We'll come back. He'd gone off shift.'

'Come back? We're up and down these roads a lot, aren't we?'

'Look, we get Sayer to examine those scrapings off your boot. I bet we get a match.'

'So you go for his twice-hung theory then? And you think hanging number one was from those gates back there? That wouldn't be easy if they're closed all the time.'

'Don't know about that.' Challis mulled it over. 'If they were closed they'd make a nice ladder to get up to the desired height.'

'Then what? Somebody obligingly activates the gates to open for the drop?'

Ruff was staring at Challis who briefly returned the stare. Back to an assisted suicide again?

'I made a note we should check the cctv footage,' Ruff told her.

'I asked...him about that,' Challis said. 'It's on constantly for monitoring but only recorded during days when they're open for business. So, not much good for us.'

*

'Meredith, where's Chas?' Stuart Devlin asked as he came out of his room into the office.

'I thought you told the copper he'd gone off for the day. That wasn't a porky was it?' she replied.

He smiled.

Before he could answer, the door from the hallway opened and Lord de Cottel came in, still wearing his outdoor top clothes.

'What's been occurring here, Stuart?' His lordship had this occasional tendency to use phrases he'd picked up from trendy television programs in the belief that he was being knowledgeably amusing but his rendition was usually pathetic. 'I don't much care for having the police here, unless they're clients. What's all this talk about a death? Was it one of ours?'

'It was a neighbour of Meredith's.'

de Cottel looked at the woman. She didn't fit in, the way she looked, but he'd been persuaded she was good at the tasks asked of her.

'This is not good enough.' His chin was set as he spat out the rebuke at Meredith. 'Why could you not have ensured that any questions they might have for you were not asked where you work. It's not good enough; bringing police here, chasing after you.'

Meredith looked to Stuart Devlin to explain but he didn't. 'I've already told her all of this,' he lied. 'It's a typical police tactic, to pressurize a witness in this way.'

There was confusion written on de Cottel's features. 'She mentioned suicide, the short brown one did, to me. I found her snooping around. Now how did that happen as well? What sort of security are you operating here, Stuart?'

'Lionel,' he addressed his lordship in the more usual informal way, 'again, a police tactic.'

'What do you mean? Without a warrant they can't just wander around without permission, man.'

'Kay...the short, brown one...was sent out to find Meredith...'

'Fucking chaos here,' was de Cottel's attitude towards Stuart's attempts to explain things. 'You're on first name terms with them. Is that your tactic?'

'I've met them, previously.'

'What, both of them? Shagged them too have you? If not, you're slow.' He looked down at a piece of paper in his hand. 'It is Kay; Kay Ruff, if you can believe a name like that.' He handed it to Meredith. 'Here. Her address is on there too. Add her to our mailing database. Now, where's Chas? I've got another job for him.'

*

'Harry called in sick,' Lockett told them as they arrived back late afternoon.

'He is fucking sick,' Ruff said to no-one but everyone as she hung up her coat and sat at her desk. Lockett knew immediately what Ruff was getting at and her open comment told him she'd probably told Challis what had been said by Muench.

Challis wanted to know more about Muench's absence; nothing else.

'He dashed out not long after you'd gone and then phoned me later.'

'What's wrong with him?'

'I hope it's nothing trivial,' was Ruff's sympathetic offering.

'Gut ache, I think,' Lockett said, smiling at the quip as he caught the look from Ruff. She did not smile back.

Challis looked up at the board to confirm to herself that Muench's long-running case was now off the books. It was.

'Get that bag of goodies from Cottel Court down to Sayer,' she instructed Ruff. 'Make sure you tell him what we think it is and where it's from. Tell him about the coat that Chas was wearing.'

'Guster was wearing one too,' Ruff remembered. Challis frowned at this. 'Yeah,' Ruff nodded. 'I wondered if they were company issue and how many more they might have. Don't you want coffee first before I go?'

'I'll get 'em,' Lockett volunteered.

'Not yet. I want you to bring me up to date on Timothy Bush's family.'

'First things first,' Lockett began. 'I ended up going back to TorfGov Software Ltd to get Timothy Bush identified. I asked the boss there but the girl I'd spent time with yesterday ...her name is Barbara Jeffery...insisted she would do it. She's known him for seven years. I fixed up for her to come in tomorrow. She wouldn't be put off.'

Challis was unsure. 'What about the family then?'

Lockett took a deep breath. 'Right...' and opened a file on his desk while Challis stood in front of him, across the other side, apprehensive at what he may admit he'd done. How far had he gone with the task? Who had he approached? What had he said?

'James Wheeler called on your direct line. He was mostly interested in how we'd found him, found his number. I explained the emails. Then of course he wondered why we were looking at them. He sounded worried actually, as if he'd been caught out. I don't know; perhaps they don't like their system being used for personal emails. Anyway, I ignored that and told him we were looking into Timothy Bush's sudden death.'

'What, just like that?'

'Yeah. His whimpering was pissing me off.'

'Okay, so you came right out with it. What'd he say?'

'He was shattered, speechless to start with. I had to shout down the phone to wake him up. Then, he went on about having just found him and now he was gone. Ironic I suppose. Cruel fate. He wants to see the body.'

'He can't identify him.'

'I told him that but he's coming anyway; tomorrow sometime.'

'Okay. So who was next? Did you get hold of the daughters?'

'I was going to.'

Challis knew he wouldn't. She knew he'd chicken out. Difficult call to make, she knew that, but she was disappointed he hadn't even tried. He saw her face.

'I was going to,' he repeated forcefully, 'but then I got a visit from Mr. Sayer.'

Mr. Sayer, Challis noted.

'He dropped this off for us.'

Lockett picked up a sheet of A4 paper and handed it to Challis. She was reading it a second time as Ruff came back in, interrupting. 'Well, Sayer's in a funny mood. All very mysterious. Glint in his eye which he didn't bat when I handed him the bag and told him what we thought of the samples in it. Hardly looked at it.' She soon realized she was talking to herself. Challis had heard every word.

'No doubt Mr. Sayer was gloating over this.' She waved the paper. 'Toxicology report on Timothy Bush. No sign of any drugs that would have rendered him incapable. However, there is evidence of drug taking. NRTIs and a protease inhibitor to be exact.'

This information rang a bell with Ruff but there were gaps that refused to fill. She looked for help from Lockett who simply raise his eyebrows and blew out softly.

'Drugs,' Challis continued, 'that are used in the treatment of AIDS. He was HIV positive.'

'Is that why he killed himself?' Ruff questioned.

Challis had no idea. What she did know was that she had revised her opinion of Lockett. This latest news gave them food for thought.

Sayer had shown a great sense of timing, calling her on her phone within minutes of her passing on the HIV news to Ruff. He told Challis that the cocktail of drugs that Timothy Bush was on indicated that he had been under treatment for some months. He repeated his previous advice that the man's GP should be tracked down.

There were many possible implications of this latest revelation and Challis's stomach turned at the very thought of some of them. With Cottel Court still fresh in her mind and Timothy Bush a known visitor to and participant in the activities of that place it could not help but be construed that the two together could spell disaster. She had no idea what the rules and protocol of that place were: where did they stand on safe sex? were there medicals? Did participants have to prove they were clean? How responsible was Timothy Bush, especially as he knew what he carried? How careful had he been with the girls who turned out to be his own daughters? Perhaps he hadn't been careful at all; perhaps he realized that he may have infected the two girls.

Ruff was ahead of her. 'Shouldn't we contact the daughters now?'

*

Kay Ruff was repeating this sentiment over and over again to herself as her homeward bus set off. It had to be the right thing to do but Challis did not seem to be convinced.

They both agreed it had all become a bit sick; even Lockett was on the same wavelength but more concerned how Timothy Bush had become infected in the first place. The two women gave him a long censorious look as they saw he was pushing the original sin back onto some unknown female.

On her walk to the bus station she had called in at a chippie and bought small chips, open, with lashings of salt and vinegar. They were hot, just what she wanted. Now, seated on the bus, she chewed on the last chip. What to do with the plastic container, a puddle of vinegar in the bottom, and the soggy white paper. She should have eaten them all before boarding the bus and got shot of the wrappings in the nearest litter bin. Now there was no alternative but to hang on until she got off.

She was cheered, more normal, and was going to get even more normal when she got home to her nice warm terraced house half way up a mountain.

She had decided she was going to have sex tonight, even while she was still seething from the eavesdropping in the office. At that point in time, though, she had felt inhibited about deploying those parts of her anatomy that had been verbally dirtied by Harry Muench. Now, however, having endured the silver tongue of his lordship, she was heading home determined to give Alex an evening of special treats. She was failing to be totally unmoved by Lord de Cottel's matter-of-fact, realistic commentary that had accompanied his imaginary misguided tour of Cottel Court's inner workings. She had not been entirely forced to give him her contact details and now she was in two minds. She would be sent information and she wondered if it would be as stirring as his lordship's tone and vocabulary. Alex wouldn't be entirely opposed to some experimentation. They had spoken of it before now, of various fantasy scenarios. But would it be safe? Could it ever be as safe as in the comfort of her own home, just her and Alex?

There had been one exception. It was hard to imagine now in mid-winter but his lordship had described in silky detail Cottel Court's outdoor facilities: the scene he presented was a balmy summer evening, clear skies with a pale moon hanging there and one acre of night-lit lawn alive with fleshy mounds, heaving and rolling, as if born from the very soil to serenade the stars with their cries of ecstasy; hot bodies, he concluded, on cool grass. Ruff had never had totally naked alfresco sex. She was sure she could persuade Alex.

The bus was hot and people were getting on and off at every stop, making the ride up the Valleys as slow as a fast train up the Himalayan foothills. She looked at her watch; Alex should be home by now, she very much hoped.

* * *

Angela Plumitis turned over in the bed so that she could see the red-haired girl in the doorway. The girl saw the effort it had taken etched on the features of her beautiful partner. Beautiful she was, normally, but her whole being had been made ugly by the pain that seemed to be getting worse again.

'You look nice,' Angela gasped. 'Like your hair tonight. Colour suits you.'

'Chas said you were still bleeding.'

'A bit.'

The girl could see that Angela was having a painful spasm; teeth gritted. She stood over her. 'Why? Why do you do it?'

'You know why.'

'I hate it. You're a stupid whore. You're in my bed but we've only been together once in the last I don't know how many weeks. I miss you, you daft bitch.'

'I know. I'm sorry.' She grimaced. She wanted to reach out and grab the girl, bring her to her but a spurt of agony was too much. 'I love you,' was all she could get out. Gradually it eased and she breathed more regularly, raising her head to look at the radiant girl in front of her. 'You're going out aren't you?'

'I have to. You know me.'

'Where?' Angela asked almost apologetically.

The girl shrugged. 'Anywhere. I just have to.'

'I know,' Angela capitulated and sank back.

'You're the love of my fucking life!' The girl sounded despairing, stiff with conflict and disbelief. 'What have you done to yourself?'

'I'll be okay. You go. You need to. Just be careful.'

The girl melted. She bent and kissed Angela on the mouth. The taste was unbearable but she smiled as she withdrew. 'I love you too Angel. Don't worry; we're getting the bastards.'

Twenty-Three

Challis thought again that she should get a new car, one with a heater that warmed up before she got home. Dark now early evening, she was glad to be wending her way home after the day she'd had.

Ruff and Lockett had been at loggerheads. The news of Timothy Bush's condition had driven a wedge between them, Lockett insisting he must have caught it from some woman and Ruff retorting that, for all they knew, Bush could have swung both ways and received the "gift" from some bloke; far more likely, she said, statistically speaking.

'Stop,' Challis had ordered.

The whole thing was becoming emotive; they were losing all objectivity. 'This is getting way outside the scope of this investigation.' Ruff didn't agree but Challis overrode her. 'We have absolutely no remit to go about warning people of potential health hazards, especially when all we have is circumstantial evidence. Even if we did it wouldn't be you or me doing it. Specialized training for that kind of stuff.'

'It was covered on my last course,' Ruff insisted, ignored by Challis.

'We don't know what Timothy Bush did to anyone, his daughters, if they are his daughters, or anyone else. There's absolutely no evidence that if he did indulge in any sort of sexual activity that he did it....'

'Bare-back,' suggested Lockett.

'Irresponsibly,' Challis corrected with heat.

'There is precedence,' Ruff challenged. 'Deliberate or even reckless infection of others with diseases such as HIV has been through the courts. People have been found guilty of grievous bodily harm. Since 2001 men...'

'And women,' Lockett added, getting an impatient frown from Ruff as she went on unchecked.

'...have been prosecuted and got sentences of three years and upwards.'

'Yes but crucially here in this case Timothy Bush is dead,' Challis pointed out. 'If we have no potential perpetrator that we can pursue then potential victims are irrelevant.'

Ruff was not happy. She still thought they had a duty towards the Wheeler sisters but she conceded that there would first have to be evidence that they had had unprotected sex "of an incestuous nature with their father." She couldn't resist spelling it out like this. Challis closed the discussion with the calm decision 'We're doing nothing, is that clear?' but she wished that Redland was around to make that decision.

*

She hadn't fully convinced herself about the rights and wrongs of it all. She desperately wanted someone to talk it over with. Redland was on her mind as she drove into Usk, so much so that she thought she should make use of the keys he had given her and go check out his house.

Passing Twyn Square on the right she drove the short distance to Redland's semi. She pulled into his drive, behind his car. She noticed that bins were out for collection the following morning. That was one thing she could do for him.

The house was cold. Obviously the Scrooge-like Redland did not have his heating system on automatic timing. Understandable. As a policeman his hours were irregular and he would not want an empty house to be warming up unnecessarily.

Her breath came out in a cloud as she walked into his kitchen. It could stay cold and she would worry about a cold house causing the bursting of water pipes. Perhaps she should shut off the water, if she could locate the stopcock.

She would address that issue later.

She placed the mail from behind the front door onto the kitchen breakfast bar. None of it looked in any way urgent; no brown, demanding envelopes. The pedal bin had a quaint whiff about it as she lifted the lid so she pulled out the plastic bag inside, knotted it and carried it outside to the wheelie bin. As she turned she gave a start. An elderly man wrapped warmly in coat, headgear and scarf had appeared behind her.

'I heard you drive up,' he said. 'I live next door.'

Challis in fact recognized him, she'd seen him earlier that day, waving a camera around in front of a Dutch lorry driver's face.

'Ah, I'm a colleague, from work,' she explained.

'I know,' he said, though how he knew she didn't know. 'How is he, Alan?'

'Not too bad.' Challis didn't want to say too much. 'He should be home soon.'

'Good news, good news,' the old man enthused. 'O, this is for him.' He held out a large brown envelope. 'Came this morning. Recorded. I had to sign for it.'

'O, okay.' Challis took it from him. 'I was wondering if you could help me turn off his stopcock. There's no heating on in there and it would be a bit of a bugger if the pipes burst.'

122

The old man followed her into the house. Challis added the large envelope to the pile on the breakfast bar without giving it a second look. While the man knelt under the sink she looked for any more rubbish to throw out. She opened the fridge to check for anything furry or smelly. Nothing looked too far gone but the bread in the bread bin had a bluish tinge to it.

'He doesn't feed the birds, does he?' she asked the man who was slowly making his way up to a standing position.

'No but we do.' He took the half a loaf. 'Water's turned off.'

She wanted to thank him but he was already heading back to his house.

'I saw you earlier today,' she called after him. 'Bit of a problem at the bridge.'

He turned. 'Aye. We were doing your police work for you, again.'

Food was her next requirement. She didn't fancy cooking when she got home. There was a choice of take-aways: Indian, Chinese, English and fish and chips. The chip shop was close to Redland's house and she hadn't had fish and chips for ages, so she wheeled the wheelie bin down to the pavement and walked to the shop. There was no queue but she still had to wait ten minutes for the fish to be cooked. At least it was all piping as she laid it on the passenger seat. It would still be hot enough to eat straight away when she reached home.

She didn't bother with a plate, washing her hands quickly before sitting in her warm lounge with the unwrapped paper on her lap. No knife and fork either but with extra vinegar. Much nicer with the fingers. She was hungry and ate the lot, batter and all, something she could not always do as too much oily skin sometimes made her feel sick. A pint of water washed it down and she felt all the better for it. Fish and chips with all its unhealthy deliciousness had its usual feel-good effect.

She was energized. For some reason the tiredness she'd had when she left work had lifted.

She was abuzz.

It had been an adrenaline filled day on the Timothy Bush case. A lot of revelations had assailed her senses and then there had been the confrontation with Stuart Devlin. His conceit that her life had been empty since the days with him had got under her skin. His departure had not left her bereft of hope and self-esteem. On the contrary, she had used him as a bit of a springboard. His patronizing attitude today had fired her up to prove him wrong.

She gave the lounge and the kitchen a quick once-over. Nothing really needed doing in the lounge and the kitchen only required the vinegar put away and the chip paper disposed of in the swing-lid bin.

Unlike her mother who had been a permanent housewife Challis was never drawn to house chores. Her job was all-consuming; she had no desire to be overly busy when at home. The house ticked over. When her parents had died suddenly she had continued to live in the family home. Her mother especially had been one to be continually plotting and planning what she would like the place to contain. New stuff arrived; old stuff remained. As a place to put something new became an issue, her mother would simply relocate items and as a result Challis could never find anything, be it clothing or utensils in the kitchen. It had taken nearly a year after their death before she could bring herself to rationalize the household and then she had begun a clear-out. Things were put in a place where they had remained ever since. She could lay her hand on anything blind-folded. Acquisitions were based on need not want. She and Ruff had many a debate on the subject of shopping. Ruff thought her a traitor to womankind. Ruff would have got on well with her mother.

She showered; cleaned herself. It was Thursday and Thursday night in the Eastgate Hotel was music night. She had seen a notice in the chip shop that the group tonight was Storm Petrel, a folk-rock ensemble fronted by a couple of female singers, accompanied by guitarists, one of whom was a long-standing occasional buddy of hers, Jonathan Watkins. He'd be there tonight, playing. She'd last spent the evening with him two weeks before, at The Eastgate, but he hadn't been performing that night, until later in her bedroom.

As she dried herself and looked about her wardrobe for something to wear she brazenly admitted to herself that he was more than just a buddy. He was the kind of buddy that Stuart Devlin seemed to appreciate but she wasn't going to think of him like that; she wasn't going to lapse into Stuart Devlin's vernacular.

She had to drive back into Usk so she had to pledge that she wasn't going to drink much.

It was eight-thirty as she pulled up opposite the hotel. Live music issued forth as she entered and she caught sight immediately of Storm Petrel set up at the rear of the second bar area. The two girls, Eve and Carla, were hand-in-hand, belting out a Mamas and Papas song. Not bad harmony, Challis thought; bit loud though in the confines of the bar. On their right, the fiddler's elbow was going like crazy, the bass guitarist in a far too small space behind them and Jonathan on rhythm guitar away on the left. In front of him, on display, were copies of Storm Petrel's CD, cut the previous autumn in some recording studio up the valleys.

Jonathan caught sight of Challis as she leaned in a gap at the bar and he smiled at her. She gave him a wave.

A girl coming into a bar on her own always caused heads to turn; on this occasion both male and female. Eve and Carla were "partners" and their fan-base was like-minded females. So the looks that Challis got were mainly from the unattached females. There was one such right next to her now who turned, eying Challis, watching the wave to Jonathan. She moved her mouth up to Challis's ear to talk over the music. Challis was ordering a pint of John Smiths and didn't flinch at the close proximity of the woman.

'You here on your own?' she asked.

'No!' Challis replied, not bothering to put her own mouth anywhere near the other woman's face.

She had nothing against lesbians; as a policewoman she had to be at least neutral, but she had never had a desire to get too familiar. She had once had a close encounter. During her police training days she went out one evening with a fellow female cadet for a much-needed drink after a particularly stressful day. They had ended up in a bar where an all-female group was playing. The fact that virtually the entire audience was female did not register with either of them. They sat on a bench-seat with dykes either side. Still in all innocence, Challis, quite inebriated, got chatting with the girl next to her who asked if she was an ardent follower of the group.

'No,' Challis slurred. 'It's purely random. Me and my...' she was stuck as to how to describe her companion '...girlfriend just popped in.'

'Girlfriend.' the girl had repeated. 'That's nice.'

They talked until the girl said she had to move on and before Challis could do anything about it the girl landed a powerful wet kiss right on Challis's mouth.

'That's nice too,' the girl said, then got up and left the lip-smacked Challis gasping for air. Her colleague had missed it all and seemed a trifle envious when Challis, spitting all the while, described the whole experience as they staggered back to the hostel.

That had been all of ten years ago but Challis had never forgotten it. Men could be hungry kissers but that girl had left her imprint. It served as a warning, a near miss – a pun she enjoyed - and thereafter she had maintained a forced stiff manner whenever a lesbian came anywhere near her space. She was scared how she might react a next time.

'You're not with him are you?' asked the woman derisively, gesticulating towards Jonathan.

'Well I'm certainly not with anyone like you,' Challis said in no uncertain terms. 'So kindly piss off, there's a good girl.' Now she stared at this intruder as she raised her glass to her lips and took a long swig. The woman was a lot younger than she had first thought, a girl in her early twenties she guessed.

'You stuck-up cock-sucker,' the girl breathed as she disengaged herself.

'Better than...licking...' Challis struggled to find a suitable retort and immediately retreated, moving around the bar to stand closer to the band.

She was not particularly pleased with the repartee that had laboured from her lips. And she couldn't even lay claim to its originality. She had pinched a bit of a Muench description of a group of gay women: *a lick of lesbians*. He had come out with that during a quiet hour or two in the office. It had been a rare afternoon when light banter had ricocheted between the unsupervised four of Redland's team, inoffensive in the main, comical even, with Ruff coming back at him with a collective phrase for the male equivalent: *a gag of queers*. A one-off time that afternoon was, not anywhere near repeated since.

She chanced a quick glance back at the woman who surprised her by smiling at her, raising her glass in a toast that had a feel of touché about it. Challis smiled back, surprisingly relieved, wondering if she'd just taken part in some kind of lesbian foreplay.

The song "Both Sides Now" had followed the Mamas and Papas "Creeque Alley". Now the band broke for a fifteen-minute rest. Challis was at the bar as Jonathan approached. He kissed her on the lips and she grunted her appreciation.

'What you drinking?' she asked him.

'Pint and a whisky chaser.'

'What? Are you driving?'

'Nope. It's a drinking night.'

She put her face into his face. 'Don't you dare get drunk tonight!' Her eyes bored into his and her free hand reached around and clenched one of his buttocks. They were firm, she knew that, and there was nothing like gripping the two of them as she pulled him into her. She was living it already.

She bought him his double drink. His backing vocals had made him dry and the beer didn't touch the sides. The whisky he watered down a little and sipped. He didn't want to be too drunk either.

The fifteen minute break passed quickly and he returned to the podium. Challis had offered to buy a drink for the others in the group but they had not come over.

She watched Jonathan as he plucked his strings and belted out occasional vocal accompaniment. They didn't enjoy each other's company that often and it was usually Challis who instigated it. Neither of them enquired about what the other was getting up to in the intervening periods. She knew very little about his friends, sexual or otherwise. At this point in time he was the only one invited into her bed.

Unbidden, the events of the day crept back into her mind. *Timothy Bush. HIV. Deliberate or reckless infection.*

She took a large swig of her pint, hid the half-empty glass on the bar and headed for the Ladies, inadvertently following the woman who had earlier accosted her. She pushed the door open. The woman heard and saw her coming behind her and held open the second door for her. They were both in the inner sanctum. Challis had not come in to use the toilet but to purchase condoms. Two pound coins clicked in her hand. The woman was quick to detect that Challis was not heading for a cubicle and assumed that she had followed her in, hoping to catch her alone no doubt.

She approached Challis. 'I knew it,' she whispered as she reached out to catch Challis's arms.

Challis held up a hand. 'Back off, please. I'm here for the machine.' Challis walked past her and up to the condom dispenser. She looked the transparent windows up and down. They were all empty.

Then the woman was right behind her, her hands coming around Challis to land one on each breast. As she squeezed, Challis's arms shot up, the pound coins spurting out of her hand. She broke the hold and spun round. The woman was a few inches shorter, bulkier though, but easy enough for Challis to push back against the sink. As she stood over her Challis was able to get a good look at her for the first time. She was wearing tight-fitting jeans and a pink top that dipped low enough to reveal a sharp cleavage between the tanned mounds of her generous breasts. Challis was positively over-dressed by comparison. She always wore tops up to the neck. There was little that she could expose anyway.

'You're a persistent little dyke aren't you? How many times do I have to tell you? One more move like that and I'll run you in for sexual assault.'

'What? You a copper?'

'But you're in luck. It's my night off.'

'Sorry.'

'Really?' Challis was disbelieving.

'Yeah. I thought you were at least bi.'

Challis looked at the woman who was devoid of any pretence.

She was indeed younger than first appeared. Young woman; girl even. Her short hair was dyed red, nuclear red if Challis had but known. The girl's heavy makeup was aging her. She was a pretty girl underneath it all, wide-eyed now, brown, dark orbs. Breathless from her mistake.

Challis still held her by the shoulders and was beginning to feel she should reassure her captive who was feeling too relaxed and comfortable under the firm grip of Challis's hands.

She stared Challis in the eye, thinking 'cuff me or kiss me'.

Challis suddenly swallowed as if her breath had been stuck in her mouth.

She let go.

There was more than a hint that the girl had enjoyed the hands-on moment.

She scoured the floor looking for her two pound coins. The girl joined in, found one of them and handed it to her. She took it without utterance, picked up the second one and walked out and straight into the Gents, luckily empty, although she could hear some activity in the furthest cubicle. The condom machine was well stocked and she quickly retrieved a packet, not caring about its particular properties but thinking all the while how sexist this was; full in here; empty next door!

She was caught coming out of the Gents by that girl again who was herself just exiting the Ladies. She stared, amazed seeing this bold woman coming unashamedly from the men's room. Challis smiled and tapped her pocket. 'They've got plenty in there.'

The girl appeared to be fascinated by her, hanging on her every word and trying to anticipate what this copper might do next.

'Are you going to buy me a drink then?' she demanded.

Challis was surprised again by this bright-eyed girl whose face was now next to hers. It was the only way any conversation could be carried out with all the background noise.

'I'm Jackie by the way.'

'You've got a bloody cheek.'

'If you don't ask you don't get.'

'I've got a drink already thanks.'

Challis elbowed her way to the bar. Storm Petrel were just starting "California Dreaming" and Challis looked for a glance from Jonathan but he was engrossed in his music.

She retrieved her half pint, deciding to put the other half in it; that would have to be it if she wanted to drive herself and Jonathan back to her house later.

'I'll have a pint of Carling.' Jackie was right behind her, breathing in her ear. 'What's your name?'

Challis rounded on her only to see the girl gazing upwards in expectation. 'Wait back over there,' she ordered Jackie.

Jackie removed herself to the fringe of the crowd, out of the crush, turned and watched Challis push herself closer to the bar.

She'd been in the pub for over an hour when Challis had walked in. She had been struggling to forge a promising new relationship for the evening; most of the faces were familiar but distant. She'd had looks down her cleavage from several men. Her breasts were her pride and joy and it turned her on to put them on show but she hated the pull they had on the males of the species.

Challis's early rebuttal had made her think the evening was not going to get any better, forcing her to admit she probably shouldn't be here at all really. There were times when her needs were selfish, she knew that but so did Angel. She was as bad. Worse! Poor sick Angel. She should have stayed by her bed, miserable.

But no! Now she was drinking Challis in deeper.

Attractive. Dark and slim; tall. Strong character. Had to be. And her tits had felt nice in her hands. Small. Firm. Too brief to tell much else. Couldn't see her bum properly, partially hidden by her coat. Looked cheeky, what she could see..

She, she smiled, would be a nice conquest. Nice fit body, kept in good shape. And she was befriending her. She knew why. The woman had never been groped by another woman. She was intrigued. This kind of reaction had happened to her before. She'd always enjoyed making it happen.

Challis returned with the drinks. She tried to hand the lager to Jackie but the girl led her away into the bar-room nearest to the front door where the music was not quite so loud and punters were watching darts on the big screens.

There was an awkward silence that Jackie encouraged at first, speaking with her eyes. 'Cheers.' She sipped her drink.

Challis was uneasy. She had allowed the girl to dictate to her.

'I still don't know your name. How can I thank you if I don't know your name.'

'Mel,' Challis confided before taking a long swig. Jackie nodded. A small victory.

'Mel,' she repeated. 'Hi. Look, I'm sorry about earlier. I'm not very good at reading signals. I think it was wishful thinking.'

Challis shrugged inwardly. This girl was keen to converse. She wasn't but she wasn't going to allow awkward silences to make her look juvenile and tongue-tied. She knew she must be appearing nervous, jittery, looking everywhere but at the girl.

'Look I think I'll go back in there and listen to the band.'

'I have got a girlfriend. She's not here tonight,' Jackie said. 'I'm free tonight.' Her mouth lowered to her glass but her eyes remained fixed on Challis who was treating any revelations with a pinch of salt. 'You're very attractive but I could see you wanted him tonight, the musician bloke, but that didn't mean you were exclusively hetero. I knew a girl once, well a woman really, who was bi.' She came closer, her mouth near to Challis's ear to exaggerate the confidence she was about to share. It was all Challis could do to not visibly recoil. 'She used to say she loved screwing girls but loved being screwed by men.'

She drew back a little and watched Challis's reaction. There wasn't one.

Jackie kept their cheeks close. Still silence from Challis.

In the absence of any light riposte, Jackie's face adopted a serious countenance. 'I don't know how any fucking woman could have done that,' she said as if wrestling with a deep issue, pulling right back from Challis to see if this new found acquaintance had an inkling. 'From beauty to the ugly beast,' Jackie resolved her conundrum, lightening her mood. 'I don't know if that was all at the same time, mind, if you know what I mean, a threesome. It was always just me and her when we were together.'

Challis found she was reluctantly juggling with the concept of one woman screwing another.

Jackie pulled on her pint of lager, some of the refreshing liquor catching her lip and dribbling onto her chin.

Challis was glad the girl was taking a breather. She had interviewed people who liked to babble on. There was always a reason. Nerves maybe, sometimes camouflage and sometimes an attempt to impress. Jackie was trying hard to get onto an intimate level as quickly as she could. It didn't bother her. It was just another facet of the game.

'Are you really a cop…policewoman? You look too young.' Challis let the compliment go by. 'I've never been with…in the company of a policewoman before.'

'Don't worry. I don't bite.'

Jackie giggled. 'Shame.' She really couldn't stop flirting, Challis thought, beginning to believe getting stuck with this girl could be an enormous bore.

'I do some…modeling.'

'Really?' She didn't smile. The description could cover a multitude of activities. 'I've never been with…in the company of a model before.'

Jackie got it. She liked it.

'Nude modeling. Mainly.'

Challis doubted the truth of this statement. The girl's body seemed to be striking an exaggerated pose. 'Artistic I hope.'

'Sometimes.'

Challis nodded slowly, her eyes adopting a far-away thoughtful look. Probably 'modeling' was euphemistic.

'So when it's not nude could we see your work and your name in lights?'

'You might.' She doubted it. 'Though I may have to change it to achieve real fame.' She had. 'Jackie Davrot doesn't sound good enough, does it?'

Now she had Challis's full attention.

*

On the three mile drive home Jonathan interfered incessantly with the driver. His hands were everywhere on Challis's body and would have been even more invasive had she not been well wrapped up against the cold. She hurried, as much to get back to her place before he forced her into a driving error as to get down to proper bodily exploration.

'I saw you chatting up that young lesbo,' he laughed.

'So? Jealous?' she teased.

'No. I was hoping you'd bring her along.'

She laughed. She thought the thought would cross his mind but Jackie had disappeared into thin air. She couldn't see her anywhere. Jonathan finished the set and Challis had gone up to him while he packed his gear. When she looked round the young girl was nowhere to be seen.

She had spent nearly an hour sparring with Jackie Davrot, allowing her to top up her beer with half a lemonade. It had been an intense time. Jackie had enjoyed it; other women had passed her with an admiring look, obviously thinking she had pulled Challis. The looks that Challis received from those females who knew of Jackie Davrot ranged from amazement to sympathy but she had not noticed.

Initially, Jackie's topic of conversation had been all sex. She talked and talked. She was twenty-two and was in a long-term relationship but tonight was a "night off". She'd used two fingers of each hand to coquettishly emphasize the quotes. Challis always hated that gesture.

She lived with her father in Monmouth. Her mother had left them years ago. Her father was in a kind of relationship with some woman he worked with; she'd only met her once or twice. Strange woman.

Challis eased out of her without too much difficulty that her father was indeed Chas Davrot and got out of Jackie that he worked mainly at Cottel Court, which was where he reckoned she could find work. With feigned innocence, Challis asked her about Cottel Court, what they did there, but Jackie was cagey, saying that she thought it was all very arty.

'Have you been there?' she asked Jackie.

She had. She had even met Lord Cottel 'Lord de Cottel,' she corrected herself. He was a dirty old queen in her opinion. 'Makes me cringe.'

Challis wished she'd met the old man. Ruff hadn't described him like that. She'd called him a charmer.

Challis watched Jackie closely. She wasn't as naïve about Cottel Court as she tried to make out. Artistic? That's one way of putting it. Sex can be an art. But she'd get Ruff to find out if there were weekends of more aesthetic pursuits.

In the meantime, to join in the game, she issued a note of caution to the girl, telling her to be careful about modeling jobs. Must be careful not to sound like Ruff. But anyway, it was probably all right; after all, her father was looking to get her into the place and he surely wouldn't pimp his own daughter.

'Just make sure you check it out thoroughly,' Challis advised her, as seriously as she could manage.

Jackie raised an eyebrow. 'Yes, mother.' She beamed broadly, happy to receive Challis's maternal advice.

This bugged Challis. 'I am serious,' she went on. 'We see lots of cases where young girls get lured into situations that don't exactly pan out the way they envisaged.'

'Aw, I'm sorry.' Jackie moved her head to snuggle up to Challis's breasts, by way of childlike apology. Yes, they were firm, Jackie noticed again, wishing she could get her lips on them.

Ruff had a theory that lesbians look for a surrogate mother. It came to Challis' mind at that moment.

So, not wanting to give out the wrong impression, she moved back to re-open the gap between them, her free hand on Jackie's shoulder gently reinforcing.

Jackie's large brown cow-eyes were locked onto Challis; her full lips daubed with bright red gloss were parted in a contented smile. The scent of her hung in the air. It would be very easy to take advantage of this pretty young girl.

Any protective urge that Challis may have had gave way to a sudden realization that this worldly young woman needed no warnings. She played this game very well and probably enjoyed much success.

She wasn't looking for the love and guidance of an older woman. She wanted to win. But this single-minded intent left no room for any doubts.

Challis looked back over her own shoulder to see if Jonathan was anywhere near finished playing. He wasn't and she hated herself for looking for an escape. This girl could be handled quite easily. There was no threat, for God's sake. She spun her head round. The girl was in her space again. Jackie was mind-reading. She guessed Challis might possibly be making a decision.

Twenty-Four

The shit hit the fan as soon as Challis walked into the office the following day, Friday. She was a bit late. She'd had to drop Jonathan in Pontypool.

She had not had time to remove her coat before Superintendent O'Halloran was through the door of the office. He looked around to see who was there: Ruff and Lockett; no Muench. He glanced up at the case board before almost dragging Challis into Redland's office.

'What the fuck's going on here, Mel? That case of Muench's is off the board I see. How come?'

'He brought in his perps yesterday and was going to charge them. He...'

'He offered no evidence and told the custody sergeant to let them go. Not even on bail. Did you check them out?'

'Why no. I left it to him. I was out with DC Ruff on the suicide case...'

'You didn't get involved in questioning them'

'No. Harry was full of it, like a cat with two...'

'Dicks is the word you're looking for.'

'No, I was going to say...'

'Dicks is the appropriate word, Sergeant.'

'I don't understand, sir.'

'No, surprisingly. But I've got a bloody good idea! And I want you to find out. Where is he?'

'He called in sick yesterday, later.'

'Did you speak to him?'

'No, Ray Lockett took the message. Can I ask what it is you want me to find out?'

'A complaint has been made. Mr. Henderson, the owner of the timber place where Muench was investigating an alleged theft, has complained of inappropriate behaviour by one of our officers in relation to his wife who also works at the business. Muench has been shagging the man's wife, Sergeant.'

'Is that what the husband said?'

'Not in so many words but I can't imagine Muench is one who would waste his time with platonic friendships.'

'If there's been a complaint it's out of our hands surely. Professional Standards will be in.'

'Yes, well, they don't know yet and I want to know what's what first.'

Challis was not happy with this. This was not the correct procedure. She was of course not privy to the thinking of higher management: times were hard, money getting tighter; more jobs would be shed; recruitment dry up. Nobody wanted manpower reduced by lengthy and unwanted external investigations.

'I want you, just you, to get onto this case and pull somebody in for it. I want to know why Muench changed his mind. You've got the rest of the day then I'll have to start the other ball rolling.'

'Has Muench been suspended?'

'Not yet.' Suspension of officers was the last thing that he needed.

'Well surely he should be, sir!' she exclaimed as he effectively ended the conversation without further response.

She cursed the man as he marched off. There was nothing worse than being in full flow with one investigation and being yanked off onto something else, especially when the first case was complex and the second one all about arse-saving, and somebody else's arse at that!

'Kay,' she called out. Ruff came to the door of Redland's office. 'You and Ray crack on with Timothy Bush. I want you to check a couple of things. One, Chas Davrot's background; see if he's got a record. Two, see if Cottel Court runs other activities, non-sexual activities, weekend breaks, conferences, artists retreats, whatever. O, and three, track down Timothy Bush's GP. And chase Sayer for results on yesterday's samples.' She paused for thought. 'Actually, number two is lower priority than the others. Do what you can. I've got to pick up something else for O'Halloran; has to be done today.'

She walked out of Redland's office with Ruff. Challis headed for Muench's desk, attracting Lockett's attention as she began to rifle through files.

'Ray,' she snapped, not looking up. 'You assist Kay. She knows what's wanted.'

'Don't forget,' Lockett objected. 'Timothy Bush's being id'd today. I've got to be up there with the girl from TorfGov Software and his son coming down from Cheltenham.'

'O, shit. Right. Okay concentrate on that then and don't give anything away to the son about his sisters' involvement; possible involvement.' She caught Ruff's eye and didn't want to sound positive about the tenuous link between Timothy Bush and the Wheeler girls. 'By all means sound him out about his family members but you know nothing, all right?'

She lifted a couple of files from Muench's desk and, watched by the other two, took them into Redland's office, closing the door behind her. She flung her coat on a chair near the door and dumped the files on the desk. They looked thick enough to need a week to absorb all the details.

This was really pissing her off.

She was tired and had been looking forward to a day of consolidation on the Timothy Bush suicide, working with Ruff and Lockett, easy paced.

Now, she was so upset by O'Halloran that the previous night's failures with Jonathan began to assume more importance as something else that was conspiring to make her feel real miserable. She had almost seen the funnier side of it earlier but now in retrospect that was really pissing her off as well.

*

The late night with Jonathan started off badly. They'd got to her house, still with a fit of the giggles, although she did not feel totally relaxed with him for some reason. They got undressed quick enough and spontaneous passion was rising until she couldn't remember where she'd put the condoms that she'd bought in the pub. They were in one of her coat pockets or her bag. She'd had to put glaring overhead lights on to relocate them. Jonathan was questioning why they were needed this time and the longer she searched for them and the more he went on she couldn't help but recall Jackie's words in the pub. 'You wouldn't need those with me!'

How true.

Then she had to work on Jonathan to get him fit to receive the condom and they had just got down to it in earnest when he had to get off her and go and relieve himself. This was followed by a lengthy debate as to whether or not the condom he'd had to remove could be put back on again. Now that it had been extended once it was not very flexible for re-application and their protracted efforts didn't do Jonathan's manhood any favours.

In the end, Challis told him to forget it, meaning the condom, but in his half-cut state he thought she was calling the whole thing off.

They flopped back on the bed, eventually pulling the duvet up to cover their naked bodies. Jonathan fell asleep.

Challis lay there for ages, thoughts whirling around in her head. Jackie Davrot was in there and for the first time ever Challis thought how simple it would have been not to have to mess with a temperamental penis.

She dozed but woke as Jonathan got out of the bed again. She heard the toilet flush and then his chilled body got back under the duvet. By now she was awake and she let him come to her and start working on her body. She knew his every move; where he'd start, where he'd go next. At other times she keenly anticipated this predictability, now she just wanted him to get on, get in and get it done. It was pleasurable enough and she enjoyed it as far as it took her.

In the morning she woke earlier than usual as she knew she'd have to take him to Pontypool. Even so, he rose clearly ready for more action but she was irritable and leapt out of the bed and into the shower, giving him instructions to go put the kettle on. They left after a quick cuppa and a round of toast and after she had dropped him she juggled with a tired confusion of ideas. She was really looking forward to the normality of the office, until she got there and was confronted by O'Halloran.

*

Challis switched on Redland's computer.

First things first though, she thought. She took out her mobile and called Harry Muench. No answer despite her quiet urgings of 'come on, Harry.'

She grabbed the files and opened them. The crimes reported, thefts of timber products, seemed simple enough. Regular stock checks had consistently thrown up discrepancies, not huge differences but stock levels of certain items were being repeatedly written down. Anne Henderson had spotted this trend and decided to do a spot check herself. There was always natural wastage but she knew that some items were more likely candidates for this old stock controllers' excuse than were others.

Unannounced she had walked into the main warehouse. She had with her the on-hand stock figures from the computer inventory system. The first thing she did was to check those figures with the balances held on individual stock cards in the warehouse office. The manual system was the original that had been retained even when the computer system was introduced. Originally it was to be updated only until the computer system had proved itself but that had been three years ago now and was still in place. It was a useful audit tool. Or should have been.

She noted the figures from the stock cards on her computer printout and then went out to count for herself. By this time she had attracted the attention of a number of warehouse workers. Some just enjoyed watching the attractive woman taking her high heels for a stroll down the aisles. She was wearing a tightly buttoned white coat that showed off her figure beautifully.

The supervisor asked her if he could be of assistance. She declined his offer. For the rest of the afternoon she checked and re-checked the count of items until she was confident that she had arrived at the truth. There were more discrepancies but the difference between the actual count and the book count on certain items was unacceptable, unbelievable even. Somebody was on the thieve.

She interrogated the supervisor and others who handled both the goods themselves and the recording of stock movements. She got nowhere and that was when she called the police.

Muench's files were full of statements from just about anyone and everyone. His enquiries spanned days. He went back there and back there again. No new statements were taken and very few notes of actual activity on those days, except the odd input of fairly useless information from Anne Henderson.

It was immediately obvious to Challis who the main targets were. It could only be the supervisor and one of the warehouse workers. She checked with the custody sergeant. He confirmed that the two guys brought in by Muench the day before and released later that day were in fact the ones that Challis had top of the list.

*

'Sarge.' Ruff had knocked the door and walked in carrying a cup of coffee which she placed on the desk. 'D'you want an update yet? On the suicide case?'

Challis sighed. 'No, not yet. What time is it?' She looked at her watch but Ruff answered anyway. 'Quarter to eleven. What's the Munch been up to?' Her question was put with an upbeat tone. She wanted Muench to be in trouble.

Before Challis could say that she couldn't say she heard her desk phone ringing in the other office. She motioned Ruff to go get it.

'It's the switchboard,' she shouted back. 'They have the Argus on the line with questions about the suicide at Llanhelog and the links to Cottel Court.'

Challis wanted to use the "no comment" approach to the local newspaper's enquiries but she knew that the standing order in relation to public information was to not use this phrase but to say something but give nothing away. She knew of the reporter; Amelia Griffiths, a freelance, actually. She was persistent. Challis asked her right out what made her think any connection existed between Timothy Bush, who Griffiths named, and Cottel Court? The reporter fell back on quoting a source and would not be deflected. She seemed to know that Challis was running with the investigation so she was coming to the "'voice of authority" for an update. Challis thought quickly although she was determined not to appear rushed. She said that there had been a suspicious death that was being treated as suicide and no other person or persons were being sought. Investigations into the circumstances were continuing and the coroner had been informed.

'And the Cottel Court connection?' Griffiths insisted.

'There isn't one,' was Challis's measured and, hopefully, confident response. It was not accepted by Griffiths who continued to press the point but Challis could not be drawn and ended the conversation with a sigh of relief. She had almost conceded to the reporter that the person who had found the deceased worked at Cottel Court but that would have made Meredith Guster easy to trace and easy to be pressurized.

As always in situations like this the source of the leak, for that was what it must have been, was a gnawing annoyance. Was it someone at the top with a political motive or someone at the bottom with a more pecuniary incentive or just someone with a grudge or an axe to grind.

Having got shot of the reporter, Challis decided it was a good time to take the task handed to her by O'Halloran out on the road and get to Henderson Timber.

She let Ruff give her a quick update as she put her coat on.

Chas or Charles Edward Davrot was ex-Army, employed in tanks during his service which spanned most of the Nineties. He had seen action in the first Iraq war in 1991 but was out just as the next one started in 2003. He had a police record. After he left the Army as a captain he had been done for driving without insurance and then later there had been an assault charge following a drunken brawl in a pub in Newport. Fined and bound over. An interesting item in his record was in connection with the death of a girl in Wiltshire in 2005. He was questioned at length. He was in charge of security in a resort where the girl worked as a cleaner. There was no clear evidence of foul play but the police in Frome kept him in custody for nearly two days.

He had a daughter in her early twenties; wife not living at home. They lived in Monmouth and she had the address. He'd worked for Stuart Devlin's security company for nearly five years.

'We have his prints and DNA if we need them,' Ruff stated.

'Anything on the daughter,' Challis asked, surprising Ruff.

'Well, no, I haven't looked.'

'That's okay,' Challis covered herself quickly. 'Just wondered.'

She repeated to Ruff where she was going and went. Ruff, her curiosity raised, decided to do a quick search on Jacqueline Amelia Davrot.

*

Lockett bumped into Barbara Jeffery on their way into the morgue. He nervously chatted about her early arrival. They stepped inside the warm building although they both agreed it was considerably milder today. Lockett relaxed; it was after all his responsibility to gently guide the girl through this ordeal. She was in her mid-twenties, a natural copperknob, hair tight and wiry. Glasses shaded her lime-green eyes and the large lenses covered her upper cheeks. She was wearing a grey skirted suit, looking formal unlike the shirt and jeans that he'd seen her wear in her office.

She had none of his edginess, seeming keen and eager to get on with the job in hand. Lockett had noticed her enthusiasm on the previous two occasions he had met with her and she had been adamant that she wanted to be the one to carry out the formal identification.

'I've known him for seven years,' she'd said in her Mancunian accent. She was married to a man from Gwent who she'd met on holiday in Spain. 'Tim was great when I arrived. Really nice. One of the few that didn't make fun of me accent. He used to translate for me.' She'd smiled at this joke.

Lockett could not decide if she was being helpful or if she was just a real nosey beggar who couldn't bear to be left out of the action.

As they stood in the vestibule loosening their topcoats he began to explain what was going to happen with the identification process.

'Don't worry,' she said. 'I've seen it all on telly.' And she went ahead and began to describe what she perceived would happen. She was still in full flow as two other people came in through the outside doors; a man and a woman. The man approached him without hesitation. He was bent at the shoulder, leaning forward, not a hunchback but his head lowered sufficiently for his eyes to peer from beneath his manicured eyebrows.

'Detective Lockett? I'm James Wheeler. This is my sister Jennifer. She wanted to come. I hope it's all right. Our other sister Liz...Elizabeth...couldn't face it. She thought it might be too...' He left the sentence in mid-air as he shook Lockett's hand.

Lockett's eyes were already on Miss Jennifer Wheeler. Unlike her brother, her body was unbowed. She was tall, her blonde hair long and straight, down below her shoulders. Her clothes were smart, she too dressed in grey but in a trouser suit. Like Barbara Jeffery she seemed to exude confidence and her grip on shaking Lockett's hand he found to be extraordinarily firm for a woman. The perfume she was wearing knocked him sideways. She must have been drenched in the stuff. Perhaps she'd thought a powerful nosegay would be required in the presence of a corpse but heavily-scented flowers in front of her face would look too obvious. He noticed Barbara Jeffery screw up her nose.

Her arrival had taken him completely by surprise; there had been no hint from her brother that she would be coming with him.

He couldn't help the first thought that came into his head. Her looks totally belied her apparent appetite for the things on offer at Cottel Court.

This shouldn't really have surprised him. He knew full well that not every criminal looked like a criminal or that every sexual deviant looked anything but normal. But he was staring at Jennifer Wheeler, her hand still in his; he was unable, unwilling even, to imagine her cavorting with her sister and her albeit estranged father.

Muench would have summed it up immediately with no holds barred.

There had been that time when the two of them were downstairs in reception and that very pretty young civilian girl had been on duty behind the desk. She had one of those faces that acted like a magnet and Lockett was locked onto its perfection.

Muench had whispered in his ear. 'To look at her you'd never believe she loves it in the mouth. Eh?' He had grinned that grin of his and watched for Lockett's drooling reaction that failed to materialize. 'Donahoe told me,' he added the extra evidence. 'He's been there, done that.'

But Lockett was still transfixed by that girl. She was eminently kissable, capable, he had always thought, of a romantic liaison. Muench had shot that down in flames, whether it was true or just one of his slanderous fantasies, and he hated him for it. Lockett was ashamed to be of the same gender. Too scared to tell him that, of course. He had been obliged to snigger at his colleague's obscene observations.

Now, the eyes of the three visitors were all on Lockett. He had gone silent for too long and he knew it. He could stare at Jennifer Wheeler all day long and still not know her. Her secret would be hers, except that he'd been given a privileged insight that made him shiver as he recalled Timothy Bush's disease. Did this beautiful girl have it too?

He tore his hand and his gaze away from her and let his eyes drift over the other two. What were their secrets? They were looking at him too but they couldn't possible know his personal quirks. Only the disconcerting Muench seemed to have that ability. He'd got close to guessing Lockett's foibles more than once.

'Fab'lous,' he uttered, shuddering. 'Before we make a start I have to make a quick call.' His mobile was in his hand as he stepped outside.

'She's not here,' Ruff told him. She'd answered Challis's phone. 'She's on her way to Henderson Timber. Only just left. What's up?'

Checking over his shoulder to make sure none of the three had followed him outside Lockett told Ruff that one of the daughters had turned up with the son. 'He's here to see the body and I assume she is as well. What if she recognizes him, from Cottel Court?'

Ruff went quiet as she thought it over. Christ! She had said all along that the daughters should be told but not like this.

'Can't you talk her out of it? You know, stress the…stressful nature of it all. Could be upsetting and all that shit.'

'Yeah, I could, but then she'll see Barbara Jeffery going in there bold as brass, almost savouring the experience she is. Raring to go.'

'Okay, okay, here's what you do. Let's imagine we know nothing about the Cottel Court connection. Mel says it's all circumstantial anyway. Names on a list prove nothing she reckons. So, if she wants to see the body, you don't stop her. But watch her, closely. See her reaction. That might actually tell us a lot. Okay?'

Lockett took his time replying. 'Okay. You're right. Absolutely.'

'Okay then.' Ruff thought that would be the end of the conversation.

'I can't believe it myself,' Lockett blurted out. 'You should see her; she's beautiful.'

'Great a grip, Ray,' she said. Probably not very appropriate advice. 'Stay objective. Looks can be deceptive, you know that full well.'

His voice was low and shamed. 'I said "fab'lous", would you believe.'

*

'What do you mean you want to drop the charges?'

Jeff Henderson had made the declaration as soon as Challis had entered his office and introduced herself.

'I've had enough of this,' he explained. 'We should have sorted this out ourselves in the first place. My wife made a bad decision calling you lot in. Totally unnecessary. The two men you were unable to charge were sacked this morning. That's the end of it as far as I'm concerned.'

'Excuse me, sir, but you made a complaint this morning concerning...concerning our handling of the case and...'

'The complaint was about more than handling just the case!' Henderson made the point forcefully. 'But you can drop that as well. I'm withdrawing it, if that's what you need me to do. I'll even put it in writing.'

'A lot of police time has been wasted on this investigation.' Challis strained to fight the corner as best she could but she knew she didn't have a leg to stand on. Henderson sank into his chair as if he was weary with it all.

'Sergeant, somehow I don't think the officer – I won't call him a detective - wasted his time at all, but please don't make me spell it out. If there are rights and wrongs on all of this I think I'm ahead on points. The whole episode has been a shambles from your perspective. You allowed it to drag on. No action was taken to conclude it. As far as I can see this is the first occasion that anyone more senior, marginally more senior, has been anywhere near the case. Don't you have targets? Don't you measure progress or lack of it and take action as and when required or do you just not care enough about the dull and boring cases?'

'I can assure you, sir, that every case is treated very seriously and...'

Once again Henderson would not let her finish. 'I think you'd better leave before I change my mind about the complaint. It's all been totally unprofessional and I'm not impressed by your attempts to make it seem otherwise. That to me is equally unprofessional.'

He was right, Challis knew it. She made her farewells and left. Ah well, she sighed as she sat in the car, at least the fucking case is closed. Somehow though she did not see O'Halloran being pleased.

She started the car and pulled out onto the main road. What a waste of a day and what a waster that Harry Muench is. She could have been getting further with the Timothy Bush case. She cursed both Muench and O'Halloran. What would happen now, she wondered. O'Halloran wouldn't have a scandal on his hands but what to do with Muench. At the very least there should be an internal enquiry and some disciplinary. Muench should have his knuckles severely rapped and be exiled to the local Siberia, either traffic or Complaints. He certainly should be taken out of CID; she didn't particularly want to work with him. How many other witnesses or vulnerable females involved with cases had he got into bed? Personally she couldn't see the attraction. His attitude towards the female of the species was sickening. What Ruff had overheard the day before was nothing new to Challis. She'd known all too well his tasteless sexist remarks.

She accelerated away and the wheels spun. Tyres, she remembered.

The day was warmer, the road wet and spray was coming up onto her windscreen from vehicles in front. She pulled the screenwash lever. Nothing! And the wipers had gone through their five automatic sweeps and severely smudged the windscreen.

Bollocks.

If she took it steady she'd be all right. Then she heard three beeps. She looked at the dashboard. The battery warning light was on and a bright red 'STOP' was lit up.

Double bollocks.

She was contemplating stopping when the two warning lights went out and she breathed a sigh of relief but before she had reached HQ those lights had come back on twice. She definitely needed another pool car.

*

Jeff Henderson sat at his desk absentmindedly shuffling papers and staring blindly at his computer screen. Part of his problems had been got rid of but one major portion was still gnawing away at his insides.

Anne! He could bloody strangle her!

He powered off his laptop, stood and collected his topcoat from the coat-stand near the door that he then opened with a sweep of the hand.

He went straight home. He was there within minutes. He had forbidden his wife from going anywhere near the office that morning but who was he punishing, her or the business? Despite everything, she was an integral part of their company. She had been the one who had discovered the fiddle going on in the warehouse. He had admired her diligence, her quick grasp of the situation, but what a disaster had followed. He was right in what he'd said to that detective sergeant: they should have sorted it out themselves. But who was to blame for what had happened subsequently? DC Harry Muench was clearly the predator but why had she been such easy prey? Was that his fault?

Anne Henderson heard her husband's car and saw him through the sitting room window. She was fearful now. That morning when all hell had been let loose she had been amazed at his calm reaction. He'd made it clear he knew what had been going on; how he knew she had no idea but she suspected that the two miscreants although having been released from custody had decided to inform Jeff after all, perhaps in a bid to save their jobs. Probably they threatened that they'd go public with it if he chose to take any action against them. Well, her husband had called their bluff and no mistake.

She decided to stand her ground. He'd stood his. She was waiting in the hallway as he let himself in. He glanced at her as he removed and hung up his coat.

'Well, it's over,' he told her. 'At least, the police are dealt with. What other repercussions there may be we'll have to see but it'll only be words. No problem. Sticks and stones and all that…'

'Jeff,' she began, wanting to explain, perhaps even apologize, but the words wouldn't come. He closed on her.

'I'm not going to ask you why,' he said into her face but not with anger. 'I think I probably know why. Look at me!' He raised his voice a little at last. She obeyed. She was a lovely women, he could see that; he wasn't blind but perhaps he had been short-sighted. 'I want you to tell me what happened.'

The look on her face was quizzical.

'I want you to tell me the details; all the details.'

Her jaw dropped. 'Jeff, what…?'

'The first time,' his voice was becoming more urgent. 'Tell me about the first time, with him. Tell me what, tell me where, tell me everything.'

She went to turn away but he gripped her shoulders. Her face was scalding. 'Jeff, I….' She wanted to refuse him but there was passion in his face; she wasn't sure what kind of passion it was but it had been a very long time since she had seen from him anything like it. He was demanding an intimate confession.

'It was in the office,' she breathed, 'that first day, in the evening when he came back to go through the figures.' She paused and shrugged, hoping that would be all.

'And?' Jeff urged. She hesitated but he repeated more urgently. 'And?'

'We were at my desk, sitting close and it just happened.'

'Who started what?'

His eyes had a flash of excitement and from them she read that he was not being an aggressive interrogator. Far from it, he wanted her to go on and instinctively she realized there was something symbiotic going on.

'I did,' she said unashamedly, moving imperceptibly closer to him. 'I kissed him. We started undressing each other and he swept everything off the desk and...'

He grabbed her hand, frightening her, but he pulled her into the study. Across the other side of the room was the desk between two windows. It was pre-war, oak, a token sheet of blotting paper on it with a fake antique pen and ink stand. He'd inherited it off an uncle he never really knew.

He led her to it, the firmness of his grip on her hand easing. He looked down.

'Show me,' he said, letting go. She felt the hard edge of the desk pressing into her flesh.

Twenty-Five

Dr. Jill Scott walked into Lassman's office. He and DS Laurie O'Toole had their heads together as they leaned over the desk on which were spread photographs extracted from the memory stick found in George Medlyn's place of work. Lassman, in true old detective style, was examining them through a magnifying glass. O'Toole had the same set of photos lined up on Lassman's computer screen and was zooming in and out as Lassman requested closer scrutiny.

As a team they had spent a lot of time with the photo-manipulating experts, trying to get as clear an image as possible. There had only been a one minute and fifty-two seconds worth of video imagery on the memory stick. The opinion was that it was a mere segment of a much longer show. At first they had thought it was just part of Medlyn's collection of pornography, like the stuff they'd found in his study, but an eagle-eyed WPC Olluwala thought one of the males in the video looked like George Medlyn. They had retrieved photos of Medlyn from the house in order to get a clear picture of him: post-mortem shots of his face were rendered pretty useless by the fatal gunshot. Zooming in on stills of the video did indeed reveal that a naked George Medlyn was a principle participant in the scene.

This discovery had led to the isolation of other persons in the video clip: one female and three men. Two of the other men were seen only from the back; one other had a profile and half full-face visible. He was six foot plus, about one hundred and eighty pounds, dark hair, a bit of a pot belly that put him around fifty years of age, so they reckoned. The two other males could be seen flitting in and out but never in full view, just a hint of torso here and there. It did appear that they were wearing masks of some sort, leather perhaps, tight-fitting. Their height was less than six feet, weight harder to gauge.

The girl was plain to see; completely full-frontal at times and exposed enough for all her personal details to be deduced: age early thirties; height five feet seven; weight one hundred and twenty pounds; dimensions thirty-six, twenty-four, thirty-six with her breasts c-cup size and some debate over whether or not work had been done on them. She was blonde, a strawberry blonde according to Olluwala. Her accent, albeit emanating from a somewhat limited vocabulary that fitted the scene being enacted, was analyzed and said to be Home Counties. Facially, she was a good-looking woman although her face was contorted much of the time. The colour of her eyes could not be seen for sure but greenish-blue seemed favourite.

Much of the debate centered around what exactly was going on in the video. Clearly it was all about sex and equally clearly she was restrained by ropes. The issue was that some opinions said she was not ritually restrained, in other words she was not tied à la true bondage fetishism. Somebody described her as being hog-tied; rendered helpless.

'We're looking at rape here,' one of the detectives observed.

'Yeah but is it staged?' somebody asked. 'I mean is she a willing victim? Without the beginning of the tape you can't tell.'

'If it is staged she's a bloody good actress.'

'It's a rape version of a snuff movie,' someone else put forward.

The scene was horribly degrading for the woman. She could not resist. In less than two minutes of video they saw enough to get a very good idea of what was going on but most of the action was of George Medlyn having brutal anal sex with the woman. Clearly this had been "his moment" but the other men could either be lined up waiting or had had their turn already, as somebody crudely commented..

It had been WPC Olluwala who spoke up after the video clip had been played over and over again.

'Is this relevant at all to the killing or are you lot just getting off on this?' Her blood had been coming to the boil for some minutes, recognizing the change of tone of the mainly male audience gathered in front of the plasma screen set up in one of the side offices. Male voices objected to her observation but Lassman could see she was genuinely upset by the situation. Lassman had a lot of time for this WPC. She had made useful contributions to the investigation all the way through.

'I think we've seen enough,' he conceded but added 'for now,' not wanting to give all the ground to the WPC. There was a mumbling of some discontent as O'Toole closed the computer file but Lassman raised his voice. 'I think what we have seen is relevant. O'Toole, I want you to go through all the cds, dvds, that we brought from Medlyn's house. This piece of shit that we just watched is a small bit that has come off something else. Now, is it on a disc? If he downloaded it to his PC we're buggered because we don't have it. Is there any way we can find out what he downloaded without having his PC?' There were negative whispers. 'Well find out anyway,' he ordered. 'Olluwala,' he'd mastered her surname. 'I want you to take charge of this video evidence. I want stills printed off, enlargements…' that caused a ripple of laughter to which he frowned '…the best clear images we can get of the people in it; faces are what we're interested in, okay? Unless there are any distinguishing marks you come across.' More tittering. 'You happy with that?' She nodded. 'You sit on it and if anyone…' he looked around '…juvenile wants access to it you refer them to me. Clear? I want this investigation to get objective and to stay objective. I have a gut feeling it's only going to get uglier, so everyone be alert because…' he fed them one of his favourite lines and a couple of the younger DCs rose to it 'because we need more lerts,' they chanted.

'Exactly.' Then he continued on a more serious vein. 'For all we know, what we have just been watching may be a significant reason for the killing so we take it all seriously. Remember, all the crap in the world gets dumped on us so we can digest it. We're the worms in the shit-heap. I want some good clean leads out of this lot. And if I find anyone using any of this material for titillation they'll be off the case before you can say soixante-neuf. You may be regarding this stuff as pure adult porn and not the sick kiddie stuff that we often have to sit through but nonetheless its evidence and we're professional enough, or should be, to view it as just that. Clear?'

He allocated another DC to follow up on the file title on the memory stick. 'Try and find out what 'VKS' is about,' he instructed him. 'January 2011,' he added pessimistically.

That had been two days ago and now Dr. Scott had come in to impart the results of the forensic tests. He looked up as she came in. 'Scotty! About time an' all.'

'O my apologies, o great one. If only I had the powers of alchemy to perform instant miracles.'

Lassman smiled, O'Toole ignored what was their usual verbal sparring and pseudo-insulting backchat.

'First things first,' she said, opening a brown file she had in her hand. 'I think your shooter used a silencer. Lots of lovely extra markings on the bullets, especially the one that went through the soft belly and into the seat of the car. Not much damage to that one unlike the one in the head.'

'That explains why nobody heard a thing,' observed O'Toole.

'Gun?' Lassman asked.

'Hand gun. Nine millimetre. Could be anything. No spent cartridge cases found. Our man seems to be tidy minded. Gun could be Smith and Wesson or Browning – much favoured by the SAS...'

'I knew that,' said Lassman and was stared at by the other two, neither of whom wanted to question his alleged knowledge. 'They're well known assassins.'

'This does look a bit professional,' O'Toole said. 'Except for the gut shot. What was that all about?'

He directed his question at Scott.

'Might need a profiler for that one,' she suggested. 'The shot was aimed almost vertically, from around about the chest area. There was residue there from the discharge as there was on the left temple. It was all close range stuff. Shot to the head first, in the nether regions next by which time he was dead. That shot entered behind the pubic bone and went on unobstructed through the bladder and the prostate and out of the anus. Missed the genitalia completely.'

Lassman was thoughtful. 'Not necessarily.' He went thoughtful again.

'Not necessarily what?' O'Toole asked.

'Well,' said Lassman slowly. 'The shot may have missed his old boy but was that the target? I'm just thinking like a profiler.'

O'Toole saw where his boss was coming from. 'You're thinking back to the video.'

Lassman would not commit himself to an answer so O'Toole continued. 'You think, what, a revenge attack? Somebody, or somebody hired by somebody, tried to shoot Medlyn's nuts off, killing him first of course. I would have thought if that was the case they would have shot off his bits first, properly, and then perhaps finish him off later. Make him really suffer. And all of that is only if the video has anything to do with it in the first place.'

'What is it you guys are talking about?' Scott asked.

'Just thinking out loud,' Lassman answered quickly. 'What else have you got?'

'We got fingerprints. Lots. All over the cd and dvd cases but they're nearly all different. Trouble with items like that is they get handled by all sorts of people like whoever Medlyn got them off in the first place. Anyway, they're all logged and are being scanned for any matches. We'll probably get some that are complete red herrings. I mean, guys who sell that stuff are likely to be on the wrong side at some time in their illustrious careers. None of the prints in that room are Mrs. Medlyn's. In the car, nothing. No prints other than the victim's, no detritus...'

'Detritus?' queried O'Toole.

'Yes. Droppings of a criminal nature,' Scott replied sarcastically.

'It was a clean job in more ways than one then.' Lassman ran his fingers through his beard. 'I don't like this. We need to find any prior shootings like this, if there are any. Ask the Serious Crime lot if it rings any bells. We need to find out more about this George Medlyn. His movements. Credit card activity. See what he's bought, where he's been. Go back three months for starters.'

'We need more publicity. Ask for witnesses, anybody in the area.' O'Toole turned to Scott. 'Time of death?'

'About four p.m.'

'Okay. Need to find out who was about around at that time. I'll get the team back out there.'

'Please do,' Lassman pleaded. 'Them upstairs will not be liking an execution in the greater Windsor area. Such things came to an end centuries ago.' He then seemed to go into a dream state.

'You haven't asked me about the sheets,' Scott said, bringing him back.

'Then tell me,' he breathed wearily.

'Semen, from George Medlyn. Some blood spatters and other dried fluids, not from George Medlyn.'

Lassman waited for more. 'Are you deliberately teasing me? Is there more?'

'They're from Mrs. Medlyn.'

'I thought she refused a DNA test.'

'She did but there was a hairbrush in the bedroom that we removed as evidence and the DNA matches the blood and stains on the sheet, so we can assume that the long hairs in the brush, too long for George, were the wife's.'

'The wife! Didn't think you feminists liked that expression. The wife; the little woman...'

Scott ignored him. She knew that he knew that she was far from a feminist of that ilk.

'We can also tell,' she continued, her stride unbroken, 'that the stains are over fourteen days old. Don't ask me how; it's all clever stuff.'

'That,' O'Toole began, consulting some notes, 'coincides with the departure of the wife. Makes sense; she ups and leaves, bed stays unmade, untouched. Do you think, sir, that the bed and whatever happened was the final straw?'

'Yes, could be,' Lassman said, eyebrows raised in interest. 'But what happened? I think we'd better bring her in under caution. I want to know if whatever happened was sufficient for her to see her husband off. Scotty, I'd like you to be in on the interview. Woman's touch may be needed to unzip Mrs. Medlyn's lips.'

'Bring her in under caution,' said Scott, 'and we can legitimately get her DNA.'

Twenty-Six

The assistant forensic examiner told Lockett everything was ready and led him and his party of three through the security doors and to the viewing room.

Lockett had decided to take Barbara Jeffery through first to do the formal identification. He checked with her that she was ready to go. She barely controlled her eagerness. She was right behind the assistant. A green drape covered the body of Timothy Bush. The assistant stood one side and Lockett gently eased Jeffery forward on the other side so that she was alongside the head.

'I have to tell you that there are some visible effects of the deceased's last moments,' the assistant warned quietly.

'Are you okay?' Lockett asked, his hand lightly on her elbow. Jeffery looked less sure but she took a deep breath and nodded.

The assistant drew back the cover so that the face, neck and shoulders of Timothy Bush were in view.

Jeffery gasped, imperceptibly. Then a smile slowly crept across her lips as she twisted her head to get a better look full face. She stared for a while, a long while Lockett thought, and then nodded.

'I have to ask you,' Lockett spoke. 'Do you recognise this man?'

The face was swollen and still discoloured.

'Yes,' she said volubly. 'This is Timothy Bush.'

'Thank you,' Lockett smiled and turned expecting Jeffery to do the same and head for the door. But she stood where she was and then did something that totally surprised him. She bent forward and kissed the cold face of Timothy Bush, not on the cheek or the forehead but full on the lips. Lockett was open-mouthed and he also saw the look of amazement on the face of the assistant. This was not something you saw every day. Even close loved ones thought twice about kissing a corpse on the lips.

She was unabashed. She rose, smiled contentedly at Lockett and led the way out. She was stared at by James and Jennifer Wheeler but she simply smiled at them as well.

'It is your father,' she told them. 'I know you didn't know him much but take no notice of what he looks like now. He was a good-looking man. I loved him. He made me laugh.' She was re-living memories and her face showed it. No sign of regrets or sadness.

The Wheelers didn't seem to know how to react to her gushing accolades. They held back, looking to Lockett.

'Okay,' he almost whispered. 'Miss...Mrs. Jeffery has formally identified Mr. Bush. So, do you wish to come through?'

'Can I go now?' Jeffery asked him.

'Can you wait a few minutes. I need your signature.'

Lockett returned his attention to the Wheelers. James was ready to go into the viewing room; Jennifer, he noticed, held back.

'That's fine,' Lockett held up a reassuring hand. 'I'll take Mr. Wheeler through and you can...decide...'

He pushed the door open and the two men walked through. The assistant was standing in the same position and this time Lockett joined him so that they were both facing James Wheeler who stepped gingerly alongside Timothy Bush's bare shoulders, his own curved shoulders seeming to push his face right over the body.

He drew in a sharp breath.

'He looks different,' Wheeler croaked. 'The same man as the other day but different. His face, is it that colour and everything because of the...the...?'

'It's the effects of the constriction on the blood supply,' the assistant explained and Wheeler nodded.

'It is the man you had recently come to believe was your father?' Lockett asked.

'Yes.'

The door opened and the pale faced Jennifer Wheeler came in.

'Jen.' James Wheeler offered her his hand. She took it at full stretch, not advancing any closer. Lockett tensed himself, getting ready to follow Ruff's advice and keep a keen eye on the girl.

James Wheeler gently pulled his sister closer and he moved further along beyond the top edge of the gurney to give her room. She had her eyes on her brother but gradually lowered them. She recoiled and her hand slipped from his fingers. James went straight to her and held her.

'It's all right. It's okay.'

'I'm sorry.' There were no tears in her voice. 'I can't do it.' She turned and quickly left the room followed by James who gave his father one final glance.

That was inconclusive, Lockett thought.

Lockett found an empty office with a bare desk where he took Barbara Jeffery to put her signature on a document to confirm her identification of Timothy Bush. His pen wouldn't work. Barbara Jeffery had one in her bag, she said, somewhere, but rummage as she might it could not be found. He asked her to bear with him and went back out to see if the assistant had one.

He turned the corner to the viewing room. The corridor was empty; he'd left the Wheelers there a minute ago. He drew level with the viewing room door and looked through the glass top to see if the assistant was there. He wasn't but he saw Jennifer Wheeler, standing over the completely uncovered body of Timothy Bush, her eyes scanning the entire length of the corpse. The green cover lay in a heap on the floor. He walked in.

She turned to face him, her eyes flickering in a way that he recognized. She was searching her brain for some excuse, some reason for her being there and for the body being in such an exposed state. Everything was in full view: the stitched work on the chest, the discoloured skin, the scabs.

'James needed the toilet,' she began, speaking quickly. 'The man took him through the security doors. I thought I should try again, having come all this way.' She bent to retrieve the cover. 'I pulled too hard.' She half-heartedly tried to drape the cover over the body. Lockett moved forward to grab a corner. He looked up at her as she looked up at him. She was trying to see what Lockett was thinking about the situation.

'Do you recognise him?' He decided to come right out with it. This was all suspicious enough to warrant the question. This time she slowly and calculatedly gazed down at the still largely uncovered body.

'Not at all,' she said and Lockett saw a faint frown. 'Of course not.' She pulled back the lower part of the cover. 'What happened down there do you suppose?' Her hands were full so she nodded towards Timothy Bush's scarred hairless genital area. Lockett saw her eyes were fixed in a downward stare. No shock registered on her face.

'We...they're still carrying out tests.'

'What do you suppose happened? I mean, why would anyone do that to him?'

He was surprised that she assumed the wounds were not self-inflicted. That had not occurred to them.

He was thrown and had no reply.

He pulled the cover from her hand and re-positioned it over the body. This broke the spell and Jennifer Wheeler's clear blue eyes bore into him with the same question.

'What sort of avenging bastard would want to do that?' she persisted. She asked without anger or bitterness. It was a puzzle that she wanted him to solve, almost a challenge to Lockett to come up with the right answer. As if she knew the answer.

Lockett kept his cool, unfazed by such words coming from such gorgeous lips, more disturbed by her suddenly taking this high ground.

'Can I ask if this is the first time you have seen your father since he and your mother split up?'

'I can't remember him so I can never be sure he is my father. We've only got the word of that strange girl this guy worked with.'

'And the chance meeting with your brother.'

She was silent.

'And you don't want to believe it, do you?' Lockett asked. 'Why not?'

'I've said why not.' She turned to leave the room.

Delicious though she looked Lockett was unhappy with her manner. She was hiding something and he of course knew what it was.

'We know why not actually,' he called out after her, making her return to search his face for an unspoken hint.

He was about to blurt out that it was known she and her father had met at Cottel Court when the assistant came in, with James Wheeler tagging along. Jennifer Wheeler and Lockett had to break eye contact; her mouth had the beginnings of a smile. She brushed past the assistant, grabbed her brother with a calm 'Let's get out of here' and marched off. Lockett went to pursue but thought better of it. As he came alongside the assistant he asked him if he had a pen he could borrow. 'And I'd get a lock put on this door if I was you,' he added.

Twenty-Seven

Challis appraised O'Halloran of the Muench/Henderson situation as soon as she returned to headquarters.

'Well done, Mel,' he enthused when told that Mr. Henderson's complaint against Muench had gone away. He didn't want the full report she offered, in fact he wanted no report at all.

'Just tie off the loose ends on the case,' he ordered. 'Investigation dropped by the alleged victims i.e. Henderson Timber. Case closed.' He'd had a gut feeling that it would end like this. Nobody wanted the hassle and embarrassment.

'What about Muench, sir? He can't get out of this without some action. What he did was out of order. I can't work with that.'

'Don't be naïve, Sergeant. Having relationships with a witness in a case is a risk of the job.' He glared knowingly. 'Could happen to any of us. We could all declare a compromising intimacy, whether it be a current one or…historical.'

He was alluding to Stuart Devlin. She knew it and she could tell that he knew she knew it. But she didn't know how he knew that **a.** she and Stuart Devlin had once been an item and **b.** that he was connected with the case she was working on. The answer to **a.** had to be Redland and the answer to **b.** was that O'Halloran was taking a closer interest in the Timothy Bush case than she had thought. He must have been reading the case notes on-line. He was watching how she worked.

He showed her the door. His last words to her were 'get Muench back to work.'

*

Early afternoon and Ruff was still on her own in the office. In Redland's office Challis had had no lunch and was starving. Ruff was licking her lips and there was a smell of pesto in the air. Challis casually looked at Ruff's desk to see if there were any crumbs remaining.

'D'you want coffee?' Ruff asked her.

'Yeah, why not. But should I drink it on an empty stomach?'

'D'you want some crisps out of the machine?'

She declined the offer, feeling guilty all morning about the fish and chips the previous evening. And she hadn't been for a run for ages, something else that narked her. The dark mornings and evenings plus the freezing conditions of late did not lend to footslogging the lanes near her house. But the evenings were drawing out and it was a bit milder this morning so who knows? Maybe the weekend.

Her mobile rang as Ruff headed off. The caller was unknown and that amazed her. She knew that she had given her number only to people who were identified in her contact list. 'Hello.' She decided to try to be personable.

'Melanie. How are you? You sound odd.' It was Stuart Devlin.

He was the last person she wanted to speak to. There was still a taste in her mouth from the previous day's conversation with him at Cottel Court. He had really got to her. But he had been questioned about the case so she had to discover if he was contacting her about that. She couldn't help the first thing she said though.

'How did you get this number?'

'That's a fine greeting.' She knew he had a smile of his face. 'Uncle Alan of course.' He waited a very short time for a response from her but then carried on. 'I thought you'd like to know; he's being released from hospital today. They're sending him home. I'm on my way to pick him up right now.'

This was unexpected information from Stuart.

'Is he going back to his house?' she asked.

'Yes.'

'It's freezing in there. I was there last night. And the water's turned off.'

'No, it isn't, not now. I called in there on my way through Usk. Spoke to the bloke next door, Jared whatever his name is. He told me of your concern. Thanks. Anyway the water is back on and so is the heating.'

'Is he all right to look after himself?'

'If that's what he wants. You know what he's like.'

'I'll call in on my way home. Tell him I'll call in, unless you're staying there with him.'

The last thing she wanted was to be in his company so soon again.

'No. I have…some business tonight.'

'Okay.' She was relieved but hoped it didn't show across the satellite. 'Thanks for telling me. Everyone here will be delighted.'

He tried to continue with idle chit-chat but she told him she was in a meeting. She thought about adding his number to her contact list but decided not. She'd had to type his name when she had updated the report of the visit to Cottel Court and that had been bad enough but putting it in her mobile would be invasive in the extreme. She didn't like to recall that, once upon a time, her mobile had practically smoked with the sheer number and heat of the calls between her and Stuart.

Ruff came back in as Challis slumped back in her chair. She made herself think of the good news.

'Kay, the boss is coming out of hospital.'

*

'I think she recognized him,' Lockett told Challis and Ruff as they sat in Redland's office recapping the case. He was half-hearted about this assertion. Driving back to the office he asked himself what difference did it make if Jennifer Wheeler knew Timothy Bush or if she had shagged him, alone or with her sister? He was also disheartened by the fact that the gorgeous girl had those predilections. You just can't tell, can you? Unless you're Harry Muench. And that thought sickened him too.

'Oh fuck,' Ruff spoke under her breath but she was heard. She didn't care. She now had the urge to let Ray know she could be crude off her own bat too. It wasn't entirely Ray's fault but he did encourage Harry the Munch. She looked at Challis who looked back sternly.

'Unless it's pertinent to the case, we have no cause to tell anyone anything.' She was spelling it out, clear and simple. They'd had this debate before about passing on Timothy Bush's positive HIV status to his family, to his daughters in particular. They had opposing views but Challis had the casting vote.

'So, Ray, the girl from the software house identified Bush, yes?'

'Yes, Sarge,' and then he recounted the kiss that Barbara Jeffery had planted on the lips of the deceased. 'She also told the Wheelers that she loved him.'

'Were they at it as well?'

'Well she's married so if they were then she was being a bit obvious about it don't you think?'

'Depends on the marriage,' Ruff offered. 'But if they were...'

'Don't even go there,' Challis warned. 'We're not telling anybody!'

'It'll come out at the inquest,' Ruff pointed out. 'It could be a key factor, the key factor, the reason he topped himself. How are we going to look then?'

Challis desperately wanted to sign this case off; pass all the info to the coroner. There was enough to confirm it as suicide, except for the one niggling point; Sayer's Sherlock Holmes moment. The man was hung twice, second time in the field, first time off something metal painted black. Possible crimes committed: interfering with and disposing of a corpse; perverting the course of justice; assisted suicide...

'Anything back from Sayer on what we found outside Cottel Court?'

'Yes,' Ruff replied crisply, not happy with this change of subject. 'The black specks we found are of metal paint identical to that found on the rope.' Challis and Lockett both raised their eyebrows. 'But,' Ruff continued, 'it's common as muck. A popular brand. However, neither those flakes nor the ones on the rope were painted onto clean metal. There's bits of rust on all of it. Tests done on the rope indicated the metal would have been wrought iron, so fairly old. He says it's not used these days.'

'I've seen wrought iron gates for sale on the internet,' Challis said. 'I was thinking of getting some for my driveway.'

'Ah, yes,' Ruff dug out a piece of paper. 'Sayer says stuff called wrought iron today is usually mild steel.'

'So, what are the gates at Cottel Court made of? We need a sample.'

'Need a warrant,' Lockett advised.

Challis was thoughtful. 'Yes but first I think I'll pay a surprise visit on Ms. Guster.'

*

By the time she escaped from the office it was half-past four. She had just assigned new tasks to Lockett and Ruff when yet more all-hell broke loose.

Detective Sergeant Ken Tart from Homicide came in at a gallop. His DCI, Harriet Moray, had sent him along on orders from above. A triple murder had been reported in the Sirhowy Valley; a woman and two children. A massive hunt for the perpetrator was about to get underway and extra CID officers were required.

'Partner or ex-partner,' Ruff exclaimed. 'Always is.'

DCI Moray had been told she could take two from Challis's team.

This was another thing that pissed Challis off. She could understand the necessity but her first reaction was to resent it. She thought quickly.

'Okay,' she told Tart – an unfortunate name she'd always thought and she was sorry for his wife and especially his daughter. He looked like a tart of the strawberry jam variety, somewhat circular and red-faced with pimples. 'You can have Ray and Harry.'

Tart looked around. 'Where's Harry?'

'Out at the moment but you tell me where you want him and I'll let him know.' She said this with such sincerity that Tart accepted it without question. He left with Lockett in tow, telling Challis to send Harry Muench straight up to Blackwood. He gave her the location of the mobile police unit being set up there.

'Leave it with me, Ken.'

'Where is the Munch?' Ruff asked her.

'No fucking idea,' Challis replied as she dialed his mobile and left him instructions on where he should go.

'You didn't want to work this weekend did you?'

'No thanks,' Ruff said with a shudder.

Challis had another thought that she probably shouldn't have. This will keep that reporter off my back about Timothy Bush.

Twenty-Eight

Challis had cursed as she'd driven over Usk bridge. Ruff had discovered that Timothy Bush went to the same doctor's surgery in Usk as did Redland. She'd rung them but they would say nothing over the phone. Challis realized that she could have got Ruff to make an appointment with the practice manager so she could call in on her way to see Meredith Guster. It was only five-thirty. May as well try it, she thought.

The surgery practice manager had gone home for the day. Challis identified herself but the staff of two still on duty behind the desk, one of them Meg Ryan, would not or could not help with any information on Timothy Bush. Finally, Challis managed to make an appointment to see the practice manager, at nine-thirty Monday morning.

*

As she approached Meredith Guster's house Challis saw a car parked outside, a blue Mini Clubman. Guster's car was parked on her hard-standing leading up to the house.

The lights were on, both upstairs and downstairs, at the front at least. She slowed down. She drove on the short distance to the gateway to the field on the opposite side of the road. The police tapes were still there, drooping, on the metal gate, as they were at the front of No. 3, Timothy Bush's house. She walked across to look at the house. Timothy Bush's car was gone having been removed by Sayer's team. She had often questioned what was the point of leaving "Do Not Cross" tape around an unguarded building.

The lights were also on in the middle house of the terrace of three and a car, an estate of some kind, was parked in front. So, the Smiths were home.

The Smith's downstairs curtains were open and Challis stopped and looked inside through the net. She could see a man, hard to tell his age or his appearance but she heard his raised voice. Who he was shouting at she couldn't see.

She walked on. She'd give them a little while to calm. Perhaps they'd only just got home from the holiday and were tired, tempers stretched. Later would do, when she'd finished with Ms. Guster.

The Mini Clubman was by no means new but it was in good condition. Obviously its presence indicated that Ms. Guster had a visitor. Challis made a mental note of the registration number and casually checked the windscreen for current road tax.

She was in two minds. Should she have the chat in front of the visitors or maybe do the Smiths first after all?

Meredith Guster's front door opened. A young woman came out, shouting back over her shoulder a 'goodnight Chas'. Her face was lit by the hall light. It was Jackie Davrot.

She was dressed much as she had been the night in the Eastgate. Different colours but same plunging neckline and tight trousers. Hair was a different colour too; a different shade of red. Almost tangerine. She pulled a top coat loosely around herself.

She jumped as Challis stepped into view as a dark image out of the dark road.

'Hello, Jackie.'

Her face, shaded now that the house lights were behind her, would have shown Challis that Jackie, having been briefly surprised, now assumed a look of feigned excitement as the same house lights illuminated the policewoman. Instinctively Jackie stopped wrapping her top coat around her and let it flop open.

'Hi, Mel. Did you come for me?'

She was a precocious little thing. Too young to be so unashamedly available but then perhaps that was the prerogative of the young.

'No,' was all Challis would say.

'I saw you in the pub, looking around for me after we'd spent that time together.'

Challis chewed her lip as Jackie went on.

'But I saw you with the guy from the band. He looked cute. Did you have a good night?'

Her eyes sparkled, seeming to be confident of the answer. Challis knew that Jackie was leaving the question open to interpretation: did she have a good night talking to her or did she have a good night with Jonathan? There was no answer to that.

Jackie continued her walk down the pathway. 'I've just dropped Chas off. He's letting me have the car tonight.' She was blurting words again. Challis thought this girl could either hide nothing or drown the truth in a torrent of words.

'I enjoyed last night,' Jackie went on. 'Sorry I just disappeared at the end but there's always next time. It's so nice to see you again so soon.'

'Is Meredith Guster in?' Challis asked as officiously as she could.

'Mmm, with Chas. Cooking something nice I think. I couldn't stay. Got to go to … somewhere. What's it about, why you here?'

Challis saw the front curtain twitch. She wanted to get inside the house now and edged past Jackie.

'Is it about that poor man in the field? The one who hung himself? Meredith was really cut up about that, Chas said. She didn't seem too bad this evening.'

It was funny but she found it unsettling the way Jackie kept referring to her father as Chas. Maybe he was her stepfather. 'Look, Jackie, some other time. I must get on.'

'Okay. Did you really enjoy last night? I did.'

Persistent, wasn't she? Had she enjoyed being in Jackie's company for an hour or whatever it was? Yes, in the ambiance of a drinking establishment, it became interesting. That's what pubs were all about after all; places to talk with or listen to people who you otherwise wouldn't. She preferred not to recall some of the thoughts she'd harboured about this girl because that would make her recall the physical disappointments with Jonathan and reveal all sorts of other imponderables.

'I mustn't keep you.'

Jackie nodded slowly. 'Sure. Okay. See you.' She walked to her car and Challis made herself turn to the front door and knock it too loudly.

Jackie Davrot drove off with one quick backward glance to see if Mel was watching her go. She wasn't.

The night before, she had waited in the dark outside the Eastgate to see if Mel would leave with that musician. She did. If she hadn't she would have pounced.

She hadn't wanted this latest chat to end. Mel had been so abrupt. She would have loved to have told her she was off for a porn shoot just to see what the reaction would have been to that kind of modeling job. It would have been a hoot. Mel had come out with words of warning the night before when she'd thought she was getting into the risky world of the model. God knows what she'd say if she knew the truth. Didn't matter.

The issue had not arisen. Mel had her copper face on, that was obvious. *Couldn't wait to move me on, could she?*

Twenty-Nine

Ruff slowly lowered the phone as her call to Pearwood Independent School for Girls came to an end. It had been a call that followed her earlier on-line search of the national police database for anything on Jacqueline Amelia Davrot.

She'd had no idea where Chas Davrot's daughter fitted into all of this but Challis's interest in the girl, albeit casual, had sparked her own interest. A good detective, she'd reminded herself, should ignore nothing, no matter how insignificant at first glance. Witnesses, she had been taught, say things they shouldn't or perhaps didn't mean to. Unlike hardened criminals who are used to being tight-lipped and careful with their words one-off suspects and witnesses have little idea what they should say or how they should say it. They give things away. Many may babble but often in the nervous outburst there will be a little gem or two of priceless information. That understanding of the guilty or not-too-innocent mind – everyone has something to hide – applies to all statements, even those seemingly aimless comments made by a detective sergeant.

Ruff wasn't any the wiser, though.

She had discovered that in 2004 Jacqueline Amelia Davrot had been investigated by the Wiltshire Police following a complaint by the parents of a girl at Pearwood School. Jacqueline Amelia Davrot was accused of sexual harassment or, in the words of the parents making the complaint, of being a "voracious lesbian", preying unrelentingly on their daughter. The school, in the parent's opinion, had sought to cover up the incident, probably, they maintained, because the school saw lesbianism as something into which some girls had a natural right to evolve. There seemed to be a laissez-faire approach, it being regarded as inevitable in that apparently enlightened but misguided environment, that some girls would drift into such relationships only to drift out again later. So long as older girls did not force their attentions on younger ones a collective blind eye was turned.

All of this was in the statement provided by the offended parents. The school played it down. However, the phone call that Ruff had just made revealed that at age sixteen Jacqueline Amelia Davrot was asked to leave Pearwood. Expelled, in other words. The police had issued her with a reprimand.

Since 2004, the girl had been clean.

The database record also answered another question that had been bothering her since she first realized that the girl had attended a fee-paying school. How did Chas Davrot afford it? The answer was the Army paid and even though he quit in 2003 he seemed to have been paying the 2004 fees himself.

Jacqueline Amelia Davrot was also questioned in the same 2005 investigation into the death of the girl in Wiltshire as was her father. She had been a close friend of the dead girl, with a suspicion of a more intimate relationship.

Ruff found nothing worthwhile in these revelations. What continued to bug her was why Challis had mentioned Chas's lesbian daughter in the first place. That was the second out-of-the-blue query from her; first there had been what did she know about Vikings and now this. Ruff knew that superior officers often treated subordinates on a need-to-know basis but she hadn't ever thought Mel was like that, not with her anyway.

The phone rang. It was Sayer.

'Is your lovely leader there?'

'No, but her lovely assistant is.'

'Ha-ha, you certainly are. Good news and I hope you're duly grateful.'

'Depends.'

'On what?'

'On who's telling me.'

'Oh, I see. So no swapsies then. No tit for tat.'

Ruff lapsed into silence, wanting him to get on with it and strangle the innuendo at birth.

'Right,' he carried on. 'The rope, or to be more specific the knot in the rope, you remember, the more exotic knot, we found a drop of blood on it when we undid it.'

'And you got a match,' she stated the obvious. He wouldn't have called otherwise.

'Aren't you the clever detective. You should go all the way. Yes, a match with a guy called Charles Edward Davrot. Ring any bells?'

*

Jackie pulled up at the closed gates in front of Cottel Court. There were no lights to be seen beyond the gates.

The gloomy overcast day was just about hanging on. It was darkening and quiet. The car engine ticked over quietly. It wasn't usually shut up like this. She sat, wondering what to do next.

She had smiled to herself on the drive up, still thinking about Mel. She told lots of girls she was a model, just as she had with Mel last night. It was a good opener; a good chat-up line, got girls hooked. But she thought better of over-exaggerating her experience when talking to a policewoman. She may check up on her and discover she'd not done much actual modeling at all. She'd done some posing for photographs but that had been just after she'd left school at sixteen.

Then, her father was still living in Wiltshire, in Warminster where he'd bought a small house as an investment early in his Army career. Initially he rented it out but on leaving the Army he moved in, Jackie with him.

He worked as head of security at a safari – leisure park and he got her a job there, too, waitressing in Café Rouge. She met a girl there, a Polish girl, Teresa. They became lovers even though Teresa had a boyfriend, Marc. Teresa was in Housekeeping and had the keys to empty chalets where the two girls could go after work for an hour or so to try out every bed in the place.

Teresa lived in Frome, with Marc, who was into photography. She was amazed to discover he was a policeman and the stuff he was into. As she got older she realized how normal that could be. He persuaded Jackie to pose for him. She wouldn't do nude posing, not even just topless, not for him, but she managed some good-looking and enticing attitudes. She had a good body and her face could pull some teasing shapes. Teresa told her Marc fancied her and wanted her to fix something special up for the three of them. Much as Jackie enjoyed the sex with Teresa the idea of Marc joining them did absolutely nothing for her.

She had had sex with a boy when still at school; once. Disappointing. Since then, as far as males were concerned she signed the pledge.

Teresa was exciting to be with. She was experimental too and equally voracious. Jackie knew the name that had been pinned on her in school and she rather liked it but Teresa was far more deserving of the accolade.

Unfortunately they got carried away with their affair and their daily disappearances became noticed by a security colleague of her father's. They began to make use of lunch breaks to visit empty chalets. The security man saw them entering a chalet and, an hour later when he walked back that way, saw them coming out highly excited, giggling uncontrollably. He arrived at the more normal worst conclusion, that they were pinching stuff or on drugs so he thought a quiet word with Chas was the preferred option.

Chas began to keep an eye on them and he too soon noticed their regular ritual but there was no evidence of loot being hidden away anywhere and no reports of anything missing. One lunch break he followed them. They took one of the internal buses and Chas had to follow on a bike. They didn't go far before alighting and he watched them approach a chalet half-hidden behind a screen of trees. It was one of the more upmarket chalets, well detached, away from neighbours. They went in. Chas dropped his bike and crept to the nearest window.

Probably because of the chalet's location the girls didn't bother with the curtains and were immediately in each other's arms, kissing energetically, undressing each other at the same time. Chas was amazed. He had not seen his daughter naked for a while and his eyes were fixed on her. He moved back, not to lift his gaze away but to reduce the amount of himself that might be visible to those on the inside should they bother to take their eyes off each other. He checked quickly over his shoulder to make sure he could not be seen from the road. He had no intention of not watching.

He was in awe of Jackie's body. She was no longer his daughter. He ignored her face except when she bent to suck on Teresa's nipples, one after the other. She had magnificent breasts, large but not overly so, contrasting with Teresa's which were slightly smaller but firmer and becoming more so under what was obviously Jackie's expert ministrations. She bent lower, her rotund buttocks coming around and her generous thighs parting as she knelt. His breath caught in his throat. He didn't flinch. Teresa's hands were all over Jackie's shoulders and breasts and Jackie was squeezing Teresa's buttocks, one arm through her legs, the hand curling up, cupping her tightly. He could hear moans coming faintly through the window before Teresa lifted Jackie up, took her by the hand and led her to an open bedroom door.

Chas's lips were dry. He tried to lick them. He was out of breath and he hadn't even moved. Before the two girls had even disappeared into the bedroom he was on his feet, quickly judging the quickest way around the building to find another window. Out of the corner of her eye Jackie spied the movement, knew who it was and smiled with confirmation yet again that Chas was a pathetic man.

Chas Davrot told his colleague there was nothing to worry about; the girls were just fantasizing about living the good life, pretending they were the holiday-makers. They were doing no harm. Nothing to worry about.

Without a twinge of guilt or an ounce of shock at what he had not only witnessed but had enjoyed for over half an hour, he began to plan. What he had seen was a great display of lesbian love and he meant love; not the constructed lust that he was used to watching. That one of the participants was his daughter made no difference, probably enhanced the experience if he bothered even to think about it in that kind of detail. He was hooked, his taste buds tickled, his desire for more definitely aroused and unashamedly he wanted Jackie to continue to play a key role. It wouldn't be the same without her!

There were security cameras all around the site, some obtrusive, many unobtrusive. His idea was to designate a chalet as non-habitable, on some health and safety grounds or for urgent repair. That would be the reasoning for higher management to keep the chalet unavailable. For his own security team he told them it had been agreed to reserve a chalet for training purposes, part of which would require covert cameras to be set up. He explained that even pleasure resorts had to be cognizant of the threat of terrorism. What better place, he argued, to plan terrorist activity than somewhere dedicated to relaxation. A bunch of guys could come there for a week and hatch all kinds of plots. They had to be prepared.

A chalet was selected and cameras installed and only he had access to the control system that operated them.

Next, he let it be known to Teresa that a chalet was going to be permanently empty. He brought it up casually one day over coffee, making it sound as if it was just of interest from a housekeeping point of view. He made sure though that a key was available and that Teresa knew how to lay her hand on it.

That was it.

Teresa took the bait and she and Jackie started to enjoy the chalet. The cameras rolled, action was recorded and Chas soon found himself the owner of numerous recordings of the most genuine lesbian porn he had ever seen.

For five weeks he collected recordings. It would have gone on longer but for the fact that management came querying the unavailability of the chalet. He actually told them the terrorist story he had come up with earlier and was surprised that they were impressed by it. Some of them altruistically recognized the need to be just as vigilant as any other citizens should be. But then the summer bookings started coming in and the chalet was required and Chas was asked to dismantle his surveillance gear and return the chalet to normal use.

'Never mind,' Jackie said when he told her. 'You got what you wanted, didn't you?'

She was something else, his daughter. He took a lot of the credit himself but she hadn't needed a lot of coaching. She followed her mother and yet she had no desire to go live with her. Her mother's bisexuality had become something he couldn't live with; it had been that bad and probably Jackie felt that too.

'Yeah,' he agreed. 'It was okay. D'you want to see for yourself?'

She did, but she showed disgust at his suggestion. She knew where he kept his stuff. She could help herself anytime she wanted.

'When's the chalet becoming unavailable?' she asked.

'Work starts day after tomorrow. Time for another session or two.'

Work actually started the very next day so there was no time for any more of the same. She and her father hadn't talked about the monitoring while she and Teresa had been going at it full bore. Now that they had spoken of it the bubble had burst. She did go past the chalet one more time to see what was happening.

Unfortunately there was less secrecy over the decommissioning than there had been for the installation. While the cameras were being removed Teresa was ordered in to clean up the place.

She had adopted an innocent, dumb blonde inquisitorial style with the truly dumb guys who were removing the cameras from the chalet. By bending and dipping her body in flesh-flashing poses she quite easily got out of them that the cameras had been linked up to recording machines. One guy, a Romanian who worked in security, looked down from his step-ladder into her blue eyes and her revealing blouse and told her that Chas Davrot had set it all up as a training exercise 'for trapping terrorists' but that not much actual training had taken place.

When she told Marc his initial reaction was to beat the shit out of the guy but Teresa calmed him down, told him to think a bit more because she was convinced that there were videos that they needed to get hold of. Marc surprised her with this lateral thinking. 'Did Jackie set you up?' he asked.

That was a question that Teresa did not like to contemplate. It was sick enough that a father would video his own daughter doing what they had done together but if Jackie had been in on it, in on the planning, then that was even sicker. She couldn't believe it; wouldn't believe it.

'Have you told her?' Marc persisted.

'No.' Teresa was adamant in her answer but unsure deep down. She had always thought she was the controlling one in their relationship but you never know.

That was a surprise to Marc. 'You should. See what her reaction is.'

'I cannot,' Teresa was angry. 'It was her father for God's sake. How could I tell her that?'

'Did you know?' he asked quietly but firmly. 'Did you know you were being filmed? Did she tell you?

'Yeah,' she said. 'O' course. We both pose, show everything, what you think?'

Men! They think with their dicks. He's probably getting turned on by all this. 'But you would still like to fuck her wouldn't you, with me too?'

After that, they concentrated on what to do about Chas Davrot. Teresa told Marc he would be no pushover. He was a big man, ex-Army, ex-Duke of Wellingtons, tough guys. 'He keeps fit too. Always working out.'

Marc concluded he had to do things semi-legally. He was a policeman. He would raid Chas Davrot's house. He had to make it look official, get his mates involved. He needed to mock up a search warrant. Easy enough; plenty of examples around.

It took him a couple of weeks to get his mates on board, telling them the story that Teresa had been videoed in the showers, and to get the official-looking paperwork. The reason for the raid could be anything they liked: thefts from the leisure park, drugs or even the real reason, pornography; child pornography. Didn't matter. There would be four of them on the raid. Chas Davrot would be in no position to argue with them.

Marc and his colleagues were all from Frome. They could not be seen in uniform in Warminster or in a police car. They drove in a plain car to a park near Chas Davrot's house.

Chas Davrot had the shock of his life when he found four uniformed police officers at his front door. One of Marc's mates was a sergeant and he was well equipped to deal with Chas's objections. Another came in wielding a video camera.

'We have to record our activity,' the sergeant told a questioning Chas.

The fake search warrant was thrust into his hand and he gave it the most cursory of glances.

The videos were found among the large collection in Chas's bedroom. They were dated and had 'J&T' written on them with sequential numbers. Everything was bagged up. Chas was told that they would be examined and any found to contain illegal material would result in another call and serious charges would follow. He was not a man to be easily frightened but it put the wind up him and he let them go heavily laden and unchallenged.

By the autumn of 2005, Chas Davrot had met Stuart Devlin, his old mate from Iraq days, sold his house in Warminster and resigned his security job.

Jackie was long gone.

She had met a new female friend, an older woman, late twenties, on a short break at the park, and had gone off with her, for good she said, to Windsor where she lived. The woman was the new love of her life. Chas could see why. The woman could quite easily be the love of his life: strawberry blonde, blue-green eyes, full lipped, perfect face.

Chas knew his daughter. She would tire and come back. She'd find him in South Wales where his new job was, with Stuart Devlin's security company.

On his last day at work he was surprised when Teresa came to see him. She gave him something wrapped in leftover Christmas paper. She wished him good luck. He opened it after she had gone. It was a video, marked 'Raid on a pervert' and dated the day of the visit by the four policemen.

He cursed her. He had not heard anything from the police since that day and he had not bothered to enquire with them about the return of his property. His collection was gone. He was resigned to that and he just had to start again.

So she knew, everything, this Polish cow. He wondered if she still lusted after his daughter but Teresa had never thought of her again.

Marc, however, was a different case. He often played the videos, one-handed, when Teresa was out. It was the nearest he would ever come to realizing his fantasies.

*

A tap on the passenger window broke the silence. Her heart was in her throat. Lord de Cottel grinned at her through the glass. He opened the door and got in.

'Jackie my dear. You're early.'

She didn't know that she was.

'We're not in the main house,' he said, coming closer, his breath on her. 'We're in my cottage, at the back. Drive that way.' He pointed to the right. She turned the wheel, put her foot on the throttle and stalled the car. His lordship smiled and patted her trousered thigh reassuringly.

Thirty

'That bastard policewoman is outside.'

Meredith Guster closed the gap in her front curtains. Chas Davrot sat forward on the edge of the settee.

'She's talking to your daughter,' she told him as if accusing him. He couldn't think what the conversation could be about.

He stood, pulling his khaki jumper down. This was a cold house, he always thought, and dressed accordingly. He had on thick khaki socks, jeans and under the jumper was a denim shirt. At least her bed had an electric blanket. His own house in Monmouth was a lot warmer and cosier than this place but he didn't like taking Meredith there. This place of hers suited her better.

'Don't leave me alone with her,' Meredith pleaded but he ignored her.

'You'll be fine. Be helpful. Just don't tell her anything.'

There was a loud bang on the front door.

'By Christ,' he said, 'She sounds like some drunk coming back late to the doss house. I saw her yesterday. Looked like a puff of wind would blow her away. Go on then. Answer it before she knocks the bloody thing down.'

She made her way to the front door while Chas headed for the kitchen which was as far away from the front entrance as he could get without going upstairs.

'Miss Guster, we need to talk some more.' Challis was brisk and brusque. Guster barred the way or at least did not step aside to allow her in. 'More evidence has some to light. We can talk here or you can come to the station again.' Challis peered over her shoulder. 'You, too, Mr. Davrot. I need to talk to you.'

Guster looked back down the passageway as if to seek advice as to what to do. This gave room for Challis to slip by. She walked on leaving Guster to close the door behind them. She caught sight of Davrot's parka, hanging on the hallstand, deciding that she had to get it for analysis.

Instead of turning right into the room where she had been taken previously she walked straight on and into the kitchen. It was surprisingly modern. The units looked new, only mdf but new, the wall cupboards too. It was well lit by a strip of four low-energy bulbs in the ceiling.

Davrot was a big man. He leaned against the sink. He looked as if he was still Army wearing his khaki but his greying hair was not regulation length.

Challis waved her warrant card. 'Detective Sergeant Challis. You are Charles Edward Davrot, right?'

He made no sound or movement to deny or confirm. Challis out-stared him.

'You were here on Monday evening. Your company vehicle was seen parked outside here for some time.'

He grudgingly nodded. 'Yeah.'

'You weren't in the vehicle and you,' she turned to Guster, 'have stated that you were out shopping. So,' she turned back to Chas, 'where were you all this time?'

He remained silent.

'I have to remind you,' Challis went on, 'that Timothy Bush died that evening.'

'Suicide,' Chas mumbled.

'Timothy Bush died that evening. His body found early Tuesday by Miss Guster here.'

'In the field, over there, where he hung himself,' Chas insisted.

'Wrong. Timothy Bush did not die in that field. He actually died some miles away. He didn't hang himself from a tree at all. He hung himself from a wrought-iron gate, recently painted black.'

Chas remained impassive; stubbornly silent. Guster shifted from one foot to another, a movement that Challis caught out of the corner of her eye but she concentrated on Chas.

'D'you want to tell me about it? No? I didn't think so. Come on. Let's take a ride shall we?'

He stiffened. Challis knew he was too big for her to tackle. She had to appeal to his common sense.

'Captain,' she raised herself up and smiled. 'I like that, that you're able to retain your Army rank and use it as a title in civvy street. It must mean something to you, that. With me if I retire I could be known as ex-detective sergeant or former detective sergeant but you can actually still be known as what you were. Nice, I should imagine. Your achievements remain with you.' She smiled at Guster. 'Nice, eh?'

'Captain, I need you to come and make a statement. In fact I have to issue you with a caution now because I believe you have committed a series of offences in relation to the late Mr. Bush. O, we believe he killed himself, probably unaided, so there is nothing too serious, illegal nonetheless but not worth doing anything silly about. No need to make things worse.'

She turned again to Guster. 'No need for you to come again, Meredith. Not this time.'

Chas eased himself away from the sink and followed Challis back along the passageway. There was a distinct chill shooting through her. She's said the right things but she was not totally convinced that he was going to come quietly.

She shivered as she passed the foot of the stairs. 'Don't forget your coat. It's cold outside.'

He hesitated. 'It's not mine.'

'O but it must be. Meredith doesn't have one of those. She told us so the other day, didn't you?'

Guster said nothing and Chas didn't reach for the coat.

'I'll carry it for you,' Challis offered, pulling the parka off the hallstand.

As she opened her car door for him she switched on her smartphone to report in and got an immediate waiting message alert. She read it as Chas hesitated before getting in to the front passenger seat. It was from Ruff, about Chas and the blood on the rope.

She asked Chas to hold up.

'Standard procedure I'm afraid, Captain. Could you please put your hands behind your back for me.' She withdrew her handcuffs. He watched her. 'Turn around please and face the car. As I say this is standard procedure when an officer is bringing someone in alone. I'm sure you understand.' She hoped he fucking did!

For a long second or two he looked as if he might resist. She looked up into his eyes. 'You remember what we said inside, Captain.' She kept using his rank in an attempt to elevate his status, in his own mind at least.

He looked back at the house. Challis followed his gaze. Guster was standing in the doorway.

'Please,' Challis asked him again.

'This is totally unnecessary,' he said at last.

'I'm sure you understand.'

'No I don't as a matter of fact. If I wanted to take you out I could have done it at any time.'

'Yeah but that would have increased your problems dramatically.'

He thought and then grabbed her hand that held the handcuffs. 'No it wouldn't. You came to see her, not me. Didn't even know I was here.'

He was right about that, Challis realized, but she also knew that it was irrelevant.

His grip on her hand was strong. This was a new experience. In all her years she had never been grabbed like this by anyone taken in for questioning. It was weird; all she could think of to say was 'unhand me.' She tugged but his grip tightened, so much that she winced.

'Chas, cut it out.' It was Guster walking down the path with purpose. 'What good's that? Making things worse.'

He looked at her but Challis's eyes were still on him. 'She's right,' she breathed. 'Let go now and I'll forget to mention assault.'

His lips parted angrily but he eased his hand away from her. 'No cuffs,' he demanded.

'Get in the car please.' She shook her hand, changing the handcuffs to her left hand before slipping them back in a pocket. 'In the front.' She bent to pick up the parka that had slipped from her hand.

As he got in she looked back at Guster wondering if she should invite her along, as a bodyguard. The woman stood in the chill air with her arms wrapped across her chest. Grudgingly, Challis mentally gave her a thank you.

Before she drove off Challis turned to Chas and quietly gave him an official caution.

Thirty-One

Two hours later, Charles Edward Davrot had been charged with perverting the course of justice, illegal handling of a corpse and interfering with the coroner's investigation. He had denied it all. When confronted with the DNA evidence from his blood found on the suicide rope he maintained he had given Timothy Bush the rope some time before when his car had broken down and needed a tow. Ruff had made sure she had a good look at his hands as he'd come in and she spotted a nice cut on his right hand between thumb and forefinger.

She had also done her homework. She had followed one of Sayer's initial suggestions and had traced purchases made by Timothy Bush and found they included the purchase of the rope from B&Q in Cwmbran the weekend before. When they asked him Chas couldn't come up with a plausible story as to where the rope came from or precisely when and where he had given it to Timothy Bush. He knew if he did they would be able to check dates and places.

His parka had been sent off to Forensics.

Challis expounded their theory to him.

Timothy Bush had hung himself from the gates of Cottel Court. Bad for business if that got out. So Chas had moved the body. Either he was a very diligent employee...okay, contracted employee...and did it off his own bat for the good of the employer or he had been asked, ordered, to remove it. Could have buried the body but why bother when the death was nothing to feel guilty about. Or was it? Come to that later. So just move him to look as if he hung himself somewhere else entirely. Near his home, for instance. Next door but one to Miss Guster, a colleague and a lover of Chas. Was it her idea? String poor Mr. Bush up from the oak tree in the field using a very intricate military knot and bring his vehicle back to his house. Sorted. And, of course, not forgetting his clothes. The big question of course is why he hung himself at Cottel Court and why naked? An interesting question for a criminal psychologist. Any ideas yourself?

Chas remained silent.

'Oh dear,' Challis continued. 'Captain, you know what goes on a Cottel Court, I guess. The jollies at weekends and other times.'

'Not particularly.'

'But enough I reckon. Now, your Miss Guster had encouraged Timothy Bush to join in the fun and games, for some months now. She knew all about it so you must have too. But at the last... meeting something rather unfortunate happened. It was a rare coincidence we think; we hope. And it seems that he got involved with an activity that really got to him later. Deeply. Troubled him deeply. He may well have flipped completely. He did himself some self-harm – you must have seen it; Miss Guster did and that's why she had to cover it up with an old pair of her ex-husband's y-fronts. She could have used Timothy Bush's pants brought back in the car but they were awful grubby. She's surprisingly fastidious, your Miss Guster. Anyway, back to the why and where he killed himself. I believe, and I'm no expert, that he, at the very least, blamed Cottel Court for what he done that last weekend or he realized that what went on there was truly abhorrent and that the whole world should know. And thanks to your efforts the whole world will probably know, when this comes to court, both for your trial and the coroner's inquest. News of the World; right up their street. You could of course minimize the impact of your case by pleading guilty, after all you went to great lengths to keep it quiet, shame if it all proves to be a waste of time.'

She rose, indicating to Ruff that the recording should end. 'We'll leave you to mull things over.'

*

Jackie had never been in his lordship's cottage before. From the outside the place looked modest, too modest for a peer of the realm, she thought.

Lord de Cottel led Jackie into a fairly large room. It must have been an extension to the original building, she surmised.

'This is our Art room normally,' he told her, his hand propelling her gently across the threshold. 'During daylight the large windows let in a lot of natural light, ideal for the artist.'

Jackie saw large brown curtains over on the right-hand side of the room and guessed the windows were behind those. There was a dais up against the far wall, stretching virtually the whole length. An arrangement of coloured drapes hung from the ceiling at the back of the platform. A selection of seatings was available: a flat quilted bench, a plump armchair with a very upright back that made her think of a dentist's chair and a couple of foot-stools.

In front of the dais, at each side, were two tripods waiting for cameras. The dais itself reached forward so that it took up at least half of the room.

'The models pose up there,' he said, pointing. 'Please, step forward.'

He charmingly offered her his hand to assist her up onto the platform. She declined, stepping lightly upwards. He followed her up, stiff at the knees.

'Depending on what our artists want, the model will be standing or seated on one of these…I have no idea how these things are arranged. I may sometimes come in at the start and introduce myself but I'm not at all artistic myself. I doubt if could draw a state pension.' He laughed.

'I thought all of this would be in the big house,' she queried.

'Oh, no, no. We did try that but the natural light is no good. And people find this more sympathetique, more intimate.'

He had a leer in his voice that convinced Jackie again that he was a dirty old man. She was glad to see the film crew of two come in through the door. She knew them both from previous sessions. One was a make-up, continuity (that was a joke) and sound man; the other was the cameraman, director and script-writer (another joke, at best he could be called an ideas man).

They greeted her and straight away started to set up. She could see from the camera angle that she would be performing on the dais.

'Who'm I with tonight?' she asked the director.

'It's Sue, just for you,' he replied with a flourish of his hand and a smile at his little bit of rhyming.

Sue Chance or, as she liked to be billed, Sioux Chaste. She and Sue had performed before, she under the name of Jacqui Davroux.

171

'As you can see from the camera setup you two will be on the stage. The initial shots will be from floor level, up into the action. We're calling this one 'Lust in a Studio'.'

The ideas man was out of ideas.

'Can we have the heating up?' Jackie asked his lordship.

'Really? It's warm enough isn't it?'

'If you're wearing a coat like yours, yes, but Sue and I will be less well protected.'

'We don't want shots full of goosebumps,' the continuity man added.

'I'll turn it up nearer the time.'

Sue Chance came in with Stuart Devlin close behind her. Jackie knew Stuart better than she did Sue. She'd known him since Chas started working for him. Stuart had tried to make them into an item but he soon understood that Jackie was not and never would be interested in him. Sue was his current companion.

Jackie and Sue kissed and embraced. She gave Stuart a casual hello.

Top coats came off. The two techies completed their setup and took the girls through a quick camera and lighting check.

'We're ready to roll,' the director man said, trying to sound as if he was about to shoot a masterpiece that would win a dozen Oscars.

Jackie stood centre-dais, hands on hips.

'Heating turned up now please. And no spectators. Bye Stuart. See you later.'

He gave her a watery smile. She could be an arrogant bitch.

'Okay, Jackie,' he whined. 'O, by the way, before I forget. Chas has just been arrested.'

There was a message waiting on Jackie's phone. Back in her car, her breathing recovered, she had powered it on and heard Meredith's icy voice. She was telling her that Chas had been arrested.

Stuart Devlin had come back into the room after the filming. By the look on his face he'd been watching everything they'd been doing somehow or other. He made a smiling beeline for Sue, obviously turned on.

Jackie wanted more information about Chas. Stuart's bombshell had put her off and from the start of the filming she had been uncontrollably rough with Sue. Not only that but Sue's expert ministrations had no pleasurable effects on her at all. Jackie was pro enough to make the right noises and the director man said it was one of their best sessions he'd ever filmed.

'You were something else tonight Jackie.'

Stuart could tell her nothing more about Chas.

It was pitch black outside his lordship's cottage. The motion-sensor light had gone out. She turned on the car's interior light and called Meredith. She and Meredith did not get on and it annoyed her that the woman should know of Chas's arrest before she did. The other thing that was making her seethe was the realization that it must have been Mel who had arrested him.

Meredith confirmed it; that was what had happened just after she had left them. Later he had phoned her to tell her he'd been charged with various offences that she couldn't recall specifically but were all to do with moving the body of Timothy Bush. She was his one phone call and he asked her to ask Stuart Devlin to get his solicitor on the case.

'Then why didn't you?' Jackie shouted.

'I did. What d'you think?' Meredith shouted back. 'He said he'd do it.'

Then why hadn't he said anything just now? Because all he could think about was humping Sue, that's why. And on film more than likely. That man's every emotion began and ended with his cock.

She hung up. There was nothing more to say. She thought quickly and realized there was much that she now had to do.

Thirty-Two

Angela Plumitis stirred in her bed when she heard the front door close. She winced. She hadn't really been asleep, just dozing. Sleep was difficult when you couldn't get comfortable, when you couldn't find a position that didn't hurt.

Footsteps came up the stairs. They were light and took the steps quickly. She recognized them. Having lain up there in bed off and on for nearly three weeks she had had plenty of opportunity. It was Jackie.

Good.

Jackie came in through the door, already ajar.

'Hi, Angel.' Jackie saw the pain etched on the face of the woman she loved. Her lovely blonde hair lay lank and stringy on the pillow and those perfect lips were drained of all colour. Angel's hands pulled at the duvet as she tried to raise herself up.

Each time she entered their bedroom Jackie hoped to see the unblemished beauty returned. Angel was always a joy to behold and so easy to love.

Jackie had seen that the bedside light was on as she parked the car. It was gone ten but Angel was still awake. She had hurried back to Monmouth as she knew that Angel would have been on her own for some hours. She had to go out again, now, straight away but she would spend a moment or two at the bedside. She'd be back later.

Angel lay in a three-quarter bed. There was a double duvet on it and the room was warm from the double-radiator under the window. The gown she borrowed off Jackie was draped across the foot of the bed. It was Jackie's room normally and her things were very evident on the dressing table. The large wardrobe close to the door was full of her clothes. Angela's suitcase was on the floor near the radiator, the lid was up and the small pile of clothes within it was beginning to look more haphazard, roughly sorted through.

It was not easy sharing the bed. Much as she loved sleeping with Angel she had to be so careful how she moved. Once she had inadvertently put her knee into Angel's abdomen bringing out a heart-rending cry.

'How is it?'

'Not too bad,' Angela lied.

Jackie stroked her forehead. She was hotter.

'Angel, you must see someone…'

Angel shook her head vigourously. 'No. You know I can't, especially not now.'

Jackie knew all the objections.

Hospital could mean the police getting involved; Angel kept warning them of that. The pain in her back passage had been bad from the start. All those weeks ago she had limped out of Cottel Court, bleeding. Chas had been there, thank God. He held her up; he held her close. He'd decided to take her to his place rather than let her go back to Meredith's house. Meredith would have no sympathy but he knew that Jackie would do anything for Angel.

'God, they're fucking animals.' Jackie's anger had boiled as Angel told what had happened. 'Why do you do it, Angel? Why do you let yourself get into these things with those men?'

Jackie could never understand how Angel got turned on by the extreme Vikings scene. She couldn't or didn't want to understand why Angel would want men at all but to offer herself up to be callously ravished was completely out of her zone. She knew injuries had happened to her before but not as bad as these seemed to be.

She'd put Angel in the bath which seemed to ease her. She gave her a brandy, then another, as she bathed her all over, removing all the stains from her body and gently, very gently, swilling between her legs. Angela took over the douching of that particular area. She couldn't trust even Jackie to be careful enough and even then tears flowed as she tried to dab the soreness. That was only treating the external manifestation of the injuries inflicted upon her. She guessed that, internally, she was equally torn. Give it a few days, it'll go; it had before.

She knew the risks. She enjoyed the risks. Men wanted to brutally rape a woman and she wanted to be brutally raped. There was a safety code but a couple of those guys were new and didn't know it. She had screamed all the way through; that was the thrill they all wanted. But her screams and shouts to stop became more genuine, simply stirring the men to greater excitement and she just had to wait for them to come to their conclusion by which time she was silent and in a virtual dead faint.

Chas blamed himself. One of his duties was to keep an eye on things so they didn't get out of hand. But it was a busy weekend and that day, the last day, a Sunday, saw day members come in to join the weekend people. And he told his daughter he was distracted, called back to the big house. When he saw the state that Angel was in he could have gone for the men there and then but they had vanished, leaving Angel in the abused heap of reeking dampness that she had become. The *Vikings* had all admired her greatly and were bent on returning another day to repeat the experience. But not if Chas could do anything about it!

She seemed to be on the mend. A week later she was up and about, at least some of the time. But something happened, some traumatic episode in the bathroom, and she re-appeared down the stairs bent double, bleeding again. She tried to maintain that it was not too bad but Jackie heard her in the middle of the night, trying not to cry out in bathroom as she tried to move her bowels. She stopped eating. If nothing went in, nothing could want to come out. But it did little good and for the last week the pain had been constant.

It tore Jackie apart. She and Chas did what they could but they couldn't be with her all of the time. When they went out they carried on as normal; Chas with Meredith, Jackie prowling the pubs.

But together they berated the men who had done this to Angel. They both knew that they loved the woman.

Angel had always enjoyed the loving ministrations in which Jackie was expert; Jackie the love she wanted but men were the brutes she needed.

Chas had let Jackie rave. But the men had been bastards and they must never be allowed to do that to Angel again.

'I have to go out again. Chas has been arrested. So I have to go out instead.'

'No.'

'Yes.'

Jackie bent and kissed her forehead then ran her fingers lightly through the greasy hair.

'Is there anything you want before I go?'

'No, don't go.'

'You have water here. Anything to eat?'

'My spare inhaler. In my bag. Just in case.'

Jackie retrieved the inhaler from the suitcase.

Angel had one leg out of the bed.

'Where are you going?' Jackie asked her anxiously.

'With you.'

'No you're not, my lovely girl.'

She took Angel by the shoulders and eased her back down to a near horizontal position. The leg that was out looked flabby and Jackie pulled a silent face. As Angel lay back to allow her leg to be put under the duvet she took Jackie's hand.

'Please don't do it, it's stupid. You'll get arrested too.'

'Chas has been arrested because he messed with the suicide man. Nothing else.'

'I still don't want you to go. God I wish I'd never said yes in the first place. Stop it now. Nobody's to blame but me. It happens. It's one of those things. Remember what I told you: pleasure and pain, same beast.'

She tried to sit up again but moved too quickly. A spasm of intense pain shot through her abdomen. Her tightening hold on Jackie's hand drew a loud scream from her lips. 'Angel!'

But Angel was gripped by such agony that she heard nothing. She was groaning loudly, her whole body stiff, motionless, as if she was scared to move a single muscle. Her breathing stopped then started again until gradually the pain subsided. Her face was grey. Jackie pulled her hand clear.

'When I get back I'm taking you to the hospital. No ifs, no buts.'

'Take me now then. Don't go anywhere else. Take me now.'

'I won't be long.' Jackie leaned forward and kissed her on her dry lips. 'I love you.' There was no response from Angel. She was drained of all energy.

In Chas's room Jackie found the key to his cupboard. It opened, squeaking on its stiff hinges. Chas had prepared everything for tonight. She took his operational bag, lay it on the floor, unzipped it and peered inside. Gently, her hand slid inside and moved the contents around. Everything she needed was within.

She closed the cupboard doors slowly, pausing to examine items stored there. On a top shelf she saw the dvd with its printed label where Chas had left it. "Vikings 30th January 2011. Mr. George Medlyn. Paid in advance" and on the floor of the cupboard two laptops, a couple of external hard-drives and a bag of memory sticks.

*

It was ten-ten as Challis walked down the stairs, only two flights from the office to the exit. Her feet rang on the steps. She would have run if she'd had the energy. Her lack of fitness worried her. Perhaps a jog in the morning.

She had sent Ruff home half an hour ago and then sat down at her desk to finish off the Charles Edward Davrot paperwork. He had signed a statement, admitting his guilt on the charges. Both she and Ruff were pleased with the result. Smiles all round. A good way to end the day; end the week! She'd decided to keep Chas in custody overnight. He could be bailed in the morning; she'd have no objection to that. The offences were serious but not enough to take up cell space and resources.

But it was late. She had planned to call in on Redland. Not at this hour though. He's probably in bed. Certainly should be.

Rounding the last bend she found herself face to face with Superintendent O'Halloran.

'Challis,' he shouted into her face. 'What the fuck do you think you're playing at?'

My God, that smacked her in the guts all right.

'Sir?'

'You gave DCI Moray Lockett and Muench. He's not even in work. She wanted two people. No, she needed two people. Now! And you gave her Muench who's on the sick.'

O Christ. She'd hoped she'd got away with that. Her tired brain juggled with possible retorts but all she could think of was Redland's favourite expression when the savages from upstairs were on the warpath: *shoot your horse and take cover!*

'Sir, there's no sick note from him. He'll be in. I've emailed him…texted him…to tell him he's reassigned and where to report. If I'd handed over Kay…DC Ruff…I'd have been down to a team of one, me, and we were at a critical…'

'If he's not on-site with DCI Moray first thing tomorrow…'

'It's Saturday…'

'If he's not on-site with DCI Moray first thing tomorrow you and Ruff will be up there in Blackwood. No arguments.'

'He'll be there, sir.'

Muench would jump at the chance of getting in on a big murder enquiry; she was banking on it. In her mind though she couldn't help thinking that one more body on the team that already numbered over fifty, so she'd heard, would not make that much difference.

'How is the case going, sir?'

'Some of us have been up there all day, getting nowhere because we're pissed about by the likes of you, Challis.'

Charming, she thought.

'He'd better be there or your arse won't touch the ground. This is the biggest case we've had here for years. There's no motive, no suspects, but a lunatic out there somewhere with a gun, frightening the entire populace of the western valley.'

'We've just cleared up the suicide case, sir.' She thought that might cheer him up.

'Suicide? It's taken you a week to sort out a suicide?'

'Four days, sir. Not straightforward. We've just charged a man with obstruction, perverting the course of...'

'What?' he sounded weary.

'He moved the body, to save his employer the embarrassment of finding it on his property.'

'I think you and your team are a fucking shambles. First the Henderson fiasco now this...embarrassment. Drop it.'

'Sir?'

'Is it a suicide or not.?'

'Well, yes, but...'

'Then drop it.'

'Can't do that. The coroner will know all the facts.'

'Then caution the man and send him on his way. Just clear it out. Don't clutter the system up with unnecessaries. Times are changing, Challis. Wake up woman. Time to streamline. We won't have the resources; haven't got the resources. Cut-backs up, sick leave up, so get the workload down. Got it. Caution him. Get it sorted.'

He jumped onto the first step. 'And make sure Muench is there first thing.'

She watched him go. She caught sight of the back of his neck. The boss was right; it was as red as a stop light.

*

Jackie Davrot got home at ten minutes past one. The drive back to Monmouth had been uneventful although her fuel light had been on for most of it. She cursed Chas for forgetting to top it up, the tight arse! That could have been very awkward.

The front door slammed behind her, slipping from her hand as she tried to make a silent entry. She halted inside, leaning back on it, listening for any sound from upstairs. She didn't want to wake Angel because, now, with no petrol in the tank, there was no way she could get her to the hospital. Unless she called an ambulance.

Quietly as she could she leapt up the stairs, Chas's bag banging on the rails. Dropping it on the landing she went into her room.

The bedside light was on, dimly. The room was warm, too warm, she thought. Angel seemed to be asleep. There was a packet of Ibuprofen on the bedside table. She had told Angel to pop a few to ease the pain.

Angel was very still. Her face was pale. Jackie was breathing hard after the run up the stairs but she tried to silence her gasps for air. As she got closer to the bed she saw again how frail and fragile her beautiful Angel was. She looked so weak but she was breathing, she could see her chest rising and falling, albeit shallowly. She leaned forward and tested her temperature by laying her lips on Angel's forehead. Still warm but so was the room. Angel was no warmer than that.

Jackie had always loved looking at Angel when she slept. Bill Withers came into her mind yet again: '*when I look at you then the World's all right with me*'. Lovely Day.

She loved this woman. She made love to other women but she loved this one; had, since day one. Chas did too. Chas had fallen for Angel. For all her desperate needs Angel was a woman you could not help but love. They had both realized all along that this was a woman for whom they would do anything; hence they were where they were now.

Chas had not had Angel, Jackie knew that. She had though, many times, because that too was where Angel expressed her love and tenderness. All the rest that Angel did with men was animal instinct, a gruesome inborn fetish that had to be sated from time to time. Jackie understood. She too needed other things from other women, never from men. Chas had found Angel's extremes too extreme for him. He consoled himself with Meredith Guster.

Angel was lying right down the middle of the bed. Much as she would have loved to get in with her and give her close comfort Jackie could see she would only disturb the sleeping beauty.

She decided to leave the light on.

Picking up the bag where she had dropped it on the landing she took it into Chas's empty room. He would not be home tonight. Locked up for the night, by that Mel!

His bed was free.

The cupboard was still unlocked. She opened the bag and removed a laptop and an external hard drive. She had no idea why Chas insisted on retrieving all this hardware but she thought she'd best comply. They went on the floor of the cupboard.

She took a dvd from the bag. She was shaking, trembling from head to foot. Chas hadn't warned her about what she might find. She had found the dvd, that had been easier than she thought. She stared unblinking at it before lowering it slowly, her hand all pins and needles, to the pile on the top shelf.

There was an unpleasant smell emanating from the bag. She knew what that was. Clean it in the morning.

She locked the cupboard, undressed, got into bed in her underwear and fell asleep immediately. At two-thirty, she was in a deep sleep when a piercing scream from her own room next-door woke her, eyes immediately wide and fearful.

Thirty-Three

Challis woke at six-thirty. She had deliberately left her bedroom curtains undrawn the night before so that emerging daylight would get in unhindered. Barely awake she was not sure that the resolution of last night was still burning in her breast.

On her back she stared through barely open eyelids out of the window opposite. The morning was grey and she could see mist over the ancient volcano. Not really a volcano but a lava pipe from umpteen million years ago. Geologists said it drilled down many kilometers into the Earth's crust. She had gone up there when she was much younger and was disappointed at the miniscule crater she eventually found. Hell of a view from up there though. You could see northwards into the heart of the county and westwards towards the iron age/Roman/Norman hilltop fort of Twm Barlwm. It never failed to stir her.

That thought was enough to rouse her. She searched out her tracksuit and some warm under-clothes, good thick socks and her trainers. No shower now; she'd have that later. Just a quick swill in the en-suite.

Downstairs, she did herself a glass of orange juice and grabbed a couple of chocolate biscuits.

Phone!

She jogged up the stairs to get her smartphone. This was a must. A young neighbour had recently cycled into a bed of potholes on the Usk flood route, a quiet lane that skirted the flood-prone river valley. She'd had no phone with her and had to limp with a fractured leg to the nearest house. Could have been worse; she could have lain there for hours unnoticed.

She made sure she did some hamstring stretches and toe-touching before setting off. Her usual route would be up the hill to the alms-houses but this was her first serious exercise for a couple of months. She decided to run up to the main road and then the gentler slope up the other side.

At a slow pace she set off.

It was a still morning, no movement of air to shift the mist and pall of stale wood-smoke hanging over the brook that ran through Capelgwm. The village was quiet, sensible people taking their time this Saturday morning. She could hear a cockerel some distance off and a dog even further away she guessed. As she crossed the brook early morning blackbirds flew up from the leaf litter. Overhead, high up, a mistle thrush was trying out a song. Challis recognized the blackbirds but was no good with birdsong. Her father had been an expert and tried to educate her but it all went in one ear and out the other, his words and the birdsong.

At least she could hear all these sounds of the country. She had foresworn the use of an MP3 player. There was something completely wrong about running through the still countryside with incongruous music pounding in your ears. Not even country music and least of all folk rock would be compatible.

Anyway, as a police officer, she had to believe the advice of her colleagues in the Road Traffic section who were about to launch a campaign to dissuade joggers and cyclists from wearing anything on the ears that impeded their ability to hear other traffic. There had been an increase in road accidents of late where these audio machines were in use by one or more parties. There were moves afoot to begin to lobby for a change to the law as per the use of mobile phones to make it illegal for cyclists to cover their ears.

Not too far behind Road Traffic's concerns were those of the Crime Prevention Unit. Female joggers in earphones had been assaulted by assailants coming upon them completely unnoticed. One girl had been abducted by a vanload of youths who pulled up right behind her and bundled her in. One witness said the girl appeared to have no idea they were there until it was too late. She was raped and dumped.

Though she was a country girl Challis had not absorbed some of its aspects: no pony for her, a bike, yes, and later, a motorized version. But she did like to run through the lanes, to have them all to herself. Good for thinking. Although this morning she didn't know what to think about.

O'Halloran, Chas Davrot, Timothy Bush, Cottel Court, even Jackie. And Stuart Devlin. All had plagued her mind the night before. She'd forgotten about them this morning, until now. Not much of an achievement. Relax. Breathe. In a while, stretch the legs and concentrate on not getting the stitch.

She crossed the empty main road and straight on, passing the village hall on her left. Now she was back on a narrower road, a main road nonetheless that cut across the plateau that eventually dropped down into the Wye Valley. But that was kilometers away. She would get nowhere near that spectacular scenery, not on foot.

Half a kilometer further on she felt good enough to take a right that led up a single-lane track. It was a fairly steep pitch in places but had level bits and the odd dip down again but its general inclination was upwards. She'd done it before, last time last autumn. It was good route in that you had to work hard up the steep bits but could then coast on the flat bits. Her aim was to not stop at all until she reached the summit where there was a detached house on one side and a farm gate on the other, on which she would lean, suck in air and try to relish the view through watering eyes.

She was doing all right. She didn't overdo it, keeping within herself.

The lane, for that was what it was, was bordered by high hedges with occasional gaps that allowed a spreading vista to be seen. The centre of the track was a strip of grass at best or a muddy streak at worst. She zigzagged from one side to the other as much to vary the run as to ease the steepness of climb. If within herself enough she would jump the central reservation to give even more variety to the exercise.

There were birds everywhere, flying up ahead of her. Most were strangers to her but they were uplifting. On the first flat stretch the hedge to the north disappeared giving a breath-taking sight of a blanket of mist through which bare branches stood high as if growing out of it. It was good, good for the soul. Even in the depths of late winter this was a beautiful county.

She was inspired to up the pace and covered the flat bit at speed and maintained it up the next slope, for a little while anyway. Three more bends and she'd be at the top. She tried to look ahead and was sure there was no mist or low cloud up there.

Her heart was pounding but she was okay. Her legs were holding up. She put her head down, ignoring more opportunities to look at the scenery. She'd done a half-marathon once; thought she was Paula Radcliffe when she was out pounding the roads. A few times she'd had to pop over the gate at the top of this lane for a pee.

There it was, the farm gate. She sprinted to it. O shit! She'd forgotten to see what time it was when she'd set off. She should have started the stopwatch app on her smartphone.

The metal gate was cold. It reminded her of last Monday afternoon at Pontderry Lane and the boss came into her mind as she struggled for breath, probably like he had when he had his seizure.

A dog startled her. She looked down. An off-white hairy thing was snuffling around her feet. It wasn't small like a lapdog and it wasn't large like an Alsatian. It was somewhere in between. She wasn't good at dog identification, always useless at it. When she was a PC out on the street and some old girl would come up to report her dog was missing Challis was expected to fill in most of the description just from the name of the breed. Hopeless. No chance.

Challis looked up and down the lane. People walked their dogs up there but no-one was in sight. Where d'you come from? Must be the house, the Mack's house.

She knew of Peter Mack. She knew who he was and that he lived in the detached house opposite. She'd seen his wife about but never spoken to her. He was a solicitor in Newport but she'd never come across him in work. He didn't do criminal. He was into the more lucrative strata of the legal profession.

The dog was still round her feet. He was picking up and dropping something, obviously wanting her to play. It looked like a slipper, dark brown, a man's judging by the size and style. She bent but the dog immediately grabbed it in its mouth and growled. Challis knew little about dogs and could not interpret the canine sounds and actions. The dye in the slipper must have been running due to the dog's saliva; there was dark red juice on its muzzle.

She put her hands on her hips and began deep breathing recovery again; chest in, chest out. She began to stroll on towards the gate into the Mack property. The dog ran on, managing a muffled bark with the slipper in its mouth. It dived under the bottom rung of the wooden gate and on towards the front of the house.

As Challis drew alongside she could see that the front door was open. The dog had dropped the slipper and was trying to take hold of another one, the other one of the pair but it wouldn't budge. It was still attached to a foot. The body that the foot belonged to was lying inside the door. Its feet protruded outside and bare legs could be seen but the rest was hidden.

Challis froze for a moment and then unlatched the gate.

She stepped up the drive, calling out. 'Hello, hello.' And then, making an assumption, she called. 'Mr. Mack?'

She moved at an angle so that she could see through the gap in the doorway. It was a man all right. He was on his back, clad in a beige gown that had ridden up and exposed his lower abdomen. She could see a patch of red there, between his legs. She hurried forward but not before she looked left, right and behind her, a full three-sixty degrees, to check for anything that her police brain should log. The Mack's garage was on the right-hand side of the house, the drive bent towards the door that was in a closed position. Nothing else of note.

'Here boy.' She called to the dog, ignorant of its sex but hoping it would come away from the body. It looked up at her but put its head down again, now licking the pool of red between the man's legs.

She couldn't hesitate. The dog was engrossed in what it was doing and she was able to reach down and grab the collar. She dragged it away from the body. Now what to do with it? She needed to check the man's vital signs. Pulling on the collar and probably half-strangling it she dragged the dog to the garage. It wasn't locked. She heaved the door up and threw the choking dog inside, dropping the door before it could run back out. If there was an open connecting door to the house, too bad; she had a window of time to do what was needed.

The man was dead and he was Mr. Peter Mack. There was a hole in his forehead, some blood had oozed from it but there was a lot more under his head where the bullet had come out. His thinning, greying hair was coated. It looked as if the dog had licked there too and there were bloody paw-prints everywhere.

Peter Mack was a tall man, a big man in all departments. She allowed herself the thought; Sayer would be vindicated by her noticing. It was odd. The Meredith Guster urge to cover him up hit her. She resisted the temptation, reaching for his hand. The body was stone cold.

She took out her smartphone and dialed Control direct. Her speech was constrained by urges to retch. Thank God the stomach was empty!

The dog in the garage was howling.

'Mrs. Mack.' Challis had called the name several times. Other than the barking dog there was silence. No birds singing now.

She didn't want to compromise the scene but she had to ascertain if Mrs. Mack – what was her first name? – was in the house. Peter Mack had been dead for some time, so where was his wife? If she was okay why hadn't she called for help?

Challis checked all the downstairs rooms. There were three: a study at the front, a dining room and a lounge. The study was a mess. From the threshold she could see dvds, cds and papers scattered on the floor. There was no computer but there was peripheral equipment like printers. She was reminded of Timothy Bush's house, one aspect of the suicide that she hadn't satisfactorily explained as yet.

The dining room and lounge room doors were closed. She pulled her track suit sleeves down over her hands and opened them. No sign of any disturbance in either room. Across the wide hallway was a door into a large kitchen. The cooking area was at the far end, an eating place this end. All clear. In the far wall another doorway led to a rear room, a scullery. She carefully crossed to it. It was a white-goods room with a toilet off it.

She retraced her steps. Out of the kitchen door the ornate staircase swept up and around to the bedrooms. There were bloody paw-prints on the stair carpet. She went up, staying close to the wall.

Her flesh was tingling as she reached the top of the stairs. More deep breaths.

On the left, was a bedroom door, ajar. She eased it fully open and immediately found Mrs. Mack. The woman was lying in the bed. Unlike her husband she was naked, at least her chest was naked. Her lower half was under the bed-sheet. She seemed to be in an upright sitting position, leaning back on a pile of pillows. Near her left breast there was a mass of blood. It had run down her body, onto the bedding and the TV remote control that lay near her right hand. Challis drew closer and could see the clotted blood filling the bullet hole that was as near as damn it to the heart. Standing over her, Challis let her eyes run up and down the flesh that she could see. The woman was well-rounded, her face subtly made up, her full lips glossed. Oddly, one eye was half closed, the other, green, wide open, staring straight ahead as if still looking at her killer. Challis followed the eye line. The killer had been at the end of the bed, slightly to the left, between the bed and the plasma TV screen, a forty inch, still on but no picture. Looking back, she saw that Mrs. Mack's blonde hair was a wig. It had pulled to one side, probably as the bullet had jolted her. Her own dark hair could just be made out: probably not natural either.

This body too was stone cold.

Challis felt stone cold herself. Shouldn't be after the run and the fact that the heating in the house was going full blast. She made sure her eyes scanned the room for anything obvious, no idea what, but you could never tell what might jump out at you.

Nothing as far as she could tell.

She couldn't remember if the Macks had children. She hoped not. Except for the unhappy, yapping dog, the house was so still.

There were three other bedrooms and a communal bathroom. All doors were shut. The carpeted floor on the landing and down the passageway was clear of bloody paw-prints so she was less circumspect about where she placed her feet. She had to step into the bathroom to check inside the shower. Clean. In the first bedroom the single bed was made up but unused, certainly last night. The next was in a similar state and the final one was not kept as a bedroom but had two wardrobes, one built-in, a chest of drawers and a wooden trunk.

All clear. Thank God.

On her way back down the stairs she heard the siren of a police car. With a long stride she stepped over Peter Mack.

She ran to the gate in time to flag down the car. She recognized PC Billy Bell before he'd got out. Tremendous relief at seeing him. He was alone. For his own part, he saw this slim, dark-haired, tracksuited woman who looked familiar but he couldn't recall how he knew her.

He stepped out of the car, putting his hat on. He was wearing his tunic and he thought for a moment about retrieving his yellow waterproof out of the back.

'Billy Bell,' Challis called, smiling inside if not facially.

He looked at her and it dawned on him. 'Sarge?' He approached her. 'They said officer already on-site. What, you called it in?'

She nodded. 'Two dead. Both shot.' Her voice was shaky now.

'You okay?'

'Yeah,' although she was sure she didn't look it. 'Come out for an early morning run and you find a dead couple. Happens all the time.'

She noticed now that Billy Bell's car was blocking the lane. 'Pull into that gateway over there,' she suggested. 'It's going to get a bit busy here soon.'

'You live around here?' he asked as he returned to the car.

'Capelgwm.'

The face that he pulled showed that he was impressed with the distance and terrain she'd covered.

When he'd parked as she had instructed she got him to take cones out of his boot and block the lane. She couldn't be sure that other vehicles would come up the same way that he had.

'Where's your mate?' she asked.

'On a sickie.'

He'd just have to operate both ends of the road block on his own, moving cones as required.

'Is there a dog in there?' Billy Bell asked. The Mack's dog was barking again in the garage.

'I had to lock him in. He was…interfering with the evidence.'

'Who are they? D'you know?'

She told him the names and then she went on and told him precisely what she'd seen in the house.

'Shit,' he said. 'First Blackwood and now this. Not the same guy is it?'

She couldn't see how. She'd forgotten about Blackwood.

This is going to test O'Halloran's resource allocation.

The next hour saw scene-of-crime officers arrive in dribs and drabs. Sayer was not among them. He'd called Challis to ask her where the hell she was; he was lost. She had already sent her location co-ordinates and that had clearly helped Billy Bell get there quickly but Sayer was in his own car, without sat nav. Challis recognized the feeble excuse. He had a sat nav app on his smartphone, like the rest of them.

'You're lucky,' he said when he finally arrived ten minutes after the rest of his team. 'This lot was just about to go up to Blackwood to relieve the night shift.'

'What d'you mean, lucky?' Challis pointed out to him that this was a homicide case and would be nothing to do with her. She just happened to have come across it.

'Chief witness then,' he insisted. 'Okay, come clean. How have you contaminated my crime scene?'

'You're such a joy to work with,' Challis returned the sarcasm.

She recounted what she had found, where she had been and what she had touched.

'We'll need your shoes,' he told her. 'Now! Before you pick up anything else.' She leaned against the gate and took off her trainers, placing them in a bag that Sayer fetched from the SOCO van. He gave her some white wellies to put on. They were too big but she said nothing.

She made a point of telling him that the Mack's dog, still in the garage, had messed things up a bit, chewing slippers, licking bodily fluids and traipsing blood all over the house. The dog was howling, like a Baskerville hound, Sayer grumbled, before ordering that it be got out of the garage and secured. It would need going over with a flea comb to see what it may have picked up. Challis grabbed Billy Bell, still the only uniform on the site, and told him what needed doing. She suggested he get coated up. He suggested fetching a length of rope out of the boot of his hedley as he couldn't get into the house to look for the dog's lead.

At the garage, she lifted the door just enough for Bell to get under and in. The dog tried to get past him but he got hold of the collar. Once he was inside Challis lowered the door. She could hear him in conversation with the dog, which he addressed as 'good girl'. He banged on the door and Challis let him out.

'She's a lovely dog,' he enthused. 'Tibetan Terrier. This breed won best in show at Crufts a few years ago.'

Amazing, was Challis's ironic thought. Men and their pursuit of trivia.

'There's a dog cage in there,' he said, 'folded up against the wall. Hold this girl a minute and I'll get it. She can go in the van then, keep her isolated.'

She heard another car, out of sight as the lane was bursting with vehicles now and any new arrivals had to park some way back.

DCI Harriet Moray, grubbily trouser-suited and wearing dark glasses to hide the tiredness in her eyes from eighteen hours straight at Blackwood, came into view with a rough looking DS Ken Tart in tow. He was unshaven and his shirt, open at the neck, was distinctly non-white. Moray saw Challis but, dressed in a tracksuit, she was not recognized. PC Bell in a white forensic gown was recognizable as a police officer as he was wearing his peaked cap. He was coming out of the garage with some wire contraption in his hands.

'You should be on this gate, constable,' she yelled at him.

'Securing a witness, ma'am,' he replied. It made Challis smile. She liked this Billy Bell. But she thought he should tread carefully with Moray and Tart as neither of them looked particularly full of humour this morning.

Moray, of course, thought Bell was referring to Challis which at last made her look more closely at the woman in the tracksuit.

'Mel?' she said, incredulous. 'Is that you?'

Challis handed the rope with dog attached to Bell who had to juggle to grab it and maintain his grip on the cage.

'Yes, ma'am.' She approached. 'I guess I'm your primary witness in this one.'

DS Tart was poised, pad and pen in hand, to record Challis's witness statement. She told him he needn't bother. While she'd been waiting for SOCO to turn up and had been supervising PC Bell's securing of the scene she had entered her observations directly into her smartphone. They were fresh in her mind; in fact the whole horrible scenario was fresh in her mind and her typing flowed. She got Tart to get his own smartphone in hand and bluetoothed the info. He was then sent to go check how Sayer and his team were getting on.

'So you ran here, what, from Capelgwm? That's miles, isn't it?' Moray looked Challis up and down.

'About four and a half k's to here,' Challis replied.

'Huh, more than I could do, especially right now. Not in those boots, I suspect.'

Challis looked down at the white wellies. She explained Sayer's insistence that she change her footwear.

'By the way,' Moray assumed a more serious look, 'I should be giving your arse a good kicking according to the Super. You gave me someone who doesn't exist.'

'O he does exist. Just been on the sick a couple of days.'

'Well you're lucky. I hear he reported at seven this morning.'

Challis knew he would.

'How's that looking?'

'Not a clue. No partner, no ex-partner, no motive yet. Nothing. And in an area of terraced housing nobody saw anything.'

'Shooting?'

'Shotgun! Close range, the woman and her kids.'

'And nobody heard anything?'

'Nope.'

They had been ambling towards the front of the house. Tart was in view at the front door, peering around it, not daring to venture in past Sayer. He raised a hand and beckoned Moray to come closer.

'You may as well come,' she said to Challis. 'It's your baby.'

Challis had no idea what she meant by that. It was her discovery all right but she was not homicide.

Sayer looked up as Moray and Challis poked their heads round the door.

'I blame you for this,' he said to Challis. 'You have a habit this week of finding disturbing corpses.'

Moray gave Challis a half-interested questioning glance. But Challis did not know how to respond to this jibe.

'Your suicide was ugly enough,' Sayer went on, 'but this guy takes the biscuit.'

Moray removed her dark glasses. 'Can you say something I might understand? I'm fucking tired, smell to high heaven. I need my bed, even if it's just for a couple of hours.'

'Right. Ma'am.' Sayer was on his haunches. He leaned back against the wall to give a less restricted view of the head of the deceased.

'Peter Mack, or so I understand,' he glanced at Challis who nodded imperceptibly, 'has been summarily executed I should say.' Moray stiffened. Sayer enjoyed the reaction and went on. 'He opened the front door and got it in the forehead. He's a tall guy, six two, six three, and the assassin was a good few inches shorter, even allowing for the door step. How short I'll tell you later. See, the entry wound almost slap bang between the eyes. I turned him over and the exit wound is at least an inch higher, so the guy with the gun was a short-arse, comparatively speaking, of course. And he fired from probably about a yard, or so. As I say, as soon as the door opened I should think.'

'What's the blood down there?' Moray pointed at Peter Mack's thighs.

'Ah yes, now this is where the Challis curse comes in. Greg, come here again a minute.' Greg was one of Sayer's team. He stepped forward as Sayer moved down the body and grabbed the far leg. He raised it. 'Cop hold,' he instructed Greg. He himself now grabbed the right leg. 'This is a bit crude and undignified but...' He pulled the right leg up and Greg did the same with the left. This action like pulling a wishbone raised Peter Mack's buttocks off the carpet revealing an oozing of blood, now clotted, around the anus.

'Christ almighty,' Tart gagged.

'What the hell?' Moray was trying to stay focused. Challis went rigid.

'*Cum vero ignito inter celanda confossus,*' Sayer said with an effort as he strained to keep the stiff limb elevated. 'Lower it down Greg.' Both legs returned to the carpet.

'Are you familiar with King Edward the second?' he asked them. 'I was on a forensic course once where they used his death experience as an interesting case study and we were made to memorize some of the detail in Latin.'

'Berkeley Castle,' Challis whispered but Sayer heard and raised his eyebrows in a celebratory gesture.

'Y..e..s..' he waited to see if more was forthcoming. Challis obliged.

'Roughly translated as *a hot iron up the backside.*'

'Top of the class, Challis.'

How could he find his work so jollifying?

'Only in this case I fancy it may have been a hot bullet. And not just fired at point blank range but at point blank range plus an inch or two.'

'You mean someone shoved the barrel up there and then fired?' Moray asked.

''Sright. He was lucky though.'

'What d'you mean lucky?' Tart failed to grasp his meaning.

'Well at least he was dead and didn't feel the intense pain of it.'

'They apparently heard King Edward's screams for miles,' Challis offered.

'Exactly. But also when we find the gun there should be some real tell-tale evidence on or up the barrel.'

His confidence was admired by the three detectives but they were all trying to get their heads around what this discovery implied, let alone the pictures that Sayer was drawing in their minds. Challis was thinking 'was Peter Mack a closet homosexual like King Edward?' Tart was physically wincing and crossing his legs at least mentally.

'What did the bloke do to deserve that?' was Moray's considered question, looking at Sayer for an answer.

'Need a psychiatrist to answer that one I reckon,' was Sayer's considered opinion. 'You see, head shot, typical execution style. The other shot...rather more personal I would say. Making a point, a statement.'

'Homosexual signature?' Moray put Challis's thought into words.

Sayer pointed his finger at her approvingly. 'Like the way you're thinking. I guess you'll have to do some digging.' Then he added as an after-thought 'Check for any precedent.'

The four of them stood in silence, heads down, seeing but not understanding.

'Mrs. Mack,' Challis began. None of the others had been up the stairs yet, not even Sayer. Peter Mack had taken all the attention. They stared at Challis, wanting more.

'I looked for her. I thought she must be here, in the house. And I didn't know if they had any kids at home. I had to check.'

Moray nodded her approval. 'Go on.'

'She's upstairs, in the bedroom. Shot as well I assume. She's flat on the bed.'

'That's all in your report that you gave Ken?' Moray asked.

'Yes but if...he' she pointed hesitantly at the body at their feet 'opened the door and was shot twice I would have thought she'd have been down the stairs like a...shot...but the killer must have been right next to the bed when she got it.'

'Not necessarily,' Moray observed. 'She may have come down or halfway down and been forced back up either at gunpoint or retreating from what she'd seen. And we're rushing things here a bit. I mean, did she shoot her husband, her homosexual husband and then kill herself? If not, was she shot in the same way as her husband?'

'You mean, twice?' Challis was alarmed at the thought. And she quickly juxtaposed in her mind the case of Timothy Bush, the word "twice" being the link. She thought she even saw the same connection in a look from Sayer. 'I didn't notice anything like that...like this. I didn't see a gun either but I only did a quick check to make sure she was dead. That's in my report.'

'I'm sure it is. Okay.' She turned to Sayer. 'What time of death?'

'I'd say...between ten last night and two a.m. I'll tell you more...'

'Yeah, later,' Moray finished. 'Okay. Ken. House-to-house. A car coming up and going down in the middle of the night. Somebody must have heard this time, please God!'

'Who am I going to get?' Tart queried. 'We're off now, you and me, before we drop. We've got all our guys and half of east Glamorgan up the valleys, CID and uniform.'

Moray rubbed her tired eyes. 'I wish I could think straight. Mel,' Challis thought she was about to be co-opted, 'how many houses?'

'Ah, o, right,' Mel was surprised by the question. 'Nothing back down that way, the way I ran up here earlier. The way you came up there's a farmhouse on the...right going back down but it's a good half a kilometer off the road. Ty-Gwyn, I think it's called. Nothing then until you get to the junction at the bottom. One cottage either side and then you've got the roads back to Capelgwm one way, away to the Wye Valley the other way and all points in between and a left turn on that road that goes north.'

Moray led Tart away from the house, continuing a discussion on manning the house-to-house to start with. She would have to bend the ear of the Super or whoever else was in control at this point in time. There was so much shift work going on it was almost impossible to know who was where and doing what. Hopefully somebody had their eye on all the balls.

Sayer was busy organizing photos. He'd ventured a little further into the interior of the house and was peering into the study. Challis, ignored now, turned to follow Moray and Tart.

'Hey, Mel,' Sayer shouted after her. He had no respect for the dead, did he? 'There's a hell of a mess in here. Bit like that other house in the sticks the other day. No computer again.'

His tone was almost one of blame. He'd implied that from the start, as if it was her fault. Ugly deaths. Twice hung; twice shot. Wally!

Moray was on her smartphone; Challis had heard it ring out with the theme from The Avengers of all things. She could hear the word "sir" repeated. It must be O'Halloran or some other sir maybe. Moray's head was bowed. Whatever argument she was having or request she was making she didn't seem to be winning. Tart was within ear-shot of the conversation and was pacing, trying to appear uninterested but clearly frustrated the way he was kicking gravel around.

Out in the lane, PC Billy Bell had the back of the SOCO van open. He had installed the cage and the dog inside it. Now he was stripping off his white cover-all, talking all the while to the dog, words of quiet reassurance. He had actually applied to become a dog-handler but nothing had come of it. There were jokes of scale-backs in that area too; Alsatians replaced by Jack Russells.

Everyone was busy. Except Challis. Her eyes came back to DCI Moray. She was only about five years older than Challis but a DCI, two rungs higher up the ladder and heading further. She had transferred to the Mon force on getting her last promotion. Challis couldn't recall where from. Although Challis had had brief attachments to homicide none of them had been since Moray had arrived. She had seen her around and whenever spoken to by the DCI she had the feeling of 'I'm on your side, girl' and she had heard on the female grapevine that Moray was a champion of the female police officer. On the male grapevine the rumours were far more unkind.

She wore a wedding ring and Challis had heard she was married with a couple of kids but when they had talked it was always about work and how was she doing and never about family. Work was work with Moray. Private life was strictly that.

'Mel,' Moray called across to her. Challis plodded over in the flopping white wellies. 'I don't imagine you can run back home in those. I'll give you a lift.'

Thirty-Four

'I need the loo,' Moray said in response to Challis's invitation to step inside Daubwthyn Cottage. 'So I'll say yes.' She added 'Nice' as she stepped out of her BMW and, removing her dark glasses, followed Challis up the drive.

Once inside, Moray was directed towards the stairs and told how to find the bathroom. Challis headed for the kitchen. It was gone ten; she was starving. First thing she did was to slip off the annoying boots and put her moccasins on.

The short drive home had been an interesting one. There was always good entertainment to be had watching a townie negotiate narrow country lanes.

Before starting off Moray with Challis had stood for half a minute in the warming sun that was pushing the damp mist to one side. The DCI was holding at bay the complete collapse of her eyelids. The view below stretched away into mid-Monmouthshire and, though sunny at this vantage point, strands of mist hugged the trees and fields in the valley. 'This is lovely,' Moray had commented lifting her dark glasses to refresh her eyes. Challis swelled with a homely pride, like, this is my beautiful country. Really grim behind them in the murder house but look at this out here. Life full of contrasts, light over darkness, thank God.

Then came the fun, so Challis thought, as Moray found she had to back down the lane to look for a suitable turning spot. She was clearly terrified that another vehicle would be coming up as she was reversing down and sure enough an ambulance, siren going, blue lights flashing, came screeching to a halt almost on her rear bumper. Neither driver knew what to do. Challis suggested that Moray drive forward a little into a field gateway so the ambulance could get by. That accomplished, Challis consoled the DCI with the fact that the entrance to Ty-Gwyn Farm was around the next bend and she could turn there.

The rest of the journey was impeded by a tractor traveling at twenty miles an hour behind which they were stuck all the way to Capelgwm, Moray bouncing up and down ever more rapidly on her seat.

'I raided your cabinet in the bathroom,' Moray confessed. Challis raised an eyebrow. 'The curse started last night and I only had one spare tampon in my bag. I was getting desperate. I hope you don't mind.'

'Of course not,' she had to say but she would never have presumed in someone else's house.

'I was gagging for the loo all the time up there but I didn't want to upset Sayer.'

'I've got coffee on or would you prefer tea?'

Moray looked at her watch. 'Jesus, look at the time. My poor husband. O bugger it. Tea would be better; coffee might prevent sleep later, if it'll come at all.'

'I'm starved, I don't know about you. I've put some toast on.'

Moray ambled out of the kitchen and into the lounge. Challis watched her nervously.

'Crikey,' Moray exclaimed. 'Three sofas. They're not new are they?'

'No,' Challis shouted from the kitchen. 'My parents bought them.'

'You live alone?'

'Yes. They died a few years ago. Car crash. I haven't changed a thing really. I'm not much of a house-frau.'

Perhaps you think it's still your mother's house, Moray ventured to herself.

'Tea's ready. And toast.' Moray returned to the kitchen. 'I've got butter or spread and jam, marmalade, marmite...'

'Thanks.'

They both sat at the breakfast bar, Moray taking a good swig of hot tea. 'Aw that's better,' she said, going for some toast with butter and marmite. 'That hit the spot.'

'Isn't it amazing,' she said through a mouthful. 'We've just come from a gruesome crime scene where we saw enough to put us off food for at least the rest of the day, and here, half an hour later, we're having tea and toast as if we just rose from a good night's kip in the arms of a loved one. What does that make us? The hard-nosed bitches that most of our male colleagues think we are anyway?'

Challis chanced a thin smile. 'Poor buggers,' she said seriously. 'They do get very confused by non-stereotypical females.'

Moray took another piece of toast. The first slice had disappeared fast. She'd had sod-all to eat all night.

Challis watched the DCI closely. She had square teeth, bright, white, that bit cleanly through the bread. Her slim lips closed as she chewed. Her face was angular, her nose prominent, her face in need of make-up. She had sharp blue eyes, dark rings under them, thick eyebrows over them, and her hair was dark brunette, cut short and business-like. Challis had always thought Moray's eyes were icy keen, as if they could see through the crap, which was confirmed by the fact that the DCI rarely seemed to indulge in trivial small-talk. Blue-eyed blondes looked soft and sexy; blue-eyed dark women brooked no nonsense. More stereotyping!

'What are you working on, Mel?'

Challis could not tell if this was a professional enquiry or an opener for some true confessions. She was in her own house but Moray was a natural inquisitor; no question asked without a need to know more than the obvious answer.

'A suicide, last Monday. Not straightforward. That's why Sayer was having a go at me.'

'Why?'

Challis outlined the Timothy Bush case as briefly as she could, excluding the Bush family issues but up to and including the charges laid and the dumbing down of the whole case by O'Halloran.

'He's probably right,' Moray conceded, 'the way things are right now. Resources, eh? Wait til the cuts really bite. You'll be here on a case one minute and then out on loan like some under-performing premier league footballer at the other end of the country, probably for weeks on end.' She paused. 'Cottel Court. I've come across a Lord de Cottel. In London I worked on vice...' *London! That was where she had come from.* 'He has his fingers in a few sex clubs. We closed a couple down. Drugs and a smell of prostitution. He was a minor player or should I say hid himself away well, out of the limelight. But he was one of the backers. Sure of it. Cottel Court; his country seat?'

'He seems to be there.' Challis was mad with herself. She hadn't thought of getting Ruff to check his lordship's background. No reason to now. Moray had scored a point.

Moray licked butter off her fingers, drained her teacup and rose from the stool. 'You happy with your lot at this point in time?'

Feeling vindicated, Challis knew this was no friendly chat or if it was Moray had no skill at it. It was not easy for her, talking to a relatively unfamiliar superior officer about personal stuff like her ambitions. Even with Redland she never went down avenues like this, unless perhaps they were under the influence in the Queens Arms.

Was she happy with her lot? No, she wanted to be an inspector.

'Ah, happiness.' She began with the option to be jocular but the blue-eyed Moray showed no inclination to be amused. 'In the great scheme of things, yes. But we could all be happier.'

'I'm surprised to hear you say that. I'm not happy and you're not either. Thanks for the breakfast. You need your shower. I need a long soak in the bath and ten hours sleep but it'll be a quick shower and forty winks if I'm lucky. The other case needs all hands to the pumps. It has the signs of being a case where goats of the scape variety will be hunted down, butchered and stuck on a spike. Enjoy your weekend.'

That was meant to make Challis feel guilty.

She followed Moray to the door. 'Any decent plans for your days of rest, Mel?' That didn't help either.

'Not much. I'll go into Usk later and visit the boss. See how he is.'

'Redland? He's in hospital.'

'No. He was discharged yesterday. I was going to pop by last night but I was too late coming…'

'No. I think you'll find he was kept in. Had a relapse according to the Super.'

Thirty-Five

Jackie had no choice but to call for an ambulance. There was nothing she could do to ease the pain that was creasing Angel. She could only imagine that Angel was going through something that was ten times worse than childbirth. Angel's hands were clamped to her lower belly, perspiration pouring off her and she had a temperature that made her almost too hot to touch.

The ambulance took an age. Friday night Saturday morning not a good time.

Repeatedly, Jackie swore at Chas and his tight-fisted forgetfulness. If only there was petrol in the car. There may have been enough but she couldn't or wouldn't chance it. What if she only got halfway to the hospital? She went outside once, switched on the ignition and watched the needle barely move from its bottommost position.

When the ambulance arrived nearly an hour after the call Jackie gave the paramedics, one male, one female, one hell of a mouthful. Angel would not allow them to lay a single finger on her, so fearful was she of the bulging tenderness in her abdomen. Her temperature was enough for them not to hesitate. They carried her cradle-style down the stairs, too narrow for a stretcher. That was torture for Angel even though they'd given her a shot to try and dull the pain.

In the ambulance Jackie sat as close to her as she could. The male paramedic was in even closer attendance, fixing up a drip to get fluids in. Angel was in a fitful torpor, the pain having abated slightly. But she looked like a stick insect laying there with a dampness that made it seem she was melting away. Sitting in the shadow of the paramedic, Jackie cried her eyes out.

In the Emergency Department they allowed Jackie to give the required details: name, address, age, allergies, next of kin but not to follow Angel through to the treatment area, despite her pleadings and her exaggerations about their relationship which she kept short of claiming it was a civil partnership.

She knew nothing about any allergies. She gave Angel's mother's address in Windsor; she'd met her when she'd stayed with Angel just after they'd first met. Her name was Greta.

She was told to take a seat in the general waiting area. A little later she went back to the desk to tell the woman that Angel used an inhaler.

It was gone five in the morning when a doctor came out and took Jackie through to the treatment area. She thought she was being taken to see Angel but was guided into a side-room. Without asking her to take a seat the po-faced doctor closed the door behind them. Jackie looked through the glass windows, trying to scan the cubicles for a sight of Angel.

'Miss...?'

What? she wondered until she realized he didn't know her name. 'Davrot,' she told him.

'Miss Davrot, what is your relationship with Miss Plumitis?'

'I told the woman. We're partners.'

'I gather we're not talking business partners. You and Miss Plumitis are in a romantic partnership?'

'Yes, of course.'

'A fully sexually active partnership?'

Cheeky bastard, she thought. He had already assumed a disdainful look of disapproval. 'So what?'

He took this as an affirmative which removed any doubts about what he had to say next.

'Miss Plumitis has a very serious internal injury. Her lower colon has ruptured and there has been a leakage of bowel fluids into the perineum. She has chronic peritonitis. She's being examined now to see if surgery is an option. In my opinion it is. There are tears and lesions from the anus up through the rectum. We need to know how this happened.'

Jackie was caught flat-footed. She hadn't considered being questioned about this but she remembered Angel's reluctance all along to get medical attention, probably because of this kind of inevitable interrogation.

'Miss Plumitis appears to have been a healthy young woman,' the doctor went on. 'These injuries did not occur as a result of a bout of constipation for instance.' He was contemptuous; judge and jury.

'We...we were experimenting.' She had to convince the doctor that it was a sexual thing between two women. No way could she hint that men had been involved in it, especially now that two of the bastards were dead.

'Experimenting with what?' he insisted. She studied him. His eyes were on stalks and she could not decide if he was pushing her out of morbid curiosity rather than a need to know medically.

'I'd like to talk to a female doctor,' she said.

'Miss Davrot, we're wasting time?'

'No, you're wasting your time, in here, with me. You should be out there getting Angel better.'

My God, he thought, you could see what this orange-haired dyke was all about, not caring to help her friend, her "partner"; more concerned with hiding her own embarrassment. His had been a long night of drunks, drug takers and abuse. And now this woman... He turned and left without a word.

Jackie stayed put even though he'd left the door open. She stared hard through the surrounding glass to see where Angel was. The doctor had walked away out of sight. Bugger this, she thought. I'll find her.

As she reached the door a nurse in a dark blue uniform eased her back in. 'Miss Davrot.' Inside the room with the door closed again she went on in a gooey tone. She was a woman of middle-age, plump, grey-streaked hair back in a bun. 'We really do need to know what happened to your friend.' She leaned forward looking for signs. Jackie recoiled a little. 'Please, love, explain to me your relationship.'

'We're partners,' Jackie volunteered impatiently. 'You know, lovers, okay? We have sex. Lots. Different varieties. We were experimenting using...'

'Using what, my love? Come on, we've all been there.'

Jackie doubted that very much. She'd see how much she thought she knew.

'Anything prick shaped. Dildos, vibrators. Stuff from the fridge, and the fruit bowl.' She piled it on and got not even a twitch from the nurse. In her lengthy career she had seen people defend by attacking.

'You'd be surprised what we get here; things you would never have thought of, stuck in every imaginable place; male and female. But we need to know what actually caused these injuries.'

'No idea,' Jackie stated.

'Some considerable force was used.' The nurse's face was serious. Jackie could guess where this was going.

'It was all consensual,' she said slowly.

The nurse shook her head. She and her colleagues had seen the lot in A&E. The things that they saw, disbelieving, they usually laughed about later. Of course, it was always consensual but the seemingly erotic or exciting became totally different when the private became public. Occasionally though, the bizarre was hazardous: tissue damage sometimes irreversible, infection, psychological trauma. As a nurse she was not there to pass judgment but this time this girl's attitude riled her.

'What, she wanted you to rupture her bowel did she? You can't think very much of her if you indulge your...pleasures in this kind of uncaring way. I don't believe you people. That girl in there could die.'

Angel could die!

Now Jackie was shaking the head. Of course she would never go that far with Angel. She couldn't look at the nurse's face, at the accusation in the eyes, the contempt. But she had to brazen it out. There was no other way. Her eyes were moistening. She fought it to stay looking unbowed.

'When?' the nurse asked. 'When did this happen? This consensual activity? How long ago? The doctor thinks the wounds should have been treated some time ago.'

She's calling them wounds.

She tried to sound contrite. 'Couple of weeks. Wasn't too bad at first. Got worse a couple of days ago that's why I called an ambulance. Angel will tell you.'

The nurse didn't tell Jackie that Angel couldn't say anything at the moment. They'd knocked her out.

'Okay. I'm sure she will. And we'll be asking the questions.' The nurse half-turned to go but her training as a carer reminded her she had spoken out of turn, justifiably and understandably, but out of turn nonetheless. This girl could have problems as well. She was obviously trying to ride out this incident but it seemed the seriousness was penetrating a little. 'Are you all right?'

'Me?' She saw that the nurse was wondering if the use of phallic substitutes had been one-sided. 'I'm fine. No problems.'

'Nevertheless, I'd get yourself checked out with your GP or a sexual health clinic. I can get the address for you.'

'No. I'm fine. I want to see her now.'

The caring went on hold again. 'No way!'

The nurse took her back to the waiting area where she sat resentfully. She had had to lie, to sound callous even, but it hurt like hell to give the impression that she would ever hurt Angel the way the medics had concluded. She could never do that. Their love-making even with accessories had always had emphasis on the sensuous, the slow eroticism. Angel got her masochistic kicks from men.

Now Jackie hated those sadists on the dvd more than ever, all of them, not just the two who had caused these injuries but the other two as well, just as guilty.

*

It was relatively easy to park in the hospital car park on a Saturday afternoon Challis was glad to discover, but she was gob-smacked to find she had parked next to a blue Mini Clubman that looked remarkably like the one she had seen Jackie Davrot drive away the night before. Surely not. These coincidental encounters were becoming nerve-jangling.

She made her way into the hospital still unable to come to terms with Stuart Devlin's selective dissemination of news about his uncle. It was clear that his call to say Alan Redland was coming home was to ingratiate himself by including her. That failed to cut any ice so any further updates were not worth his effort. It all fitted with her analysis of what Stuart Devlin had always been like.

At the main door she came face to face with Chas Davrot. They were both stunned. He had a packet of cigarettes in hand, going outside for a smoke. She didn't know that he did and she couldn't work out why that thought was the first thing to go through her mind. The second thought was what on earth was he doing there? But at least it confirmed who the car belonged to.

Neither of them moved.

'Well, look who it is,' she began first. He came the rest of the way out, releasing a cigarette from the packet, saying nothing. She followed him 'Free man today then, Captain. Look, what you did was reprehensible.' She glanced around at the other smokers; none were too close. He still ignored her. 'You're out on bail but that's not the end of things.'

'We'll see about that. My solicitor's on the case. He reckons you're making an awful lot out of very little. So does my boss. You know him; Stu Devlin. He knows you. He says he knows you very well. He was surprised, no amazed, at how far you were taking this. Not how he remembers you; so he tells me.'

'Your Mr. Devlin has absolutely nothing to do with this. Or has he? Is that what you're saying? He's as mixed up in it as you are?'

'I'll tell you something.' He moved forward conspiratorially. 'Drop all this nonsense. Or I'll set Jackie on you.' He smirked and puffed and blew smoke. 'She likes you, you know, and she reckons it's mutual. She thinks you'd prefer her to that Jonathan Watkins.'

Challis was distinctly uneasy about how personal this was getting. People, suspects or perpetrators, often sought to undermine investigating officers but this was different, more threatening. She was beginning to feel she should fight O'Halloran about reducing the seriousness of Chas's offences. Chas was getting her hackles well and truly raised.

She was not in best frame of mind when she walked into the boss's ward, the same one as last time. Same bed too.

'What happened?' she wanted to know.

'Doctors,' he snorted. 'Need the bed, don't they. Go home they said. Got out of bed, got dressed and all. Legs kind of gave out. Next thing I knew I was on the floor. Just there. I'd only gone a foot.'

To Challis he looked about the same as he had the other day. A bit greyer in the face perhaps. He wasn't sitting upright, sort of lolling on his pillows. He sounded as if he was wheezing.

'I'm sorry,' she commiserated. 'It sounded as if you'd mended quickly; going home. I didn't even know you were still here until this morning. I was going to your house this afternoon.'

'Stuart phoned you did he? I gave him your mobile number.'

'I wish you hadn't,' she pulled a face. 'Phoned me yesterday to say you were coming out. Didn't phone me to tell me you were still here.'

'Who told you then?'

She told him it was DCI Moray that morning. Then she had to go on and tell him about her discovery at the Mack's house. She didn't go into detail, just mentioned the double killing and that it was early days and nothing to do with her anyway.

'That on top of the Blackwood killings,' he said, blowing out his cheeks. 'O'Halloran and Moray'll have their hands full. Chance for you there.'

She told him she was still trying to put the suicide to bed, in the way that she wanted but O'Halloran didn't. He made no comment. It was as if he was too tired to think of a solution for her. He was glazed and drifting somewhere, elsewhere.

'You know that, if and when I get out of here, my days are numbered.' Now he looked lost. 'In fact my days are over already. Ex-police inspector Redland.'

'Not necessarily,' she said too quickly. She tried a joke. 'Anyway I prefer the phrase "former police inspector Redland".'

'Dr. bloody Carys,' was all he could say.

She stayed with him nearly an hour, reassuring him as best she could. He smiled and said he had no intention of being shunted off to the Complaints Section. That would finish him off for sure. She told him about Harry Muench and his alleged adventure with the wife of Henderson Timber.

'Not the first to do that,' was his cheerful observation. 'Don't take it too seriously. The worst aspect is his letting the case slide. Getting his end away he sees as a perk in a job that is attracting fewer and fewer rewards, in financial and ambition terms. Holding down wages is going to hit us all. If he didn't have his little sideline he'd probably pack it in.'

He was philosophical that his team was temporarily down to two in number. The best two, he said, but that cut no ice with her as far as his defence of Muench's conduct was concerned.

'I can't believe you're condoning his behavior.'

'Mel, I couldn't care what you believe right now.' He fell back on his pillows. 'I'm finished in the Force. This has done it for me, this heart thing. I know that. So, I may be sick but at least my blind eye is better; no longer needs turning. Seen lots of shit in my time. There's been lots more that I haven't seen, if you know what I mean. You know. Don't fool yourself that you don't. The only way to get on in the job is to accept the obvious even when it isn't obvious because you know it's there. As they say in the Army, *it's a good life until someone starts shooting at you*. In our job, it's a good life so long as you stop believing it is.'

When she walked away from his bed she looked back from the doorway. He'd shrunk further into the pillows and was watching the low afternoon sun through the west-facing window. He'd looked lost but so was she. She'd wanted to ask him what he'd told O'Halloran about her and Stuart Devlin. His gossiping about her was disappointing. Who else had he told?

*

When Chas got back to the Assessment Unit after his smoke break he found an aggressive Jackie pacing up and down.

'If she dies then they all do,' she told him. She'd said the same sort of thing to him from the moment he'd arrived. He was sick of hearing it.

She looked like a wild thing. Her heavy makeup from the night before had flaked off and had not been patched up. She had the appearance of a demented clown.

'I've just been on the phone to Lordy. He says you fucked up last night's shoot.'

'What?'

'They've looked at the film and it's as false as he's ever seen.'

'That's not what was said at the time. And don't you suppose I had a lot on my mind; Angel and then Devlin telling me just before we got going about you being arrested. What do you think I am? I may be a sex factory to you but there's more going on up here than just erotic fantasies. I don't suppose you stood up for me. Too busy tugging your forelock. And who the fuck cares what his fucking lordship says?'

'I don't care. We have to keep it looking as if everything's normal. No-one knows about Angel but they're going to be asking where she is soon. And it's not going to go down well with Lordy or Stuart if they find out some of their clients won't be coming back again.'

She turned her back on him.

'Don't get me wrong, Jack. Angel did not deserve any of this. I let her down. I feel as bad as you do but whatever we do next we've got to do it with a clear mind.'

'You said you'd do what was necessary.'

'Anger is dangerous if it's out of control, that's all I'm saying. I have done what's necessary; what's right. I hate it that Angel is going through all this. They said anything about her condition while I was outside?'

'They're pumping her full of antibiotics. There's going to be more tests.'

'Do they still think they'll have to operate?'

'I don't know. They didn't say.' Tears ran down her face. 'She'll have to have one of those bags if they do.'

Chas drew her to him. That prognosis was not worth thinking about. He'd seen a couple of guys in his regiment after Iraq who'd had gut wounds and ended up with chunks of bowel removed. Young guys they were who hated those bags and so did their wives. He knew little about the mechanics of those appendages but he had it in his mind that sex would be damn near impossible with one of them attached.

Angel was young, too. She and Jackie were close and their physical relationship was top of their agenda. He knew Jackie loved her but those young wives had loved their husbands when they had gone off to war but in at least two cases it turned out to be not strong enough to cope with the outcome.

He was scared for his daughter. This kind of stress was so unheard of within their sex-worshiping lifestyle that he had no idea how to deal with it. Going for the other men who had stood by playing with their dicks while the lovely Angel was being crippled was just not on. That wasn't the deal; he knew that. He would like it to have been an option but it wasn't. The first two had been sanctioned for elimination.

There were other potential problems that had come to him while he was smoking. If Angel was questioned about how she got the injuries what would she say? She and Jackie had not agreed a story. Jackie had had to make one up quickly, that she had caused them, but Angel may say otherwise especially if drugged to the eyeballs.

When they had spoken to the medics he could tell they were in two minds about how to regard Jackie's description of events. He could see they were thinking GBH but the saving grace was that Jackie had brought Angel in and was genuinely concerned about her. As the doctor and nurse had walked away he had heard their whispers. Police! He had heard the word police. And, outside, just now, he had seen that policewoman, that Detective Sergeant Melanie Challis. What was she doing here? She'd better not go for Jackie. He would never let that happen.

'I tell you, Chas, they're all going to get it.' She was right under his nose. Nobody else was around but she kept her voice low and harsh. It came through more threatening. She had this capability; he knew of old. 'You can help but you'd just better not get in the way. I'll do it. You know I can do it.'

'Jack...' With her up close he could tell from her eyes that she was not seeing him as anything other than a tool to get done what she wanted to get done. He towered over her but, not for the first time in her short life, she worried him sick. There was no doubt in his mind that she would do to him whatever was necessary to get her own way. 'Jack, go and get scrubbed up and do something with your hair. You look a real dag.'

*

Late afternoon Alan Redland was taken from his bed by a hospital porter, put in a wheelchair and wheeled to the lifts. He was being taken for a scan.

'On a Saturday?' he had joked with the ward sister when told where he was going. She explained that they needed a better look at the heart. He protested, but not very convincingly, that he could walk to the lift. Nobody listened to him. Wheelchair it was. He had a dressing gown on but his legs were bare from above the knees down to his ankles. Every draught sent a shiver up his spine but he said nothing.

When they got to the room where the scanners were located he was parked near a row of seats. It being Saturday there were no outpatient appointments and the waiting room was empty. The porter went off to announce their arrival.

Through a glass paneled door Redland could see the tube-like scanner waiting to receive him. He could see it but he wasn't that much interested in studying it, trying unsuccessfully to pull his gown lower down his chilled limbs.

The porter came back with a young girl in a white coat, coming out of what looked like a control room.

'Mr. Redland, you'll be done shortly but we've just had a call that an emergency case is coming down and we'll do that one first. It shouldn't be too long. We'll soon have you back to your bed.'

O bugger, he thought.

The porter said he'd be back. Probably going to have a fag, Redland reckoned. The guy stunk of smoke.

The girl in the white coat retreated to her room but only briefly. The double doors into the waiting area were pushed open by a trolley propelled forward by another porter. Behind him and the trolley was a couple, a middle-aged man and a young redhead. Late forties him, early twenties her. Redland practiced his deduction skills. They could be related. The man looked a bit dour; unshaven, crusty face, wearing just a jacket. The girl was equally unsuitably dressed for the time of year, exposing far too much chest flesh, eyes puffed, no make-up, orange hair at odd angles. They both looked worn and tired.

The porter parked the trolley badly and struggled to work his way around past it to get to the girl in the white coat. She actually came to meet him with a certain sense of urgency it seemed to Redland, who now turned his attention to the person on the trolley. It was a woman or girl. Hard to say. She wasn't moving; unconscious; not looking well at all. Seated in his wheelchair he was level with her head. Nice profile, he thought. Looked a bit familiar.

The couple was shown where they could sit near Redland. They showed no interest in him. The girl was tearful but the man did not try to comfort her. Kept his distance.

Redland's eyes were now back on the trolley.

The woman did look familiar. Her blondish hair was in rat tails, splayed out either side of her head. Her face was white.

He wanted to stand up so he could look down on her but just then her porter pulled on the trolley and wheeled her off to the scanner.

I never forget a face, he reminded himself. I know that one but where from?

Thirty-Six

Sunday was once upon a time a day of rest and religious contemplation but not these days. From quite early on, nine o'clock at least, Challis could hear her next-door neighbours talking loudly as they excitedly got round to cleaning their car for the first time in weeks.

She had gone to bed relatively early the night before; nothing on T.V. on Saturday nights anymore. As soon as Match of the Day music came on she switched off, cast a cursory look around the kitchen, dishes from her uninteresting evening meal in the sink until morning, and slipped upstairs. Earlier, late afternoon, she had got round to stripping the bed that still had a whiff of Jonathan about it. Fresh bedding and clean pyjamas were good. She picked up her latest Philippa Gregory novel about another woman of great medieval strength and managed a chapter before lights out. All she wanted to do then was to sleep until midday.

Challis lay abed a while and when she did put foot to floor she realized her leg muscles were complaining about yesterday's exercise. Calves and thighs were stiff and her right ankle had a slight twinge. Hot bath required but first she limped down the stairs and made tea, giving the dishes in the sink an even more fleeting glance.

What to do for lunch today? The dilemma was short-lived.

The bath was good, relaxing. She kept topping up with more hot water and stayed in three-quarters of an hour.

It was relaxing physically but mentally she was already gearing up for Monday. Much as she tried to concentrate on what she and Ruff had to do she found herself dwelling on the Macks and their killings. The images were stuck in her mind's eye. The horror of it defied answers to questions, uppermost being why? Sayer had said an execution-shot to the head but something of completely different significance with the shot that was put into the man's rear end. Her buttocks clenched at the thought.

She'd left before Sayer had had a look at Mrs. Mack but to her it had appeared like a cold-blooded shot to the heart. *You're in my way, get out of it!*

And the study rifled. Everybody seems to be looking for something. Computers going awol.

No, it was nothing to do with her and yet there were parallels with her own case, the suicide of Timothy Bush. Ugly deaths, all of them. Houses ransacked. What else? What else might they have in common? It's those bloody unknown unknowns that Ruff was always on about.

Past the half-hour mark her skin was getting decidedly wrinkled but yet more hot water was allowed in. She tried again to shut out the memories of the previous day and the uncertainties of the following one; Monday, start of another eventful week?

She was warm, wet and wonderful. Floating. She would have liked a Jonathan to be in there with her but not actually Jonathan himself.

Lunch turned out to be a chicken and mushroom pie, from the freezer as were the vegetables – peas and broccoli – and chips. Chips again, she frowned, but they were low fat. It was just about cooked when she took the call.

It was DCI Moray; the briefest of apologies followed by a summons, non-negotiable, to be at headquarters at four that afternoon. Challis stumbled over her words as she tried to ask the simple question, 'what for'? and Moray rang off.

Challis didn't remember eating the chicken pie. She must have because she put the empty dirty dishes in the sink before she went upstairs to change.

Moray had told Challis to make for the ground floor conference room. The building was busy like any other day except that no civilian staff were working. The reception desk was manned by a young female cadet who whispered a barely audible greeting as Challis strode in. Challis didn't know the girl and she was sure the girl didn't know her but she was set to let her in unchallenged. Challis came to a halt and pushed her warrant card almost into the young cadet's face.

'Just because I look as if I know where I'm going doesn't mean I'm entitled to go there. Do your job properly.'

Cruel but would do the girl no harm. Besides, Challis was pissed off being called in and kept in the dark as to the reason.

She left the chastened cadet and walked on through to the conference room which was four doors down the corridor.

The clothes she had chosen to wear were trainers – her second best pair as Sayer had her number ones - jeans, white shirt just visible, loose thin jumper and a brown jacket unbuttoned. Her chestnut hair hung loose showing up its natural thickness. Medium makeup; bright lipstick and a bit of blusher. It was Sunday after all but she carried her trusty shoulder bag with her.

She could hear voices as she approached the conference room door, voices she didn't recognise. She slowed and looked through the glass panel in the door.

The first faces she saw made her gasp. At the head of the table was the Deputy Chief Constable Alice Jones. On her right, Chief Superintendent Mike Harper. She racked her brain. Moray had said the ground floor conference room, hadn't she? Or was it the first floor one. Then she heard

Moray's voice and, leaning to one side, caught sight of her, just her profile, sitting this side of the table.

Challis knocked the door and walked in. The room went quiet and all faces turned in her direction.

Next to Moray sat O'Halloran. Across the other side was a bearded man she didn't know and next to him Harry Muench. This was completely unexpected. Harry Muench. Her eyes were on him far too long so she made them roam around the table, searching for a friendly face. They landed on Moray who was nearest to her.

'Mel,' she greeted her without a smile. 'Come in; sit down.'

She did, gingerly. She had not been in such exalted company before, not as part of what had all the appearances of being a select group. The DCC and the Chief Super had talked morale-boosters to the whole of CID more than once but this was a new experience.

Challis checked the clock on the wall. One minute to four. At least she wasn't late.

Moray introduced her to Mike Harper and Alice Jones and then to DCI Ray Lassman from Berkshire.

What the hell was Muench doing here? She got a knowing leer from him. In other words, he knew more than she did.

'Right!' DCC Alice Jones spoke, not looking at Challis. Her attention was taken with Mike Harper and the Berkshire man. 'Now we're all here let me explain what we're up to.'

She was a broad shouldered woman, black-haired, early forties, moved to Mon from West Midlands a year ago on her promotion. She was an alleged champion of women and had over-seen recruitment of more females than males in her short reign in charge of Operations. It may be Sunday but she was in a crisp white-shirted uniform as was the Chief Super. The other three were in suits, even Muench and he was wearing a tie knotted right up to the neck. Challis wished that Moray had told her who she would be meeting. Too late now. Her only recourse was to look professional. She plonked her bag on the table, opened it and took out her pad and a pen, flipping it open ready to take notes. Her exaggerated movement was seen by all.

'No need to take the minutes, Sergeant,' DCC Jones said. 'Superintendent O'Halloran will be doing that. But feel free to make your own notes if you so wish.' She made this sound encouraging and not at all condescending. Challis smiled a thank you but she wished she had removed her jacket before sitting down. She felt encumbered but she didn't want to rise and do it for fear of attracting even more attention to herself.

'Actually, Sergeant,' the DCC continued, 'it's your fault that we're all gathered here on a Sunday afternoon.' She smiled. 'Your discovery at

Capelgwm yesterday morning. DCI Moray tells me you did a good job there.'

All others around the table kept their heads down, except the DCI from Berkshire who was coolly studying Challis. Muench was twiddling a pen. 'Which is why you in particular are here,' the DCC concluded. She looked to her left at Chief Superintendent Mike Harper, a man of some girth and a ruddy complexion. He would not look out of place in an illustration for a Dickens story.

'Thank you, ma'am,' he began. 'The Gods, ladies and gentleman, have crapped on us from a great height again. No major crimes for months then two come along at once. We were at full stretch with the Blackwood case and for those of you who may not know,' he eyed Challis and Muench, 'our man has struck again. The use of the word "man" is purely descriptive at this time. We still have no idea if the shotgun is wielded by one person or more, or male or female. Last night a woman in Cross Keys was shot, completely random by the look of it. At least she's not dead. In intensive care in Cardiff. So that investigation is escalating and that is not the reason we are all here except as background re: the strain currently placed on this Force. And on top of this we have the Sergeant Challis case.' Challis was stunned by the use of her name for the shootings near Capelgwm.

'A Mr. and Mrs. Mack gunned down, probably Friday night, late, for no apparent reason. No motive presenting itself.' Challis couldn't help but think it should be called the Mack Case. Harper continued. 'A double murder though, requiring as much investigation as the valleys case but that still has to take priority. It has a far higher public profile. A seeming lunatic on the loose terrorizing the entire community. At first glance the case at Capelgwm seems to be a professional job; clean kills and the house searched for something specific. Different emphasis. Different method so different investigation required. And as it happens we have, not so much a lead but a link, albeit tenuous, which is why DCI Lassman is here from Berkshire Police. DCI Lassman was contacted late yesterday after Mr. Sayer did a quick search for similar m.o.'s. He found a recent case in…Windsor?' He looked at DCI Lassman.

'Datchet,' he stated without apparent deference to a superior officer. 'Near Windsor.' He appeared almost bored and went back to stroking his goatee.

'Datchet,' Harper repeated before emphasizing. 'Near Windsor.' He hesitated. 'Perhaps you'd like to take it from there, Chief Inspector.'

'Yes, right.' Lassman was laconic and slowly opened a file on the table in front of him. He looked at it, then looked up and began speaking without any further reference to it.

Odd man, Challis thought. Not exactly an endearing manner.

'The case in Datchet is of a George Medlyn, shot dead last Tuesday in his car in his driveway. He was shot in the left temple at close range. That shot probably killed him immediately. A second shot was aimed downwards. Bear in mind Mr. Medlyn was sitting at the wheel and this second shot was fired vertically downwards. It entered his lower abdomen, passed through various organs but exited just about dead centre out of his anus. If that was the target it was a hell of a great blind shot.'

'So what are we saying?' Moray interrupted. 'That the two murders are both execution style and that the secondary shots were both...anal...albeit one from an impossible angle. Is this the link?'

'It's not a bad place to start,' Lassman said. 'But as Mr. Harper said, a bit tenuous. But there's more.'

'Is there a Mrs. Medlyn and if so was she shot?' This was Challis. Lassman could have been smiling behind his beard and moustache; Challis wasn't sure, but he raised a finger in her direction.

'Yes,' he replied, 'and no. I think probably luckily for Mrs. Medlyn she had walked out on her husband some days earlier. But yes, Sergeant, before you ask, the house was turned over. No computer, no hard disks and a mess of all his somewhat dubious collection of, shall we say, colourful dvds. Link number two, Sergeant.'

'We also had a suicide down here this week where the house was in a similar state,' Challis added knowing this would be news to her senior colleagues as well as to the DCI from Berkshire who raised an eyebrow. This young sergeant was getting excited; he could tell.

'So,' drawled O'Halloran, speaking for the first time. 'There are these similarities. Both cases...all cases...could be burglary gone wrong.'

'Indeed they could,' Lassman agreed in a slow and muted tone. 'But we have a clincher.' He now withdrew a wad of photographs from his folder. 'As they say on T.V., even after the nine o'clock watershed, these contain images of a sexual nature right from the start.'

He passed them around the table. He was one short so Moray and Challis ended up sharing.

'Mr. Medlyn was a devotee of...erotica, shall we say. He had many dvds depicting many sexual deviations. In his defence we found none of a child porn nature. They were all of adults indulging in various activities. This photograph however comes from a video on a memory stick found in his office in the city of London where he worked as an accountant. It appears to be a segment of a longer video and has always been significant to us in the investigation of Mr. Medlyn's murder.' He paused and looked around the table. His eyes skipped past the DCC and the Chief Superintendent but dwelt longer on O'Halloran, Moray, Challis and Muench, longest on Challis. He saw her stare at the photograph, lowering her head as she gradually eased it away from DCI Moray's fingers.

She pointed at the tall, thinly fair-haired, well-endowed man standing observing the man who was penetrating the girl. She could only see him in profile but she knew.

'That's Mr. Peter Mack.' Her face lifted, glowing. 'Isn't it?'

Lassman beamed. 'Eureka!' He banged the table with his fist.

'The link, Mr. O'Halloran,' Lassman spoke triumphantly. 'Your murdered man standing three feet away from my murdered man, murdered one hundred and twenty-six miles apart. I looked it up on Multimap. One hundred and twenty-six miles from Datchet to Cap...'

'Capelgwm,' Challis obliged.

'Exactly. Now what's all that about, eh?' His eyes lit up.

'DCI Lassman's boss,' DCC Jones interjected, 'has allowed him to come down here and work on the murder of the Macks with us, seeing as there is an apparent link with his own case.'

'Cast iron!' Lassman insisted. 'Cast iron dead end,' he qualified.

'As Mr. Harper said we're up against it here with the Blackwood shootings and are very grateful to accept Mr. Lassman's secondment here even be it short-term. But he can't work alone obviously. Harriet must stay on the Blackwood case but she has put forward DS Challis to act as Mr. Lassman's sergeant and Mr. O'Halloran has released DC Muench to assist. I think it's a good idea to keep DS Challis on it as she was there at the start.'

'Ma'am,' Challis dared. 'That will leave Mr. Redland's team with a compliment of one.'

DCC Jones looked at O'Halloran for input but he was quiet and did not appear to be listening to the conversation.

'Superintendent,' she prompted. He came round with a jerk.

'Ma'am?'

Jones was clearly irritated but controlled it well. 'DS Challis made the point that DI Redland's team will be down to one if she is to work with Mr. Lassman.'

'Yes. Yes, I've looked at that. The major case they were working on has been put to bed more or less. I discussed it with DS Challis late on Friday and told her how to proceed towards tying up the loose ends. It was only a suicide. Fairly straightforward.'

Challis wanted to object to that summation but this was not the time or the place. She couldn't help but straighten up and her body language revealed to just about everyone her dissatisfaction. But she said nothing.

'Sergeant?' DCC Jones enquired.

All eyes were on her. 'I'll fill in DC Ruff first thing as per the Super's instructions.'

'Case load other than that?' the DCC quizzed.

'Well...' Challis began but O'Halloran jumped in.

'Insignificant. Minor stuff, that one DC can get on with.'

'Okay,' she said brightly, glad there were no obstacles to the plan she had just announced. 'I'll leave you to get on. Harriet, you make sure Mr. Lassman has everything he needs.'

She rose as did Harper and O'Halloran and all three left the room.

'That O'Halloran's a bit of a dick isn't he?' Lassman stated coolly. He got no verbal response but an eyeful of agreement from Challis.

* * *

There was a distinct note of panic in his voice as his call was answered. He hated the blasé attitude at the other end of this phone conversation. He had explained the situation, coherently he thought, but his concern over his position did not seem to be appreciated. It was the same position for both of them, it should be fucking obvious, but he considered that, out of the pair of them, he was in the worse peril.

'Where's the gun I gave you?' he pressed on.

'Chas has still got it of course.' The response was pretty laid back.

'Why? He's finished with it now. I want it back or I want to know it's been got rid of.'

'I'll sort it. Don't worry.'

'Listen, our tracks need to be well and truly covered and you've got to keep all this just between the two us. No blabbing to that crowd you frequent. My name was supposed to be kept right out of this, remember? No more fuck ups. Anonymous you said. Dressed me up like the man in the iron mask. Well a lot a good that did. You're in this as much as I am, now don't forget.'

'Okay, okay. I get it.' He was deeply regretting now that he had told the guy he had been seen and identified without the mask on and the deal that had been forced on him to clean up that particular mess. 'This is going to cost you.'

'Cost me? You seem to forget who's kept who out of trouble all these years. Are you listening?'

A tired 'Yes' came back at him.

'How are you going to do it?'

'Never you mind.'

'It has to be done today. Tonight.'

'O fine. Are you going to come out and help?'

'You know I can't, you idiot.'

'Fucking great!' The phone went dead, leaving him unsure where that had left him. He wanted to call him right back but he heard the outer door of the gents toilet open then the footfall of someone coming in and standing at the sink right outside his cubicle.

Thirty-Seven

It was late. Challis was still at HQ, the meeting with Lassman and Muench having only just ended.

DCI Moray had left hours ago. She'd laid case details of the killings at Capelgwm in front of Lassman and left for Blackwood. Challis, she told him, could guide him through anything else he needed to know. They worked on a press statement that went before the Chief Super and the DCC for rubber-stamping. A press conference was scheduled for the following morning to address both the Blackwood and Capelgwm cases but it was not something that needed to concern DCI Lassman and his cobbled-together team or divert them from their investigative work..

The latest news on the case was that neighbouring properties close to the Macks' residence had been visited. The people in one of the two cottages down at the junction heard a vehicle go up the lane towards the Macks' house at around midnight. They didn't hear it come back down. The people in the other cottage heard nothing but the elderly female occupant vaguely recalled seeing car lights trailing across the bedroom ceiling but she was half asleep by then.

'Considering all the work done by the perpetrators at the Mack's house they were probably there at least an hour, perhaps more,' Challis observed.

'So the old dears were asleep by then,' Lassman guessed.

'Or our killer or killers went back the other way, the way I'd run up there myself. There may be tyre tracks. It's a lane with grass or even mud washed across it. Harry, follow that up in the morning will you?''

Everything at the murder scene was being examined. There was a study downstairs that had been searched and computer equipment removed by the killer or killers. In a small room upstairs, in locked cupboards, dvds were found. Many were pornographic. The cases were well covered in fingerprints that included those of both the deceased. Lassman observed that unlike Mrs. Medlyn Mrs. Mack clearly enjoyed them as much as her husband. Moray added that early forensic tests on the two showed that there had just been an exchange of bodily fluids, seminal, vaginal and anal. Their state of undress indicated that perhaps 'their post-coitus had been interruptus', as Moray put it, by the knock on the front door. 'Happens all the time,' she added with weary remembrance. 'It's the law of Sod.'

'A happy couple,' Lassman concluded wryly but resisted saying they died happy.

She went on to say that in the bedroom where Mrs. Mack had been found the TV set and dvd player were both on. There was no dvd in the player. If they had been watching one it must have been put back in one of the cupboards in the other room. Challis winced as she recalled seeing the TV was on but she hadn't put it in her notes.

Rounding off her summary, she said that examination of the dog and Challis's trainers had not so far revealed anything significant. She enjoyed the fact that she had caused Lassman's eyebrow to rise.

During a break and left on her own, Challis called Ruff at home.

'Kay, I know it's late but I need to tell you a few things you'll need to do tomorrow.' She went on to tell her of the events at Capelgwm and her move to the team investigating the murders. 'You'll need to wrap up the Timothy Bush job.' Ruff was less than enthused when Challis told her that O'Halloran wanted the whole thing dumbed down. 'Just wrap it up, Kay, but first go and visit his GP in Usk. I fixed a meet for first thing tomorrow morning with the practice manager. I don't know where I'll be tomorrow. Have you got transport now?' She had. Her car was back on the road.

Lassman and Muench returned to the conference room from their calls of Nature.

'This building has seen better days,' Lassman commented. 'Never seen rusty walls before.'

'We're supposed to be having a brand new building in a few years' time, so we're told.' Challis, like most of her colleagues, was skeptical about the promises.

She had started gathering together all the case papers that were strewn over the large table.

Muench's first question to Lassman had been to ask if the source of the photograph was available to view. Lassman said the video clip was on his laptop and they could view it tomorrow. He did say that the clip indicated that at least two other men were present but were wearing those tight-fitting black plastic masks that seemed to reveal just ears, eyes and lips.

'The big question,' Challis pointed out, 'is how these two men, now dead, actually got together in the first place?'

Lassman nodded his agreement. 'And, of course, who is the girl?'

Challis had studied the photograph and, sure enough, the girl was the central character in every conceivable way. She was bound and powerless. Her arms and legs were well secured, her body at the mercy of the men. Lassman had conveyed the feeling that the scene was staged to look horrific, that it was all being acted out as per some agreed script. He couldn't work out if the full video was aimed at the porn market. Unlikely, he said. A city accountant and a South Wales solicitor were improbable porn stars.

'What then?' asked Muench. 'Some private club?'

'It looks very vicious to me,' Challis observed.

'It is,' Lassman confirmed.

'I can't help wondering,' Challis shuddered at what she was thinking, 'about this girl. She's blonde, isn't she? I mean, could she be eastern European, imported specially for, I don't know, sacrificial purposes? How far does the video go? I mean, we're not dealing with a snuff movie here, are we?

'You're not the first to suggest it but the clip didn't show anything like that.'

'But you don't know. Not for sure.'

Lassman stroked his beard. Challis challenged him further.

'You say there are two other men, in the video. We have to find them. For one thing they'll know what went on and for another they could be next.'

Muench hadn't thought of that and was hated that Challis had. Lassman had thought of it; thought of it a lot on the train to South Wales.

Lassman took Challis and Muench through all the other evidence surrounding George Medlyn's murder. He had a folder full of crime scene photographs: Medlyn dead in his car, the front of his house, the state of the various rooms, their separate bedrooms and the study. He spent some time going over the condition of the bed in what had been Mrs. Medlyn's bedroom and what the forensic analysis had come up with.

'Mrs. Medlyn would say nothing to us about that but Medlyn's semen was on the sheets mixed with blood that we know was his wife's.'

'You don't suppose he was doing to her what he had done to this girl in the photograph?' Challis put forward.

'If he did then I think Mrs. Medlyn didn't like it much. She was out of the house rapido. Didn't even tidy up her bedroom, as if she didn't ever want to go back in there.'

'D'you think she did it?' Muench asked.

'No.' Lassman was unequivocal. 'But I do think she was lucky not to have been around when the shooter came to call.'

Challis was thoughtful. 'What do you suppose the motive is?'

Lassman was equally thoughtful. 'No set ideas. What you said about this girl being sacrificial…If she didn't survive it then revenge could be a motive. But we could be barking up a red herring.' Challis frowned. She'd never heard that one before. 'This video could have nothing to do with it. The relationship these two men had could relate to something other than this. An accountant and a solicitor, involved in a scam of some sort? We need to dig more into their backgrounds and that's a job for you to get stuck into tomorrow, Harry. I want to know all there is to know about solicitor Peter Mack and his wife. I've got my people back in Berkshire doing the same for Georgie Medlyn.'

'One other thing will be the weapon.' He flourished pictures of the bullets extricated from George Medlyn's head and the driver's seat. 'Nine millimeter and a silencer was used. I understand we have to wait until the morning to get the ballistics report on the bullets that killed the Macks.'

'Do you think they'll match?' Muench asked.

'Oh, I'm bloody sure they will.'

Lassman stepped outside into the corridor to make a call on his mobile. The papers were all tidied. He had stuffed his case with all of his material. They had sent Muench off to make photocopies of much of it for Challis to take home and study for what was left of the late evening. Muench took care of the files left by Moray but not until he had made copies of that as well. He was less than happy with the role that seemed to be coming his way.

'Harry.' Challis checked that Lassman was still on his call in the corridor. 'Are you well now?' He looked up slowly. Her slow tone smacked of sarcasm. 'Fully recovered?'

'Fine,' he replied sharply. 'Thanks.'

'Good. Glad to hear it. There's lots to be done. Clear heads required.'

A strained silence as Challis stuffed files into her shoulder bag.

'O'Halloran obviously thinks you're the man for the job.' She actually thought that O'Halloran had lumbered her with Muench because she had earlier implied that she had no wish to work with him again. Lassman was very shrewd; O'Halloran *was* a dick.

'What job? Photocopying? And, yeah, working for this guy isn't doing us any favours is it?'

'O, I don't know. Could be the shape of things to come. Itinerant detectives.'

'Wages going down and we have to tramp round the whole country. Fuck that!'

'Really? You could end up shagging witnesses everywhere you go.'

He grudgingly gave her a cocky smirk. 'Only if they pay for it,' he mumbled.

'But just don't do it again on our patch. Next time O'Halloran will have your balls.' The continuing slanting mouth on Muench's face made her realize he was proud of his notoriety and believed he'd got away with it. He was wearing it like a medal for outstanding service. O'Halloran didn't care if one of his officers was taking advantage of his position so long as he didn't lose that officer as a resource.

She stared hard at Muench, waiting for the sly grin to disappear. It was too slow in doing so. 'Unless Kay cuts them off first.' Her face was straight. 'While I shove my lawn-mower up your arse!'

Slowly, it dawned on him what she was alluding to. He wanted to see if she saw the joke. There was no such sign from her.

Lassman re-entered and cast a satisfied glance around the table and an enquiring look at his two new assistants who appeared to have distanced themselves.

'Eight o'clock start in the morning. First thing, chase forensics for ballistics and everything else. I don't know what your guys are like here but ours are top-notch. That was my sergeant just now, forensics have confirmed the blood stains on the sheets were Mrs. Medlyn's.'

'I thought that was a known,' Challis queried.

'It's known now from official DNA from Mrs. Medlyn.' Challis and Muench understood. 'He also withdrew several hundred pounds of cash from a savings account during the last week of January. Unusual apparently. And according to his wife he was away the following weekend and she doesn't know where.'

'How did he pay for his porn collection?' Challis asked.

'Paypal we think. Still checking. Are we all packed up here?'

'Where are you staying?'

A room had been reserved at a motel in Pontypool. Cheap. With a McDonald's across the road. It was on her way, if she went that way.

'Young Harry's a bit sullen,' Lassman commented as they drove to his hotel.

'Are you always this quick with character assessments?' Challis asked. 'What about DCI Moray? The Chief Super? Me?'

'I've known many a sergeant, Sergeant. Many of them were happy being sergeants but they thought the grass was greener. It wasn't. But this business doesn't like to put people back to where they were happy so they were stuck being miserable inspectors. And some of them were so miserable they got promoted again to try and cheer them up.'

What was he trying to say about her, she wondered.

'I wouldn't say you were miserable, sir.'

'Me? Of course not. Happiness personified, me. And you, Sergeant, just get on with the job, that's my advice. Make me happy; that's all you have to do and give Harry a hug to let him know you really love him. I like a happy ship.'

He cast his eyes around the interior of Challis's car.

'This vehicle is without doubt the cruddiest I have ever seen. I wouldn't have sex on the back seat if I was you. You could get a severe case of litter rash on your tender backside. Ever considered the vehicle equivalent of a one-way ticket to Dignitas?'

Thirty-Eight

Jim Jenkins, builder of Usk, had waited weeks to make another move. It was nearly a month, the last Friday of January, when he'd followed Angela Plumitis to Pontderry Lane.

She had come out of the chemists in Bridge Street carrying a large paper bag. He turned away, gazing at the window display, watching her reflection as she walked behind him. She went back to the car park. It was dark and overhead lamps made pools of light. She crossed to a vehicle waiting with engine running, a vehicle Jenkins recognized. She got into the passenger seat and the Range Rover moved away.

For a moment he stood watching as it weaved its way round the one-way system. It passed right by him and as it did so Angela Plumitis was lowering her scarf away from her face and this time he saw her clearly, close. Her profile reminded him so much of Greta Plumitis, her hair, in colour and shape, seemed the same.

In retrospect he should have left it at that; a glimpse of the past in the present. But she was the right age and he'd heard her date of birth in the Surgery. He couldn't let her just disappear.

He ran to his own vehicle, his truck that he took home every night, naming J.J. Jenkins, Builder. As he drove off, the wrong way round the one-way system, he saw there were two other cars between him and the Cottel Court Range Rover. That was no problem. They all had to go slow to negotiate the narrow roads back through the Square. The two cars turned left towards the river; the Range Rover went right.

He followed it up the incline, through the treed bends and up to the ridge where the hamlet of Llanhelog sat sprawled. He kept a respectful distance; he had to; the Range Rover had dealt with the gradient from Usk far better than his truck was able: it was ancient and needed coaxing. His quarry was out of sight by the time he reached the brow of the hill but the long downward stretch allowed Jenkins the spectacle not only of a far distant Raglan Castle but a view of the Range Rover turning down Pontderry Lane.

The 4-by-4 stopped outside No 1 Pontderry Lane. Jenkins slowed down; he had to squeeze by. He saw a woman standing on the doorstep. He knew her by sight. The driver of the Range Rover got out first. A tallish man wearing an Army khaki jumper. Angela Plumitis started to open her door but saw Jenkins about to pass. He stopped and flashed the headlights. She opened the door fully, smiling in his direction. His chest heaved in tingling remembrance. She gave him a little wave of thanks as she shut the door and hurried around the front of the vehicle. It was her; daughter of Greta, daughter of his. It had to be.

Jenkins drove on past, aware that the man was giving him a hard stare. He kept on looking back in his mirror to observe her that little bit longer. His study was rudely interrupted by Farmer John Gee, in his tractor, coming down the lane in the opposite direction, sounding his horn.

That had been nearly a month ago. She had been on his mind ever since. It had gnawed away at him. He had convinced himself that she was his daughter, a child he never knew for certain that he had. A gut fantasy, that was all. There was no denying that it would be a shock for her if he just bowled along and told her but it had to be the right thing to do.

But she was probably gone by now.

He had tossed and turned in bed at night, indecision giving him nightmares. Beryl had suffered because of his insomnia. His excuse was that he was worried about the business, slow in this cold weather, which was true. Contracts were on hold or cancelled altogether. He'd laid off one guy already. It was a worry.

But what really tied his intestines in knots was Angela Plumitis. He had neglected his work of late, driving around Usk in the hope of seeing her. Idiotic, this hesitancy. He knew where she was or at least knew where she'd been.

So now, this morning, he had driven through Llanhelog and was slowing at the right-hand turn that led to the row of ex-council houses. He was of one mind as to his intention. He would march up to the door and ask to see Angela Plumitis. What would come next he had no idea.

He stopped at the junction. That same Cottel Court Range Rover was coming out of the lane and he would have to let it go before he could make the turn. It hesitated, which allowed him to see the two people in the front seats. One was clearly the same driver as before. Next to him, in the passenger seat. was Angela Plumitis. So she was still here but he'd missed his chance again.

The driver saw that Jenkins was waiting to let him out. A car was coming the other way so he had to wait. Jenkins stared at the woman and it slowly dawned on him that this was not Angela Plumitis. She was blonde, yes, and the face was similar.

Jenkins was a man who remembered faces and the names that went with them. Beryl was often embarrassed by him. He would approach people when they were out shopping, spouting their name and dates and places. She cringed as she watched them wrestling with all this information, sometimes remembering the dates and the places but not him. Usually all he got was a look of bewilderment and the deflating words 'I don't remember you.'

The face in the car was older than Angela but Jenkins recognized her. Greta Plumitis, Angela's mother. She could be no-one else.

Her eyes turned toward him as the Range Rover edged out across his front. She saw his truck but not him. He saw her clearly. Her face was lined, her eyes dark underneath. Aged. But her lips were the same, that bow shape, full. There was no spark though. Sadness was what he saw in her face.

The Range Rover drove on. Jenkins still held his truck in the middle of the road, his indicator light blinking and clicking. He cancelled it and moved straight ahead.

'You still haven't told me,' Greta said. 'Nobody has told me yet.'

Chas's concentration was on his rear-view mirror. The truck that had indicated a right turn was now behind him. A flash of déjà vu went through his mind but was gone as quickly as it had arrived.

'What is wrong with my daughter?'

He continued paying attention to his mirrors. 'Didn't Meredith tell you?'

'Meredith?' Greta shuddered at being reminded of the morose woman who had picked her up at Newport Station and taken her to that cold, damp house that smelled of dogs. And where it was situated was to her one of the grimmest places she had ever been; bleak countryside, grey distant hills, mud-covered pot-holed roads and a view into a field full of police tapes that Meredith would not explain.

'She said fuck all.'

'Jackie's at the hospital. She'll fill you in.'

'She? She? That daughter of yours.'

'It was her idea to call you. She'll tell you about Angel.'

'Her name is Angela! Just tell me what has happened.'

He paused. 'I can't.' He said it with such force that it was end of conversation.

Greta looked at this man.

She had met him only the once.

He had come to Windsor to pick up his daughter. Stayed the night.

She disliked the look of him and besides he reminded her of Jackie, the girl who had taken her daughter away from her, physically as well as altering her character unrecognizably.

His reticence could only mean that he or his daughter had something to do with Angela being in hospital.

She had fought with her daughter repeatedly. She had tried to tell her of her belief that Jackie Davrot was an evil influence.

The girl had come into her house, years ago it seemed, had occupied her daughter's room as if it were her own, bedded her own girl barefacedly, night after night, sounds emanating that were exaggeratingly loud for humiliating effect.

Mornings followed that were unreal; Jackie Davrot seeking her out to make sure that she knew what had happened the nights before.

Your daughter is mine, her eyes said. It was almost as if she was trying to oust Greta from her own house and from anything to do with her own daughter.

She had stayed strong, somehow, but almost longed for a man, anyone, to be with her to help. She had no-one. Her choices in life had left her with no-one.

Greta had always believed that her daughter was a normal heterosexual; she'd had boyfriends, men friends. Many of them. Never without a man in tow, dating more than one at a time.

Healthy. A healthy young woman.

Reminded her of herself when she was young.

Now, she had no real comprehension of what her daughter had become but she had a belief, a fear, that it was way beyond even her experiences.

Once, in Angela's bedroom, she had found her laptop left on, a page of pictures displaying with captions that explicitly and succinctly described the context: gang-bang, group sex, girl can't get enough.

Had Angela left it on accidentally or Jackie Davrot intentionally?

What did it mean?

Was she now a lesbian or was she still into men? Bi-sexual. She knew all about that of course. But Angela…?

That Jackie was evil and looking at the father now there could be little doubt where it sprung from.

They had reached the outskirts of Raglan. The impressive ruins of the 15th century castle were now at eye level. It dominated the skyline but Greta didn't see it at all. Her eyes were cast down as Chas bore left onto the dual carriageway to Abergavenny.

In his truck, Jenkins was suddenly torn. He had assumed they had been heading for Raglan, now he saw the Range Rover heading for Abergavenny, some nine or ten miles further on. He hesitated at the roundabout. A car behind him grew impatient and sounded off. That made his mind up. He took the same road.

Thirty-Nine

'You were supposed to pick me up at eight.'

Lassman was waiting outside the Travelodge, wrapped up in his smart topcoat and scarf he carried his laptop case about his neck. It was eight-ten. There was no 'good morning' from him as he got into Challis's car.

'I sent you a text,' Challis offered.

'Texts! Good Christ, woman! Communication like savages using drums or smoke signals. I hate 'em. If you want to tell me something, speak! Too many people hide behind texts. It's like emails, carriers of unwanted trivia most of the time. People are too scared to speak face-to-face or even mouth-to-ear. I want to hear your voice, Sergeant, not have to try and decipher your abbreviated ramblings.'

'I wasn't looking for a conversation, sir. Just a quick update.'

'A weak excuse most likely.'

'Not at all. I was on the job.'

He gave her a double-take. 'I have absolutely no interest in your sex life, Sergeant. I hope it wasn't on this back-seat. I warned you last night and you haven't exactly spring-cleaned it since, have you?'

She could not help herself colouring up. 'I meant the job we are currently working on.'

'O really,' he said, unconvinced.

'Yes. Really.' She reached back between the two front seats and pulled an A4 glossy photo through and thrust it into his hands. 'Just look at that.'

She pulled away from the hotel entrance as he turned the photo the correct way up. 'Well fuck me stupid,' he breathed. 'Georgy Porgy.'

Challis let slip a sly smile. 'And there's more.'

On the way to the office she explained the photo's provenance.

She had set off from her house in good time; seven-thirty. At that time of the day she would pick up Lassman well before eight. It was a good morning for driving. No ice on the windscreen and the roads comparatively dry. No fog either. In just five minutes she had passed the thirty mph signs outside Usk. Two hundred metres further on, where the road narrowed at the school traffic lights, there was a queue of vehicles. Nothing was moving in either direction. Two artics seemed to be jammed in the narrows. She opened her window and put her head out for a better view. No, the lorries weren't jammed. They were being held up by Jared Edwards and his wife. She was standing mid-road with a school crossing lollipop in her hand. He was busy with the camera.

Challis was near the entrance to the school. She could use it, drive through the crescent car park and out the exit at the far end, beyond the holdup. She indicated left and pulled off the road, over the pavement, driving slowly, eying the situation on her right. It was heating up, that was plain to see. Drivers of all vehicles seemed to be advancing on Jared Edwards. Like the other day, there was no sign of any officers of the law. She couldn't leave it as it was. She parked, grabbed her shoulder bag that contained her warrant card and hurried up to the road.

As she approached the melee that was fast developing she was amazed to be confronted by Alan Redland. He was well wrapped up against the early morning chill.

'I thought it was your car,' he said over the rapidly escalating noise behind him.

'What the hell are you doing here?' She was very nearly in castigating mode with him. Why hadn't she been told he was home and what was he doing here, outside, in the cold, at this hour of the morning?

'They let me out,' he replied lightly. 'Yesterday. Afternoon. I can die in my own bed.'

'Are you okay?' She adopted what she hoped was a more compassionate tone because he didn't look okay. 'You're up and dressed early.'

He nodded. 'I don't sleep now that immortality's been taken away from me. What d'you plan to do with that lot?'

The atmosphere around Jared Edwards was supercharged. 'Sort out that neighbour of yours.' Yes, she pondered, why was he acting the amused spectator? 'Which you could have done.'

'Me? I'm a sick man.' He smiled, enjoying himself, feeling better. 'And besides I think old Jared Edwards and his wife do a grand job.'

'Well do something useful. Hold this.' She thrust her bag into his gloved hands, opened it and delved inside. He acquiesced, not objecting to her curt manner towards a former superior officer. He liked watching Challis when she was in full flight and his near-death experience persuaded him to make the most of her while he could.

Her warrant card had slid to the bottom of the bag. She pulled out a thick file, shoved it under Redland's armpit and finally located the card.

She gave him one last reproving look and headed for Jared Edwards. Redland was left juggling with her bag and the file under his arm, gravity taking it downwards. He could see loose leaves of paper edging out, threatening to fall to the ground. He dropped the bag and caught the file but not before some of its contents had spilled out.

'Police!' Challis identified herself to Jared Edwards and the lorry driver with whom he was standing toe-to-toe. The driver was pulling at the straps of a bulging shoulder bag that his aged opponent had around his neck. Clearly there was a considerable age difference between the two and the younger man was to some extent curbing his anger.

'I'm a police officer,' Challis iterated. 'Hands off. Now.'

'Get this geriatric old fool and that old biddy off the road.' The driver was red-faced as he released his grip on Jared Edwards but too late. The strap snapped and the bag fell to the road.

'This vehicle has no right to be going through this town,' Jared Edwards was vehement. 'Nor that one.' He pointed at the lorry that had been coming out of the town. 'There are signs at both ends of the town.' He put his face into that of the driver. '7.5 tons limit!'

'Not if he's delivering in the town,' Challis put forward.

'Look at his paperwork then,' Jared Edwards challenged her. She was walking the thin line here, trying not to take sides.

'Papers,' she quietly demanded. The driver was less than happy at what he perceived was police bias. Challis held her hand out waiting. He fished a document out of his top overall pocket. Jared Edwards leaned over her shoulder and spotted the delivery address before she did.

'Pontypool! There you are. Ponty-bloody-pool. He should be up to the Raglan turn-off on the A449 and then the A40 to Abergavenny and down the 4042 to Pontypool.'

The driver did not wilt. 'Sat nav sent me this way.'

'Bloody sat nav. Haven't you got a brain of your own?'

Challis was mentally calculating what best to do.

'Okay. Your lorry is way over the legal weight limit and I'm not going to let you proceed through the town.'

'What?' the driver was aghast. 'How the fuck…?'

'Watch your mouth or get arrested.'

He took a deep breath. 'How the hell am I going to turn this round in these roads?'

He was right. There was no way.

'What you can do,' she began slowly, 'is drive on to the second turning on the left. That's the Square. Get in there and turn around the roundabout and come back this way and then out onto the A449, going north.'

'D'you realize how much extra diesel this is going to cost me?'

She ignored the point. 'And don't even think of carrying on through the town.'

Jared Edwards tapped his camera. 'Don't worry, officer. I've got him and his juggernaut on camera.'

'Now go. Mr. Edwards, get your wife off the road. You,' she called to the driver of the lorry driving towards the A449, 'get out of here.'

'I've got him too,' Jared Edwards muttered, waving his camera in the air.

Then Edwards and Challis, picking up his broken satchel for him, retreated to the pavement as vehicles began to move. Car drivers were less than appreciative of the hard work done by the vigilante and his wife. Despite the icy morning windows were down and colourful advice dispensed.

'Mr. Edwards,' Challis turned her attention to him as Redland sauntered up to join them, 'your actions are totally illegal. If anyone should be run in it's you.'

'Somebody has to make a stand. You lot do nothing.' He addressed his complaint to both Challis and Redland. 'Have you seen the latest damage to the bridge. Not just a few stones off the top but a bloody great hole down to road level. Six feet wide!'

He snatched his bag from Challis's hands. 'Look at this lot.' He extracted a thick photo album. 'We've been collecting all this evidence for months.' He flicked through pages and pages of photos: lorries, damage to the stonework of the river bridge, illegally parked cars, drivers using mobile phones. 'Look. An illegal lorry and he's on the phone. Look at it all.'

Challis did. This man was very serious about his hobby and, yes, he was recording breaches of the law. If Mon Police was able to operate a zero-tolerance policy it would all be good stuff but really the old man and his wife were simply wasting their time. Still, she thought whimsically, at least it keeps them out in the fresh air.

A photo grabbed her as it flashed by. She threw her hand into the page as Jared Edwards went to go on.

'You lot do absolutely nothing about any of this.' He looked down at the page she had caught. 'Yes, just look at that one. Look at it. Did you ever see such a stupid cow? A woman with a car-load of kids, turning a corner with just one hand on the wheel.'

She eased the album out of his grasp. It was not the irresponsibility of the female driver that had caught her eye, it was the car waiting at the junction. It was an old Saab, registration number M769 ZWO.

'I'd like a copy of that,' she said, unable to look up from it.

'Great!' Jared Edwards was elated. 'Action at last.'

'A4 if possible.'

A claxon sounded long and loud as the artic came back from its manoeuvre in the Square and headed towards the A449. The driver's fingers added to the insult. Jared Edwards didn't care. He'd got a good result at last. 'You can have it glossy!'

Challis waited outside Redland's front door while the A4 copy was printed in the Edwards's house. Redland handed the shoulder bag back to Challis and then the file but he held onto one document, a copy of the photo of Mack and Medlyn in action with the girl.

'Is this what you're working on at the moment?'

'Yeah. It's related to that murder last Saturday I told you about.'

He examined the photo again.

'It's not turning out to be very nice at all,' Challis told him.

He slowly looked up as he handed it back to her. 'No, I can see that.'

'Those two men have been murdered. Shot...and mutilated.'

'The girl...'

'We don't know who she is yet.'

He stared at Challis, unnerving her, as if accusing her of something. 'I know who she is.'

'He knew who she was?' Lassman was astounded as yet again something significant to a case happened along by pure chance.

They were in their conference room office in Police HQ. Lassman was digesting the information that had come Challis's way en route to pick him up. He uttered no words of congratulation. All this stuff had fallen into her lap as far as he was concerned.

'Angela Plumitis,' Challis confirmed. She was sure in her own mind how well she had done that morning and it wasn't nine o'clock yet. 'Here, look at this.'

She put in front of him the one page list of attendees at Cottel Court, found in Timothy Bush's printer. She pointed to the name that Redland had now admitted he recognized but at a time when it could have had no connection to anything they were interested in.

'Last weekend in January this list refers to and the photo of Medlyn's Saab was taken in Usk that same Friday. He, Peter Mack and Angela Plumitis were at Cottel Court that weekend. That's where your video was shot.'

Lassman put his finger on the list. 'Vikings equals VKS January 2011.'

'I guess so,' she mused. 'Vikings.'

'Yes. Rape and pillage.' Tight-lipped, he let that sink in with Challis. 'So, we have her address on this list. It's in our neck of the woods. I'll get my sergeant onto it.'

'She won't be there. The boss reckons he saw her in the hospital where he was, just two days ago. At least he's pretty sure it was her. She was out for the count, lying on a trolley waiting to go into the scanner. He thought he knew her but he now realizes she must have been really sick because she did not much resemble this picture.'

'Probably had more clothes on,' he quipped. 'So that boss of yours is on death's door one minute and a prime witness the next.'

Challis took exception to this. She was finding this traveling detective from the cultured metropolis more and more overbearing with just about everything he said and did.

'Mr. Redland loves this job. He could have retired by now but chose to work on. It's his life.'

'Very commendable.' His insincerity was palpable. 'So he still thinks it's her?'

'Yes. He has the best memory for faces.'

Muench came in. Lassman had wondered where he was. The young man had the air of a skiver about him. He was about to question where he had been but Muench beat him to it, slapping a piece of paper on the conference table before picking up a cup of chilled coffee he'd left there before going off to do his errand.

'Angela Plumitis is in intensive care,' he announced.

'I sent Harry a text asking him to follow up on the boss's sighting,' Challis explained, delighting in getting across to Lassman that some people read texts and action them. Lassman was unmoved.

'She was taking in by ambulance on Saturday,' Muench continued. 'They wouldn't tell me what the problem was. Waiting for next of kin to turn up.'

'We need to speak to her,' Challis said enthusiastically.

Lassman was less excited. 'Mr. Muench. Do you own a tie? If so I suggest you put it on.'

Muench went to his jacket hanging near the door and took out a tie from the pocket.

Lassman ignored the movement and paced the floor. He stared at Challis as he stroked his beard. He stared long and hard.

'Why?' he said at last.

'Why?' Challis was incredulous. 'Why do we need to speak to her?'

'Y-e-s. That was the question.'

'Angela Plumitis...Angela Plumitis is in these photographs being...being buggered by one man while another one stands ready and waiting to have his turn.'

'Okay. Georgie is doing the deed but we don't know that Mack the knife followed suit.'

Challis was not going to be thrown off track. 'O, I think we do. Both men, Peter Mack especially, were repaid in kind.'

Lassman shuddered. 'Ugh! Don't remind me.'

'Sir...'

'Sir! She calls me Sir, at long last.'

Muench was enjoying this interchange. Now Challis did not want to repeat the word.

'I don't think you're taking this seriously.' But she did repeat it with feeling. 'Sir.'

'What about this guy Jenkins that your boss told you about?'

Challis was nonplussed by his change of tack. She herded her thoughts together.

'He's a builder, in Usk. I've seen his lorry around.'

'So why did he get all worked up about Angela Plumitis and charge out of the doctors after her? I think we need to work out a plan of action for you and me for today. Harry, you get on with background checks on the Macks. Mel, you and I have to consider the third element.'

'The third element?'

'Yes. The one you identified yesterday. Remember? No, obviously not. First element, we need to speak to Angela Plumitis.' He ignored Challis's open mouth. 'Second element, we need to speak to Jenkins the builder…that's how you say it down here in Welsh Wales, isn't it, boyo? Jenkins the builder? And the third element, look for the other two guys in the video. You need to see the full clip that we've got, Mel.' He opened up his laptop and powered it on. 'While that's warming up I'll get my lot to check the lovely Angela's address; see who she lives with and so on. Your boss says she was at the doctors getting an inhaler and had to fill in a form. Harry, contact them and…'

'No need,' Challis interrupted, looking at her watch. 'It's nearly nine. DC Ruff is on her way there at this moment to speak to them about our suicide case. Another patient of theirs. I'll get her to do it.' She flipped open her smartphone.

'Another text?' Lassman asked incredulously.

Forty

Greta Plumitis would not allow Chas or Jackie to go with her into the intensive care ward.

Her daughter was in a bed behind curtains, on a monitor with drips of one sort or another snaking into her arms and up her nose. The nurse who took her in tried to explain the situation but most of the words went in one ear and out the other.

Greta was offered a chair but stood rooted looking down at the pale wraith that they said was her daughter. Yes, it was Angela, she knew that; she didn't want to believe it.

She heard the words "very poorly" and "can't operate yet".

She gathered her daughter's body was "poisoned".

Antibiotics were doing what they could but making little head-way.

She asked more than once what was wrong but the first reply mentioned something about the peritoneum. She asked again and heard ruptured intestine.

Was that a burst appendix?

No, the gut had lesions.

What d'you mean? She was in tears with the frustration of not being able to understand. The nurse sat her down and slowly enunciated the fact that the rectum…? Greta nodded…was badly torn in a number of places and waste from the gut had leaked into the abdomen causing a massive infection.

The rectum.

The lower gut.

Greta understood that, but how? She wanted to know how.

The nurse could see that this was not the time to go into what they had deduced about the cause of the injuries. The mother was extremely upset already. She deflected the question by saying that the main priority now had to be recovery and the doctors were waiting for the right moment to take Angel...she made the mistake of using the name used by those other two, Greta angrily corrected her...Angela! The nurse coolly repeated this version and went on to explain that surgery was the probable course of treatment.

But how did it happen?

The nurse lost her resolve and suggested she ask Angel's...Angela's friend.

Then she quickly excused herself to go find a doctor. Somebody else needed to explain more fully that there were concerns about strain on Angela's heart and could it cope with the trauma of an operation.

Greta held the hand of her sleeping daughter. She was only sleeping, yes, but her breathing was shallow and all effort.

With fingers of her other hand she wiped tears from her cheeks before stretching forward to unnecessarily move hair back from Angela's forehead.

She is my angel; not theirs.

O good God what have they done to you? How could you get such...such...? She couldn't even articulate the nurse's words in her own mind.

What have you done, you stupid girl?

She had thought she knew what Angela had become. But why had she? That was the burning question. The lure of sex, that was what it was. The addiction.

She'd had it once. For years. Never with a woman though.

They were her selfish times, she knew it, but even now she couldn't regret them. Young Angela, asleep in the room next to hers, while she entertained her men friends.

Thin walls.

Much noise.

Angela sometimes woke and tottered in. Saw nothing surely. Eyes full of sleep. Didn't matter if she did. She wouldn't understand.

Once or twice though Angela was wide-eyed in the doorway, standing there how long? She had no idea.

She had read that a paedophile can persuade the abused child that what is happening is normal. She had never read what impression is left with the voyeur child. She had found amateurish blogs that either exalted voyeuristic exposure of children to sexual acts or condemned it outright as evil.

It seemed that, if not traumatized by what is seen, the child's mind may be imprinted, even excited, eager to emulate.

That proved to be certainly the case with Angela. From a young age she had had a predilection for boys and the contents of their trousers. Greta had caught her innumerable times, at first saying nothing, later conducting a conciliatory inquest with her. But she had never interjected or stopped the childish experimentation while it was happening.

After all, it was natural.

It was what she had done while growing up.

But she had never wanted her daughter to become the butt of innuendo as she had become. Her addiction had stripped her naked, literally; the need outdoing any shame. There was hardly a single man that she could remember wanting to please. Whatever she did to them she did for her own pleasure; to get her to where she needed to go. Such was the pull. When inevitably satisfied she would cast them off.

There was an old male joke: *I have never been to bed with an ugly woman but I have sure woken up with a few.* Greta had an equivalent: *I have never been to bed with a man whose face I needed to remember in the morning.*

Was she to blame for what Angela had become?

But not, ever, for the terrible state her Angela was now in. Never ever!

But the journey that had led to this had begun with Greta. She never knew. She never knew that her fourteen year-old daughter had been alone in the house when one of Greta's gentlemen friends – Greta loved that quaint old secret-sounding euphemism – had come to call. Angela knew him. She had heard him and her mother and even watched them through a crack in the bedroom door.

'Your mother likes me to be rough with her,' he told her and she knew it was true. Her mother would beg and then scream her enjoyment. It sounded like such good fun and when he attacked her own youthful lips and neck with his rough unshaven face and then ripped her clothes from her body she fell naked beneath his still clothed body, urging him into her. There was pain, bearable pain but then delirious pinnacles of unprecedented pleasures.

Angela was addicted.

For all her self-recriminations, Greta had no idea how much she had unknowingly groomed her daughter.

Now, any token feelings of remorse and guilt were brought to a sudden end by a piercing alarm emanating from the monitor. She glared at it but could not interpret its readings. She looked at Angela, whose chest lay flat. Unmoving.

Forty-One

Kay Ruff made good time to Usk. The pool car performed without a hiccup, much to her relief, but the satnav wasn't working. The only holdup had been at Usk bridge where traffic lights were in operation as road gangs were repairing an enormous hole in the bridge wall.

The drive through the early morning had been good, she loved it, dropping from the U-shaped valleys and round-top mountains in the west down to the gentle green land of the Usk valley. She would love to live here but there was no chance. For at least two reasons. One was that Alex was an valley boy and loved it there. The other was that they could never afford it. A terraced house up a mountain was in their price range; a terraced house in Usk was not and she wouldn't want one of those cheaper pokey ones anyway.

In low moments when the mountain rain hung in curtains of grey and you couldn't see the other side of the valley she was jealous of Melanie and the boss. Alan Redland, single, no ties, nobody pulling on his far from meager resources; nice house. And lucky Melanie, a place inherited from her parents. Well, okay, they'd died in a car crash but jammy nonetheless.

She'd been to Melanie's a couple of times. Capelgwm; spaced out houses, hers actually made up of two cottages, one once higher up the slope than the other so that, now, the lower part of the single dwelling was living area, studies and an enormous kitchen to die for and the upper part all bedrooms and bathrooms. Four bedrooms! For one person! She bet the council tax was band F at least, or should be, but as a single occupant it would be discounted.

Jammy. Fair play.

Each visit her face had betrayed her feelings. Verbally she had been upbeat, telling Mel how lucky she was but after the second visit Melanie had read the signals and had not mentioned her house again let alone put out another invite.

She reached the Surgery before the appointed hour. Nine-thirty Melanie had said was the time of the appointment with the practice manager.

She sat in the car, listening to music she didn't like. Radio Wales was just coming out with traffic news. Accident on the M4 westbound between Newport and Cardiff; traffic backed up to the bottleneck tunnels. She could just imagine Alex stuck in it on his way to his call-centre job in Cardiff. He'd be late most probably.

Her phone rang. It was Mel, Mel of the detached house in Capelgwm.

'Hi, Mel.'

She had to get her pad out to write down Mel's additional instructions.

'What's this woman got to do with Timothy Bush?' she queried.

There was a temporary silence from the other end before Mel came up with an explanation. 'There's a link with Cottel Court. You'd better get a move on. It's nearly nine-thirty.'

As she was going in through the door, Alan Redland was coming out. Ruff couldn't believe it.

'Sir! I thought you were in hospital.'

He was equally surprised. 'Well, Kay. What on earth are you doing here?'

She explained about Timothy Bush; the suicide. 'This is his doctors, too.'

Redland nodded. 'You'll like Terry, the practice manager. Right up your street. Do you want me to come in with you?'

'Er, no, sir. Thank you. You should be at home with your feet up.'

'Plenty of time for that I fancy. How did you get on with that hotel robbery? He's a friend of mine the guy who owns it.'

'Pushed back to uniform, sir. Mel had to shelve a few things as we got a bit short-handed and things got hectic with that Blackwood killing.'

'Yes, right. How's that going?'

'No idea, sir. Not involved. Still on Timothy Bush. How are you anyway, sir?'

'Just been in for the early morning gloat test. The doctor excelled herself this morning.'

He waved her on to keep her appointment. Ruff blew out a sigh of relief as she approached the reception desk.

Terry, the practice manager, was *right up her street* because he was of obvious Asian descent. Redland's little joke, she realized. Terry's full name was Tareq Rahman but the receptionist called him Terry as well.

He was very co-operative. Offered Ruff a coffee that she declined and sat her down close to himself in his small office. He pointed out the intricacies of the Data Protection Act but Ruff showed him the document from the coroner's office that confirmed Timothy Bush as deceased and gave him the warrant that authorized access to the records.

'Right,' Terry began, bringing Timothy Bush's details onto his laptop. 'Don't see much of him. Last consultation here was five months ago and before that, last April, he had his ears syringed.'

'You realize we'll need a printout of his records.'

'Yes of course.'

'Can you do it now please so that I can see what you're seeing.'

Lethargically, Terry produced a single sheet of paper from the printer at his elbow.

'Is this all?' Ruff saw that Timothy Bush's last consultation with a doctor was in the previous September. He was concerned about a back strain caused by lifting something heavy that was giving him sciatic pain down his left leg. The doctor prescribed strong painkillers that must have done the trick because he didn't come back. Before that, he had had his ears syringed as Terry had said and going further back to his date of registration in 2000 he had come in for two other minor problems: left knee cartilage and/or ligament strain from jogging and tennis elbow, thought it was RSI from keyboard use.

No STIs. No mental or behavioural issues.

'Afraid so,' he said, unmoved by the thin history.

Ruff didn't know how to approach the fact that the autopsy had shown Timothy Bush was HIV positive. Her smartphone was already on – she should have switched it off before this interview started – and she retrieved the case notes, especially Sayer's.

'If a patient here sought treatment elsewhere would not these records be updated? I mean, wouldn't the other medical outfit have to keep you informed, as his doctor?'

Terry scoffed. 'Well, not if he – I assume you're talking Mr. Bush – went direct to a chiropodist or physiotherapist or some other pseudo-health johnnies.'

'What about…' Ruff was struggling with confidentiality issues herself now. 'What about sexual health clinics? Aren't they part of the NHS network?'

'What's that got to do with Mr. Bush?'

'It's hypothetical. I mean could I go to one without a referral from my GP and would they keep my results to themselves?'

With a look bordering on incredulity he said 'Yes, you can and no, they wouldn't unless you give them your permission.'

'Where are the nearest clinics to Usk?'

'You can find them on-line. NHS Wales.'

'Let's assume there is a sexual health problem, something that could be transmitted to someone else, is there no system for contacting other people that he could have passed it on to?'

'He? So we are talking about Mr. Bush? His post-mortem showed up some condition, an STI.'

She realized she'd slipped up. 'Possibly.'

'It would be good to be honest with one another here, you know. What was it?'

'I can't tell you that, precisely. But I'd appreciate your assistance in answering my questions.'

'I've done everything your search warrant requested. You have Mr. Bush's records. If you want me to act as a consultant it'll cost you, I'm afraid.'

His beady brown eyes were boring into her. It was obvious he wasn't interested in an off-the-record helpful chat. She began to put the printout and her phone away.

'Have a drink with me tonight.' His lips curled unflatteringly. His suggestion was not put like a question but a certainty. She frowned.

'We're not really encouraged to do that kind of thing. Besides,' she held up her wedding finger, 'I'm married.'

'I'm not proposing marriage.'

'That's no comfort.'

'Just a drink. Plenty of nice pubs in Usk.'

She had no idea if she'd even be anywhere near Usk come evening.

'Six o'clock,' he said believing she was contemplating his offer.

'Okay,' she said, trying to sound enthused. Saying yes could get her what she wanted and did not promise anything.

'Right. Six o'clock in the Queens Arms. You know it?'

'O, yes.' She didn't. 'Great.'

'Yeah. Right then. Let's have some coffee, shall we, before we get on with…your questions.' The conspiratorial look on his face was comical but she quietly demurred.

'No coffee thanks. Better get on with the business so I can then get on and finish before six.'

'Okay. What did you ask? O yes, system for notification of contacts of person with some dread disease.' He was so upbeat now that he had got himself an assignation with this wholesome female that he was verging on the hyperactive. 'There is no system.' He shook his head in a whimsical exaggerated movement as if he was checking his neck was still supporting his head. 'STIs are not notifiable diseases. It's all about privacy. Again. Data Protection.'

'What? That's crazy.'

'I don't believe so. There has to be confidentiality especially about a person's private sex life'.'

'That is crazy,' she reiterated. 'Deliberately or recklessly giving someone else HIV is a criminal offence so surely there has to be public concern; a right to know.'

'HIV is it?'

She recovered quickly. 'For example…'

He shrugged his shoulders with great exaggeration. 'I see. No, it is no public concern. Hitting somebody over the head with a hammer is a criminal offence but you don't have to notify anyone that you own one.'

'So the people you are currently treating here for H…for STIs you don't ask for names and addresses of their sleeping partners.'

He smiled. 'Lovely Officer Ruff, now you are beating a hasty path up a cul-de-sac. They are advised they should do, that is all.'

She did manage to move onto Angela Plumitis for Mel but she could see there was no argument to win.

Terry showed her out of his office and back to the reception area and a "see you later", wink.

Crazy bloody country, she thought, fuming. Privacy getting in the way again. P.C! Privacy had far more success than PCs like her!

Maybe she should lobby the Welsh Assembly. Now that it had been given extra powers from that last referendum in which she hadn't bothered to vote maybe they could enact in Wales that HIV be made a notifiable disease. And even stop anyone infected putting it about by cutting their cocks off. Her belief was that men were to blame, not women as was the opinion of proponents of Original Sin.

Redland was waiting for her.

'Thought you might fancy a coffee. There are a couple of cafes in the main street or we could go back to my place.'

Ruff was flummoxed by his unexpected presence and yet another invitation for coffee. She'd thought he'd headed off home. The fact that he had waited for her to reappear was disconcerting. What was he doing? He did not sound like the boss she had worked for for four months. He was giving her a look that seemed to have nothing to do with work.

'You've been to Mel's place I believe, out in the sticks,' he persisted. 'But I live just a short walk away. You could leave your car here.'

She recovered her poise and offered him a weak smile. 'It's all right for you, sir. On sick leave. Some of us have work to do. I haven't finished here yet.' She waited, hoping he'd melt away. 'Some other time perhaps, sir. We could all get together.'

'Yes, yes. You'd better get on.'

He seemed to shrink and she felt sorry for him. She didn't want to watch him go so she headed for the reception desk.

She'd told Terry that she needed to see the form Angela Plumitis had filled in on the last Friday in January. He'd playfully put on his data protection hesitation but then told her to enquire at reception on her way out. He'd clear it with Meg on the desk.

Meg Ryan had the form ready for her to peruse. Ruff read it, her eyebrows rising. She got a photocopy and left.

Outside, in the car park she looked around for the boss but he was nowhere in sight, much to her relief. She hurried to her car to call Mel, not totally put-out by two offers already today. Flattering but a bit of a laugh.

'I've got the info on Angela Plumitis,' she blurted out to Mel. 'You'll never guess what she put down as her local address here.' Challis couldn't guess and didn't offer one. 'No. 1 Pontderry Lane.'

'Well, well,' was Challis's take on the news.
'D'you want me to go there? I'm only just down the road.'
'No. She's not there. Wait a minute.'
Ruff could hear Challis talking to someone but her voice was muffled.
'Kay!' She came back. 'We want you to go to the hospital in Abergavenny instead. That's where Angela Plumitis is, in intensive care. Find out if she's available for interview.'
'Can I ask if this is still to do with Timothy Bush?'
'There could be a connection. I'll tell you more later. First get up there and find out if she can speak. Let me know.'
'Where are you?'
'In the office.'
'Who's "we"?'
'What?'
'You said "we" want me to go to Abergavenny.'
'Look, you're wasting time. All will be explained later.'
'D'you want to know what they said about Timothy Bush and his medical history?'
'Later. Write it up.' And Challis was gone.
Ruff switched on the car engine, face strained with frustration. Does she think I'm a fucking bimbo? Later! Write it up; when for Christ sake?
Angela Plumitis! Never heard of her. It's fuck all to do with Timothy Bush. Mel's on that other new case now. The murder.
What about finishing off this case first? And those daughters of his should still be told about their father's…disease!
And how the fuck do I get to Abergavenny from here without satnav?

Forty-Two

Greta Plumitis was asked, ordered, to leave her daughter's bedside.
The nurse had come hurrying in as the monitor sounded off. As Greta emerged through the plastic curtains she was brushed aside by other medical staff racing in. Disorientated, she stumbled this way and that, seeking a way out, eventually finding the door that took her back to where Chas and Jackie were still standing.
Hatred for the pair of them coursed through her entire body. She fumbled in her pockets for tissues to dab on her eyes. Jackie saw and offered her one. Christ, what had Angela ever seen in this ugly caricature of a person, this hideous orange-haired dwarf?
'Get away,' was Greta's greeting. 'What have you done to her?'
Her voice was loud and Chas looked around to see who might be within earshot. The only other person anywhere near was a guy in overalls, hovering, trying not to look in their direction. Chas was unable to tear his

eyes off the guy. His instincts said the bloke was tempted to muscle in and join them. His attention returned to Greta and Jackie as the volume of voices increased further. Greta was in full flow.

'Those injuries, those...penetrations were all you, weren't they? Say yes. You know it.'

'No,' Jackie tried to protest. She had always had a swagger in front of Angel's mother, a cruel pleasure in rubbing her nose in the fact that she was Angel's intimate.

Greta's hostility to Jackie and the role she was convinced she had played in her daughter's slide into extremes had always been plain to see.

Jackie reveled in the anguish she caused. She told herself she was more to Angel than this sexual has-been of a mother could ever be again. Greta's past and her occasional present were not unknowns to Jackie. As far as she could see, Angel had always had to endure her mother.

This time was different though. Jackie's antagonism towards Greta slid away as all that she wanted to convey to the older woman was her love for her daughter, a love that would never entertain the sadism that Angel had experienced.

Christ, shit, bugger!

Why had she let Angel carry on down that path? For all her bluster she had always let Angel do whatever she liked.

'Greta,' that was a first, using her name. 'I didn't do it. I never could.' She pleaded but Greta was disdainful.

'You bitch! You and your evil father. You preyed on her, both of you.'

Chas advanced on her until they were virtually toe to toe. The man in overalls twitched and lurched forward a pace.

'Listen to what she's saying,' Chas breathed, forceful but not aggressive. 'She's telling you the truth. She told the doctors it was her to save your feelings and to protect Angel.'

She clenched her teeth at the sound of the name but bit her tongue. 'I'm not telling you anymore. It's up to Angel to tell you, if she wants to, but I doubt she does. She knows what you're like. We all know what you're like. So don't come preaching to us.'

The tears had dried, now her eyes were like hot daggers.

She hated this man.

She knew exactly what he was getting at.

He'd come to her house once, just the once. He got under her skin then, straight away.

He came to pick up his daughter. He stayed the night. She gave him some blankets on the sofa.

They all went to bed. Jackie led the way, turning at the top of the stairs, looking down on her with that grin.

The bedroom walls were thin as ever. She had lain silent in her bed, listening to her own breathing and the noises, mostly for effect, coming from her daughter's room.

At first they kindled flaming hatred in her breast but between the gasps and groans from Jackie's mouth she could make out the genuine sighs from her daughter's lips and they had an unexpected effect on her.

She was without a man at that time. Her last lover had departed some time before and she had come to ask herself "what am I going to do now?"

She slipped out of the bed, stepped out of her nightdress and stood, her flesh creeping, for several seconds in front of her wall mirror. She then put on a sheer robe and went downstairs.

It had been half an hour since they had all retired, supposedly for the night. Chas was still awake, wide awake, laying back bare-chested, one hand behind his head, the other beneath the blankets.

The sounds from above were audible. The deep-throated moans from Angela were clearly discernible.

Greta sidled silently into the darkened room, moved to the sofa and stood alongside, saying nothing, having no wish to beg.

His free hand was on her thigh immediately, almost as if she had walked into his outstretched palm. But this touch was just for him to get his bearings. As soon as he found her flesh his hand shot up between her widening legs, his fingers slipping easily inside her.

'Why should they have all the fun?' he asked. He pulled the blanket aside. He was proudly naked. Her hot breath steamed up her eyes but she could see what she wanted and took possession of it.

God, how she regretted that night and the addiction, now especially. She hated him. She hated him then. But she hated herself more.

Now he twisted the knife. 'Turned on by your own daughter,' he hissed. 'And too arrogant to admit it.'

She broke away from him, giving him and then Jackie a stabbing stare. 'Unlike you, I suppose.'

'Listen, leave her alone.' He half-waved a hand in Jackie's direction. 'You really ought to believe this but I don't care if you do or you don't. We both love Angel.'

This time she rebutted him with 'Angela'.

'She is the love of that girl's life,' he insisted.

'I wouldn't...' Jackie began.

'You wouldn't, you wouldn't! I've seen the things you email her.' Greta was scathing. 'They're in there now, trying to save my daughter's life. If she dies...' She gulped in air. 'If anything happens to her, I'll make you pay. Both of you.'

Jenkins had watched the scene develop, seeing it but not hearing it all. He thought the big man was going to grab Greta Plumitis and he was ready to step in. But they just spat at each other, she more than him. Her body language surprised him. There was still passion there but it was aggressive, no way inviting. If he hadn't recognized her she would be unrecognizable.

He averted his eyes as Greta stepped away from the other two and meandered in his general direction. Again, she was dabbing her eyes but with her back to the others so that they couldn't see. She looked winded, standing unsteadily in the middle of the floor as if likely to topple. The other two, the bloke he knew by sight, were together at the far end, not speaking, not touching, looking lost he thought.

Greta continued her ambling until she was passing him, so close he could see her large green eyes, her skin unblemished, her lips full. She seemed vulnerable.

'Greta.' He'd taken a deep breath. 'Greta Plumitis?'

Her face had turned up at the first sound of her name. The second more qualified greeting made her try and focus her wet eyes on the source.

A man in overalls.

She blinked, vision blurred.

Was he hospital staff?

He looked scruffy; hair unkempt, face unshaven. The overalls were just that and none too clean.

What did he want?

He glanced across the room to the other two who were now watching him.

'Who are you?' she asked curtly.

Jenkins was suffering the rebuff again. It had never occurred to him that his appearance may actually put people off wanting to recognize him.

'Jim Jenkins,' he blurted. 'Jimmy Jenkins.' He remembered how he was called thirty years ago.

'I don't know you, do I.' Not so much a question but a firm put-down.

'Greta. Newport Construction, 1979.' He eyed the other two before bending closer to her to whisper. 'Christmas. 1979.'

The name of the firm was familiar to her. Yes, a job long ago.

'I left at Christmas,' he continued. 'After we'd....I never saw you again, until I saw Angela...'

'Angela?'

'Our daughter, in Usk.'

'Our....' She struggled to grasp his meaning.

'I never knew. You should have looked for me. The lads kind of said but I thought they were joking. I've thought about you, off and on, over the years. Thirty years. Angela's thirty, born twenty-ninth of September 1980, nine months after we'd...'

She remembered now. She'd forgotten his name. She'd forgotten it again already. What did it matter? That Christmas Eve; the one time she'd not been careful. The one day she'd not been careful.

When she found out she was pregnant she had gone over that day in her mind.

If this guy was the one who had worked there back then, yes, he had been the first that day but she had pushed him way to the back of the queue. He'd fucked and run, leaving her high and dissatisfied. She remembered him, barely, as a frightened little prick.

It had become a long Christmas Eve night. A party and several men. And remembering, there had never been any way of knowing which one was Angela's father. She could have taken her pick but she certainly wouldn't have picked this one.

She ignored Jenkins. That this half man would presume to be the father of her Angela...

Her Angela!

The door into the intensive care ward swung open. The nurse she had been with earlier stood there, a doctor alongside.

Chas and Jackie took a half step forward but the two white-coated figures brushed past them and on to Greta. They muttered something, the nurse taking her by the elbow. She was guided past Jenkins and into a side-room, the door closing behind them.

Chas and Jackie came closer, in Jenkins's space, just as they heard from inside the room a rumbling, escalating scream like an approaching earthquake.

Jackie gave a loud gasp. Chas looked down at her as if wanting an explanation. Jenkins's mouth was agape. Panic was in his eyes. 'That's my daughter,' he told them before taking in a huge sobbing gulp of air.

The screams in the room went on, eventually subsiding, then came the shouting. 'I want the police! I want the police!'

Jackie had walked away while the screaming was going on. Chas was glued to this guy in the overalls. The truck! He was the driver. What was he saying? Angel's his daughter?

He looked around for his own daughter, catching sight of her going into the ward. He raced after her.

Medics were still hovering over Angela and at first they didn't notice Jackie behind them. She barged through.

A high-pitched wail came from her lips as she saw the lifeless face of her lover. Arms restrained her as she tried to get to her. She needed to embrace her, to shake her into life.

'Come away. Jackie. Come away.' Chas had hold of her arms.

'I want to see her.' It was a screeching demand.

'Come away now. Later.'

He pulled and she was surprisingly weightless, no real resistance.

'We have to go. Now. The police will be here.'

'I don't care.' She wriggled violently, still in his grasp.

'Jackie, it's finished. We've got to get away from here; get you away from here. This way.'

'It isn't finished yet, Chas. I told you. It isn't finished.'

He led her to the left so that they would not have to go past the side-room. The direction surprised her; she was already looking the way she thought they would be going. The man in the overalls was still there waiting outside the door which burst open and Greta Plumitis stormed out, glaring, her face red and wet, scouring the corridors.

'You!' she screamed as she caught sight of Jackie and Chas heading for the side stairs. 'You bitch! She's dead. You killed my girl!'

Jackie's first instinct was to home in on the woman and she would have done but Chas restrained her, pulling her towards the exit. Jenkins too had a firm grip of Greta's arm. She tried to wrench it away but he would not let go. The anger in her face was now on him but by the time she looked back to where Jackie had been there was nobody there. She screamed her frustration and finally tore herself away from Jenkins.

Forty-Three

Lassman loaded the video clip on his laptop.

'This is a short clip, a minute or two, all of it my Georgie in action. I reckon he took this bit off a much longer video so that he could keep viewing his moment. He's not interested in the other guys. It's only good luck that we get a sight of your Mr. Mack. The other two blokes barely come into view. Are you ready?' He checked with Challis who attempted a nonchalant nod. Muench had been called over to join them although this made Challis nervous. She knew how his mind worked.

Lassman was seated at the keyboard, the other two stood one over each shoulder.

'Okay. Same watershed warning as last night, only more so.'

Before his finger could hit the Enter key the door opened and DCC Alice Jones came in.

'Ah, morning, ma'am,' Lassman said cheerfully. She did not return the greeting.

'What's this?' she asked.

'We're about to view the video clip from which the stills were taken,' he explained.

'Really.' She approached at a matter-of-fact pace that matched her tone. Challis made to move but DCC Jones halted her. 'May I?'

'Why, certainly, ma'am.' Challis noticed Lassman was a lot more proper with the DCC this morning than he had been yesterday.

'Okay. Rolling.'

He kept up a commentary as the video played. He had seen this material so often now that he was striving to keep the viewing objective. It could disgust, nauseate or, he suspected, arouse. He had seen all permutations back in the office in Windsor.

He spoke slow and deliberately, choosing words carefully, highlighting when Peter Mack came into view, the brief sight of the two masked men and the interpretation of Angela Plumitis's screams; that is, she was either a bloody good actress or was in considerable pain. Either way, George Medlyn was spurred on by it.

'You know who she is,' the DCC spoke after clearing her throat.

Lassman allowed Challis to tell how DI Redland had identified the woman. She was glad to do this, it allowed her to avert her eyes from the screen in order to address the DCC. She strung it out; lots of detail.

'Good copper Alan,' the DCC said. She too was struggling with the pictures.

The video ended.

'That's it,' Lassman concluded. 'Short and...' He let the next word die in his mouth.

'Could this woman be your killer?' the DCC asked.

'She could be.'

'If you know where she is shouldn't you be picking her up?'

'DC Ruff is on her way to the hospital now,' Challis informed her.

'She may need backup.'

'Ma'am,' Muench spoke up. 'Angela Plumitis is in intensive care.'

'So the hospital says,' the DCC glowered. 'Until it's confirmed I think we should act accordingly. You need to check her movements. See if she could have been in both places at the times of the shootings.'

'We're also concerned about the other two men,' Challis said. 'The ones in masks.'

'Why would you be?'

Lassman picked it up. 'They may be next. And if Angela Plumitis is not our man then the killer or killers are still out there. We need to blow up the limited view that we have of them; see if we can id them.'

The DCC nodded. 'I'd chase Miss Plumitis first if I was you.'

She was on her way out when she paused. 'O, I nearly forgot, why I came in in the first place. Superintendent O'Halloran called in sick. Don't know for how long but as Chief Super Harper is busy with valleys case you can report to me. Keep me updated. Find me this afternoon when you've something to report.'

Lassman was less than impressed but waited until the DCC was out of the room.

'On the sick. I dread hearing those words. It's almost become a communicable disease.'

'Goes with the job,' Challis put forward. 'We've all had time on the sick.'

'Have we?' Lassman asked, looking distinctly tired of hearing once more what he considered had become a policeman's God-given right to be unwell.

To Challis Lassman had a ruddy glow about him so perhaps he was the exception. But then the boss was the same. It had taken a heart-attack to lay him low and even now he'd be here if he could.

'DC Ruff found out where Angela was staying in this area. It's an address known to us. It was part of our recent investigation into a suicide.'

'Ha, the famous suicide.' Lassman almost scoffed.

'The woman who lives there works at Cottel Court.'

Lassman's eyebrows lifted. 'Coincidences. I hate coincidences. Usually they're not.'

'She's probably there right now so I suggest we get up there. Kill two birds with one stone.'

'More than two I wouldn't be surprised. Could be a whole flock.'

Muench's silence attracted them. He was still standing at Lassman's left shoulder staring at the laptop screen even though there were no longer any moving pictures. Lassman was thinking this guy is getting dumber. Challis was more disturbed, wondering what thoughts were in Muench's head after the video show.

Their silence jerked him to life.

'Harry, are you still with us?' Lassman asked with an edge.

'I was just thinking...'

Good, at last, Lassman thought.

Yes but what about? Challis thought.

'This video, a snippet as you say of something longer. Their houses, both houses, were ransacked, computers removed, dvd collections searched. Could it be that the killer, or killers, were trying to make sure that any copies of the full-length video were destroyed? And aren't we forgetting that now we know, or think we know, where those three met and had their orgy that the original images must be there too.'

Forty-Four

As Ruff came to the junction out of the Square in Usk she saw a sign for Abergavenny. She turned left and then right and drove out of the town along the bank of the River Usk. This road would take her through countryside. She was not in a hurry. Mel had implied no urgency. She was able to do fifty, sometimes sixty, but preferred coasting more slowly.

The early morning greyness was lifting, the sun striving to come out. Her spirits were lifting too. The forecast was for the return of snow but she didn't believe it.

It was a pleasurable drive through the Monmouthshire countryside, green fields either side, tree-topped hills rising up from the verge and the occasional glimpse of the river, its waters untypically low for the time of year. The winter had been cold, freezing, but with little prolonged rain. The snow that had fallen off and on since December had been slow to thaw, giving no rush of fresh melt into the Usk.

She would love to live among all this but she didn't let that infertile thought deflate her. On the contrary she experienced a steady flow of relief. All weekend she had been burdened with the crimes that had suddenly plagued the county: Timothy Bush, the valleys shootings, Mel's murder near where she lived. In her small valley town, people who knew her and knew she was a policewoman came up and made a point of asking what was going on and why didn't the police do anything? She had come out with the usual platitudes; nothing else she could say. Even Alex had given her that look of accusation as if she wasn't doing enough to prevent all these deardful things.

This morning, the beauty of this slow drive helped dispel the ugliness of work.

She drove through or past little hamlets with big Welsh names; she'd never heard of them but she liked their sound even if she was mispronouncing them. Her tongue was full of their flavour as she recited them. And white cottages. She was passing dazzling white cottages. She loved white cottages. She wanted one. This would be a fine place to live.

*

The small side-room near the intensive care ward was full. Greta Plumitis was seated there, a nurse next to her, holding her hand. A doctor stood talking to a uniformed police sergeant who had come with a WPC in response to an emergency call from the hospital.

Just inside the door stood a man in overalls.

The doctor was explaining that he could not sign a death certificate. There was a great deal of concern on their part as to the circumstances surrounding the injuries. A scan had revealed their serious nature and in his opinion they had not occurred naturally. The police sergeant asked him to elaborate and the doctor said that no bowel disease was apparent, there appeared to be no inherent weakness in the bowel lining, no evidence of diverticular disease for example, which in any case would be unusual for a person of the age of the deceased though not impossible. The case should be referred to the coroner.

'There's one other thing.' The doctor glanced at the distraught mother. He waved his hand towards the door to lead the sergeant out of the room. A man in overalls opened the door for them.

'Thank you.' The doctor gave the man no second look but the sergeant did.

In the larger waiting area the doctor drew the policeman to one side but couldn't help notice that a woman who had been standing there was closing on them.

'Excuse me, Sergeant,' said Ruff. She produced her warrant card for the sergeant's benefit. She looked awkwardly from one to the other. 'I've been sent up here by my boss in HQ to look for an Angela Plumitis. I understand from a nurse back there that I should come and speak to you.'

The sergeant seemed struck dumb. The doctor had been about to tell him more about the death of Angela Plumitis and here was a DC from HQ with an alleged interest in the woman. He excused himself from the doctor and moved Ruff a short distance.

'Can I ask why you are looking for this woman?' he whispered.

'It's to do with a murder investigation.' That was about all that she knew of Mel's current case. The sergeant appeared to be waiting for more. She thought quickly. 'There was a murder just outside Usk on Saturday. Angela Plumitis may be connected. I'm here to see if she's fit for interview.'

The sergeant puffed his cheeks. 'Hardly, constable. She's dead, under suspicious circumstances. It's for the coroner. The doctor has been telling me.' He looked around. The doctor was checking his watch, advancing on the two police officers.

'I'm very busy but you need to know something more.' Without hesitating and ignoring any possible protocol issues that may exist with the two officers' relationship he revealed the "confession" of Jackie Davrot.

'She had brought Angela Plumitis to casualty and had been joined later by her father...' he checked his notes '...a Charles Davrot.'

'She confessed to having inflicted the injuries on the deceased?' the sergeant queried.

'Confessed, yes, but under the guise of consensual sexual activity.'

'What did the deceased have to say about that?' he asked.

'She never said anything. She was unable. We had her sedated she was in so much pain. We would have had to operate but her heart was compromised by the severe infection in her abdomen.'

'Charles Davrot and Jackie Davrot?' Ruff asked. The doctor nodded. 'Where are they now?'

'They left, very quickly, when Miss Plumitis died. The girl tried to get in to see her but her father dragged her away.'

'Who's that in the room?' she asked.

'That's the mother of Miss Plumitis. I don't know who the man in the overall is.'

'Do you have an address for the two Davrot's?' the sergeant asked.

Again the doctor checked his notes and shook his head. 'The address for Miss Plumitis was given as Slough Street, Windsor.'

'Vikings!'

Ruff's one-word outburst startled the two men. The sergeant was the first one to ask. 'What?'

'O, nothing, Sergeant.' Ruff tried to appear collected but inwardly she was tingling. The name had been familiar but it needed the extra bit about the address to jolt the memory into place. Angela Plumitis was the name at the bottom of Timothy Bush's list. Requirement: Vikings. And she had found out from his lordship what that activity was all about but, o shit, she had never told Mel.

'What was the nature of the sexual activity that Jackie Davrot allegedly confessed to?' she asked the doctor.

'There was no allegedly about it. She told one of our nurses in A & E that…various sex aids had been utilized. That kind of thing is not unusual. We encounter all kinds of devices used on or in. You'd…'

'But this was unusual?' she persisted.

'In its obvious violence, yes.'

She recalled the suspicion of lesbianism in that Wiltshire case she had found, the one that involved the Davrot's. And a girl died then too. Jackie Davrot: *voracious lesbian.*

She also knew that she had an address for Chas Davrot on her smartphone or rather she could use her smartphone to look it up in the database. Very briefly she toyed with telling this sergeant. But no. She'd follow it up herself.

Forty-Five

'Billy Bell, are you stalking me?'

Challis had pulled up at the front of Cottel Court to find PC Billy Bell's hedley parked there.

'Sergeant,' he snapped.

'What are you doing here?'

'Break-in, Sarge.'

'Where's your mate? Inside?'

'Still on the sick.'

Lassman winced as he heard what Bell said.

'PC Bell, this is Detective Chief Inspector Lassman from Berkshire. Working with us for a while.'

'What's this *headloo* on your car?' he asked.

'Heddlu, sir' Bell pronounced it correctly. 'Welsh for Police.'

Lassman's lips contorted as if struggling to comprehend. 'Strange language,' he said. 'We've just come through a place that has "bugger" in the name.'

Bell frowned. 'Usk,' Challis explained. 'The Welsh name for it, Brynbuga.'

'Ah,' Bell understood. 'No, sir, the U is pronounced like an E and then you have W that's pronounced like…'

'Thanks, Billy. I have tried to educate this Englishman.'

'And this Englishman is very glad that he is. Do you speak this weird tongue?' he asked Bell.

'Welsh? Yes sir.' Bell was beginning to colour up. He glanced at Challis, for support she thought, some protection from this pig of a patronizing Englishman.

'Odd. You look normal.'

Challis bit her tongue, for now, and decided to get back on track. 'Who are you liaising with here?' she got back to business.

'Um,' Bell adopted a secretive pose. 'His lordship.'

'His lordship, eh?' Lassman's eyes lit up. 'I do so enjoy interrogating the peers of the realm. Hereditary is he?'

'Yes,' Challis confirmed. 'Lord de Cottel, umpteenth baron I believe. Did he call it in?'

'No, Sarge. A Miss Meredith Guster.' He spoke from memory, not consulting his notes. His eyebrow raised in Challis's direction to indicate that he recalled this same woman at the scene of the suicide the previous week. He got a nod from her.

'What's the story?' Lassman asked.

'Well, sir, Miss Guster came into work this morning at about eight-thirty. The door had been forced.'

'No alarm?' Lassman asked.

'Not working, sir.'

'Really.'

Bell continued. 'She found items were missing.'

'A word of advice, constable. If you're called to give evidence in Court on this please avoid using the words "found" and "missing" when they relate to the same thing. It confuses the jury and the judge too very often. Learn to select your words carefully.'

Bell again sought out input from Challis but she was looking away. Can't Lassman change his tune?

'Carry on,' Lassman instructed.

'She found...discovered...noticed that all the computers in the office were missing. Stolen presumably.'

'Possibly,' Lassman qualified. Challis was beginning to feel that Lassman was taking too much pleasure out of making Bell a nervous wreck.

'No security officers here, Billy?'

'Er, no, ma'am...Sarge. Just Miss Guster and his...Lord Cottel.' By now he was red in the face.

'Thanks, Billy.' So, no Stuart Devlin or Chas Davrot around. 'Where are they now?'

'I asked them to wait in a room opposite the office. I tried to seal the office until the SOCO guys get here, if they do. They say they're real busy. They're still up at your murder site so they say and still up the valleys. I just came out to get a drink from my flask.'

'Well, Billy, this is your baby for now. We're here for something entirely different.'

Billy pointed them towards the room where he'd left Meredith Guster and Lord de Cottel. He was told to wait outside.

As they walked up to the house Challis rounded on Lassman.

'I didn't want to say anything in front of the constable, sir, but I have to say it doesn't go down a storm to criticize someone else's language, especially to someone like Billy Bell who wouldn't dare defend himself to someone of your rank.'

'I should hope not!' Lassman stopped and gave her a stare. 'I don't believe it's such a good idea to say anything now either, Sergeant. You speak Welsh?'

'No...'

'But you're Welsh. I'm English and I speak English. You're Welsh; you speak English, the national language. I bet you're one of those the Welsh wheel out on rugby days. I've seen them at Twickenham, sat next to them, half of them miming, the other half coming out with some made-up noises while that God awful anthem is playing.'

She was riling. 'I think it's got a lot more passion to it than God Save...'

'I'll stop you right there before you malign the person you have sworn to serve.'

'That's ridiculous. That's not…'

'The Queen, Sergeant, not some Ku Klux Klan look-alike arch-druid. Let me tell you that multiple allegiances do not work, especially not for the good of society; they're divisive and downright subversive. Why d'you think we keep a close eye on the Muslim community in this country?'

'That, sir, is stereotypical bigoted bollocks.' She realized this debate was getting out of hand and personal.

'O, right. Is it.'

'We're in no more danger from minorities like the Muslims than we are from anyone else although we like to think we are because they're easier to pull over and harass except that we think everybody brown is a follower of Islam.'

He caught her arm and pulled her towards the wall of the building.

'Let me tell you something, my provincial innocent. July the seventh, 2005. My son and a work mate on the tube, just left Kings Cross. You know what happened next. My son's mate lost a leg, my son got away with facial scarring. He saw stuff that morning that in twenty years being around all kinds of shit I could never witness. Don't talk to me about allegiances.'

She yanked her arm.

'I guess your boy was lucky.'

If that was intended as some sort of fence-building consolation it was a tame effort. Lassman's look was unappreciative.

'O, yeah. Lucky. But it's our job to take luck out of the equation.'

This was heavy stuff, Challis knew. She felt sorry for his son's encounter but he was carrying a grudge too many and that could really fuck up impartiality. But that was a something of a myth in the Force anyway.

'Some day,' he continued, 'you'll acquire enough experience to understand what I'm talking about. Until then listen and learn.'

'I resent that, sir.' He couldn't stop patronizing.

'Tough.'

She wanted to say *grab me like that again and I'll flatten you*.

Challis remembered the layout from her last visit. The admin office was on the left. She hadn't been in any of the other rooms, unlike Ruff.

Only Meredith Guster was in the room on the right. It was a large bare room and she was seated on the only suitable piece of furniture; a tatty chaise under the window. There was a whiff of something sweet in the air. Baby oil. Challis recognized it immediately. It was sickly stale.

Meredith Guster rose to her feet.

'Meredith, we meet again,' Challis greeted her. 'Trouble does indeed seem to be following you around. This is Detective Chief Inspector Lassman.'

Meredith Guster stood her ground, shiftily. Challis turned to the DCI. 'This is Meredith Guster, sir.'

He smiled blandly. 'Carry on, Sergeant.'

He sounded distant, as if not wanting to get involved. A legacy of their last discussion, she wondered. And he wandered away, several paces.

'Meredith, please, sit down.'

Meredith tentatively felt for the chaise with her leg and flopped at one end. Challis moved forward, loosening her bag. She sat at the other end and then shuffled closer to Meredith as she extricated what she needed from her bag. In front of Meredith she placed the list they had found, together, in Timothy Bush's printer.

'You see the name at the bottom, Angela Plumitis. Do you know her?'

Meredith stared long and hard at the name, using it to defer eye contact with Challis.

'Come on now!' Lassman sounded impatient. His voice at least made her look up but without any urgency. 'If there's one thing I can't stand,' Lassman's eyes seemed to pop as he spoke, 'it's people about to deny something that we know full well will be a lie and will really piss me off.'

Meredith was unmoved by this blast from Lassman. She had not been around the likes of Chas Davrot and Stuart Devlin for years without becoming hardened to all kinds of verbal bullying.

'I know her.' She spoke quietly but directly to his face. He had taken steps closer and had bent his head towards her in an attempt to intimidate her more but she hadn't recoiled.

'How well do you know her, Meredith?' Challis, immediately recognizing the part that Lassman wanted her to play, had to force the Christian name out. She would have much rather come down hard on this woman herself!

'Not that well.'

'But she stayed with you, in your house,' Lassman persisted.

'Yes.' She was cool. 'But I don't know her that well.'

'Where is she now?'

Meredith looked at Challis this time. 'I have no idea. She moved out weeks ago.'

'What, after this weekend? This weekend that this list is all about?'

'Yes.'

Lassman jumped in again. 'So you don't know where she is now, this very minute?'

'No.'

'Show her one of my photos,' he ordered Challis who hesitated. 'Show her, Sergeant.'

Hand in her bag Challis located the photo of Angela Plumitis, George Medlyn and Peter Mack. She withdrew it and placed it on Meredith's lap.

'Look at it!' Lassman barked. She did so.

'Recognize anyone?'

No response.

'What about the woman, eh?'

No response. He allowed a longer pause.

'That's Angela Plumitis, being buggered by a George Medlyn while a Mr. Peter Mack looks on.'

No response.

'That's Angela Plumitis isn't it?'

'Can't tell.' She was casual, lifted her eyes up to meet Lassman's. 'As I said I don't know her that well.'

'Meredith,' Challis slipped quietly into the discussion. 'The two men that the Chief Inspector mentioned have both been murdered in the last week. We're concerned that everyone who knew Angela Plumitis could be in danger. She herself is in intensive care in Neville Hall as we speak.'

This brought the first hint of a reaction from Meredith. It was hardly anything, just the quicker flicker in her eyes. Challis could tell she was wondering how they knew that, which meant that she knew already, which meant that she had lied. She decided to divulge what she had spotted.

'But you knew that didn't you Meredith? You knew she was in hospital.'

Meredith's body language had returned to non-committal.

'Meredith, Meredith.' Lassman sighed. 'What are we going to do with you? You're obstructing us, you know that. Of course you do. It's quite deliberate. But I don't know why. You see when people are this reticent when being questioned in a murder enquiry it's usually because they are heavily involved in it. I think the best thing that we can do is to take you somewhere more appropriate and let you take your time telling us everything you know. Shall we? But before we do let me tell you another story. That photograph that you have on your lap is from a video clip that we have. It's a very short video clip, cut from a longer one but on it we can just make out that there are two other men in the scene but we can't see much of them. Now, what we need is the full original video or dvd. I'm so old-fashioned, I keep forgetting which is which. My son tries to put me right. Anyway, we need you to give us the original, for our investigation.'

Meredith laughed. 'Me?'

'Yes you. You work here so you can go and dig out the original for us. You see we know that you sent copies to these gentlemen but they...mislaid them, so we need the original from you. If you would be so kind.'

'Why would I have them?' She was still smiling.

'Because the thing was recorded, filmed, here, in this building somewhere. The Vikings were filmed here. See, on that list, Angela Plumitis. Vikings.'

'I'm sorry to disappoint you but nothing is filmed here.' It was Lord de Cottel, standing in the doorway that led from an adjoining room.

*

Harry Muench arrived at Cottel Court with a search warrant and two male uniformed officers who Challis recognized as newly qualified, just out of their cadet courses.

'It's all that was available,' he told Challis as he led the way up to the front step where she was waiting. 'We can use him as well though.' Muench nodded in Bell's direction. 'What's he doing here?'

Challis told him of the break-in and the fear that she had that their search might now be pointless. The whole idea of the warrant was to look for the source of the video clip. That would have meant a surprise visit, the impounding of computers and any hard copies of videos, dvds and the like. It looked as if someone had pre-empted this and removed everything that would have been useful to them. In all probability she should have cancelled the search warrant and saved Muench and his two novices the trip.

*

His lordship had been adamant that filming of activities in Cottel Court was forbidden. He was candid about the kind of activities that took place during their "special weekends" but, when pushed, insisted that the Vikings activity was a costume drama that represented an enactment of a raid by Norseman where there would be pillagers and pillagees who would carry out their roles with enthusiasm and feigned reluctant ravishment, respectively.

'Whatever turns people on,' he quaintly summarized. 'You'd be surprised.' He dwelt on Challis as he said this which she interpreted as *perhaps you personally wouldn't be*; an indication to her again that her former relationship with Stuart Devlin was an open secret.

Lassman got his lordship to concede that the partial list of attendees for the weekend events at the end of January did originate with them but only after Challis told him that Meredith Guster had already confirmed it.

'We need to see the full list of people who were here that weekend,' she demanded.

His lordship looked at Meredith. 'It'll be on computer,' she said with a distinct smirk.

'All of which, conveniently, are no longer here,' Lassman observed.

'Quite,' his lordship agreed. 'And what are you doing to investigate the break-in and the theft of our property?'

Lassman shuffled his feet and stroked his beard. 'That will be the subject of a separate investigation. Nothing to do with our enquiries.'

'Well, I...' his lordship began to protest but Challis interrupted to put another question to Meredith.

'What about your system backups? Off-line data storage, for just such an emergency as this?'

Meredith was hesitant.

'Surely your highly paid security consultants would recommend you regularly backup all your information without which your business could not operate. Fire-proof safe, for instance, like the one I saw in the offices here the other day. I'd like you to open it, please.'

His lordship had refused the request but now Challis handed him the search warrant and asked him for the key to the safe.

'Meredith, do you have the key?' he asked.

It was in her desk drawer, in the office behind the police tape that PC Bell had put in place.

Muench tore down the tape and they all followed Meredith to her desk. She opened one of the drawers.

'It's not there,' she said, not bothering to search for it, clearly expecting to see it in full view.

Challis and Muench pulled open all of the drawers in the desk and rummaged through them. No sign of any keys. Challis turned to his lordship.

'Don't look at me,' he said. 'I haven't got one.'

'Any spare keys anywhere?' she asked Meredith, who shook her head and twitched her shoulders.

'Do your security consultants have a set?' Lassman this time asked the question.

His lordship and Meredith exchanged dumb looks.

'Where is Stuart Devlin today?'

'Sergeant Challis, don't you know?' His lordship's creepy smile really got up Challis's nose.

'Harry, the safe is in that room through there. Take the boys and carry it out to the car. We'll take it with us and blow it open if needs be.'

'You can't do that,' protested his lordship.

'We most certainly can,' Lassman assured him.

'Sarge!' Muench called from the other room. Challis and Lassman followed the voice. Muench was standing at the safe. Its door was open, the key in the lock, and it was empty.

Outside, away from the front of the building, the three detectives were gathered. The uniformed men, including Billy Bell, were still searching the offices, going through every drawer in every desk. They had been told to move on to the rest of the downstairs rooms when they'd done that. Everyone realized that the building was far too big for this small team of searchers to do a thorough job unless they were willing to spend the rest of the week there.

'This is not break-in,' Lassman observed. 'This is a systematic removal of evidence. Anything that could store information electronically has been lifted.'

Muench's mobile rang. Lassman grimaced at the sound of Muench's ring-tone.

'Hello. Yes, Detective Constable Muench. Yes, I did enquire. What? When?'

'Why do people always shout down a mobile phone?' Lassman shouted at Challis.

'That was the hospital.' Muench's call had ended. 'Angela Plumitis is dead.'

'What?' Challis was stunned. 'Who was that? Was it Kay?'

'No, it was the hospital.'

'Well, where's Kay? I sent her up there.'

Muench didn't know; they didn't say anything about Kay.

Shit! Challis remembered she'd switched her own phone off when they'd arrived here. A voice message was waiting, timed over an hour ago, from Ruff. The message confirmed that Angela Plumitis was dead and that the local plod had been called by the hospital.

'Get this,' Ruff went on excitedly. 'Chas Davrot is involved. His daughter brought the Plumitis woman to the hospital. They're not here now but the hospital believe the Davrot girl may have contributed to her death. She as much as admitted it. I have Chas Davrot's home address. I'm going there now. O, Vikings. Sorry Mel I forgot to tell you I found out what it was. Rape, Viking style, Angela Plumitis's requirement, remember? Don't know if it's relevant.'

Fuck, Challis breathed and called Ruff's number. Her phone was switched off. She left a message. 'Kay, don't go there without backup. D'you hear me? Wait!'

Challis quickly told Lassman what had happened.

'Harry, get Billy Bell and get to the hospital. Find out what the score is with Angela Plumitis. Get hold of Sayer. Tell the other two you came with to do what they can here. Remind them what we're looking for. Sir, we need to get to the Davrot's house and can you contact DCC Jones and get her to call off the local plod at the hospital? It's our baby, this.'

Forty-Six

'Do you suppose that guy was really Angel's father?'

Chas was at the wheel of the Cottel Court Range Rover. The question from her surprised him. It was the first thing she'd said since the hospital. It came so much out of the blue that he had to forcibly think who she was talking about.

'The guy in the overalls? Never.' That could never be. No-one, especially no-one looking like that guy, could usurp his position with Angel. That's what it amounted to. He was Angel's father, in all but name. Only known her six years but...

He had to blink his eyes clear.

Jackie noticed but considered any tears of his a mere token; crocodile ones even.

'Good, cos he was an ugly bastard. Chas, you know what we got to do. We got to get the others.' It was quietly said but a severe test on her part. She was testing his tears. 'We got to do it for Angel.'

'No, we haven't.' He failed her test. 'They didn't do that to Angel. We've got the two who did it.'

'You don't understand, Chas. Angel thought they were going to do it. She could see them priming themselves. The fear of another two ripping and tearing at her was as bad as if they'd actually gone on and done it. Worse probably.'

'But they didn't, did they? You saw. You've seen the whole show.'

'Makes no difference. I want to shoot their cocks off.'

The rest of their journey was done in silence. Chas wanted his daughter to forget her vendetta and decided it was best to say nothing at all about anything. Sly glances to his left revealed little of her continuing mood. Her face was mainly angled away from him.

She was in thought, not deeply in thought because her next moves were clear as day. Chas's reticence would not deter her. She wondered how compliant he would be, how supportive, how much he would assist. He'd better assist.

When they reached their rented house Chas drove down the lane at the rear and parked on the narrow hard-standing. As soon as she was in the house Jackie ran up the stairs. He hoped she was going to the bathroom to see to herself, tart herself up. Two days of neglect had left her looking and smelling really gross.

'Jackie, you hungry?' He was. The kitchen beckoned. She did not reply. Noises up above told him she was in his room. He heard the door of his cupboard creak open.

'What are you doing?'

She came back down carrying the large bag in one hand and a dvd in the other.

'If you won't help me I'll find out myself. I'll hunt the bastards down on my own. I don't need you.'

She opened the lounge room door and walked in, dropping the bag to the floor. She took the dvd to the dvd player. While she was powering it on and unboxing the dvd Chas grabbed the bag. She saw out of the corner of her eye but concentrated on loading the dvd.

Chas unzipped the bag and a rotten smell assailed his nostrils.

'Good God, what have you got in here?'

Jackie had not cleaned it out. Angela had become her priority.

Gingerly Chas ferreted around in the dark corners of the bag, pulling out each item and sniffing them. Before long the Browning automatic with silencer still attached came to light. Unfortunately he had not picked it up by the butt and the smell transferred itself to his hand.

'Aw, God. This is shit.'

On another occasion Jackie may have apologized but she was busy with the dvd.

'I'm going to clean this.' He was already on his way back to the kitchen.

The dvd had started to play. Jackie sank to the carpet in front of it.

She had sat through it before. It had never turned her on, not like that Maggie Mack. She'd been reveling in it, right up until she'd put a bullet in her chest.

There was Angel, fully clothed at the start, seemingly alone in some mock house. Her role was to look like the unsuspecting housewife, doing pretend chores with a smile. Jackie recognized the room. It was the filming room in the cottage that belonged to his lordship. There was a knock at the imaginary door and Angel almost skipped across the floor to open it, her face alight with some kind of faked expectation but her smile was there, genuine, lighting up the frame. Jackie gave out a cry that was half sob half yell of joy at seeing the lovely Angel bright and beautifully expectant for probably the last real time in her life.

Two masked men stood there but not for long; they were immediately all over the horrified Angel. Roughly they pulled her to a conveniently located low straw-covered bed. One held her tightly while the other began to rip and tear at Angel's clothes, slapping her to stifle her objections. Angel was good. She sounded genuinely fearful but Jackie knew how much this action fulfilled Angel's fantasies and the angry sadness that came with the realization was gut-wrenching. She growled a stifled curse at the rapists as they began their work, not wanted to watch it in its detail but wishing she could put her hands through the screen and throttle the life out of them.

The naked Angel was tied to the bed, arms and legs outstretched, wriggling, pleading. One of the men motioned two other men into the room from outside the door. These were George Medlyn and Peter Mack. They were naked, except that George Medlyn was still wearing unlaced shoes. The two masked men slipped out of picture only to return soon also naked but facial features remaining hidden.

Jackie waited for these two to move closer to the camera so she could pause and study them, hoping for some recognition. She had done this before. All she could make out with one of the men was some scarring on his ribcage. The other was taller and looked older; the skin on his chest wrinkled when his arms came forward. His mask was bigger and covered his neck as well as his face. He seemed to have long red hair that peeked from the back of the mask.

'This gun was filthy.' Chas came back in, brandishing the automatic in his hand. 'What have I drummed into you about looking after your weapon? Did you do with this what I think you did with it?'

She gave him a "stupid-fucking-question" look.

'By Christ.' He knew where she had put it. 'Turn that fucking stuff off.'

He could only see her defiant back so he headed to the kitchen. He changed his mind and went up to his room instead.

The cupboard was wide open. He'd gone up there with the simple intention of wrecking any other Vikings dvds. He should have destroyed them straight away but he'd had no idea that Jackie would have carried on with this vengeful mood for as long as she had. If Angel had survived then her revenge thing would have died a death, he was sure of that. But now Jackie had this sickness. It may pass but he was seeing something in her that he had only seen in fits and starts before. The worst manifestation had been when she had urged him to eliminate Teresa in Wiltshire. She had sided with him against the Polish girl. That had surprised him. But she had seen Teresa's involvement in the invasion of their personal space as the greater transgression. Underneath their debauched symbiosis there had always been a basic almost caring feeling from his daughter to himself. She was full of surprises.

Dumping the dvds would only be removing the tip of the iceberg. He looked feebly at the laptops, external hard-drives and memory sticks stacked in the cupboard and knew they would all have to go as well.

No time right now. But he desperately wanted to break the obsession that was undoubtedly controlling Jackie.

He still had the gun in his hand. Should he help her by doing what she wanted? Would she do it for him?

She probably would.

He took the weapon back down the stairs. He had to clean out the stinking bag as well.

Forty-Seven

Ruff didn't know the east of the county as much as she did the west. The industrial valleys of Monmouthshire she knew intimately; couldn't go wrong, straight up and down. Thank God for sat-nav.The rural east was another world. When she had broached to Alex that she would like to live there his retort had been 'what, over there with the knobs? No way!'

Her destination was reached in good time and she quickly located the house she wanted but had to drive on several metres before she could find a slot in which to park.

She checked her phone for messages. No response from Mel.

The house she wanted was several doors back. The terrace sported no front gardens, the front doors opening onto the pavement. A car was parked right outside the Davrot house but she had no idea if it was theirs or not. They may not be in. She looked the house up and down and tried to see in through the one front window to the left of the door. Net curtains spoiled the view.

There was no doorbell and no knocker so she shoved her fingers into the letter box and rattled it a few times.

*

Chas had scrubbed the inside of the bag, using lavender scented washing-up liquid. He had sponged it as dry as he could. Everything that had been in the bag was strewn around on kitchen worktops. The Browning had been separated from its silencer, both of which had been washed clean. He was drying the weapon with considerable care and respect.

He drained his coffee cup.

Jackie had continued to ignore his invitations to partake of some sustenance. She was still crouched in front of the plasma screen, running the dvd, pausing it, bemoaning its frequent jerky quality and its relentless fascination with the tortured Angel. Why were there not clearer shots of the men, more close-ups of their heads and upper bodies? You could see every pore on Angel's entire skin but as far as the men were concerned it seemed to be all about size and depth of penetration.

On one occasion, the cameraman had caught himself in a mirror behind the action. She paused it. My God! If it wasn't the creature with the face of a ghoul...Lordy! The bastard! Did this make him a candidate for payback?

There were one or two brief shots that showed Angel's undoubted beauty. She was thirty but looked eighteen. She was so desirable. Why did she have to sully herself with men? Why did she want men to treat her this way?

It had to be down to Greta. Jackie knew she had been right all along. Angel's mother had a cock-hungry cunt. She had ruined Angel's life from a very early age. Angel had told her about the procession of men, night after night, and of the things she had witnessed. She was and always had been an evil influence. She had led her daughter into this world of ravaging men, given her own daughter an addiction she couldn't fight, not even with her love.

When she had finished off these other men, she would finish off Greta Plumitis. That would give her just as much satisfaction.

The Browning was just about cleaned and reassembled when Chas heard the rattle at the front door. They never had unexpected visitors. He stood in the doorway of the kitchen, looking down the short straight corridor.

The letter box rattled again. This time Jackie came to the lounge room doorway. He motioned her to go back in as he turned and opened the front door.

He recognized the policewoman.

'Mr. Davrot. You remember me; DC Ruff?'

'Yes, of course.' He smiled. In all the previous interviews she had never seen him smile. She found him disarmingly different. 'Is something wrong? I've not broken my bail terms have I, as far as I know?' He smiled again. Scruffily rugged, she thought.

'No, of course not.' She was almost lulled into smiling back such was the charm he was exuding but she held back, remembering the seriousness of why she was there. 'I'm anxious to talk to your daughter.'

'About...?' he asked with almost an uninterested lightness in his voice but now his smile seemed forced.

'About Angela Plumitis.'

'Well she's not....' He began but Jackie, hearing Angel's name had moved back into sight at the lounge room doorway.

'Ah!' Now Ruff did smile. 'Miss Davrot? Miss Jacqueline Amelia Davrot?'

Now Chas's face assumed a more rigid expression. This formality of address filled him with a sudden fear for his daughter. He let Ruff enter the house, closed the front door and stood behind her.

Ruff had her warrant card out and was about to introduce herself to Jackie when something hard jabbed the small of her back. It hurt and made her spin round. Looking down, she saw the gun. There was no way she could know that it wasn't loaded. The ammunition for it was on the kitchen worktop.

'Chas!' Jackie was stunned by his action.

'I can't allow this,' he said. 'We need time. You need time. I need to make the time, for you.' He shoved Ruff with the gun barrel. 'Upstairs with you.'

'Now you have broken your bail conditions,' Ruff said in the vain hope of lightening things. Perhaps he'd see how brainless this was and put the thing away.

'Shut up,' he ordered. 'Are you here on your own?'

She remained silent.

'Is anyone with you?'

She decided on an embellishment. 'Backup is on the way so I wouldn't...'

He poked her again with the gun and she made her way slowly up the stairs, deliberately exaggerating the effects of the blow.

At the top he ordered her into his room. She saw the cupboard wide open and various laptops on shelves in there. There was a dressing table on the opposite wall and the three-quarter bed coming down into the middle of the room.

The bed had a metal bedstead, all bars and rods. Ruff was ordered on to it.

'Mr. Davrot...Chas...this is crazy. Put that gun down.'

His countenance remained set. 'On the bed.'

Ruff looked at the bed, getting distinctly nervous. Did anyone actually know where she was? Had Mel picked up her message yet?

'Captain...' she tried.

'Phone first.' She pulled her smartphone from her pocket. 'Nice,' he said as he took it from her. 'Still on I see.' He dropped it to the floor and crushed it. 'Off now.' He allowed himself the thinnest of smiles. 'Now on the bed.'

'Let's talk about this. You're going way over the top. I'm here to talk to your daughter, to clear up some...misunderstandings that may have been raised at Neville Hall Hospital. I'm sure...'

Addiction

The gun poked her hard in the stomach. 'Don't make this thing go off, there's a love. Just get on the bed.'

He wasn't messing about, she could see that. O my God!

She lowered herself near the pillows.

'Not there. Put your head down this end.'

She got up, shuffled to the foot of the bed, sat and swiveled into a prone position.

'Lay still, there.'

She saw him move behind her head. He came back with some blue rope. Where the hell did he get that from?

'Hands on the bars.'

She hesitated. 'There's no need for all of this.'

He reached forward and yanked her nearest arm, the right one, back onto the metal bars. He moved the gun under one arm and tied her right wrist to the bed. She wondered if she could do something, go for the gun, while he was tying the knot. He was too quick and was soon working on her left wrist. This time she watched him tying the knot.

'Good knot that one isn't it?' Her voice was shaky. 'What's it called? An Evenk Knot isn't it?

'Very good.'

'The same one you used on Timothy Bush.'

'It does for all kinds of occasions.'

This was now an extreme situation for Ruff. She was shaking like a leaf. Her knickers felt wet and she knew it was not from the arousing nature of being rendered immobile. She had urinated without even knowing it. She had had training about hostage scenarios but this didn't fit the pattern as far as she could tell. She had really cocked this one up.

She could see his daughter Jackie standing behind her father. Was there any point in appealing to her? She didn't think so. There seemed to be unemotional acquiescence coming from her.

'Hold this,' he passed the gun to her, 'while I do her feet.' He faced Ruff. 'This is my daughter, Jacqueline Amelia Davrot? Jackie, this is DC Ruff.'

Jackie came closer and twisted her neck to better view the upside-down woman.

'O, Chas. She doesn't look *rough* to me. She looks like a delicious chocolate brownie. I haven't had one for ages.'

Chas had finished tying Ruff. 'Downstairs now. We've really got to move.'

Jackie bent lower over Ruff's face and kissed her nose. 'Bye.'

Ruff bent her head back as far as she could to watch them leave the room.

Immediately she studied the knots. As she'd intimated to Chas she knew this knot; she remembered Sayer's description and his demonstration of how to tie one and release it. On each knot she could see the length of rope that had to be tugged in order to free it but Chas had been careful not to leave it dangling anywhere near her. If she could just get her teeth on one of them...

Jackie was straight into the lounge again, restarting the dvd.

'We haven't got time for that,' Chas told her.

'You're pathetic. We're not going anywhere until I get somewhere with this. Don't you recognise anything about these two?'

'This is a waste of time.'

'Well look at them. Look why don't you? The shorter skinny one with the scars. The taller one with red hair. Look, look! Him with the scars, he's close there.'

She paused the dvd. Chas looked and swallowed hard. She saw his discomfort.

'You know him. You do know him. Chas! You recognise the scars.' She returned to the screen and then back at Chas. 'You've got scars like that. On your legs. Great red welts. From Iraq.' She looked again at the pictures. 'Is that what they are? War wounds. Battle scars.'

She stared at Chas, trying hard to read his mind, trying hard to see confirmation of the solution that was going through her mind.

'It's Devlin, isn't it? It's that bastard Devlin. Who's the other? Come on who is it?'

'Leave it. Just leave it.'

Without taking her eyes from him she tightened her grip on the gun in her hand. She could tell from the weight that it was not loaded. She wished it was. She needed it to be loaded to get the truth out of him.

She brushed past him. 'I hate you. Keep out of my sight.'

Senseless bloody girl. It had gone too far. She had lost control. But she was right, it was Stuart Devlin, he'd known that all along. The man had more balls than sense. He couldn't resist the setup, especially as it was Angel on the receiving end. Chas knew how long Stuart Devlin had wanted an opportunity like this one. He spoke of it often enough, expecting Chas to set it up for him. But Chas wouldn't, couldn't, because of Jackie and because it was Angel. He looked again at the paused scene, halted at the point where Stuart Devlin was pulling Angel's hair as he forced her mouth onto him.

'I'm going to kill the bastard!' Jackie was back and this time she was pointing the now loaded gun at Chas. 'Now you tell me where he is right now and tell me who the other one is.'

Chas sighed. 'Give me the gun, Jackie. Stop now! Stop right now.'

'Tell me. That's all you have to do.'

He shook his head. 'No. It's enough.'

'Were you in on this? Did you set this up for him? She couldn't stand him, you know that. He'd tried it on with her for years, tried to get her for himself, for him and Sue. Angel wouldn't touch him. Did she know? After it all, after all of that, did she know he was one of them?'

He held back for a moment. 'She guessed. The scars. She knew about the scars. Remember? No, you don't, obviously. It must have been when you weren't there. He bragged about them to her, wanted to show them to her.'

'You betrayed her.'

'No, I didn't! The arrangements were nothing to do with me.'

'But you were supposed to be looking after her that day. But you didn't. You said you were ordered back to the big house. You weren't were you? You turned a blind eye, for your old mate.'

'I wouldn't do that!'

'Or did he pay you?'

'Jackie, you're talking bollocks!'

'Bollocks? Bollocks? I'll show you bollocks!'

She pointed the Browning down and pulled the trigger. Chas fell on the spot. All power in his right leg was gone as the bullet hit his thigh, high up near the groin. He screamed, clutching the wound as soon as he hit the floor. Jackie saw that she had missed her target and she stood over him taking a fresh aim. Blood was gushing from the wound, squeezing out in rivulets between his fingers. His face was white, bloodless already.

From upstairs came Ruff's panicky voice. 'Chas? Chas? Jacqueline?'

Blood was oozing rapidly from Chas's thigh. 'You mad cow! Look what you've done to me. Where d'you think that gun came from? Stuart got it, gave it to me. We didn't kill those two men for Angel we killed them for Stuart.'

'You're lying. You told me… Why would he want that?'

'I don't know.'

'You made me believe you were doing it for Angel. It was all for Angel.'

There was no further response.

'Chas, you bastard!'

His breathing-in had ceased. His grip on his leg loosening. His eyes closing. He could breathe out, just; long, slow.

'Captain! Jacqueline!' Ruff's voice came shrill down the stairs.

Jackie spun, wishing she'd shut the fuck up.

Ruff had heard the noise and knew what it was. What the hell had happened? She called out their names. For some reason, she was anxious for the two of them.

She heard the stairs creak. Someone was climbing slowly. Who? There had only been one shot.

Her head was arched back and she saw Jackie come in. At first she did not notice the gun.

'Jacqueline, what was that? What happened?'

'My useless mother called me Jacqueline.' Jackie came closer, staring down at this annoyance on the bed. But she smirked. 'You know, you are much more voluptuous than Mel. Do you know Mel? I noticed it as soon as you came in.'

'Mel?' Ruff was baffled. What is she on about Mel for?

Jackie was behind Ruff's head. The gun was in her right hand, down, by her leg. With her left hand she reached robot-like over the dip in the metalwork of the bed-end and moved Ruff's hair away from her face.

She giggled as the hand moved from the face and down into Ruff's low-cut jumper.

It was like her schooldays, when girls submitted to her, prostrate like this woman, scared or excited, she had never cared which, allowing her hands, fingers and sometimes her mouth parts to do as they pleased.

She was no child now.

Ruff tried to draw in her elbows as protection but the ropes were too taut.

The hand went on and curved around Ruff's full right breast, right around, the palm encompassing the tip. Ruff not taking her eyes off Jackie's face, barely suppressed a sharp intake of breath as Jackie slowly brought the fingertips back from beneath the breast so that they could tease the nipple. Ruff was a sucker for this normally. She always liked Alex to start with her breasts because the sensation from their engorged state went directly where it was needed. Now under Jackie's hand the assault made her tense up but she couldn't help the physical reaction.

'You are so much more of a handful than Mel,' Jackie commented and went on toying with her.

'Where's Chas?' Ruff wheezed. She wanted to convey fear not pleasure to this weird woman. No way did she want to enjoy this, but...

The whole thing was macabre: there could be a dead man downstairs, she was trussed up helpless and this woman who might have killed another woman with a sex toy was playing with her tits! This was not real. This was not happening. Worst thing was she couldn't remember what she was doing here!

'The captain is a bastard. Sorry. Was a bastard.'

Ruff was aghast. 'He's your father.'

'We only have…had his word for that. He was a bastard that's for sure.'

Any hint of enjoyment at what she was doing disappeared from her visage. She slowly began to withdraw her hand but froze to pinch the nipple hard.

Frighteningly Jackie found she got no pleasure from taunting the captive woman. She was perplexed but there was a chasm opening inside her from chest to belly. It was wide and fathomless and in its emptiness there echoed a terrifying scream of betrayal. She could no longer betray Angel because there was no Angel to return to for forgiveness.

Anger towards this compliant temptress was multiplying exponentially.

'What am I doing?' Jackie whined, pinching the nipple harder as her tone increased. 'What the fuck am I doing with you?'

Her fingers were clamped tightly, milking tears from Ruff who was yelping then whimpering as she writhed into the mattress, vainly trying to get distant from the torturer.

'Please.' Despite the agony Ruff panted out air through her larynx. Jackie's hand left her. 'Please,' she dribbled, 'untie me now. Let's get out of here and sort this out.' Even through the pain, which was diminishing very gradually, the mention of the word "untie" made Ruff realize that in leaning over the bed Jackie had brought one of the end lengths of the rope close to her face.

Jackie was staring with hatred at the woman beneath her. The bitch was still tempting her.

'You want me to fuck you, don't you? You should. You'd enjoy it, or pretend to because you're like the stuck up cock-sucking Mel. You'd turn round and reject me as well, when it came to it. I really don't understand women who don't want to be nice to other women. What is the attraction of a penis, eh? Tell me. That's all a man is, you know that, don't you?' She paused, moulding the concept into a horrible reality. 'The fucking things killed my Angel!'

Ruff desperately wanted Jackie to back off and give her the little time she would need to loosen the knot. She was blinking hard to clear the streaming wetness that was blurring her vision.

The rope, she had to concentrate on the rope. Time, she needed time.

'Okay you can, if you want to.' Jackie stared at Ruff's blubbering lips. 'But I need a wash, freshen up, and then I want you to,' Ruff was trying to sound sincere but she had misread her captor. 'I've always wanted to, with a woman.'

Jackie sneered. 'I'm not your fucking novelty lesbian. I'm not here just so you can boast to your girlie friends that you tried it once but didn't really like it because it's not as good as the real thing. No, you're not as good as the real thing. Never could be!' The last words jetted from her mouth like spitting venom. She raised her left hand and struck Ruff's face with the back of it. It stung and a smear of blood coloured her lip. She could taste it.

'What do you want me to do?' Now there were tears.

'I've just lost the love of my life, you little whore, and you think you can replace her!'

She raised the gun to Ruff's temple.

'No, don't.' She moved her head away as far as she could but it was not far enough, couldn't be, the cold metal never left her skin. She shut her eyes, fearful of seeing.

Why is this girl putting the frighteners on me? Think!

She opened her eyes but was on the edge of a black, black hole. Only one thought came to her and she voiced it.

'Alex!'

She desperately wanted him.

Jackie Davrot marched away from the bedside to the bedroom window. She peered from behind the edge of the curtain at the street below.

Two shots.

They'd sounded loud in there, in the house. Someone must have heard. Her breath caught in her throat as she saw a police patrol car pull up opposite. There were two uniformed officers, one, the driver, could be female. She eased back even more behind the wall and watched the car. They were not getting out. They may be nothing to do with her at all!

She had to get out of here. Get out and finish what she'd started.

First, she retrieved the remaining dvds from the cupboard. From one of the drawers she took some of the items of restraint that Chas liked to play with: handcuffs, lengths of rope. She had every intention of using them on Stuart fucking Devlin when she caught up with him.

Then she moved to the bed and rifled through Ruff's pockets. She took her warrant card, wallet and car keys and stuffed them in a pocket.

The policewoman's eyes were still open but looked away from Jackie, the force of the bullet having pushed her head to one side, her left side.

What a shame, Jackie thought without real regret. The skin on the palm of her left hand was barely imprinted now with the fullness of the young woman's breast. She clenched and unclenched it trying to awaken some sort of erotic memory.

Nothing.

She reached forward and burrowed beneath Ruff's jumper and onto the left breast this time. Still warm, she noticed, but the nipple failed to harden, unlike last time.

Neither was she stirred.

She buried her nails into the breast flesh; dug in and scraped.

'I think,' she muttered, 'perhaps the wrong policewoman is dead.'

She raced down the stairs, two steps at a time. Straight to the kitchen, she collected the bag, still damp, and stuffed in it what she'd need. Not much: the gun, the spare clip, the loose ammo, the silencer. She added Ruff's warrant card and wallet.

Through a gap in the lounge room door she could see Chas's feet. There was no movement there, so that was that!

She left the house by the back door. Having already decided to use Ruff's car she followed the lane around to where it came out onto the road. Which car? She pressed the key and ten metres away the hazard lights on Ruff's car blinked orange.

Forty-Eight

On receiving the call from Lassman, DCC Jones called off the local police from the Angela Plumitis death and transferred their attention to providing backup for DC Ruff. As a result, when Challis drove up to the Davrot house a patrol car was already there, parked opposite. Challis pulled into a space a bit further up the road, the very same spot where, earlier, Ruff had parked.

She looked up and down the road. No sign of a pool car anywhere but she saw Davrot's Mini Clubman parked there.

A great wave of relief swept over her and she didn't know why. There was no proof, no indication, that the Davrot's had been involved in anything but her gut was having a jig. Kay was inexperienced and had dashed off on what now looked like a wild goose chase.

Challis checked her phone. No call, no message from Kay. She double-checked the cars parked in the road. No recognizable car. So why hadn't she called in? Her gut upped the tempo.

'Why have we rushed here?' Lassman had nervously gripped the passenger door all the way. Challis had heard it rattling. She hadn't gone that fast she didn't think.

'Sir, this is the Davrot house. They took Angela Plumitis to hospital, probably from here. If Angela Plumitis is heavily involved...'

'Was.'

'...then there may be crucial evidence here. A weapon maybe. The Davrot's, especially the father, are connected to Cottel Court. He's up on at least one charge already. If they're close to Angela Plumitis then they may want to destroy any evidence.'

'So let's get on with it then. But, Sergeant, in future kindly bear in mind you are not in the Traffic Section, not yet, so watch your speed especially in a vehicle that has the danger of falling apart at any moment.'

They approached the patrol car and made themselves known to the two officers; the female driver and the sergeant with her. Lassman made use of their local knowledge and ascertained that a lane ran behind the terrace of houses. He instructed the sergeant to make his way to the rear and to apprehend anyone coming out of the house in question but to remember they may be armed.

'Okay, Melanie, how are we to effect entry?'

The three crossed the road. Challis went straight to the sash window next to the door. She cupped her hands and put her face almost to the glass. Net curtain and glare impeded the view.

'My God!' She banged the glass with her fist. 'There's someone in there. On the floor.' She banged again. 'Not moving.'

Lassman peered in. 'I think you're right.' He raised his gloved hand and brought his fist down on the pane of glass above the window catch. It shattered. He reached in and undid the catch. The window was hard to slide up, glued by paint most probably. He and Challis banged the frame itself until at last their fingers managed to ease the lower sash up.

They could see plainly now that a man was lying there, motionless.

Challis pulled herself onto the window ledge. It was high. She got one foot up on it and hesitated for a second lunge. Lassman's hand was on her buttock, heaving. She did not find it a pleasant sensation but it propelled her through the window. He then offered a hand to the WPC and got her in as well.

'Open the door for me,' he commanded.

The young policewoman hovered over the body of Chas Davrot. She was rooted, her face turning green.

'Go!' Challis told her. The girl went out to the front door and let Lassman in. He saw her face was green.

'Check upstairs,' he told her, determined to give her something to do and think about. Glancing into the other downstairs rooms, he joined Challis in the front room.

Chas Davrot was on his back, his one hand now limp on the darkened wound near his groin.

'It's Chas Davrot,' Challis confirmed.

'Gunshot?'

'Could be. Too much blood to make it out.'

'Call it in.'

Her smartphone was already in her hand and she couldn't recall how or when it got there.

'Wait!' He held her arm. 'Look.'

His hand was pointing towards the corner next to the window. The plasma screen was still on, the dvd still paused showing a close shot of the masked man with the scars, Angela Plumitis clearly visible behind him.

'Sir!' The quavering voice of the WPC came weakly down the stairs. 'There's another one up here.'

He left the room, Challis stuck fast to the image on the screen. Suddenly she was hot, hot all over. She knew she was looking at the unedited version of the full video; the thing they had most wanted to find, to identify the masked men. Here was one of them. A man with scars on his ribcage, scars she had once traced with her lips. Stuart Devlin.

'Stuart,' she whispered. 'What on earth are you doing to that girl?'

'Melanie, you'd best come up here,' Lassman called down, his voice deliberately strident.

The WPC was on the small landing, taking huge gulps of air. As Challis passed her Lassman suggested she go down and let her sergeant in through the back door.

'Tell him to secure the building.'

He followed Challis into the bedroom, almost walking into the back of her. She had stopped just one or two strides in.

Kay Ruff's head was facing away from the door. The dark red hole in her temple had let a trickle of blood ooze out down past her right ear and onto her neck. There was no mistaking her. Challis knew her hair, her colour and her clothes.

'Is this...?' Lassman knew he had a choice of two names but could not decide which one would be easier to say.

'It's Kay.' There was no life in her voice. She took a deep breath. 'Detective Constable Kay Ru...' The surname snagged in her throat.

'Okay.' One of Lassman's arms found her shoulders. 'Go back downstairs. I'll do the scene here.' He had an inspiration. 'Go check that video or dvd or whatever it is. See if it's the real thing.'

O fuck that, she thought. Fuck that. Who cares? She looked around. She saw Kay's crushed phone on the floor. She saw the ropes on her wrists and the knots, those same knots. She wanted to untie them. Free Kay.

'Go!' Lassman ordered. 'I'll be with her. I'll call the DCC. You call it in to Control. Get the team here.'

Challis tottered back out onto the landing. What did he say?

'O and don't forget the video.' Lassman's experience told him how necessary it was to get people working objectively in a situation like this; a colleague down. His experience also told him how damn near impossible it was to achieve.

The tears came as she went down the stairs. She used the wall for support, each step a blind stumble as she searched her pockets for a tissue.

The front door was open, the cold February sky beyond it attracted her, clear and bright. Snow clouds forecast for later. The WPC was there on the front step and behind her members of the public had begun to gather, peering in at her in her state of distress. That was no good. She turned her back to the onlookers. The WPC followed the gaze of the crowd and came inside, closing the front door. She moved quickly to Challis's side.

'Sarge,' she said quietly and then tears welled in her eyes as she saw them in Challis's. However, she had a supply of tissues that she shared out.

'Thanks,' Challis was at last able to speak. 'What's your name?'

'Wendy Wilding, Sarge.'

'You okay?'

'Not really. Was she your…?'

'Yes, she was.'

'Sorry.'

'Me too. Look, you'd better get back out there, if you're okay.'

WPC Wendy Wilding went back out on the pavement, leaving the front door ajar. Her sergeant was coming in from the back garden.

'There's a car out there in the lane. Not sure if it's to do with this house. It's a Range Rover. Cottel Court on the doors.'

'She's taken Kay's car. Their own car is out in the street.'

'Excuse me?' His ignorance of the situation should have been understandable but it rattled her.

She ignored him, grabbing her smartphone. She contacted Control and ordered a SOCO team. She told them that a woman needed to be located in connection with a double killing at this address, name of Jackie Davrot, probably armed and driving the car that was allocated to DC Kay Ruff, one of the victims at this address.

That information caused a big double-take from the sergeant.

When asked for a description of the wanted female she found it hard to see in her mind anything other than Kay Ruff, the living being that had been Kay Ruff, that little perfectionist, font of all knowledge, annoying pesto lover, little beauty… The contrast between that image and the brash rust-headed hard-nose that was Jackie Davrot was hard to bridge. How could she have fantasized about her? You could tell what she was: predatory, a collector of female victims. She remained as single-minded as she could as she gave her description.

'Could you keep the back of the house and that car secured?' she asked the sergeant. He told her there were more uniformed officers on the way.

Challis went back into the front room. There was the bloodied body of Chas Davrot bathed in the glare of the TV screen and the suspended animation of its pornographic picture. Some artist could make a disturbing statement out of a scene like this, she thought.

She found the remote and hit the play button. This was indeed the long sought-for original. They were all on it: Angela Plumitis, all three men whose identities she now knew and the other masked man, still anonymous, who seemed to have red hair protruding out of the back of his all-embracing neck and face mask.

'It is the dvd we wanted.' She had gone back up the stairs and spoke to Lassman on the landing. 'I've left it in the player for SOCO to remove.'

'Any better images of the other two men?' he asked.

Stuart Devlin was one but how could she admit to knowing that? As far as the second masked man was concerned she couldn't care less. What was the point now? Angela Plumitis dead, Chas Davrot dead. Jackie Davrot was their main priority surely.

'Some,' she answered unenthusiastically, hoping to convey the irrelevance of that issue. Let's concentrate on wrapping up this killing before we worry about preventing more crimes that now may never happen and may never have been going to happen.

'There's a cupboard in there full of laptops,' Lassman lapsed into practicalities. 'I wouldn't mind betting…'

Challis surprised him by brushing past and into the bedroom again. She walked on up to the bed and without hesitation took hold of Kay's tied right hand.

'Mel!' Lassman knew he should tell her to keep away from the body but the look she gave him cut him dead.

The brown eyes were still open, a blood stripe on her lip. The coat was open. The top of the low-cut jumper looked disheveled. Deep scram marks streaked Kay's left breast almost to the collar-bone. There seemed to be a damp patch on the crotch of the jeans.

She must have been petrified.

She was tied down. Degraded. Like Angela Plumitis.

Challis was angry with regrets. Why had she bowed to Lassman's prejudice about mobile phones and switched hers off? If she hadn't she'd have answered the call from Kay. She would have stopped her coming here. Why had she come here? This case was nothing to do with her.

'Kay, I'm sorry.' Lassman heard the apology and turned away back to the landing. He could do this by the book and order her out of the room but…

He rounded on her. 'You can't, mustn't, blame yourself for this in any way, Melanie.'

'Of course I can. She had no idea what she was heading into.'

'Neither did you. You do now but you had no idea. None of us did. Our money was on…'

'The Plumitis woman I know. We didn't do this properly.'

'Well she certainly didn't.' Lassman threw out a hand in the direction of the bed.

'You bastard.'

'She didn't!' He was emphatic. 'You told her to do one thing and she went off half-cocked and did something else. See if Plumitis is fit for interviewing were your instructions so what the fuck was she doing here? You remember how you reacted when you heard her blasted voice message? You couldn't believe how naive she'd been, could you? So don't you go apologizing to her. It's not your fault.'

Challis had eyes swamped with tears again. Her entire face felt like a sodden sponge. She tried to look at Kay but she was a big blur. 'If she made the wrong call then it's all our fault.'

Forty-Nine

There was no-one at home at No. 1 Pontderry Lane. Jackie banged on the door and peered through the front window.

The Guster woman must be in work.

She'd have to go to Cottel Court if she wanted to get the name of the fourth man.

She wouldn't mind betting though that there would be some evidence in the house here. It was more than likely that Chas had got his info from his whore.

She was contemplating going around the back to find a way in when the next-door neighbour, Marcia Smith, came out to see what the noise was. Jackie retreated to the car saying she'd come back.

In Ruff's car she made a call to Cottel Court. Meredith Guster answered. Jackie said she'd be coming by to talk to her. Chas needed something from her.

'Well, don't come now,' Meredith dismissed her. 'The police are here with a search warrant and there's been a robbery. All our computers are gone.'

Shit! What was all that about?

'Where's Chas? I've been calling him but…'

Jackie ended the call. She hadn't prepared an answer for that one.

Damn, she should have asked her if Stuart Devlin was there. Probably was if there had been a break-in. She needed to find out. She needed to find out his precise whereabouts so she could attach herself to him and pick her moment. She'd get the other name from him; one way or another.

'Hi Stuart.' He answered her call straight away. She'd worked out a patter now. 'Chas is not fit for work today, won't be working.'

'What's wrong with him?' This was the first time ever that Chas had got his daughter to phone in for him. He never got any bullshit from Chas. If he wanted a day off or couldn't make it in he'd always call himself. Jackie knew this so carefully framed her reply.

'He's in hospital that's why he hasn't been able to phone you.'

'Hospital? What the fuck's he done?'

'Broke his leg. My fault. I hit him with my car, squashed him against the wall at the back of our house.' She knew she could make the story as fanciful as she liked; Chas couldn't contradict her. But now she had to get close to Stuart Devlin before he discovered the truth. 'He's given me something for you.'

'What?'

'I don't know. It's in a plain brown envelope. Said it was urgent. Where are you?'

'I'm on an errand of mercy. I'm in Usk, just parked outside my uncle's. He's just out of hospital.'

'Is Sue with you?

'No, she's back up in the smoke this week. Hey, we had a great weekend, no small thanks to you for kicking it off so nicely.'

She was unresponsive.

'You're good, you know,' he continued in a low voice as if his tongue was in her ear. 'You really ought to think about joining us sometime. Sue would love it. She's said so.'

This attempt at seduction was not what she wanted to hear, not from any man, ever, least of all this little shit. All she needed to know was where in Usk he was going. She was close. Five minutes away, if that.

'I'm coming through Usk. Can I meet you?' He was hesitating. 'I won't keep you long. Just give you the package. I've got to meet someone else later.'

'Okay.' He told her the address and gave her directions. He had not given up the chase just yet.

*

Alan Redland had called his nephew that morning and asked him to come and see him. First, Stuart had to drop Sue Chance at Newport Station to catch the London train.

He guessed his uncle wanted some errands run. Now that he wasn't allowed to drive he'd probably be pestering him on a regular basis. Well, that was okay, for a while. He was his uncle's only living relative and if the old guy's ticker was dicky it would do him no harm to keep in his good books. He fancied living in Usk. Couldn't afford it yet but Uncle

Alan's house would be one hell of a good first step. As he drove there he wondered if Alan had made a Will.

There was something of a surprise, or perhaps shock, waiting for him.

The welcome from his uncle was warm enough. A hot drink was offered and accepted. He sat sipping, waiting to know the reason for the summons. He didn't want to be hanging around all day. There were things to do, especially now that Chas was not around.

Redland slapped a photograph down on the kitchen table.

'Tell me about this, Stuart.'

Stuart slowly put his coffee cup down alongside the photograph of Angela Plumitis, George Medlyn and Peter Mack. The light over the kitchen table was on so Stuart had no problem seeing the detail. No need to bend down for a closer view. This told Redland that the scene in the photograph was familiar to his nephew.

'That's your mate Peter Mack,' Redland stated. 'Didn't know who the guy is who's doing the business with the lovely Miss Plumitis. Melanie does. She said it was a George Medlyn. She, er, left this with me. I was able to identify the girl for her.'

'I don't understand why you think I would know anything about this.'

'You may have heard that Peter Mack was murdered, shot, on Saturday. You may not have heard that the other bloke, George Medlyn there, was murdered, shot, earlier last week. This photo comes from a video clip that shows that two other men were present. They are unidentified so far, wearing masks according to Melanie. She and her colleagues are worried that they may be next on the shooting list. I'm worried in case one of them is you.'

'I know about Mack and his wife Maggie. Of course I do. It knocked the valley killings off the news headlines this morning. But this George feller...'

'Windsor he lived, I believe.'

'Windsor?'

'Small world, eh? Your old stomping ground. Perhaps you did know him.' He raised an eyebrow as a question mark. 'Or Miss Plumitis even.'

Stuart's mobile rang. His eyes were still on his uncle as he withdrew it from a pocket. The call was from Mel. Intriguing. He cancelled it.

'It all means nothing,' he smiled. 'No need to worry. You shouldn't worry about anything in your state of health.'

There was a knock on the front door.

Fifty

Midday, DCI Harriet Moray arrived at North Road.

A prediction voiced by Lassman proved to be accurate: *losing one of our own trumps a mass murderer on the loose.*

DCI Moray had been sent from the mass murderer command centre by Chief Superintendent Harper to relieve the visiting DCI from the case. His presence was deemed no longer necessary but he argued with Moray that the killer or killers of George Medlyn and the Mack couple had not yet been proved one way or the other. There was still an investigation that needed to be carried out. The killer could be any one of three possibles: Angela Plumitis, Chas Davrot or Jackie Davrot. Chas Davrot was now dead and unfortunately so was Detective Constable Ruff and while it could be assumed that Jackie Davrot was their killer even that was not yet proven.

When Muench arrived he found Challis sitting in her car. She had been sent there by Moray. Lassman went to follow her but Moray stopped him.

'She doesn't need you. She doesn't need anybody right now.'

But Muench stepped out of Billy Bell's hedley, spotted Challis and got straight into the passenger seat.

'Does Ray know?' he asked her.

'Ray?' Not from her but probably the whole force knew by now.

From his demeanour Muench seemed to be affected by this business. That seemed unbelievable to Challis. He didn't care about anyone but himself.

'Does the boss know?'

Is this all he can say? Why is he asking these frigging inconsequential questions? But pausing for reflection the boss probably should have been told, or is he strong enough to take it?

The only cohesive proactive action she had taken had been to try and contact Stuart Devlin. No answer. What had she called him for? Should have been to warn him, she supposed, but she had no idea how she would couch the words. The dvd showed what he had done to Angela – she was just Angela now, just as Ruff would always be Kay. Challis had even called DCI Moray Harriet. She didn't want to see any woman differentiated by rank or by type or by anything other than a close familiarity. The one exception had to be Jackie Davrot.

'I don't know,' she snarled half-heartedly.

Okay, Muench was struggling for the right thing to say. He could be granted a dispensation. Despite his inability to think or say anything half decent about any of his colleagues he may possibly be moved by Kay's death.

'Okay, Harry?' She forced herself to ask but her tone was bitter.

'I got Billy Bell to drive me here, blue lights, sirens and all.'

So that was how he gauged it; that was how he chose to express himself. Well, it wasn't fucking good enough.

She had been told, ordered, by Harriet not only to go sit in her car but to get off home. They were all in there now, in that house.

Sayer and his assistant Twink Finch had turned up. Challis didn't particularly want his hands all over Kay. At the top of the stairs she had stopped him, the palm of her hand flat against his chest.

'Let Twink do it.' She could see he was taking offence so she spelled it out for him. 'You do the man downstairs.'

He brushed her hand aside. 'Not your call,' he countered but without malice. He walked on past her but held his stride at the door to the bedroom as she shouted after him.

'Respect, Sayer!'

Twink drew alongside her and took her hand. 'It'll be fine, Mel.'

Sayer had gone on. She was going to follow, to make sure. 'I'm going in there with him.'

Twink held her back. 'You can't Mel.'

'Well, you be...' Challis didn't know what to tell Twink to be: be gentle, be kind, be nice. Twink knew what Challis was thinking; Sayer was inclined to flippancy and lack of sympathy. Came with the job; his way of coping. But she was used to oiling troubled waters with relatives of the bereaved in situations like this. No different. She squeezed Challis's hand and followed Sayer.

Lassman and Moray overheard all this; they couldn't help it. It was then that Moray suggested that Challis call it a day.

'I'm going now, Harry, so if you don't mind...'

'Mel!' Her name came from his lips like a plea but her look into his face rejected him.

'Go and help in there, Harry. Do something for Kay for once.' She wanted to be in there, with Kay.

'There's no need for that...Sarge!'

There was aggression in his voice. He actually wanted to be as one with the team at this time. Challis was playing the martyr.

He got out. As he closed the door hard Challis called out. 'Harry!'

He walked on, unloading his phone from his belt to call Ray Lockett.

Challis started her car. Almost immediately the battery warning light gave out its three beeps, flashed for a few seconds and then went out.

As she pulled away, she saw the DCC arrive in a splendid black staff car. My God, is this a peep show or what? Isn't it amazing how a lowly DC is highly valued as soon as they fall in the line of duty? She'll be there, DCC Jones, on the News tonight giving out how sadly missed, how brave, how dedicated was DC Ruff, cruelly and savagely done to death this day. That's how it was. That's how Redland's game was played.

Redland!
She wouldn't go home. She'd go to Redland.

Fifty-One

To make good her story, Jackie went to the newsagents in Usk to buy a brown envelope. She put one of the dvds inside and sealed it, writing Stuart on the front. This had to be done because no way could she just hand him a dvd. The envelope would allow her to get inside the house with him. What next, she hadn't worked out. And what to do with the other guy, his uncle?

Stuart's car was parked up the road. She'd seen it as she drove past the house on her way to the Usk car-park. When she was driving in she realized that she'd given herself a problem by taking the policewoman's car. They'd be looking for it. She had to abandon it. She could walk to Stuart's uncle's house, no sweat. It was only a few hundred yards.

What would come after that she had no idea.

But at least her head was clearer. She couldn't remember leaving the house where Chas had bled to death. Somehow she'd got to Meredith's place. Talking to people had jolted her into consciousness. Her thinking was piercingly clear.

'Hi.' Jackie greeted Stuart as he opened the door. Redland had been going to answer the knock but Stuart said it was for him. She had the large bag over her left shoulder and the envelope in her right hand down by her side. She forced herself to smile for him.

'Jackie.' His face dropped. Her appearance shocked him. Facially she was naked and, without makeup, she was almost middle-aged. Her eyes had bags. The red of the hair was fading, the natural mousy colour appearing in streaks and smudges. Her clothes, too, were grubby with stained patches. She looked anything but the fresh-faced lesbo, rarin'-to-go. His usual meaningless phrases full of unmeant praises hung back from his lips. My lovely girl was toned down to my dear girl but he nonetheless invited her in, an unpleasant odour rising as she brushed past him.

She hadn't needed to worry about gaining entry to the house. She interpreted Stuart's invitation as just his lascivious nature coming to the fore as always. If he wasn't going to score immediately he would prepare the play area for another day. To her mind there was much that he had in common with her. He was a voracious seducer.

She was led into the kitchen where Redland was rinsing out the cups.

'Alan.'

He turned.

'Alan, this is Jackie. Jackie, my uncle Alan.'

Redland froze, his brain's face-recognition software activating. This was the girl in the scanner room, the one who had come in with the scruffy man behind the trolley on which lay the unconscious Angela Plumitis. She was equally scantily dressed as at the hospital but facially much more alive and clearly hadn't tidied herself up. There was something about her eyes. Piercing black. He would have said she gave the impression of having taken some prohibited substance.

He put his hand on the photograph that was still on the table. What did this turn of events signify? Here he was grilling his nephew about Angela Plumitis and the men in her session and in comes a girl who had been manifestly distraught at the state of same girl. Even though a policeman of many years' experience this kind of coincidence gave him the shivers. It was beyond his understanding. Other forces were at work.

Did she recognise him?

No she didn't but what had grabbed her was the back of Redland's head while he was at the sink. His hair colour! Could be construed as red. Most definitely!

Fuck! She had the two of them!

Stuart was perplexed by the reaction to his attempted introduction.

'Do you two know each other?' he asked.

There was a limp shake of the head from Redland. 'No, no.' while Jackie handed Stuart the envelope.

As he took it she eased the large bag from her shoulder and across her chest, slipping her now free right hand inside, finding, with little difficulty, the Browning, silencer fitted.

'What is this? I wasn't expecting anything.'

'It is urgent,' she uttered, her hand gripping the gun more firmly. Redland noticed how she was reaching into the bag but, as Stuart began to rip open the envelope, her eyes locked on him.

'What's this?' Stuart had the dvd in his hand.

'A present,' she said, 'from Angel.'

It was the ominous tone of her voice that jerked Redland into action. He took a stride towards her, only the one, because she was expecting him to do just that and she had the gun out, pointing at him. She went back one step to increase the space between Stuart and herself.

'What d'you mean?' Stuart spoke first.

'I mean, that Angel...Angela to you, I suppose...Angel, my love...and my bastard father are both dead.'

She could tell he was juggling with the implications.

'Just like George Medlyn and Peter Mack.'

A quick glance was exchanged between Stuart and Redland who raised an eyebrow to silently say 'well, I did warn you'.

'The gun is a big mistake, Jackie,' Redland tried to move closer but she jabbed it forward and back like a snake's tongue.

'It hasn't finished its work yet. Not quite.'

'Jackie.' There was a note of panic in Stuart's voice. 'You don't realize that Alan is a policeman. A detective inspector.'

You idiot, Redland thought. That isn't going to help.

'The fucking police!' Jackie roared. 'I'm not surprised. They're everywhere!'

'He's right Jackie.' May as well try to use it now that it's out in the public domain. 'Let me help you here. I have no idea what's gone on before this. I have no idea who the people are that you are talking about. I've not been working lately. I'm actually on sick leave but...'

'Fuck off, Alan. I saw you trying to cover up that photograph and even from upside down I can see what it is, so don't fuck me about.'

Shit!

'The photograph? Yes I have this photograph but I have no idea who the people in it are. This was accidentally left here by a colleague who came to visit this sick old man.' His attempt to lighten the atmosphere failed. Jackie believed his sickness story because she remembered Stuart saying on the phone that he had just come out of hospital.

'You don't know who's in the photo?' She looked from one to the other. Redland said nothing but Stuart blurted out 'No!'

'You have a dvd player?' It was a rhetorical question. Everyone had a dvd player. She pointed the gun towards what she assumed was the living room at the front. 'Let's play your present, Stewie. Relive some old memories. Try and jog a few shall we? Come on, let's go.'

The two men were not inclined to go anywhere and stood their ground.

'You think I'm fucking joking?' Jackie shifted the Browning a few inches to the left of Redland. A single shot spat out of the silencer shattering the door on his microwave. 'Now let's go.'

'Stuart,' Redland spoke quietly, giving the appearance of calm but shaking with uncertainty. He very slowly glanced at the splintered door of his microwave. 'I think we'd better do what the young lady wants.'

'Turn it on, and the TV. Load this dvd. Come on, Stewie, hand it over to uncle Alan. And then draw the curtains shut.' Redland did as he was told. 'Stay there where you are. Now, you, Stewie, on your knees, head on the arm of the settee. Hands behind your back.'

He ended up balancing on his forehead such was the position she'd put him in. She placed herself on one side of his angled body so that she could still see Redland. When a set of handcuffs were on Stuart she reminded him of the gun and that he should remain as he was. She beckoned Redland over and got him to kneel at the other arm of the settee, hands back.

'I just wonder where you're going with this, young lady.' Better to keep talking to her, he thought, keep her mind from concentrating on just one job.

'Don't keep calling me that.'

'Young lady? Well that's what you are, at least to old traditionalists like me.'

'Yeah, well I know what old traditionalists like you are really like. Dirty fucking perverts.'

He had watched her work on Stuart and saw that she had to loosen her grip on the gun in order to lock the cuffs.

'Oh, you can't generalize. We don't all chase little kids.'

He made his move. He had waited for her to click the cuffs on one wrist and as she did he spun away onto his back, both hands flailing at the gun. But she was quick and lifted the Browning beyond his reach. Undeterred he swung a leg at her legs. Because he was up against the settee the backlift he could employ was minimal and although his shin made contact with her calves she buckled only slightly.

His moves done, he lay helpless, floundering and could not protect his torso as she knelt on his stomach and jabbed the barrel of the gun to his chest. The same sharp pain that he had experienced in the doctors surgery some weeks before hit him again. He was gasping for air as she dragged him to the kneeling position and secured the handcuffs.

'Stay you,' she ordered Stuart but he hadn't made any attempt to capitalize on the scuffle.

'This is total madness, young lady,' Redland spoke through gritted teeth. His breathing hurt and the handcuffs were biting into his skin where she had applied them with extra spite.

'Shut up, old man.' From the bag she took out a long length of blue nylon rope. 'And I told you not to call me that.'

As she tied one end to the chain on Redland's handcuffs she leaned into his ear. 'You know a young woman called DC Ruff? She wasn't half as ill-behaved as you, in fact, at the end she tried to be quite sweet to me. Cut no ice. So I'd watch your smarmy mouth and any more sudden moves like that if I was you.'

The menace in her voice sent the sharp pain coursing across his chest.

'What about Kay Ruff?' he croaked.

'Kay? Was that her name? I never knew.'

'What happened?'

From behind, the gun came round before his right eye. She waggled it.

The pain in his chest refused to subside. What's with this girl? What is she? Twenty-three, twenty-four? Where's all this blind hate coming from? She definitely must be high on something. Hallucinating.

There was no further explanation from her.

She pulled him up and told him to sit tight in the corner of the settee. She lay the blue rope around the back of the settee, got Stuart to sit in the other corner and tied the rope to his handcuffs. The rope was taut. Neither man could move forward. She got another length of rope and lashed their feet tightly to each end of the coffee table.

'I have some tablets, for my chest. I need one,' Redland panted. 'They're...'

'Later,' she declared. 'But first some action.' The dvd player started up. 'This runs for a good hour, so make yourselves comfortable although I feel sure there will be the odd intermission.'

'Listen,' Stuart called. 'Jackie, he really has got a bad heart. He's been in hospital.'

The dvd began to play. Jackie yanked off her coat. 'Christ it's like an oven in here.'

She came and stood behind the settee, midway. She tapped Stuart's temple with the silencer. 'Is it all coming back yet?'

'Jackie.' His voice was nervous but he controlled it well. 'Did you hear what I said?'

She looked at Redland. 'He looks all right to me.'

'He's not, believe me. Why are we going through this daft charade? Look, if you're in any trouble I can get you out of it. We can get you out of it.'

There was a harder tap on his temple. 'Shut up, Stewie, and watch the movie. Your big scene comes up soon.'

The dvd had already got to the point where Angel had opened the door to let the two masked men into the room.

Now that she knew that she had those same two men in front of her Jackie could not watch the pictures objectively. She was no longer studying them for clues; instead, they played immediately on her strained emotions. Anger welled up.

The soundtrack rang out with Angel's early shouts for help and pleadings for mercy, nowhere near as full-pitch as the later genuine ones would be. As Angel became naked Jackie studied the faces of Stuart and Redland.

Stuart was red, his lips were parted and he noticeably swallowed even though his mouth was dry. But he stared at the screen.

Redland, by contrast, was ashen. She was not to know that the pain in his chest was taking over his consciousness. She saw his ambivalence as being an attempt to mask his true reaction.

'Watch it!' His temple felt the tap of the silencer. This was not the time for watching stuff like this.

'Why?' he asked her breathlessly.

'That's why!' she hit the pause button. The man with the scarred ribs was near the camera.

'Hey, Stewie. Look who it is. Big Stewie.'

'What are you talking about?' he almost squealed the question.

'Not denying it are you?' She walked around and knelt on the floor in front of him, laying the gun on the coffee table. 'Now don't misunderstand this,' she warned as she reached up, unbuckled his belt and undid the fly. She tugged on the waistband. 'Lift your bum up, Stewie.' But he didn't, so she yanked, pulling down trousers and underpants to his knees.

'My God, you fucking moron. It's fucking turning you on, isn't it?' Now his shirt was pulled up, revealing the scars of friendly fire, 1991. 'I rest my case. What d'you reckon, uncle Alan? Enough proof? Well, look, look at your nephew's war wounds. Good enough match with the dvd evidence?'

She turned and commenced play again, up to the point where there was a better close-up of Stuart's torso as he pulled Angel's face on to him. She paused it again, lifting the gun from the table.

'You're not going deny it's you, are you?'.

'So what?' Stuart questioned desperately. 'You know what those session are all about. She was getting what she wanted, you know that.'

'She didn't want what those two did to her. They killed her. You do know she's dead, don't you. Did I tell you? Killed by what they did to her. And you can see that while they were buggering her to death you two stood around playing with yourselves. Never once did you try and stop them. She screamed for mercy, you can hear it. She begged.'

Both Stuart and Redland were wrestling with what she had said '...you two...'

'Wha...?'

'You're a bastard, Devlin! And as you didn't have the balls to help her...' She looked down and pressed the silencer onto his right testicle. He jerked back in nauseating pain that was followed by an even greater agony as she pulled the trigger. He screamed. The silencer was withdrawn from the bloody mash of skin and flesh. Jackie was unmoved by the sight of the wound or the sound of his screams. Calmly she pressed the silencer down on his left testicle. This time the pain of the pressure failed to generate a reaction, it was relatively insignificant now. A second shot doubled the torture.

'I'll leave you your useless cock.'

But he didn't hear her. He had passed out.

281

Blood and bits of skin and flesh had splashed onto her coat. She casually brushed it but that only served to spread it into stripes.

'Okay, uncle Alan, let's move onto your big appearance.'

It pissed her off that Redland seemed disinclined to watch any more of the dvd. Much as she cajoled and threatened him he remained uninterested. So she fast-forwarded to the point where the second masked man pulled Angel to the floor and forced her to kneel before him. At the point where he was about to penetrate her from behind she paused it again.

'Okay, doggy. Your turn.'

His breathing was very shallow, his face white. To Jackie he was suffering from hysterical fear. He did not cooperate so she had to tug his trousers, thermal long johns and boxer shorts down his thighs. His terror, she surmised, had left him unstirred. Not the rampant rod that he had sported for Angel.

The gun was between his legs when she noticed something. She was not one to be overly familiar with the sight of the male member and she had not encountered enough to fully appreciate their potential uniqueness. But what she was seeing was painfully obvious. She looked back at the TV screen and then down at Redland.

'Fuck,' she groaned.

Redland was circumcised and extremely hirsute. The masked man had a hooded penis set on a mound of stubble.

She jumped to her feet and slapped Stuart hard across the face with her hand.

'Who is he? Who's the other one?'

He was unresponsive. Another slap and then a third did nothing to revive him.

She turned on Redland. 'Do you know who he is?'

But he by now was in a state of delirium.

She stared at the screen, desperate for any clue. A red-haired man was all she could deduce.

Grabbing Stuart's shirt she shook him. His eyes flickered. A sharp intake of breath between clenched teeth showed her his injuries were still agonizingly raw. He tried to shift his position but it was impossible . Each movement sent hot daggers searing through his abdomen and new blood oozed over Redland's immaculate settee and carpet.

'The man with the red-hair…who is he?'

'Red…hair,' he spoke from deep in his chest. 'Huh.' And he tried to smile.

Fifty-Two

PC Billy Bell, with his passenger DC Harry Muench on board, had his foot down. His hedley was doing well over eighty on the dual carriageway, blue light flashing and siren blaring. A call had come through that Kay Ruff's car had been spotted by a Community Support Officer in the Usk car-park.

As they neared the Usk junction Billy Bell pulled into the left-hand lane and braked hard for the sharp curve up to the road into the town. A car coming off the dual carriageway from the opposite direction came straight out into his path and he had to swerve into the outside lane, siren going now at double tempo.

The road was now single carriageway. A tractor in front of them had to pull over onto the grass verge to let them pass. As they approached the thirty miles per hour sign Billy Bell slowed; the roadside warning sign lit up and flashed at him. The junior school was just on the left and the traffic lights there were on red. A parent and child were crossing. He came to a halt.

'Hey!' Muench grabbed his arm. 'Look who's over there.'

Challis was standing in Redland's concrete front yard talking to Jared Edwards and his wife Margaret. Five minutes ago she had pulled up outside his house, her near-side wheels on the pavement due to the narrowness of the road. Redland's car was there, in his driveway, but there was no response to her persistent knocks.

About to give up, she heard a quiet voice behind her.

'There was a scream.'

Unlike her husband, Margaret Edwards voice was a loud whisper. She was standing on the path in her own garden.

'Excuse me?'

'There was a scream, well, may have been two.'

'A scream? Where from?'

'In Mr. Redland's house.'

'Is she bothering you with this scream business?' Her husband strode up to the hedge, their hedge that separated the two properties. 'I didn't hear anything.' He said this as if to put an end to the discussion.

'When was this, Mrs…?' Couldn't remember the name.

'Thirty-five minutes ago.'

Challis thought that was very precise. 'And then…?' Margaret Edwards wondered what she should say next. 'Did you see Mr. Redland?'

'O no,' her features lit up as she understood. 'Only the young lady. She came out about seven minutes later.' Precision again.

'Yes, well, I saw her,' Jared Edwards joined in, dismissively.

'How did she seem?'

'Flashy,' was the assessment from Jared.

'Cool and collected I would say,' said Margaret. 'She walked out, closed the door quietly behind her and walked to her car. There, where yours is parked.'

'On the pavement!' her husband said unforgiving.

'Can you describe her?'

'Flashy.'

'Dressed in the current fashion as far as I could tell. Low cut top, jeans, nice coat, brown. She carried a large bag, leather, over her shoulder. O yes,' she giggled, 'she was a red-head, faded orangey, and about five feet four. About twenty-two I think she was. Her hair though; looked like she'd been dragged through a hedge backwards.'

'Where were you? Where were you standing when you saw this?'

'Across there.' She pointed to the other side of their front garden. 'Seeing what damage this weather has had on my hydrangeas. I could see her quite clearly from there.'

'And the scream? You heard that from the same position?'

'Not quite. I was under the flowering cherry at the front there. It's amazing, after all this weather, the daffs are showing already. Standing quite proud they are. Anyway, o yes, I jumped up and hit my head on that branch. Then, well, seeing the young girl come out a few minutes later it seemed all right. She didn't look as if she'd been screaming.'

'What on earth does that mean, woman? How can somebody look as if they've been screaming?'

'I mean,' she turned on him forcefully, 'her demeanour was calm, unperturbed.'

Their collective heads turned at the sound of the police siren coming into the town. They watched it come to a stop at the crossing. Challis recognized Billy Bell at the same time that Muench saw her.

Challis ran across the road. Billy Bell pulled his car into the kerb, blue light still flashing. She had a shock when she saw that Muench was with him. He lowered his window.

'Where are you going in such a rush?' She spoke to Billy Bell, cutting right across Muench but Muench replied anyway and if looks could kill his would have.

'Kay's car spotted in the car-park here.' He'd not forgotten how their last conversation had ended. Neither had Challis. She had wanted to make amends. He'd stormed off, but she couldn't blame him. She looked at him squarely.

'I think I need your help Harry.' Her brain had already processed the latest known information. Kay's car, taken by Jackie Davrot, was in the Usk car-park. The girl coming out of Redland's house was clearly Jackie Davrot. Why she was there was unknown. According to whatshername, the next-door neighbour, the girl – Jackie – had got in a car outside Redland's house and driven off.

And then there was the scream.

'I need you both. Now.'

'What about the car in the car-park?' Billy Bell asked.

'Forget it. Come on. Leave your blue flashers on.'

Muench didn't move. 'The orders are to get to Kay's car and secure it. And the last I'd heard you'd been sent off home, rest and recuperation, or some such shit.'

'Kay's car is old news. Jackie Davrot has dumped it. And I'll fuck off home when I'm good and ready. Now shift.'

The Edwards couple still stood in their front garden. Challis detailed Bell to get a description of the car that Jackie Davrot had driven away.

'I've just remembered,' she told Muench. 'I've still got the boss's keys for the house.'

'This is the boss's house? What the fuck has this to do with the fugitive?'

'I have no idea.'

Challis found the right key and opened the front door. Slowly, she led the way inside.

'Boss? Alan?'

The door to the living room was on their right. It was pulled to. She extended her fingers and pushed it open.

The first thing she saw were Stuart Devlin's feet, then his trousers around his knees and then the bloody mess in his crotch.

'O Jesus.' She walked in quickly.

'Fucking hell,' Muench's shock was palpable. He stood rooted in the doorway.

'Call an ambulance,' Challis ordered.

Her stomach was heaving. It looked like Peter Mack all over again except she could see no wounds other than those to Stuart's genitals. She leaned forward. He was breathing. She couldn't decide if she could do anything for him or if she should move on to Redland. He too was in a state of undress, trousers down in the same fashion. No blood on him. She had to look hard to see if he was still breathing. He was, just. His heart! He needs to be put in some sort of recovery position. She tried to move him.

'Harry.' He was concluding his call for assistance. 'Come here, help me get him on the floor.'

Muench was staggered by all the blatant exposure. Challis didn't seem to be batting an eyelid. His first thoughts would be to hoist up the boss's trousers.

They couldn't move him. She yanked down his thermal vest as far as it would go.

'He's cuffed and roped to that guy,' Muench discovered. He was quickly able to untie the rope from Redland's cuffs. Challis did the same with the rope holding his feet to the coffee table.

'We need to get the cuffs off. Try your keys.'

Muench tried his keys but they didn't work.

'Get Billy Bell in here.'

Muench met the PC at the front door. 'Right, the car the girl got in was a...'

'Billy! Billy!' Challis yelled the name as soon as she heard his voice. He came to the door and immediately paled. 'Don't come in. We need some cutters to get these cuffs off. Got anything in your boot?'

He was motionless.

'Billy, have you got any cutters?'

He nodded.

'Go! Get them.'

She and Muench got Redland onto the carpet and positioned him as best they could with his hands shackled. He moaned when they moved him. Challis spoke to him, asking him what had happened but he was incapable of response. She then started encouraging him to stay with us, keep calm, lay still; all the platitudes.

Muench was prompted to go upstairs and bring down a blanket to drape over Stuart Devlin's lower half. The trousers would have to stay at half-mast rather than run the risk of damaging him further.

Kneeling next to Redland, she held his hand. It was the only practical thing to do. Looking around, she could see that a lot of blood had seeped from Stuart Devlin's injuries. Redland's carpet and settee were ruined. She couldn't help thinking that'll upset him.

Muench was breathing heavily; shock coming in nauseous waves.

'Do you reckon the girl, the Davrot girl, did this?'

Yes, she did.

'What with?' he asked incredulously.

'A gun,' Challis said with quiet confidence. 'Did you not see the two holes in the cushion under him? Two bullet holes.' She'd used the gun all right, with a silencer attached. Mrs. Nextdoor only heard a scream. No gunshots. 'And there's a cartridge case here, next to the boss.'

'She shot his...'

'Yes. She shot them off.' Just like she'd stuck the gun up Peter Mack's arse.

'And you think she did Kay as well.'

Too choked to answer him with words, Challis's face was all desolation.

'I hope she gets well and truly fucking skewered,' he said. He sounded sincere; red-faced and watery eyed. But she could only believe he was making dutiful noises; she had no empathy, not with him.

Once again though, she found it hard to comprehend how a young girl could possess such a vicious - no, sadistic - streak. But that wasn't it, surely. What was driving her? She was working her way through the men in the dvd. She was doling out justice, well her version of it.

Not to Kay. Kay had just got in the way.

Punishments to fit the crimes of the others. More like revenge. A blood feud. Stuart had not been given the same sentence as Peter Mack. He was still alive, he hadn't been given the replica treatment of what Angela Plumitis had received. No, he'd been emasculated, worse than death for him, the poor bastard. Jackie had left his genitals unrecognizable. He'd been a beautiful specimen. Challis shivered, mourning his loss, not hers. But why do this to him?

She'd seen the dvd, some of it. She'd seen what Stuart had done to Angela Plumitis.

Angela Plumitis. It all came back to Angela Plumitis.

What did he do while she was being buggered to death? Perhaps nothing. Perhaps he'd cheered them on. She hadn't seen anything of that, yet. Jackie Davrot obviously had.

'Why in here?' Muench broke into her thoughts. 'Why strap them to a settee? It's not easy. A bit of a billy-bodger job.'

Challis cast her eyes around, bending her neck. She didn't want to relinquish her hold on Redland's hand. She saw the TV. The settee faced the TV. It was on stand-by. So was the dvd player.

'Check the dvd. See if there's a disc in there.' There wasn't.

It was obvious that Jackie Davrot had confronted the two men with the dvd. She'd wanted them to sweat and be afraid, perhaps looking for confessions. She must have known Stuart was one of the two masked men. She'd recognized his scar, as she had. But why go half the way to giving Redland the same payoff? Obvious: she'd thought he was the second masked man! But then something had made her conclude that he wasn't.

Challis was more determined than ever to view the entire dvd as soon as possible. Jackie was out there and still going for the other man.

Fifty-Three

Stuart Devlin's car was an Audi S4 Saloon. Red. It was a brand new example of German technology. Forty grand's worth Chas had said when Stuart had picked it up a couple of months ago. He'd tried unsuccessfully to get her in it, convinced it was a surefire substitute for foreplay.

She had electronically adjusted the seat and pumped up the back support, adjusted the steering column and played with the enhanced climate control. There was no time or opportunity to try out the cruise control, not really appropriate on the roads from Usk to Cottel Court. Maybe later. Maybe there would be a hot police pursuit and she would burn rubber down the motorway.

He was an arrogant sod that Stuart, interested only in his own image. And in sex. Well she'd cured him of that. She allowed herself to wonder what his new condition would be like for a man with his appetites. Of course, by the time he was found he could have bled to death. Alan Redland didn't come into her thinking at all.

The car gave her confidence. She knew that if Guster was being truthful she would be driving right into the arms of the police up at the Court. But she wasn't heading for the big house. She was on course for his lordship's cottage.

The drive out of Usk up to the ridge where Cottel Court was sited provided one set of scenic delights after another. It was early afternoon and the day was more overcast, threatening, but bright enough to see some distance especially as the road climbed up higher and higher. To the left and to the right Monmouthshire stretched away, its vales and tumps undulating in green squares of fields bordered by interminable hedgerows. Left and miles off to the north the long white ridge of Mynydd-y-garn-fawr terminated with the hill that was the Blorenge, one of the three peaks of Abergavenny. Of the other two, the Sugar Loaf could be observed but the Skirrid was obscured.

All of this was of no interest to Jackie. She had never been one to look at the view. To her the joys of travel began and ended with the style in which she could do it and the excitement promised by the destination. She wanted to put her foot down, and she was tempted, but the narrow road and the strangeness of the vehicle inhibited her. Nevertheless the experience was refreshing. Behind her was the disappointment. The uncle had seemed sure to be the second man. A moment of doubt hit her.

Could he have been circumcised since the dvd? Probably not. Why would he at his age? He would never have imagined that his foreskin would be key to saving his potency. No, there was still another man to find. A red-haired man, although…

That smile that Stuart had forced through his pain bugged her. She had tried to prod more information out of him, poking the silencer into his fresh wounds, but he had just groaned a barely discernible plea for her to stop before passing out again.

A cold spasm gripped her as it suddenly occurred to her that the second masked man could be another George Medlyn, from anywhere in the entire country. She'd become hooked on the idea that, like Stuart Devlin and Peter Mack, he would be found locally but these perverts traveled miles for their peculiar pleasures. The entire UK police force would be out looking for her soon if not already but at this point in time she could guess that they would be concentrating on this area. It may be safer if she had to look for him elsewhere.

For a moment her mind flirted with the issue of what comes after this. She didn't know, didn't care. But she did not contemplate self-destruction. She would do all this for Angel but to her way of thinking she was only dispensing justice. There was no guilt attached. There could be a new life waiting beyond the last execution.

No Angel. No Angel though.

The haze returned and her vision blurred and air became hard to take in. Christ, help me! Can't give up now. No softness now. Later. Stay fixed.

It was three o'clock. Radio Wales had been on quietly in the background and now was time for the news headlines:

Breaking news: reports are coming in of a shooting incident in Monmouthshire. There are conflicting reports of numbers of casualties but early indications are that at least two people have been shot at least one fatally. Witnesses say that one of the casualties may be a police officer. It is unclear at this stage if this latest incident is related to the hunt for an armed killer in the western valleys of the county that has been going on since last Friday. News from that search which is ongoing is that the police have widened their search following Saturday's events when shots were fired and another woman wounded. Police are also still investigating the shootings near Usk on Saturday. There is concern that police resources are being stretched, a question our reporter Hywel Lloyd put to Chief Superintendent Mike Harper of the Mon Police...

The policeman droned on about being able to cope and that the public needn't worry. Jackie did not listen. Monmouthshire had been mentioned but not Usk.

Through the gates at Cottel Court she could see that there was a single police patrol car still in the grounds, parked next to Chas's Mini Clubman. She slowed as she drove past. No uniformed officers were in view; obviously they were in the big house.

289

Outside the cottage she drew up next to his lordship's grey Suzuki Grand Vitara with its pretentious number plate 69 LDC. There was no way of knowing if he was at home here or up at the Court.

She dived into the bag and took out the Browning. There were just three rounds left and no spares.

Lordy was going to help her identify the second masked man. He would have to be persuaded. She had left the handcuffs behind in Stuart's uncle's house and had used up all the rope. That's no problem, she smiled. The film room in the cottage had cupboards full of items of restraint.

And, Christ! She was forgetting who the guy filming the sadistic scene had been!

She gave the gun a swift wipe using tissues found in the glove compartment and replaced it in the bag. Next, she made sure her mobile phone was switched off. She'd remembered on the way up that the police could home in on it. She put it in the bag. Out of her pocket she brought Stuart's phone that she had grabbed when she'd searched for his car keys. She could use this.

Relying on Lordy to give the answers she wanted was not necessarily the best option. The Guster woman would be a better bet. She'd given Chas the info he'd needed. But she was busy with the police up at the big house and Jackie did not have time to waste hanging around for her to get free of them. Stuart's car would soon be missed and the police would be on the lookout for it. She was hoping that they would still be looking for the policewoman's car but there was no guarantee. Lordy would have to be persuaded to part with his Suzuki.

She only had three rounds left. Why the fuck had she wasted a bullet on that fucking policewoman?

'The lovely Miss Davrot,' exclaimed the surprised Lord de Cottel. 'Good God, what the hell do you look like. Something the cat dragged in. Not even a shadow of your former self. More like a spectre; the ghost of erotica past. I saw the car, thought it was Mr. Devlin. Don't say he's loaned out his spanking vehicle for you to drive in that state. Well, well, well. And what did you have to do to enjoy that privilege I wonder.'

*

The ambulances, two of them, had come and gone. A paramedic had turned up first. His assessment was that Redland needed immediate emergency resuscitation. His opinion of Stuart Devlin's condition was that blood-loss had ceased and although the shock of the injuries had rendered him unconscious his vital signs indicated he could wait for backup which in any case arrived within minutes.

Neither of the victims was able to speak. Redland tried but his speech was slurred and disjointed. Challis got as close to him as she was allowed. He seemed to be saying "red" but she wondered if he was just trying to convey his own name. The paramedic was concerned that Redland had had a stroke. Challis told him of the angina but his take on that was that one thing can often lead to another.

However, so concerned was she that Redland and, hopefully, Stuart would be able to say something about the attack that she ordered Muench to go in one of the ambulances.

'Not back to the fucking hospital,' he complained.

Challis couldn't go herself. Her most recent orders had been to get home but those she discounted, as circumstances had made them irrelevant. No, she wanted to have a good look around the boss's house. She was puzzled by how Jackie had caught up with Stuart here of all places.

She instructed Billy Bell to go back to the hospital as well, to set up some security around the two victims. She would wait for SOCO. Billy Bell put up tape at the front of the house – he was running out – and then left. She locked the front door behind him.

No sooner had he gone than Challis realized the report about Ruff's car being in the Usk car-park had not been checked out.

The system had to be updated. She made a quick call to tell Control of the latest developments and to get another team out to Usk car-park.

Then she started a visual scan of the room.

The ropes were where they'd fallen near the settee. The handcuffs had gone in the ambulances, still attached to the wrists of Redland and Stuart. They were non-standard silver handcuffs, non-rigid unlike police issue, with a short central chain connecting the two wrist bands. All they had been able to accomplish with the Billy Bell's cutters was to snip through the chains. The cuffs were very tight on the wrists and there was every chance that the two men would bear the marks for a time.

She stood behind the settee. The TV was dead ahead and she was convinced they had been forced to watch something, probably that dvd. She crossed to the player which was on a shelf beneath the TV itself. Muench had checked it when she asked him to but she wanted to double-check. There was no dvd in the slot but as she bent lower she could see that something had slid down the rear of the unit. It looked like an envelope. She reached in and drew it out. She recognized it. It was the envelope she had brought in the day she had come by to check out the house, when Redland had first been admitted to hospital. Jared Edwards had passed it to her; he'd had to sign for it.

It was open. She widened the opening and peered inside. There was a dvd.

She stared into the envelope. She wanted to pull the dvd out. But this was a crime scene; she should retrieve it with care, gloved hands and all that.

She tipped it out onto the carpet. With a pen she flicked it over and turned it around so she could read what was written on it.

It read 'VKS: January 2011'. This was the one.

She read the envelope again. It was addressed to Redland all right. Why was he receiving a copy? This worried her; made her feel extremely queasy. Her feet were slipping from solid ground into a quagmire. The rock that was Redland was suddenly shaken as if by an earthquake; like the rarely recalled discovery made at a funeral that a father she thought the world of had been screwing around for years.

No, wait. Jackie had let Alan off. Think! Think.

It all came down yet again to her needing to view the whole dvd. Okay, there was one taken as evidence from the house in Monmouth but that would go through forensics first. There was no time for all that. Besides, she wanted to view it on her own.

She scooped up the dvd and, for a second, thought about playing it now but she had no idea of the runtime. She put it straight into one of her pockets. The envelope got absent-mindedly folded and went into another.

She took a deep breath. She was in deep shit now if she was found out.

She jumped. A bang at the front door. SOCO.

Making sure her contraband was buried deep in her pockets she unlocked the door. It wasn't Sayer and his SOCO band. Standing there was Lassman and with him DCC Jones.

'Thought that was your car,' Lassman said, striding in. Challis was struck dumb by their entrance. 'Thought your last order was to get home,' he added, as much for the DCC's benefit as for anyone else's or was there just the remotest hint at irony?

'I had to get the pool car back to the station, didn't I?' she babbled. His attitude caught her flat-footed and all she could do was pat her pockets and their secrets. 'Called in here on my way home.'

Lassman had stopped talking but kept walking right into the lounge.

'Forensics haven't been done yet,' Challis warned, adding belatedly '…sir.'

DCC Jones joined him in the doorway.

'You found them, Sergeant?'

'Yes, ma'am.'

'Damn good job you didn't go straight home then. From what I hear you may have saved two lives.'

Lassman did not appear impressed. 'Explain what you found will you?'

Challis did just that, in some detail. Twice Lassman tried to interrupt her flow but the DCC quietly raised a hand to silence him. When she finished, Lassman got his first question in. 'How did you get in? Was the door open?'

Challis decided to lie. 'Yes.' She didn't want them, or rather him, to know the boss had entrusted her with a key. Muench would contradict her of course, if and when asked.

'Have you searched the place?'

'Why, no, sir.' She was genuinely surprised by this question. It sounded as if Lassman was applying the procedure following entry into a major crime site, not into the house of a fellow officer, an injured officer at that! 'Waiting for SOCO.' She knew this addition sounded tame.

'SOCO not coming until tomorrow.' The DCC calmly advised.

'They're too busy following your trail of destruction,' Lassman put in without much humour.

This guy has as much charm as the red-necked O'Halloran. This thought brought on a light-headed flash, a bell tinkled. The flash faded fast.

'There are more casualties in your wake than there are up at this other place; what's it called?' he ranted.

DCC Jones gave him a hard stare. 'This case certainly does demand a realignment of resources. I'm bringing some people back in from the valleys.' This explanation of tactics was directed at Challis.

'It could be this case was not given the importance it deserved,' Challis observed.

'Sergeant,' Lassman bristled. 'This case was important enough to me to bring me down here to assist.'

'You sure it wasn't just a jolly outing in Wales?' Challis was red-faced. 'Show those Welsh peasants how to run a case.'

'I...'

'Sergeant!' DCC Jones's voice was firm. She could see that Challis was close to breaking down in tears. It was only her anger that was damming the flood.

It had always rankled with the DCC that a woman's physiology meant that tears were unpreventable in times of stress. It was a natural weakness but yet a safety valve. But in the eyes of men they were a sure sign that women could not control their emotions, a weak point some enjoyed exploiting. As a younger officer she had learned to hold back until she was somewhere private, like the loo or, more often than not, at home. But her husband had tired of being with a tear-strewn wife several times a week and had gone off and found a woman who laughed a lot. Another marriage becoming a casualty of the job the DCC refused to give up.

There had been many occasions during her long crawl to the top that she would have loved to see a bastard of a man in floods of tears. Her eyes now were fixed on Lassman. 'I would suggest, Chief Inspector, that this is all totally unproductive.'

She could not give him more of a bollocking in front of Challis, neither could she over-compensate in her sympathy towards Challis. The girl had found her close young female colleague cruelly and needlessly gunned down and now her boss perhaps close to death.

She turned to Challis again. 'It was suggested you go home after what you'd been through earlier. This latest experience makes that suggestion an even better one.'

Challis had been aching to make a more constructive contribution to this debate and ignored the DCC's overtures, which tempered her superior's annoyance with no little admiration. Add a dash of diplomacy, Jones thought, and Challis could go far.

'We're still looking for Jackie Davrot, ma'am. She's abandoned...Kay's car and we believe taken Stuart Devlin's. I've asked its description be circulated. We got full details from the people next door, including the registration number.'

'You are convinced she is the perpetrator even though there are no witnesses?'

'Yes, ma'am. The woman next-door saw Jackie Davrot leaving here in Stuart Devlin's car.'

'She saw a woman who you assume is Jackie Davrot,' the DCC corrected her.

'Ma'am, Jackie Davrot took Angela Plumitis to hospital. She was distraught.'

'She more or less confessed to killing Plumitis,' Lassman interjected. 'Caused her injuries.'

'No, she didn't. Those men in the dvd caused her injuries.'

'Then why did she say she'd done them?' Lassman persisted.

'I don't know. Maybe...maybe if she'd accused men who had just been murdered then that would have made her appear involved in their deaths.'

'So what's she doing now?' the DCC asked.

'Revenge on all the men involved in the Vikings scene.'

'Stuart Devlin?' the DCC raised an eyebrow. 'Mr. Redland's nephew? He was one of the masked men? How did she know?'

The DCC could see that Challis was convinced of Stuart Devlin's involvement. Challis's face reddened slightly as she created a story that would not reveal her intimate knowledge of Stuart Devlin's body. 'She probably got it out of her father before she shot him. What I don't get is how she knew he was here.'

Lassman drew himself up. 'She phoned him. We've checked her phone-calls. From...' he couldn't remember where she'd come from '...she drove to, where was it?'

DCC Jones took it up. 'She drove to somewhere near Llanhelog. We have a team up there now, Pontderry Lane. She called Cottel Court first and then Stuart Devlin. For some reason he must have told her where he was, here obviously, visiting his uncle.'

'You realize your theory is based on circumstantial evidence,' Lassman asserted. 'At this time we have no idea who actually carried out any of the shootings. None whatsoever. We have possibles. Count them: Angela Plumitis, Charles Davrot; two for sure. Jacqueline Davrot? Doubtful. We know the two dead men enjoyed Angela Plumitis. At first she may have been a willing participant in their little orgy scene but things went too far for her liking. So, she's favourite for the two shootings.'

'She was in hospital Saturday morning. Couldn't move.' Challis put the case.

'The shooting of Peter Mack and his wife was on Friday night,' he countered. 'Now, the shootings today... For all we know right now Charles Davrot killed DC Ruff and was shot in a struggle with a third party. Shot in the groin; hardly a shot to kill. And there's no evidence at all that his daughter Jacqueline was even in the house.'

'She took Kay's car. It's in Usk car park...'

'Circumstantial again.' He paused for effect, swaggering slightly as Challis contemplated an alternative.

'Where's the gun, from the shooting? Where's the gun?'

'With the third party! Obvious I would have thought. And here? Okay, a woman answering the description, you say, of Jacqueline Davrot was seen leaving.'

'Jackie Davrot is the common link. She took Angela to the hospital...'

'After inflicting the fatal injuries, as she confessed.'

'No. She saw her die there. Okay, we don't know for sure what happened in her house. It may be like you say, Chas shooting...' she couldn't say the name '...doing the shooting and then a struggle but she came here to get Stuart Devlin. She'd seen him on the dvd and...'

'What do you mean "seen him on the dvd"?' This time it was DCC Jones. 'I thought the only men who could be identified were the two who were murdered already and that the men wearing masks were unknowns.'

There was silence until Lassman said 'Correct.'

'How then did she recognise Devlin?'

Challis sought a reason that she could phrase the way she wanted. 'He was naked.' The words came out unconvincingly. Lassman and DCC Jones worked on them.

'She recognized his naked body? You're saying she was familiar with him in a naked state. Had she had sex with him?'

Challis saw a get out. 'Possibly but he certainly had a distinguishing feature.'

'Which was?'

A white lie was forming. 'When we found him his shirt was raised…'

'As well as his trousers down,' Lassman interjected.

'His shirt was raised,' Challis ignored him, 'exposing a large scar on his ribcage. Very noticeable. Unmistakable I would have thought.'

DCC Jones nodded but Lassman was obstinately not persuaded.

'That can be checked,' she said to Lassman. 'Check the dvd and check Mr. Devlin.'

Challis was noticeably breathing quickly and her face had reddened even more. The talk had been allowed to home in on her own private knowledge of Stuart Devlin, which, she accepted, was bound to come out. She had dug a hole and was widening it. The verbal fisticuffs with Lassman and his obstinate logic had wound up her emotions. Her intuition about Jackie Davrot had been challenged. She was sure she was right and was uptight that she was not believed.

'Why were you here, Sergeant?' Lassman was eager to know.

The reason for coming to the boss's house wouldn't come out. She turned to face the DCC, speechless, eyes flooding.

'To tell Mr. Redland about Kay Ruff I would think,' the DCC answered quietly. 'Break it to him gently.' Her hand lightly touched Challis on the shoulder and that gesture opened the floodgates.

'Sorry,' Challis managed to splutter.

'Off you go,' the DCC urged. 'All right driving?'

'Yes, thank you, ma'am.'

The DCC's attitude let a guilty feeling creep over her. She liked the way she called the boss "Mr. Redland". Her hand found its way to her pocket. 'Ma'am,' she began but no, the job wasn't finished and she wasn't going to supply Lassman with any ammunition. 'I'll be in first thing.'

'Whatever.'

As she walked out of the front door she heard DCC Jones say 'Right, now, Mr. Lassman!' So, she called him "Mr". too, but she was consoled by the fact that her tone sounded less than friendly. Challis hoped he was about to get the delayed bollocking.

She realized too late that she still had the key to Redland's house in her pocket.

Fifty-Four

Lord de Cottel's cottage did not seem particularly home-like to Jackie. The older rooms smelled fusty, damp, an odour peculiar to Lordy himself. Not many men were able to make her feel uncomfortable, she could deal on almost equal terms with men of any stature, but this old man gave her the creeps.

She regarded him as an old man although if she had given the matter any prolonged thought she could have concluded that he was only in his fifties, albeit his late fifties. He was shabby. He thought he was a chic old hippy but his clothes never really seemed to suit him. She thought that, no matter what he wore, his face would always let him down. There was a sickly grin born of some kind of anticipation. Similar to Stuart Devlin, she always thought, but whereas Devlin was to all women a predator who enjoyed the challenge of the chase, Lordy expected females to drop right into his lusting lap.

Today he was wearing faded jeans, fashionably threadbare in places. Despite the coolness of the day and the relative lack of efficient heating in the old part of the cottage he was wearing a long-sleeved denim shirt, faded, and a bright red cravat. His lack of hair on the top of his head gave him the look of a gormless skull, strands of dyed blonde hair trailing down the back and sides.

He ushered her in, guiding her to the kitchen.

She knew he was right in his reaction to her appearance. Smells were drifting up.

'So tell me, Jackie dear, how did you persuade Stuart to part with his car? Coffee?'

She had no wish to concoct a piece of fiction. She eased the bag onto the breakfast bar and took off her top coat, resting it on a stool. Glancing around, she was surprised at the tidiness of the room.

She had no desire to be pissing around sharing a beverage. She'd come to this place specifically to get information out of this guy, not to have a coffee party.

'Forget the coffee!' she barked.

He turned sharply, confounded by her vocal volume. He found he was staring at a gun, pointing unwaveringly at his chest.

'What…?' he began, a laugh wanting to come out..

'Let's go into the film room,' she suggested firmly.

Full of confidence he strode towards her. 'Big weapon in such a little hand. Browning, eh? Specially machined to accommodate a silencer. How professional. Now put it away, there's a love.'

She only had three rounds but for the second time that day she let off a shot in a kitchen. This time the bullet smashed into a light fitting right above his lordship's head, showering him with shards of glass. He halted in mid-stride. They both heard the ejected casing tinkle the crockery hanging from hooks on the Welsh kitchen dresser.

'The next one goes somewhere more painful,' she warned, hoping to Christ she would not need another one. Only two precious rounds left now; she had to pile on the fear-factor.

'And don't think I won't do it. Just to let you know, I got Devlin's car after I did him. You could say he bequeathed it to me.'

There was shock on his face but he tried to mask it. He was sizing her up. There was no giveaway about her. She seemed to be perfectly serious and would have to be given the benefit of any doubt. He knew guns and being at the wrong end of one was not an entirely new experience for him. His London days had been fraught with conflicting interests, some more heavily armed than others. He had survived unscathed but never had he been confronted by a pint-sized venomous female in her early twenties, brown eyes verging on jet black, ragged fiery hair. Eminently pleasurable when cleaned up but clearly deranged now.

'Film room,' she repeated, pointing the way with the Browning.

He would have to ride the initial storm and wait his moment. She would soften.

He had known many women obsessed by sex, sex of all kinds. This one, though, seemed to be fixated on women. He had tried his routines on her, so too others, Stuart Devlin for one. But she shut them out, cut them off at source. For a long time he had been convinced that her father had an incestuous hold on her, that she was his and his alone. He had seen the way Chas used to look at her, he had caught Chas devouring videos of her in action. She was excellent at what she could do to another woman. Even he had been taught a trick or two by her. But men?

As they walked in single file, she using the gun like a cattle prod, he decided not to be totally dominated by the girl. 'You realize who you're dealing with, don't you, my dear? There's an awful lot I know about you and your father.'

All he got for his opening gambit was an even firmer jab, right on his spine. He winced. He had to admit that hurt!

'I heard your tongue was more skillful than that. Just bite on it and open the door.'

The room used for filming was in semi-gloom. As soon as the lights came on Jackie's eyes also lit up.

'Christ, Lordy, you going into the computer business?'

In one corner there was an arrangement of desktop power units, computer screens and at least two laptops. In a cardboard box she could make out various bits of ancillary equipment and in another dvds and tape cartridges. Without allowing her attention to wander too far from his lordship she eased towards the pile of electrical stuff and studied it.

'I know what this is. This is all your computer equipment. The Guster woman said it had been stolen. Is this an insurance scam? Short of money are we?'

'It was Devlin's idea. He had to shift it all for some reason, make it look as if we'd had a robbery. He didn't want the police to get their hands on it. Somehow he knew they'd be coming up here this morning for that specific purpose. And sure enough they did. They...' He realized he was talking too much.

'They what?' The longer he remained quiet the more Jackie elevated the gun to a horizontal position, targeting his chest again.

'Nothing.' The gun looked threatening and any doubts he may have had about Jackie using it were beginning to fade fast. 'Just that they wanted to know about the dvd of Angela. They wrongly assumed it was filmed here...'

'It was filmed here, in this very room. I've seen it. I recognized it. You filmed it!'

'Me?'

'Yes, you. See that mirror? Never film facing a mirror. Fairly basic. There's a perfect shot of you.'

He shook.

'You filmed Angel being murdered.'

He watched her closely, trying hard to judge this girl's intentions.

'So what else did they say?'

'They wanted the original.' He was trying to sound nonchalant. 'Let me phone Sue.'

'How did they know about it?'

'They had stills; still photographs. They said they were taken from a short clip of the dvd and they wanted to see the whole thing. They were going crazy about it. Saying crazy things. Let's get Sue here; she'll sort things out.'

'Who was? Who were they?' She would not be distracted.

'An older policeman and a younger female. Meredith knew the woman, said she was the one who had arrested Chas the other day.'

Mel!

'Go on. What kind of crazy things were they saying?'

'They were going on about murder. Two of the men in the dvd were dead. They said they were concerned for the safety of everyone else in the film. Sue...'

She leveled the gun again and he shut up.

'Concerned for everyone involved, eh? Like the cameraman?'

He was lost for words. Her manner did not bode well for him. He had lost the ascendancy, if indeed he had ever had it with this female.

'Especially the cameraman,' she emphasized.

He was looking decidedly pale.

'Sue's gone, by the way. All the way to London. And all I want to know,' she continued, 'are the names of those in the dvd; and where I can find them of course.'

'Two of them are dead,' he yelled. 'The police said.'

'There were two men wearing masks. Who were they?'

He hesitated, confused. Surely she knew the answer to that; she'd mentioned Devlin.

'You must know,' he sounded irritated.

'Why must I know?'

'You said…'

'I said what? That I did Stuart Devlin?'

Silence from his lordship.

'So are you saying Stuart Devlin was one of the masked men?'

'Why? Why are you doing this? What the hell is your problem? I don't know any names. This was a private party. It was run outside of the events in the big house. That's why it was here and not up there. It's not on any of those computers. It was privately arranged.'

'Paid big money were you, as the middleman? They even got a peer of the realm to do the camera work. Of course you know names.'

'No!'

She raised the gun, advancing on him.

'All right. I knew Peter Mack. He's a regular; him and his wife. The other guy was new, first time here, never seen him before. Something Medlar was his name. The guys in the masks were wearing masks for a very good reason. Anonymity. We guarantee it here if specified.'

'How fucking gentleman's agreement.' The gun was waving almost under his nose. 'Names!'

'Stuart. But you knew that.'

'Very good. Not difficult see! And the other one.'

The gun was touching his face. This was no time to hold anything back.

'I don't know.'

The silencer jabbed into his skin.

'He was a friend of Stuart's. You'll have to ask him.'

'I did.'

'Then you know, you know more than I do.'

'No, I don't. He didn't say even when things got more painful. So who?'

'I don't know. All I know is he's a policeman.'

'What?'

'Stuart told me. He found it amusing. He…'

'Local or what?'

'Um?'

'Local police?'

'I think so. I don't know.'

Jackie pushed the silencer harder making him jerk backwards. Automatically his hand came up to push away the pain. The barrel jerked. The gun went off, the bullet crashing hard against his temple. His head bent to the right and his body followed it, hitting the floor with a sickening crunch.

'Fuck,' she swore, as angry about wasting another round as with the sudden unavailability of his lordship for further interrogation. She stooped to examine him. He was alive. He was unconscious, either from the fall or from the bullet that may have grazed his skull or entered it. Without closer inspection she couldn't tell one way or the other.

Now the question was who was the local cop in the mask? Was it that uncle of Devlin's after all? She was beginning to feel totally incompetent. The tail she was chasing was endless, wagging close then veering away and she appeared to not have the skill to hold it and pin it on the right donkey. How come Chas was so good at this kind of thing? How can it be so difficult?

'Hello! Anyone here?'

Meredith Guster was hailing from somewhere near the front of the cottage. She was inside, the door could be heard closing behind her.

Jackie looked down at the unmoving Lordy. For no real reason she weighed the gun in her hand but she didn't need confirmation that there was only one round left. The Guster woman had to be faced and rendered harmless because, if she made her escape, then the alarm would be raised immediately. But then, it wouldn't be known that she was responsible. No-one knew she was here.

The various permutations raced through her mind but she prevaricated too long; Meredith Guster was in the doorway. She saw the gun before she saw the twisted body of her employer. A gasp escaped her lips.

'You!'

Her face was red, her eyes even redder. She advanced into the room, bearing down on Jackie who could not interpret the emotions in this woman's face. Defensively, almost timidly, she steered the gun in Guster's direction.

'Chas is dead.' She spoke just inches from Jackie's face. The gun was pressed against her left breast but she casually swiped it away as if she were swatting at a troublesome wasp. 'Those coppers who'd been here all day, they suddenly wanted to know why you'd called, earlier, looking for Stuart. D'you know, at first I wouldn't tell them. Never tell 'em anything, that's me, not less you have to, like Chas. They told me about Chas, piled it on they did. Chas shot, left bleeding to death.'

'Shut up,' Jackie warned her.

'Policewoman,' she wrestled to get the right words to come out, 'killed in cold blood they said. Executed. One of their own. They want you. They said it was you.'

'Shut...up!'

Guster didn't shut up. She grabbed Jackie's collar.

'You're in deep shit.'

There was no distance at all between them now. The silencer jabbed deeper into her top coat but if there was any pain from it she ignored it.

'You and that fucking girl, that fucking Angel. That's a wrong name for anyone if I ever heard one.'

'Shut up about Angel, you pathetic whore.'

Like the gun in her chest Jackie's insult passed painlessly.

'Pathetic? You're pathetic and you made that father of yours just as bad. I know he would have screwed that girl at the drop of her knickers, no hesitation. He was as loony about her as you, mooning around after her. And you, Angel, the love of your life. Pathetic. You'd screw any woman you could get your hands on.'

By now she was shaking Jackie with almost every syllable, pushing her backwards. Suddenly she stopped and dragged her even closer.

'How could you do that to your own father?'

'You turd! Of course he loved Angel but not like that. And you...you were just his easy shag.'

The slap came unexpectedly. The flat of Guster's hand across Jackie's face stung like hell and the force of it loosened Guster's grip on her collar. That hand now free followed up the first blow with a second that sent Jackie reeling, her feet stumbling backwards, hitting the outstretched legs of his lordship. A third swipe hit nothing solid because Jackie was falling backwards. She was unable to brace herself for the impact as first the back of her head and then her elbows hit the floor. Her brain jolted and bright lights flashed behind her eyeballs but through it she heard the spit of a bullet, the last bullet, leaving the Browning that jerked in her hand.

She was stunned. She thought she would black out. Then she realized that she was struggling for breath, the wind knocked out her, the bellows of her chest refusing to inflate, compounded by Guster's body falling forward flat onto her belly. Jackie thought she would now suffocate. She could not breathe and there was no strength in her to shift Guster off her.

Ironically, Guster's ribcage was heaving as she strove to pull air though her throat that was a fountain of blood. She was gurgling, as if suckling. One of her hands was squeezing her neck, either to try to stem the flow or find the source of the agonizing pain. With the other hand she pressed down on Jackie's abdomen in an attempt to lever herself up. The intense pressure on her soft belly made Jackie's diaphragm convulse and to her great relief she gulped in oxygen.

She managed to twist the lower half of her body, getting a hip sidewards off the deck and Guster tumbled away, onto her back where she lay in a final twitching paroxysm. Red saliva shot upwards from her mouth in mini geysers. And then there was a final choking strangulated cough.

Now a stream of air rushed into Jackie's lungs. For some reason she was clinging to the empty gun with her right hand and resorted to using the left to push herself up. The first thing she saw was Guster's face. The dead woman was bloody from nose down to waist. They were inches apart. Up on one elbow she tried to see detail but it was just a mess of colours. Try as she might she still couldn't rise any further. Her head spun every time she tried. Like vertigo.

She heaved up once more and vomited, partly over the dead woman's face. That suited her just fine. She was a woman she had never had any time for. Chas's fascination with her astounded and sickened her. And now the cow had made her waste her last round and given her one hell of a headache.

The room was spinning. She could barely sit up. There was nothing close to hand that she could use to hoist herself up. She turned onto her knees, squeezing her eyes shut and taking deep breaths to try and staunch the bile that was desperate to surge up her gullet.

Meredith's face was beneath hers, mouth agape.

I could have made her tell me who that policeman guy is, Jackie thought, still believing that she had had the power over Guster to get her to do what she wanted.

She looked at the gun, lying impotent on the floor. Only good for bluffing but that hadn't worked just now, had it? And it had still been loaded, then!

At last she got to her feet but swayed from side to side. It was no good, she had to sit. There was a chair near the door.

From it she surveyed the scene, still shadowy.

She examined the back of her head. There was an enormous lump, getting more enormous. Too painful to touch she could only trace its outline with her fingertips. No blood. Was that good or bad?

For what seemed like an age she sat there, thoughts in her bruised brain ranging from fleeting despair at this incapacity to a determination to get out of there and finish the job. For Angel.

A policeman. A fucking policeman. She hated the lot of them. She'd done that Kay girl. Wished she'd seen off Devlin's uncle. That Mel; she'd be another one. Bet she'd know who the red-headed bastard was.

The waves of nausea eased off. After ten minutes or so and a couple of abortive attempts to stand she managed to walk over to where Lordy lay. She had to bend to search his pockets for his car keys. Nothing. While she was bent double she picked up the gun and for the first time she noticed that she was covered in Guster's blood. Her sweater was saturated, her jeans sodden at the waist, streaked down the legs. Standing upright again brought a return of the wooziness and she had to stagger back to the chair for a few more minutes, staring.

Two bodies. Accidents. The gun just went off.

Two more bodies. She was derisive. His perverted lordship and Chas's whore.

Chas! He'd fucking annoyed her. Always. But he wasn't dead, surely. It was a leg shot. She'd aimed for his bollocks but had missed. She'd hit his leg. He was all right. Did she check him before she left? He'd be all right. That Guster woman was fucking mad, going on about him being dead.

The Kay girl. Why had she shot her? Her head was hurting; she couldn't remember why she'd shot the girl. *Why did I? I shouldn't have, should I?* She was gorgeous. There must have been a reason. She must have given her a reason.

Devlin was good though, worth any number of mistakes.

She found the keys in the kitchen, next to the kettle.

Her blood-stained clothes had to come off. She'd leave the jeans on, had no choice. The sweater she discarded, dumping it on the kitchen floor. She'd be cold in just her bra but her top coat would be warm enough if she kept it buttoned up. She gathered up her bag, deposited the gun in it and left the cottage that was not her idea of a cottage at all.

Out of breath and her brain whizzing she sat, suddenly depressed, in the driving seat of Lordy's Suzuki. Was it all over? She feared there was nowhere else to turn. The hunt was done. The final quarry never flushed out. The last bit of justice for Angel left unfinished. Her promise undelivered.

For a moment she had no idea what to do next or where to go. But then it came to her.

*

As she drove off, Lord de Cottel sat upright, gingerly feeling his scalp before staring incredulously at his crimson fingers.

Fifty-Five

Her car was on auto-pilot. Nothing registered at all with Challis. When she reached the top of her road she could not remember having passed any of the home-run landmarks: the straight-stretch near the showground field, the twisting chicanes of the climb to the old volcano before the long shallow descent to Capelgwm. She had no recollection of switching on her windscreen wipers but she had, or the auto-pilot had. As she'd left Usk snow began to fall. By Capelgwm it seemed heavier.

She eased the car down the slope and up into her driveway, already white. She grabbed her bag from the passenger seat, got out and went quickly to the house, not locking the car. The front door crashed shut behind her and she stood in the darkening silence. The bag slipped to the floor.

Crying was not far off. It was there, right behind her eyes, and in the tightness of her chest.

Fuck! She had let loose tears in front of the DCC, and that fucking Lassman! The only way to erase that would be to turn back time; turn back time to this morning, all the way back, to when Kay had been alive. Never mind her own fucking embarrassment! Go back, for Kay.

Why? Why? Why?

What had she done wrong? In her mind, a jumble of events, decisions, wrong ones. Where had she made a wrong one? When was that "Sliding Doors" moment?

What did she need, right now? What did she want? What would do it for her?

Alcohol!

A bath, shower. But that wouldn't wash inside her head. The vodka would. Two. Three, even better.

Food. No.

Noise. It's too quiet, too quiet in this house.

Jonathan. Some selfish sex. Couldn't imagine it.

She wanted to cry but she just couldn't.

She let out a long drawn-out shriek.

It left her exhausted.

Her top coat fell to the floor, on top of her bag.

Lights! Lights, put them on, everywhere. They lit everything up and all she could see were her mother's things. *Let's be honest, Mel, there's bugger all of you in this house.*

Well, the vodka's mine.

One drink went down quickly, the second she took upstairs. She stripped off on the landing. All the lights were on and none of the curtains drawn, just net at the windows. If the entire cluster of houses wanted to look, well they could.

The second vodka was gulped down before she stepped into the shower. Hot water hit the top of her head and cascaded down her body. No soap. She didn't want a wash she wanted a drenching. For an age she stood motionless, water beating down, hair flattened. Perhaps the jet would work like CIA water torture, rend her senseless, knock all horror thoughts out of her consciousness until she was empty.

The tears had to come.

Kay's Alex! Poor Alex.

She edged back downstairs, a toweled robe hanging loosely. Soggy footprints imprinted on her mother's beige stair-carpet. Droplets fell from her legs and spattered her mother's hall rugs. At the bottom she halted to tie a token knot in the belt of the robe.

The tears had come. And some clarity with them. She remembered the dvd in her coat pocket.

The lounge room windows had mother's net curtains. She didn't bother to pull mother's heavier drapes.

Her knees made two dark damp patches on her mother's off-white carpet as she knelt in front of the dvd player. The lid of the dvd case wouldn't open and then she noticed for the first time that the little sticky seal had not been broken.

The dvd had never been let out of the box.

Redland had opened the envelope but had never taken the dvd out of its case.

He had never even watched the dvd.

The realization sent a pulse of joy right through her body, a lonely ray of hope. But the reason for the sense of relief was beyond her.

She broke the seal, loaded the dvd and turned on the TV.

It began to play.

No preamble, no titles, no trailers of other offerings; straight to a smiling Angela Plumitis opening a door to find two masked men standing there.

Challis sat down cross-legged close, too close, to the screen.

She had seen pornography, from quite a young age, from when she was a police cadet. A group of them had got together one night, more than one night, and consumed beer and watched porn. It had been a laugh. Perhaps educational because in amongst all the laughter and jeering it had been clear that certain individuals were taking in and banking what they were seeing. Certain hints and tips had certainly stayed with her. But it had been later as a twosome with Stuart Devlin that she had been introduced to the serious consumption of porn.

A lot of it she liked, the early varieties that he brought. Later on he came with more extreme stuff that did not appeal. She knew that this dvd was going to head in that same direction, from what she had seen of Lassman's clip.

But now, these early scenes, although clearly of a woman being taken against her will or at least pretending to be taken against her will, made the simulation stimulating.

She adjusted the volume upwards, ostensibly to try to make out words or names but most of it was guttural.

Close-ups of Angela Plumitis showed what an attractive woman she was except when she pulled faces to let out a rather ineffectual scream. Could she have killed George Medlyn and the Macks? The hospital had said she had been in agony when she was brought in to Casualty early on Saturday morning. Couldn't walk. Jackie Davrot had confessed to inflicting her injuries. Why?

While she was thinking about possible perpetrators, she ticked off Chas Davrot who had been locked up that night, the Friday night, the night the Macks were shot.

So, Angela incapable through injury, Chas incapable due to incarceration. That leaves Jackie. Jackie did the Macks, perhaps George Medlyn too and then Stuart and the boss.

There was Stuart now, on the screen. His body, just how she remembered it, well built as ever. The tell-tale scar stood out, a dull vein of pink on his brown torso. The mask looked ridiculous.

The camera began to zoom in.

What was that?

The cameraman had moved and a mirror at the back caught his reflection. She paused and rewound. Several times. Well, I'll be buggered, she said inappropriately. His bloody lordship. The lying old sod. *We don't allow filming here!*

He moved out of shot as the zoom went in very tight on Stuart's close-up. The scene went on and on and the more it went on the more she twitched, the more her face heated up. It reminded her.

She tried to concentrate on Angela Plumitis but Stuart was choking her quiet.

Enough!

She put the dvd and TV on standby. She was supposed to be moving the investigation on, professional, looking for the second man; that was the whole idea. But it had been a fucking awful day and this was only making it fucking worse.

She rose unsteadily, her head light, her breath quick and hot. The urge to go back upstairs was strong.

She started up. Mid-stair she halted, realizing the loose knot on her robe belt had given way and her right hand was on her groin. She removed it, grasping the banister. Her mind was a maelstrom of conflicting emotions.

Kay! Kay was dead for fuck's sake.

If only there was some normality at the top of the stairs, someone waiting to take hold of her, some warm flesh and hot blood. Somebody to erase the taste of the whole business, make her forget everything she'd witnessed, everything her face had been rubbed into. Somebody to give her either tenderness or better still to pummel her into forgetfulness.

The staircase looked like a mountain to climb. She drew her upper arms together to shield her breasts. She was immobile. Nothing to go for in either direction. Why did she feel empty and why did she see something physical as the filler? That was so temporary.

Out of sheer helplessness she burst into tears. Christ, you could really hate yourself sometimes.

Her mobile sounded off. It was near the front door, in a pocket.

Bollocks! Who the fuck…?

She weaved back down the stairs and retrieved it, pulling out a folded envelope from the same pocket.

If it was Lassman he could take a running jump.

It was Ray Lockett. She had forgotten about Ray.

'Ray, Ray.' Control yourself Challis. Difficult.

'Sarge, it's me.'

She was sobbing, holding back most of the sound of it.

'Are you okay, Sarge?'

Her voice was cracked. Nothing she could do about it. 'Ray, where are you?'

'Aw, I'm in Usk would you believe. They got me outside the boss's house, making sure it stays secure until SOCO get here, tomorrow probably. Look, Sarge…' He was finding it hard to say what he wanted to say. 'About Kay…'

'I know, I know.' Fresh gulps.

'Harry said you were there, you found her.'

'That's right,' was all she could say which put Lockett in a quandary as he didn't know how to continue this conversation.

'Bloody awful, the whole thing,' he said, speaking his emotions. 'I can't believe it. What it must be like for you I can't think. I don't know what to say. I liked Kay. What about Alex? And now the boss!'

'Are you there all night?' She was taking her gaping robe up the stairs, mobile in one hand, crunched up envelope in the other. This was a bit surreal, talking to Ray like this. After the day that she had had there was a kind of perverse satisfaction in it but what that feeling might mean she had no idea.

'No. Another half hour or so. Uniform taking over. I've only been here about an hour but guess what. I'd only been here a few minutes when the Super turned up.'

'Who? O'Halloran?' She sniffed her nose clearer.

'Yeah. Wanted to go in the house. I told him it was secured for the night but he ignored me and went in anyway. He was in there ages. Went in all the rooms. I could see the lights. He asked about you when he came out. Wanted to know how you were. I couldn't tell him, could I, but I knew you'd gone home.'

'You'd better log his appearance there.'

'He asked me not to. Told me. No need he said.'

'Do it anyway. Do it now. Did he say why he was there?'

'No, not really. Said he was doing a pre-SOCO check.'

O'Halloran had called in sick that morning. What had brought him from his bed, out into the cold. This puzzle brought her to a halt on the landing.

'Look, Sarge, first Kay then the boss and you finding both of them. When I finish here d'you want to get together for a drink. I need one or three. Be good to talk. We probably both need to talk.'

Sweet.

'I don't know Ray. It's snowing here and I've had a few drinks already so I'm not driving.' Is Ray asking her on a date? 'You could come here.' Ray Lockett? 'It would be nice.' She had this sinking feeling that he was now the only friendly face left in the entire world.

'It's snowing here too,' he said. 'But okay.'

'You know where I live.' He'd given her a lift home once or twice.

'See you in a bit.'

'The door's on the latch. Just come right in.'

She'd put some food on, but clothes first and sort out her hair before it became irreparably tangled.

Fifty-Six

The large whisky was probably a bad idea but the theory was that it would clear her head and ease her stomach.

It didn't.

It was early to be at the bar in the Eastgate, just gone four, dusk trying to gather outside in the grey, snowy end of day. It had got a lot colder that afternoon.

'Mel?' the barmaid, Alysha, responded to Jackie's question. 'I know her.'

'She's a policewoman,' Jackie added.

'I know. I know her. What about her?'

'Well, we were in here, together, last Thursday night. That band was on, er...'

'Storm Petrel. The Gastric Band I call 'em. Can't swallow too much of their music. Like ancient, yeah? But you were all in here, in force, that night.'

Jackie understood that the barmaid was referring to the group's fan base. It was the lesbian following that attracted her. She was with this girl on the sad brand of music.

'I thought she was straight up,' Alysha continued. 'She went off with that guitarist.'

'Yeah,' Jackie smirked as best she could with the pain in her head. She was finding that just about every facial expression and neck movement pulled at the skin that stretched over the lump on the back of her skull. She had tried to give her hair a tidying up but only by dragging her fingers through it, avoiding the places where her scalp hurt like hell. 'They're the ones you got to watch.' A belch of gas and regurgitated spirit came up her gullet.

'O, right. Swinging like a pendulum.'

'Hopefully.' She tried to act a smile but bile burned the back of her mouth.

'So what d'you want? She won't be in tonight I shouldn't think.'

Jackie had worked on some words. 'Well, we had a good long chat, didn't we, and I promised I get something for her. I said I'd bring it here next Thursday but I've managed to get hold of it now. I thought I'd call in on her at home and...surprise her with it.'

Alysha was staring at her, not warming to the story yet. This dyke in front of her looked as rough as old boots. 'What is it?'

'This mate of mine works in Ann Summers. I was telling Mel about these machines she can get hold off. You know, definitely no man required...'

'O, I know.' Alysha's eyes glazed. 'I've seen them on the internet. You got one of those?'

'Yeah. In the car. Still in the box. But I don't know where she lives.'

'Phone her.'

'That won't be a surprise then, will it? I want to see the look on her face.'

'Aw, got you. Well I don't know exactly but it's definitely in Capelgwm. D'you know where that is?'

'Yeah.' She remembered it from last Friday night.

'It's not on the main road, it's opposite that pub that's closed. The road drops down. She's down there somewhere. You might have to ask.'

'I know her car.'

Jackie knocked back the last of the whisky and stood, wrestling with her balance.

'Is it still snowing out there?' Alysha asked. 'I need a smoke.'

*

Challis left her thick hair wet, teasing out the tangles down to shoulder length. As a young girl, it had reached below her shoulder blades in wave after wave of full-bodied lustre.

She shunned a bra as she often did at home and put on a light green nipple-suppressing weighty jumper that had a v-neck plunging down to just short of her wide cleavage. Looking at her top in the mirror she reiterated a long-standing promise that if she ever won the lottery – highly unlikely as she never did it – she knew the one thing, or things, she would want worked on. Envious of Kay. What did it matter now?

Light blue track suit trousers and light leather indoor boots rounded her off to her satisfaction. Her mother would have come out with the old adage about blue and green should never be seen. What a load of crap.

Hers was the one room in the house that was not her mother's. The furniture was all her choice. Stuart had once made the observation that it was far more girlie than he would have imagined. That was a description she didn't particularly like. If he'd said feminine that would have been more pleasing. It was an early indication that he had a mind full of female images and couldn't really see beyond their external attributes. Like most other men the physique of a woman was appreciated way before her intellectual muscle, which could become viewed by some males as a plus yet by others as an obstacle to be overcome or even ridiculed. She had learned to value men for their physical prowess when it suited her. To hell with their addled thought processes.

One thing her room had was a surfeit of mirrors, full-length many of them. Throughout her session on her hair in front of the dressing table mirror she tried to concentrate on her looks. But Kay Ruff had kept coming into her mind. As she repaired herself and then chose her clothes she knew Kay would never be going through these basic rituals again. The dead face of her colleague would not stop coming to her like some subliminal message; the hole in the temple, blackening, the leak of blood on her neck, all in stark detail and sharp focus.

She tried humming her way through it, picking any tune, new or old, real or imaginary. She had always done that in times of mental juggling, sounding, her mother used to say, like a frantic bumble bee stuck in a spider's web.

She had decided to forego makeup. It was Ray Lockett for God's sake. She just wanted to look tidy. One last once-over, in the long mirror on the middle panel of her built-in wardrobe. Looked okay. Whatever!

It was when she saw the reflection of her face against the reflected backdrop of her bed that the tears for Kay came again, this time in earnest. Weird the things that were uppermost in the mind at times like this, young Kay and Alex, lively in bed, no more.

She had no right to be so alive, tarting up. She had sent an unprepared Kay to her death, never mind what Lassman had said about her being headstrong and going off on a lone pursuit. Kay had been her responsibility but she had put her on the back-burner, all her efforts going into this exalted murder investigation, her head swayed by being privy to the innermost high-flying thinking in the Force and that bloody Lassman.

She flopped down on the end of the bed, head bowed, tissues out of reach on the bedside table. Sorry, sorry, sorry spewed from her lips. So sorry.

The sudden noise from downstairs shook her and halted her relentless slide into despair and pointless regrets.

It was startling. The sounds were of strident male voices and shrill female utterances of pain or pleasure. Her tears stopped. Moving quickly she grabbed a handful of tissues from the box and wiped her face clear of wetness.

It was the dvd she could hear. It had started up.

*

Superintendent Derek O'Halloran had parked his car in the small car-park that serviced the Capelgwm village hall. The dark grey snow-filled clouds had helped to expedite the closing of the day. The white precipitation made what daylight there was appear as if behind a veil. He knew he was faced with a walk of over a hundred metres to Challis's house but he thought it better to leave his car here on the top road rather than risk getting stuck lower down. The weather forecast that he had just heard said the snow could be in for the night on the Welsh Marches.

He had his top coat on already. The white flakes that had fallen on it outside Redland's house had metamorphosed to water droplets. His damp hat was on the passenger seat. His kid gloves, a present from his wife last Christmas, should have been on the seat with the hat. They were not there, or underneath it. He checked his coat pockets. Not there either. He'd had them at Redland's. That's where he must have left them. He cursed. That was a bad mistake. He'd have to go back. Later.

He didn't know quite what to expect at Challis's. He knew what he wanted to find but there was no guarantee. This might be a complete wild goose chase. Plan B was already in his head: it had been a horrendous day for Challis, she had suffered events that demanded that, as her superior, he rise from his sickbed to come forward and offer her comfort and support.

Plan A, however, would be his preferred course of action but one where the reaction could not be anticipated with any certainty. Backup precautions were necessary.

He reached across to the glove compartment. In there, on top of the car manual and service record book lay the Smith & Wesson 38 snub-nosed revolver that he had confiscated on a job some years ago. He withdrew it, studying it as best he could in the dullness of the vehicle's interior. He had never used it in anger, He had never used it at all but he liked the feel of it in his hand as his fingers moved from the wooden grip to squeeze the chamber. He slipped it into his right-hand pocket.

It was cold outside in the hush of snow. He cursed mislaying his gloves and had to put his hands in his pockets. Strangely, the gun felt warm. The single overhead streetlight cast a pallid glow through the swirling snowflakes and with careful steps testing the ground he crossed the main road and headed for the side road to Challis's.

*

Despite the sound emanating from the TV O'Halloran heard Challis moving to the landing and then coming down the stairs. He turned to greet her.

'Hello, Sergeant, or should I say in the circumstances, Melanie.' He smiled. Challis stood open-mouthed in the doorway. 'I must say I'm surprised, Melanie. I fully expected you to be inconsolable with grief but what do I find?' He had the remote in his hand and he gesticulated with it towards the screen. 'Been upstairs? I can understand that. The early scenes are quite stimulating. Couldn't resist, eh? Obviously not. I can see you're quite flushed.'

She was, from the crying, but now she flushed even more as she understood his insinuations.

He smiled again, perhaps he hadn't even stopped, and she hated men who smiled without baring any teeth.

'Sir! What are you doing here?' She'd left the door on the latch for Ray. How on earth could she have expected someone like O'Halloran to just walk in.

'And another thing. A sergeant of police and you leave your front door unlocked. You should know better, Melanie.'

A Plan C was formulating. He had not expected to find the door unlocked. The lights were on throughout the house, like a beacon in the increasing blizzard conditions. The house almost invited direct access and knocking had not occurred to him at all. Then to walk into an empty lounge, hearing Challis upstairs and find on the floor near the TV a familiar dvd case bearing the 'Co♀Co' tab was an unbelievable piece of good fortune. The dvd player and TV were on standby. He switched them both on and immediately recognized the point at which the viewing had been interrupted. Stuart Devlin's master-class. Only too well, from past experience, he understood the potency of what was on show. It had been his point of no return on a couple of occasions.

He was seeing Challis not so much in a new light but as a realization of what he had been led to believe, led to believe by Stuart Devlin. Seeing her former lover in close-up action had proved a real turn-on for her; that was obvious. Her face was getting redder by the second and he knew where the heat was coming from. It didn't matter to him what she looked like; he knew from Stuart what she was capable of.

Challis could tell what his mind was thinking. He was in her house, just walked in and had homed in on the dvd. She kept her eyes off the screen, the alternative being she keep her eyes on him. The grunts and panting protestations from the TV made clarity of thought a difficult thing. The sounds she recognized were coming from Stuart and were more and more urgent, attracting O'Halloran's gaze as he watched, eyes wider and wider.

'This is Stuart's big finale. Look.' He turned up the volume.

With his back turned to her she found the scene was a magnet and she witnessed with some disgust Stuart's extremely vociferous climactic moment.

'I bet that brings back memories for you.'

O'Halloran clearly knew about her and Stuart. How? She couldn't imagine. He knew his way around this dvd too. How?

She was becoming increasingly uncomfortable at the senior officer's increasing familiarity but they both watched on as Stuart collapsed out of the shot, replaced by the long-awaited second masked man. She studied the mystery figure as best she could, raising her gaze to catch a glimpse of the red hair below the mask before O'Halloran switched off the picture.

'That's enough of that,' he said quickly, his face suddenly unsmiling and pensive as if waiting for some reaction from Challis. She was confused by this loss of composure, but only for a minute. His manner implied insecurity.

'I need to see the rest,' she said calmly. 'Switch it back on.'

'No. That's enough.' He moved to the dvd player and removed the disc, placed it in the case which he waved at her. 'I only came to reclaim my property.'

'Sir!' She was genuinely shocked. What did he mean by his property? 'That's evidence.'

'Then what's it doing here, Sergeant? You removed it from a crime scene.'

'I needed to view it. All of it.'

'Do you have the envelope?'

'What?' She knew what he was asking for but why on earth would he want it?

'Where's the envelope?'

'There was no envelope.' She knew she had to tell a lie, again.

'So where did you find the disc?'

'It was in his dvd player.'

'That's a lie, Sergeant.' He was adamant and yes it was another lie but how did he know that?

Muench! *He* had checked the empty dvd player. He must have passed on every bit of information to O'Halloran which explained why he was suddenly all over this case.

Why was it so important to O'Halloran? Why is the disc his property? This is going beyond the professional. This is personal. Why?

But of course she knew why.

Red!

'You're the second masked man, aren't you? That wasn't red hair, it was your red mark.'

He was so pre-occupied deciding how to respond to this bit of deduction and she so uplifted by the same thing that neither of them heard the front door open and click shut.

'Thanks, Mel.' It was the voice of Jackie Davrot that shattered their silence.

They spun round to face the Browning she was pointing at O'Halloran.

'Got you, you bastard.'

*

Driving into the blizzard had compounded Jackie's increasing difficulty with her sight. The car was hot, like a sauna. There was a wet film over her eyes and blink as she might it would not clear. She nearly missed the right-hand turn at Capelgwm.

From the top of the road, lights on full beam, she could see houses on either side of the narrowing road. Alice in the Eastgate had not known which one she was after so Jackie had no choice but to put the Suzuki in low gear and drift down the snow-covered slope. The windscreen wipers were on high-speed to keep her vision as clear as possible. She had to resort to wiping her eyes in an attempt to clear her sight even more. It didn't help. Made things worse.

She reached the dip in the road and as she began the ascent up the other side she spotted Challis's car on the left. Her headlights dimmed leaving only sidelights on as she let the car glide under its own momentum until it ground to a halt at the edge of the drive of Daubwthyn Cottage. With the engine off she left the wipers running. So this was Mel's place. Not bad for a single woman.

Her bag had little in it but it was too heavy for her to lift, the strain on the shoulder muscles sending a spasm of pain to the back of her head. She only needed the gun, for what it was worth.

She stepped out, her feet crunching snow. The car door clicked closed as she carefully avoided slamming it. The gun was in her hand as, feebly, she set off up the short slope of the drive towards the front door. She realized she would have to rush it as soon as Mel opened it.

Mel's car blocked the centre of the drive and as Jackie tried to sidle around it her feet went from under her, sliding backwards, leaving her crashing face down. The gun crushed her fingers against the concrete but she managed to avoid hitting her head which was spinning in any case. She clawed at Mel's car for a hand-hold and finally stood, leaning against it, eyelids shut tight, breathing rapidly, waiting for the pain in her neck and shoulders to subside. Her head was throbbing more than ever. She swallowed back the whisky rising from her stomach.

She pushed off from the car and edged slowly to the porch and out of the snow. Before approaching nearer to the door she took deep breaths and had just about summoned up the strength to advance when she heard an ear-shattering sound from inside the building. She knew it. She recognized it. Mel was playing the dvd. In spite of her scrambled brain she thought a whole string of expletives to describe what Mel was apparently doing. It was Maggie Mack all over again.

*

'Red-haired be fucked,' she uttered coarsely, eyes on O'Halloran. 'You're fucking deformed.' She spoke to Challis with a half-laugh. 'I came here to force it out of you, who this bastard was, but you just went and announced it for me.'

O'Halloran froze. He didn't know this tramp of a woman but he knew who she was. She sounded drunk. And the Browning complete with silencer looked familiar. It should. It had been another one in his confiscation collection, the one he had loaned to Stuart Devlin.

Challis was the first to speak. 'Jackie, put the gun down.'

'D'you know,' said Jackie wearily, 'I knew one of you was going to say that.'

'Then do it,' Challis insisted.

'Don't be silly, Mel. You don't think I've come here to turn myself in, do you? Aren't you going to introduce us before I cut his balls off.'

O'Halloran saw the darkness in her deep brown eyes set in a ghostly face. There was hate there.

Mel saw something else. Jackie was a mess. She noticed that the girl appeared purposeful but although upright her weight was leaning on the door jamb. Her face was pallid but covered in beads of sweat. There was also what looked like blood on the legs of her jeans.

'Young lady,' he began nervously.

'Don't fucking call me young lady.' The gun twitched in her hand. 'I'm not any man's young lady. Christ, it's hot in here. Why are all your fucking houses so fucking hot?'

She loosened her top coat. It flopped open revealing she had nothing on up top except a black bra. Challis could see red staining on her bare midriff, lots more on her denim-covered belly. It was blood.

'Okay, okay. Just take it easy,' O'Halloran bleated, taken aback by the state of the girl.

'Jackie, are you okay?' Challis wanted to close in on her but was halted by a jerk of the gun.

'I'm fine.'

'There's blood.'

'It's not mine. Put the disc back in,' she ordered O'Halloran.

'What?'

'Put the fucking disc back in and play it from where you stopped it. I heard Devlin's scream of ecstasy now I want to see how you perform. Not that good if I remember it. What say you, Mel?'

Challis was thinking was it Stuart Devlin's blood? 'I've not seen it,' she muttered.

'Liar.'

'I've not seen it after Stuart's...I wanted to but...'

'O, he was shy was he? Put it on, whatever your name is. I know you're a copper but I'm still surprised, Mel, that you choose to entertain a shit-brain like him. Put the fucking disc in. Mel, you can drive the remote.'

At last O'Halloran followed her orders. He inserted the disc and Mel hit 'Play', turning the volume down. She wanted to talk to Jackie.

'Christ,' exclaimed Jackie, edging further into the room. 'It really is you. We'll find out for sure in a minute. Mel, where's your cuffs? Come on, I know you've got some. You used them on Chas the other day.'

'I'm not playing these games, Jackie. You've hurt enough people today. You killed my young friend in cold blood.'

'Yeah. Sorry about that one. I can't think what she did. I've been trying to remember. It should have been you, Mel. Who's Alex? She said Alex.' Briefly, she seemed to enter a dream state.

'You've hurt people today, you hurt people before today. Why? Why this crazy frenzy?'

She woke again. 'They killed Angel.'

'Angel?'

'And the ones that didn't kill her, like him, just stood and watched and wanked. That's why! I promised her. If she died then so would they...or worse. Get your cuffs.'

'Mrs. Mack had nothing to do with this. You shot her for no good reason.' She was trying to divert Jackie from her intentions, whatever they were. Nothing pleasant that was for sure. Something nasty for O'Halloran was in the girl's mind.

'She was watching this,' Jackie almost screamed. 'She was getting off on watching this. I told you about her, the crazy bitch, Maggie Mack. Remember? Liked screwing girls but liked being screwed by men? That was her. She was getting off on Angel's pain, like him. Now get your cuffs.'

The gun was on Challis now and as it swung in her direction Jackie staggered, thrown off balance by her own sudden movement.

'Jackie you're not well,' Challis spoke quietly.

'Just get the fucking cuffs.' She seemed to have barely enough strength to speak.

Now O'Halloran noticed her weakening but his advance towards her was enough to jerk the gun back up.

So many next steps were racing in Jackie's mind: get him cuffed, get him stripped, get a knife, cut his balls off, what about Mel? where would she be through all this? what will I do with her? She shook her head to re-sort the jumble of next steps but again the pain came, this time shooting down her neck, through her spine and into her belly. She began to retch. She saw O'Halloran coming toward her. She aimed the gun, heard Mel shout 'No' as she pulled the trigger.

Click. Click, click, click.

Of course! O, shit, it was empty.

She flung the useless weapon at O'Halloran who ducked but not enough, the gun glancing off his scalp.

The effort of the throw was too much, her legs gave way as more pain hit her entire torso and she fell to her knees.

Challis began to move forward, intent on preventing the girl falling completely to the floor. But O'Halloran reached her first. His left hand caught her right shoulder and while he supported her his other hand brought the Smith & Wesson 38 out of his pocket. Challis's mouth dropped wide open as she saw what it was in his hand. She stopped in her tracks as, almost in slow motion, she watched the Superintendent raise the snub-nosed barrel to Jackie's temple and fire one shot into her troubled brain.

The 38 was a powerful round, belying the small gun that fired it. The bullet came out of her skull on the left side, scattering blood, tissue and bone fragments all over Challis's mother's off-white carpet before burying itself somewhere in the mortar in the old stone walls. Jackie slumped, falling to her left in the same direction as the bullet, arms at her side, she hit the carpet.

O'Halloran lifted his head, not smiling but relieved. Behind Challis came the sound of the red-necked masked man achieving his own relief. O'Halloran smiled now in appreciation of the two satisfactory climaxes.

He walked up to the stunned Challis and yanked the remote from her hand, switched off the dvd and put the disc in its case again. It was almost as if the last few minutes had not existed for him. He was back in exactly the same position he had been when Jackie's voice had announced her arrival. The big difference now was he was holding a gun. The fact that Jackie Davrot was lying prone, bleeding, was to him completely by-the-by.

'What the fuck have you done, you mad piece of shit.'

Challis's anger was total. She had knelt by the body while O'Halloran was fiddling with the dvd. Like Kay, Jackie's eyes were open and like Kay she had a clean hole in the right temple. All the blood was escaping from the gaping exit on the other side of her head. For a second, as she pointlessly searched for a pulse in the neck, she saw a similarity between the two: size, shape, facial features; it was just a matter of colouring.

'Remember who you're talking to, Sergeant.' He had crossed to the window, bent and picked up the thrown Browning. It went straight in his pocket.

She rose to her feet. 'Fuck that! You shot her down. She was helpless. Unarmed.'

He blew through his nostrils. 'Only just.'

She was as angry now as she had been finding Kay and yet lying beneath her was the person who had caused that earlier bloodbath. But this shooting was as cold-blooded and not just that, it had been carried out by a police superintendent, a top officer of the law. Somehow she was able to grade the two deaths. Kay had been killed by a demented young woman, deranged even. Terrible, terrible, yes. But this was on a different scale, more terrifying.

'You seem have forgotten already, Sergeant. She killed your fucking friend. You just reminded her of that fact minutes ago. She executed your fucking friend!' He was genuinely furious. 'She shot and killed an unarmed police officer. *One of us.* One of your colleagues. Your closest colleague.' He was suddenly calm. 'This is what happened. She came here to confess and shot herself. Once this weapon is cleaned and put in her hands, end of story. Case solved. All down to you, Sergeant.'

She didn't recognise this man. The redness of his chameleon neck was brightening, his face too assuming the hue and even his piggy eyes as far as she could tell looked blood red.

He was right, on so many counts, but even so...

'No. I have to take you in, for murder.'

He sighed.

'I don't think you've ever fully understood what this job is really all about, Mel.' He sounded mournful as if he was sad for her. 'We catch bad people. We lock up bad people. And if we can't lock them up then we sometimes have to find other ways of removing them. Putting them somewhere they can no longer harm the good people. That girl was trash. A positive danger to the public. A positive danger to me personally. For whatever twisted reason her warped mind made her believe she was engaged in a legitimate blood feud.' He laughed. 'Look what she did to poor Stuart and all because she had the hots for a tart who loved it rough. Now how warped is that? And don't forget I outrank you by some distance.'

'Not in this house you don't. You broke in...'

'The door was...'

'You broke in, uninvited.'

'And what did I find? You, in a state of undress, wallowing in the licentious delights of pornography. And don't tell me you weren't excited by it. It's easy to tell that a woman has just pleasured herself.'

She was seething, as much a result of his mind-reading as by his smug smirking expression. The boss had been right, so too Lassman, and Jackie; he was a shit-faced dickhead. With this realization, any guilt she may have harboured faded to zero.

'Stuart was always very forthcoming about the things you enjoyed doing,' he went on. 'But I can keep his secrets secret; I can keep your secrets secret.' He paused. 'I could even help you to relive some of those...'

'In your fucking dreams,' she immediately protested. 'Who the hell do you think you are?' She was pacing now. It had been coming to this all along. She had seen the long slow build up, for days now. He knew, that fucking Lord Cottel knew. She wouldn't mind betting Muench and everyone else in the county knew about her and Stuart.

The word that Kay had used in the car the other day, the day she'd been upset – no, tamping mad – the word she'd used to describe Muench, that c-word, leapt to the forefront of her mind, a label to stick on Stuart

Devlin. It's rarity in her vocabulary made it forceful, made Devlin sickeningly unique. How long had he been slagging her off to all and sundry? She would never have done that to him.

O'Halloran shrugged his acceptance of the snap decision from Miss High-and-Mighty. He could work on her later.

She was livid, with all fucking men, but made herself return to this creep's clear wrong-doing. She homed in on him. 'I've seen what you did and how it got Jackie fired up. Her friend…'

'The dvd? Don't be pathetic. Nothing illegal there. It wasn't really rape you do realize. Everyone was performing the role that best suited them, including the tart. She was really up for it. Okay, two of the guys shall we say overacted a bit, got carried away, got really carried away when they saw through my mask and thought they could blackmail me. Don't know which one of them it was, may have been both. My money was on Peter Mack but the two of them were sorted, just to be on the safe side. That silly bitch,' he pointed at Jackie, 'got this idea in her warped mind that it was pure revenge for what happened to her beloved Angel but then she wanted to go a bit too far and punish everyone who had been there.' He watched her taking it all in and then smiled that tight-lipped smile again, dismissive over his confession. There was no culpability. There was just his continued survival. 'Anyway, I believe you once enjoyed a bit of restraint.'

Gloating, he watched her as she bit her lip, her fury towards Stuart Devlin made her wish she could have been the one to shoot his balls off.

'You can't possibly hope to keep out of all this.'

'With your help I can,' O'Halloran continued slowly. He was studying her face; she knew he was and she knew why. 'I've explained how this can all be explained, haven't I?'

He had, and he wanted her approval. He had brought her into his confidence, there could be no ifs or buts. It was brutally clear what she would be covering up.

'You obviously tried to round up all dvd evidence and all the computers at Cottel Court but you failed. There's a stack of them at the Davrot's house.'

'Not too worried. Dvds don't give much away. The mask, remember? Yours was a lucky guess. And anyway, evidence sometimes has a way of getting mislaid.'

His conspiracy plans were getting deeper and deeper but he still needed her compliance, her co-operation.

'But the way you just executed…her.'

That observation was crucial to her decision making, if she had even considered coming down on his side.

She could see that, if she chose to, she could corroborate his story but she knew that there was a distinct possibility, no probability, that a little way down the line when the investigation was put to bed and he was in the clear, he would have no qualms about organizing her own demise, some accident, some random killing. All loose ends neatly tied off.

'Put her down would be more accurate,' he quipped, 'like you would a sick, dumb animal. Tidying up the old loose ends.' There it was; he said it. 'But no different to what you'd probably like to do to good old blabbermouth Stuart right now.'

He smiled at her again and she hated him for reading her mind again. What she couldn't know was that he regarded Stuart Devlin as another loose end.

'Okay. Don't be a silly girl. Go and put the kettle on while I tidy up.' He grinned. 'You know it makes sense.'

'No...sir!' She was scornful of his soft tongue. There was no way she could acquiesce. She was about to repeat her defiance but she had a horrible feeling that words would not be enough. She would have to tackle him. Her cuffs, demanded earlier by Jackie, along with her preferred old-fashioned truncheon, were in her bag which was near the front door where she had dropped it. He had the only gun, which he was fingering thoughtfully.

'O dear, Mel. Think about it. If you were to collar me what do you think I would do? I would accuse you of pursuing me vindictively. I would get Stuart to confirm his stories of you, all the intimate details. Your painted picture would be black right through. You'd end up with more motive than me, I can assure you.'

He paused to let his argument sink in.

The implications were obvious but, in the great world of rights and wrongs, to paraphrase Humphrey Bogart in Casablanca, one of her favourite old movies, she knew they did not amount to a hill of beans in this crazy situation.

Kay, I'm sorry, but your killer has just been murdered.

'Derek O'Halloran, I'm arresting you...'

'You really are reducing my options.' Now he was shouting. She knew he didn't have that many choices. His viperous tongue had failed to sting her into submission.

'...for the murder of Jackie Davrot...'

His 38 was no longer dangling by his side. It was slowly elevating. Her eyes dropped to follow it as she continued her speech.

'...You do not have to say anything but it may harm your defence...'

'It pains me to even think this but there's only one solution.' He stepped closer. 'Miss Davrot shot you before killing herself. From about here I think.'

'…if you do not mention, when questioned, something which you later rely on in court. Anything you do say may be given in evidence. Do you understand?'

'O yes, I do.' He understood what he had to do and her script had come to an end. 'Sadly,' he concluded, 'you'll be no great loss, not to the police service anyway…'

O'Halloran aimed at Challis's heart. She held her breath as she stepped forward; a move too late, she knew.

Fifty-Seven

While positioned outside the boss's house DC Ray Lockett had kept the engine running and the interior of his unmarked pool BMW warm. The last hour had dragged and snow had fallen more heavily. He knew Mel lived only three miles or so outside of Usk but he was seriously contemplating calling her to cancel his visit: the last thing he wanted to do. He had spoken to Harry Muench earlier and his colleague had been less than sympathetic towards Mel.

Lockett was thinking of her as Mel. Harry had referred to her as "she" this and "she" that. Lockett didn't approve. He knew that Mel had been close to Kay, closer to Kay than to himself and definitely closer than to Harry. Her body language in that direction had been only too easy to read. There was no love lost there.

Harry had seemed gutted about Kay and his description of what he had found in the boss's house made Lockett think sooner him than me. But Mel had seen all that as well, a double whammy for her today. He stopped himself from implying she was weaker just because she was a woman. For all Harry's bravado he suspected that Mel had faced up to it better and the stronger.

She probably wouldn't have liked anyone suggesting a weakness because of her gender but he had noticed that since the boss had been laid up she had lost some of the swagger that she seemed to go with being "the inspector's sergeant" and had looked distinctly vulnerable. Probably Harry had spotted the same thing and she would hate that because Harry would recognise an opportunity to exploit.

Lockett had often thought that the boss was a bit of a father figure for Mel. She had no parents, killed some years before; he knew that. He'd heard rumours in the post-work bars that she hated men, that there had been some revelations about her father after he died that had fueled her anti-male feelings. Except towards the boss. Harry had made a point more than once that Mel preferred the company of Kay although without explicit speculation as to her leanings, hence his recent conclusion that she was a loner in more ways than one.

But she had said his name twice when he'd called her and he'd heard a sob or two and then she'd invited him up to her place. Thoughts of her and the day's cataclysmic events had shifted Timothy Bush's daughter Jennifer Wheeler from the position of prominence in his brain every morning, noon and night for the last four days. He considered he was in that old-fashioned state called besotted, with her and what she was. Boring duties such as the one he was currently lumbered with were normally an ideal environment for fantasies to ferment – Harry Muench had once told him that normal healthy males think about sex every few seconds; women not far behind.

But the last hour had been all Mel and in no way could his thoughts be construed as fantasy. He was concerned. The word "bonding" flickered but that didn't have the appropriate ring to it. Deep down he knew what he really envisaged: support, mutual, in a time of shared grief.

The wipers were on intermittent swipe, clearing two arcs of windscreen, one minute encased in snow, the next allowing a view ahead of large flakes falling, of headlights and red rear fog lights of vehicles slowly passing by, of the odd pedestrian bare head down trudging to the Spar for supplies that might be unreachable next morning.

Once, he had had to wind down the passenger window as Jared Edwards came out to demand to know what was going on next door and how much longer police vehicles would be parked outside his driveway. The glass dropping down had allowed a slab of snow to fall onto the seat. He'd brushed it to the floor where it now lay as a pool of water.

He had thought long and hard about Mel's advice to log the coming and going of the Super. Not so much advice, he reflected, more like "you'd better do it". But the Super had ordered him not to. Why had he done that? What's to hide? He had a terrible feeling he would get his arse kicked but he logged it anyway. He could always delete it if he woke up in a sweat about it in the night.

Just after five his relief turned up. Two of them. Uniformed. While the handover went on in Lockett's car there were now two police vehicles outside Jared Edwards' driveway, a fact that was recorded by the man and his camera from his window.

'Have a good night,' Lockett offered the officer who stepped out into the dark evening feeling the damp patch on his legs.

Lockett logged their time of arrival.

There was a case update on the system: the fugitive Jacqueline Davrot was now believed to be driving a Suzuki Grand Vitara, registration number six, nine, Lima, Delta, Charlie, stolen from Cottel Court around four. Christ, she was changing cars like she was changing shoes.

He continued looking down at his smartphone. Should he call Mel and cancel, weather too bad? Or should he log the fact that he was going to consult with her about the case?

Neither.

He'd make the visit. It was private.

The road to Capelgwm was just as he had imagined it. The gritting lorries had not been up there so the snow lay thick, obscuring any road markings. The road was a good two-vehicle carriageway under normal circumstances but snow had a narrowing effect. Vehicles progressed gingerly, unsure if there was room to pass.

It was slow going. Lockett had only gone two miles when he first thought of turning around. He came to a halt where the road split into three choices. He knew he had to bear right towards Capelgwm. He also knew that the road would climb and there would be bends to contend with.

It was still a toss-up what he would do when a tractor went past him and on up the road he needed to take. Its large rear wheels cut a nice flat track in the snow. It was enough to persuade Lockett to use those tyre marks and carry on.

The tractor turned off the main road at the point where Capelgwm could be seen in the valley below. Lockett saw his destination and ploughed on, in a low gear, slowly down the shallow hill. He thought he would never get back up this way or in the opposite direction. Capelgwm nestled low, hills on every route out of there. He could see he'd have to stay the night, if she didn't object.

He dropped down Mel's road easily enough and pulled to the left in front of her house. There were two cars. He could just make out Mel's Citroen partly hidden by a Suzuki, a Suzuki Grand Vitara, licence number 69 LDC.

He had no idea what this meant. What was Jacqueline Davrot doing here?

His first thought was for Mel. He retrieved the side-handled baton and was about to leap from the car when caution stopped him. He grabbed his smartphone and called in the sighting and then had to wait while instructions from on high were fed back to him. *Armed backup being dispatched, the weather conditions may cause delay in reaching you. Stay put and observe. Keep this call open.*

After the conversation he quickly realized he could observe little from where he was; snow on the windows obliterated the view. He got out and moved closer to the house, edging around the Suzuki and then Mel's Citroen. The baton clunked on the Citroen's bodywork as he slipped sidewards. He halted. It was awkward; baton in one hand, smartphone in the other.

He just regained his balance when he heard the shot from inside the house. It was definitely a shot, a loud one, certainly no party popper.

He cursed under his breath.

He called in. He had to wave the phone around to try and get a good signal. He cursed again as he had to retrace his steps nearer to his own car where the signal had been okay. He got through. 'Gun shot heard from within the house. I repeat, gun shot heard.'

'Hold your position,' came the reply.

'Where's the backup?'

There was a hesitation. 'Backup is on the way.'

'Where is it?' he asked again, enunciating each word carefully.

'ETA twenty minutes.'

'Twenty minutes! I can't wait that long.' He looked around at the scattering of other houses. This was rural. Someone was bound to have a shotgun. The only house with a light on was some fifty yards away. He headed off in that direction and got halfway when the lights ahead of him went out.

He looked back at Mel's house. The main curtains were not drawn. Net ones were up. From his new standpoint he thought he could make out a shape, perhaps two, inside, moving about.

Mel had said she'd leave the door on the latch.

He made a decision. 'I can't wait that long,' he yelled into his phone. 'I'm going in.'

'Your orders are to…' He lowered the phone, leaving the connection open. It went in his pocket. He may need both hands on the baton.

It was ridiculous. He wanted to sprint the last few yards to the front door but he had to walk with tiny steps and even then he slipped back every other stride.

Reaching the porch took longer than he expected; too long. He heard a shout from within. It sounded like a man's voice. Taking a deep breath he grabbed the door handle. The door opened easily; it had never occurred to him that it might not. He grabbed the baton in both hands and kicked the door wide against the wall.

Fifty-Eight

The crash of the front door was like a bomb going off. Both Challis and O'Halloran jumped out of their skins.

O'Halloran's back was to the noise and with the first tremor of shock he spun round. Challis had been expecting to hear the report of O'Halloran's gun going off, if that was something you could actually do when shot from close range, and for a second she thought that was what she had heard. She recoiled but then saw Lockett in the doorway, gripping the baton across his chest, tension written all over his face, eyes darting.

The gun in O'Halloran's hand had moved off its target, now pointing somewhere above her right shoulder. He was looking the other way, at Lockett. Challis knew immediately that two of them were now in danger.

She projected herself forward, thankful she had already advanced on O'Halloran, and grabbed his arm in a standard disarming move. She pushed it up then took it down and behind his back, putting numbing pressure on his shoulder. His grip loosened and the gun was flung across the room to end up less than a foot from Jackie Davrot's face.

Challis kicked the back of O'Halloran's knees causing them to buckle and force him down in a kneeling position, all the time keeping the painful lock on his arm.

Lockett was paralyzed by what he was seeing. Mel had the Super in an arm lock!

Despite the pain he was in O'Halloran spoke first. 'Lockett, get her off me.'

'Ray, get your cuffs out,' Challis hissed through teeth clenched as she strained to keep a tight grip of O'Halloran's arm. 'Get over here.'

Lockett didn't move. He had now realized that there was the body of a woman under his feet, a hole in her head and blood everywhere. O'Halloran, raising his head enough to look at Lockett, saw what had caught his attention.

'She shot her, Lockett.'

'Ray, he had the gun, you saw that.'

O'Halloran was keeping all options open; working on Lockett while wrestling with Challis's grip on his hand and arm.

'She tried to kill me. I managed to get the gun off her.'

Challis's hands were aching. 'Ray, please get over here with the cuffs.'

'Get the gun, Ray,' O'Halloran pleaded, using the first name. 'Before she does.'

'Don't touch it, Ray. It's not my gun. It's O'Halloran's. There will only be his fingerprints on it.'

Lockett took a step around Jackie Davrot so that he was standing over the gun. He looked at the two struggling figures. What the fuck was going on? He could not work it out.

'Just calm down,' was his advice.

'Ray!' Challis screamed. 'Just throw the cuffs to me.' Her grip was slipping. O'Halloran may be a much older person but he was strong. She'd just seen him on screen, stripped, and his body was in good shape. 'Now Ray!' she shouted.

Lockett made no move and for one awful moment Challis thought he might be another Harry Muench; an O'Halloran man. That frightening thought eroded her resolve, only momentarily, but enough for O'Halloran to break free. He went one way and she stumbled the other. But instead of getting to his feet and assuming some semblance of authority he scuttled on all-fours across the carpet, homing in on the gun.

Lockett's size nine shoe came down smartly on the 38. O'Halloran reached him and tried to lever his foot away.

'That's evidence, sir. Like the sergeant said.' He then saw that it had dawned on O'Halloran that a further assault higher up his body was his only hope of shifting him away from the gun. His hands stretched up and began to seek a handhold on his clothing.

'This is all very undignified, sir. Will you stop please?'

But O'Halloran didn't stop until Lockett brought the baton down sharply on his hands. As O'Halloran withdrew in pain Lockett passed his handcuffs to Challis who was on her feet, right behind the Superintendent.

Fifty-Nine

Lockett called Control. They thought he was chasing the backup, which was still twenty minutes away. The weather was closing in.

It took them a while to comprehend what it was he was trying to tell them.

He told them that Jacqueline Davrot was dead. He told them that Detective Sergeant Challis from whose house he was speaking had arrested Superintendent O'Halloran for the murder of Jacqueline Davrot. He further told them that the armed response unit was no longer required but some sort of rescue was necessary.

He was told to hold for further instructions.

O'Halloran, hands secured behind his back, was seated on one of the three settees in Challis's lounge room. He was still wearing his topcoat and was complaining about over-heating.

Challis had left Lockett standing behind O'Halloran, baton at the ready. She held herself back from wrapping her arms around Lockett but her hand stayed extra-long gripping his shoulder, more than once.

O'Halloran showed few signs of "coming quietly". In her absence he continued to put the case to Lockett that Challis was the culprit and not himself. He became more agitated and tried to rise to his feet more than once but each time he got a sharp tap on his collar-bone from Lockett's baton.

Lockett was in no doubt who was the most likely guilty party and O'Halloran's status was dwindling in significance.

Upstairs, in her bedroom, Challis had got dressed and was looking for the envelope in which O'Halloran had expressed an interest. She remembered carrying it in her hand when she was talking to Lockett on her smartphone. It took a while but she found it in the waste bin in her bathroom. It was screwed up. She flattened it out. It was plainly addressed to Alan Redland and was a recorded delivery. She put her hand inside, not expecting anything to be in there but her fingers pulled out a piece of paper. It was a Cottel Court delivery note for the supply of one dvd, described, for delivery to Mr. Alan Redland, purchased by...Mr. Derek O'Halloran.

She was amazed, not by the presence of the document but by the apparent cool efficiency of the Cottel Court administration systems. That would be down to the fine work of Meredith Guster, she grudgingly supposed. A complete surprise that the dozy woman could accomplish anything like that.

Lockett had a call from an incredulous DCC Alice Jones, asking for confirmation of his status update. Her concern was such that she totally ignored Lockett's earlier expressed opinion that the armed response unit was no longer required and ordered all units to make best possible time to Capelgwm.

Nothing was said by her to Lockett other than to give him ten minutes ETA and she turned down his offer for her to speak with Challis. The information coming out of that place certainly made extreme caution advisable. It was bordering on the unbelievable, if not totally bizarre. She would not believe anything until she had seen it with her own eyes. Challis had been under increasing pressure throughout the day; she could have cracked, misread signs, jumped to conclusions. She knew nothing about Lockett, how independent he might be or how easily influenced. He sounded okay on the phone, level-headed, clear in answering her questions but there was a hint in his voice that he was in the deepest water ever, perhaps out of his depth.

'Is this the envelope you were asking about?'

Challis thrust it under O'Halloran's nose and then waved the delivery note at him before bringing it up to her face and reading its details.

'A present for the boss?' She rubbed it in as she saw he was struggling to talk his way out of this one. 'Ties you to the dvd,' she added.

'Proves very little', he said, trying to dumb down any possible significance.

'Proves your link to Cottel Court. Proves your perverted interest in the content of the dvd. Proves you were one of those taking part in the dvd.'

'It does not.'

'O I think it does. You know how good digital enhancement of images is these days. It'll recognise your red mark peeking out. And then of course there is the fact that you are totally naked. Every mole and blemish plain for all to see. And that's before they even look at enlarging the interesting bits of your anatomy.'

'Sergeant, you should know that any such intimate investigation breeches my human rights and I think this lack of respect will come back to haunt you.'

We'll see, she thought. 'Bullshit, on all counts. I should remind you you are still under caution but what I would like to know is why you had this sent to the boss, to DI Redland?'

'Thank you for reminding me. No comment.'

'You're a fucking disgrace.'

'Aren't we all a bit shameful?' he smoothly accused.

She passed the envelope and delivery note to Lockett. 'Bag these too.'

The items joined the two guns and the dvd in his growing collection.

'Can't we cover up the girl?' he asked. 'It's her eyes, they're everywhere.'

The answer was a firm negative. 'The integrity of the scene must be preserved,' Challis reminded him in words that sounded overly formal. O'Halloran scoffed loudly, attracting Lockett's attention but Challis was unmoved.

Her quiet resolve and clear-mindedness startled her a little. She couldn't believe the transition she had gone through in what was just a little over an hour. The longer this waiting for backup to arrive went on the more she enjoyed seeing O'Halloran squirm. He had tried various manoeuvres: demanding the toilet – she had sent Lockett with him, handcuffs to remain on - demands for drinks – a glass of water with a straw. But he became to her just another criminal. She had nervously noticed that Lockett had had difficulty seeing things in the same light at first. But not now. His courage and belief in her were impressive.

There had been times these last few days when the job had lost her, left her floundering. But now, seeing how the mighty could be of less worth than herself she no longer felt inferior. He was an evil bastard, in every sense. And what did he think he held over her? Only what that other bastard Stuart Devlin had told him, that was all, and she had no idea what that might have been, how much based on reality, how much based on how much Stuart wanted to degrade her and elevate himself. Men's recollections of their sexual feats often made for great works of fantasy fiction. No reason now why these male myths should reduce her stature. With bravado, if she could muster it, she could bask in the notoriety. Unlike O'Halloran she certainly couldn't get locked up for it.

A quick check out of the window revealed no let-up in the snow. The tracks made by Lockett's vehicle, the last one down the slope, were obliterated.

It was a beautiful scene out there. Snowy stillness, large flakes feathering through the air: *Old mother Rees is plucking her geese*, as Gran used to say. The little cluster of houses silent. Everything white and pure.

Snowed in!

No, please God sweet Jesus not tonight.

She turned back to the unrecognizable state of her house interior. It gave a whole new meaning to bringing your work home with you.

Come on, come on, she demanded of the night outside, where the hell are you? I need to get this filth out of here. I'll go find a tractor to get him shifted if I have to!

Sixty

By the end of March, Spring had sprung. The snow was long gone but the cold persisted for weeks. Challis's mother's daffodils missed St. David's Day. They were in bud in the garden but reluctant to bloom. Forsythia was yellow, snowdrops were white but other plant life like primroses, fritillaries, sloes and plums were hesitant. The garden was nice to look at but she had neither time nor inclination for it. She had a man come in once a month but she could manage to mow the lawns, front and back, in the summer. Redland badgered her to adopt his garden design and "concrete the bloody lot."

She'd had a call from him. It embarrassed her somewhat. He had been out of hospital this time for nearly three weeks and she had only been to see him the once, the second day he was home and that was brief.

He said he wanted to see her. She said she would pop in over the weekend. That was the best she could do.

*

Work had been surreal, like nothing ever before. Straightforward in some senses though.

There had been enough DNA found on Jackie Davrot's clothes, skin and fingernails to prove beyond doubt her guilt in the five shootings of that Monday. Fingerprints on computer hardware retrieved from the Davrot house and other forensic evidence made Jackie the killer of the Macks and Chas of George Medlyn. Lassman returned from whence he had come but he went unsatisfied. He had not found his killer. The killer had been found for him.

The Davrot case was shocking enough though there was some semantic debate as to whether Jacqueline Davrot was a serial killer, spree killer or a mass murderer. But nothing had really calmed down from the major earthquakes of mid-February.

The old Redland team was a team no more. No Redland for one thing. Only Lockett was still working with her. Muench had moved on to bigger and better things. After that mad Monday when Jackie Davrot went on the rampage he had returned to the Valleys case and two days later had been instrumental in cornering the shooter, a man who had been made redundant by Caerphilly County Borough Council and had decided to go berserk with a shotgun. The two women he'd shot were council employees who had kept their jobs.

Muench had confronted the man who had been run to ground in the Sirhowy Valley Country Park. Muench may have been unarmed but the squad of men with him were not and it was lucky that they shot the man down just as he was leveling his own gun at Muench. But his bravery was noted, his stupidity ignored, and he became a more permanent member of DCI Harriet Moray's homicide team; foisted onto her. Challis dropped all thoughts of confronting Muench about his tip-offs to O'Halloran. Give him enough time, she thought, he can't help himself. He'll go that bridge too far one day.

She and Lockett appeared to have been sidelined. Generally speaking they were boycotted by just about everyone. Few new cases came their way and those they got were of a trivial nature.

O'Halloran was vociferous in protesting both his innocence and the connivance, conspiracy even, of the two junior officers both of whom could not believe he was allowed out on police bail the day after he was arrested by Challis. A theory put forward by Chief Superintendent Harper was that O'Halloran had acted in self-defence. It became well-known that it was from Harper that the unofficial directive to send Challis and Lockett to Coventry originated.

Almost immediately O'Halloran was re-arrested at the behest of DCC Alice Jones. She had been first on scene at Challis's house and had made absolutely certain that all of the evidence was collected, collated and uncontaminated. Forensic tests, done not by Sayer but in Cardiff, proved beyond doubt that Challis's story of events was correct. O'Halloran was charged and remanded in custody.

Then Challis and Lockett, especially Challis, had to run the gauntlet imposed by those who saw them as turncoats, shopping one of their own. The content of Challis's report in which she detailed O'Halloran's suggestion that Jackie Davrot's execution, and she used that word, be turned into suicide, became widely known. Many said in private huddles that an execution was justified, the dead woman had killed a copper, and that Challis should have gone along with the story. They speculated why she hadn't. They concluded that she and Jackie Davrot were more than the mere acquaintances that Challis had alluded to in her report. Challis was now the latest office dyke and there was plenty of graffiti to back it up. Also intimate details of her past liaison with Stuart Devlin became common knowledge. O'Halloran had kept his word.

Lockett struggled to balance it all in his mind but he came to the simple decision that two wrongs would not have made a right. It was wrong that Kay had been shot down by Davrot but it was worse that O'Halloran had carried out the same cold-blooded act mainly, it became obvious, to cover up other equally serious prior transgressions.

And those transgressions attracted a longer and longer list of charges against O'Halloran: the murder of Jackie Davrot; theft of evidence – another three firearms appropriated over the years from previous cases of his had been found in his home; supply of firearms for criminal purposes and even conspiring in the murders of George Medlyn, Peter and Maggie Mack and indirectly contributing to the death of DC Kay Ruff.

When this last item joined the list, the tide of opinion against Challis was turned, not by all, but by an increasing number. And whereas it had seemed that Challis's only backers were DCC Alice Jones and DCI Harriet Moray others gradually came to her, many finding the easy opener of condolences for Kay Ruff.

The funeral of DC Kay Ruff was a big affair. Her small valley town closed for the day; its entire population on the streets. Everyone was there, except Redland who was still in hospital. The media was out in force and there were speeches and quotes from the high and the mighty. Alex avoided them all, moving away in a cocoon of protective friends and relatives as soon as anyone in a uniform came anywhere near.

She was buried on Alex's hillside in Alex's town. It was a freezing cold day. A heavy fog lay across the valley; you couldn't see the other side but it was a nice spot. Challis could not believe there were no pesto-vegie sandwiches at the wake but this thought made her chest heave and forced her to slip away early.

A week later, Challis got up enough courage to call Alex, to see how he was and enquire about buying Kay's car. Alex told her to piss off as soon as she announced herself; didn't want any more to do with her. She had been prepared to tell him that his name had been the last thing on Kay's lips - that's what Jackie Davrot had said. But she had to listen to him rant on, blaming her, blaming the Force, blaming the job and came to the conclusion that telling him of Kay's last words would be of no comfort whatsoever.

*

She parked on Saturday morning outside Redland's house. His car was in his driveway. Her eyebrows raised as she spotted it had a new registration plate.

'How could you get yourself a number plate like that?' she scolded him on the doorstep.

'I didn't,' he was firm and not amused. 'You know what I think of them but they got it for me. They decided a bike was no good now as a parting gift so they got me that instead. They even sorted out the DVLA and sneaked in and fitted it when I wasn't looking.'

'Well,' Challis tried not to smile, 'if you ever get demented and can't find your way home everyone'll know you come from USK.'

'It's not funny. You know my views on these personalized number plates. Only marginally better than all those Chelsea tractors in every other driveway.'

'Come on, you old poser. Cheer up. It could have been worse. What if they'd got you X CID?'

'I prefer former CID.'

'I told you you would. Do they have a little club, all those U S K number platers? Dinner dances? Rallies across the Brecon Beacons?'

He turned his back, leaving the door for her to close. The super warmth in the house hit her.

'Hey, new carpet I see.' Her coat was unbuttoned already. 'And your sofa's gone.'

'Hardly surprising I would have thought.'

'Correct but you could have waited. My mother's carpet's gone too. We could have got a good deal on two.'

He pointed at an armchair for her to sit in.

'Actually,' she continued, 'I'm not having a new carpet. There's a great flagstone floor and I've covered most of it with rugs, multi-coloured rugs. You must come and see. What was your insurance company like? Mine was a bit awkward. They couldn't see it as accidental damage, we had to go down the criminal damage route in the end. I've got a spare settee if you'd like one. Three's too many. I'm getting rid of one.'

'Your mum must be spinning.'

'Yeah, well...' Some of these changes had been forced on her but now she'd started she could see more ahead. Redland had never heard Challis talk about household furnishings and other decoration topics. She seemed to be a bit hyper.

'I've just made coffee,' he said, 'but I don't think you need any.' He eyeballed her.

'Sorry.' She drew in breath. 'How are you anyway?'

'Okay, they say. More pills. Final medical next month then definitely out to pasture. You've had a rough time, I've heard. Harriet Moray's been by. She thinks a lot of you.'

Challis was unresponsive.

'Thanks for coming,' he went on. 'I'm not allowed to drive yet. I wanted to see you, about Kay.'

She was surprised and showed it.

'I wish I could have been at the funeral. Saw bits on TV and in the papers. I don't know but...That last case she was on, before the suicide of...'

'Timothy Bush.'

'Yes, and then my first...attack. I saw her in Usk that last morning...'

Again Challis was interested.

'...at the surgery. I'd been in for an early morning depressing chat with Dr. Supergloat and Kay was just going in.'

Challis nodded as she remembered the appointment to discuss Timothy Bush.

'I asked her about that other case, the hotel at Raglan, told her the owner was a friend. It had been shelved, of course.'

From the coffee table he picked up a thin buff folder and passed it to Challis.

'Sorted,' he said.

The folder contained one sheet of A4 paper. She looked up at Redland.

'I did it...' he stumbled over his words. 'I wanted her last case to be...sorted.'

He left the room. Challis watched him go and then could hear cups being moved in the kitchen.

She took off her top-coat before speed-reading the one-page report.

...Stake out...

Redland did a stake out?

Thefts were not of money but of stock...A barman...also worked one day a week stocking the bar...Part of the job was to take empty bottles to the recycling yard that was right next to the lock-up where wines and spirits were stored. As he took out full bottles to replenish the bar he took out extra ones that he hid among the empties. Then, at night, he'd park his car in that same yard and when he finished his shift at midnight he simply moved the full bottles from their hiding place and into the boot of his car...The owner...decided to sack the man and not pursue the matter further.

At the bottom he had dated it mid-February and put Kay's name on it. The sight of the late DC's name on a report should have got her eyes wet but she couldn't see the point of any of it. It had been a nothing case, one which would never have got their attention again. Why had he bothered?

She got up and walked with the folder into the kitchen.

'This is…good,' she said walking towards him and she didn't stop until her lips were on his cheek. This reaction by Challis was unexpected and unnecessary and so un-Challis-like. He could read her mind and was immediately defensive.

'Coffee?' He didn't know why he'd bothered. Over-sentimental. He put it down to his condition.

'I thought I wasn't to have any.'

He tried to smile. 'You've calmed down a bit now.'

They went back into the lounge. 'He must have been doing it for months,' Redland said, deciding to add some justification.

'What, the barman?'

He nodded as they both sat in armchairs that seemed too far away from each other.

'So, when you getting your DI?'

'What, you mean a new you?'

'No. I mean your promotion.'

Her face brightened. 'No chance. I'm transferring, to Newport. Next month. East Road nick.'

His eyebrow twitched. 'My dad was reprimanded there once.' The memory amused him. 'He was ten, caught writing dirty notes and shoving them through old ladies' letter boxes.'

He studied her face. 'It'll come, Mel. Soon, I reckon. You did a great job.'

'More luck than management.' She remembered what Lassman had said about luck but no way was she about to give that arsehole the credit for anything. 'I've heard people going on about coincidences and when you look at things closely that's about all it is. No deductive reasoning just reacting to things that fall in your lap. If you don't get the lucky breaks you don't seem to get anywhere.'

'You will if you chisel away at the different layers of evidence.'

They both sipped their coffees, she more than him.

'It's like archaeology,' he said, out of the blue as far as she could tell. 'You know I'm into archaeology. I'm actually hoping to get up to the 'lost city of Trellech' and do some work up there. Have you heard about it?'

She shook her head.

He copied her head movement. 'I sometimes worry about you,' he said with feeling, 'a supposed native of this county but surprisingly ignorant about its places and history. You didn't know about Cottel Court and you've never heard of Trellech.'

She searched his face to understand how serious he was being. It looked as if he was deeply frustrated by her alleged shortcomings. She could easily retaliate, she knew that. Not everyone could know everything. Depends what turns you on.

'I know Trellech,' she stated. 'I've been through Trellech. Small village. Huge church.'

His face lightened. He had immediately regretted how niggled he had been by her lack of knowledge.

'That's right,' he was upbeat, in reparation mode, 'that's the place. Well, up at Trellech, a medieval village, town really, not really a city though, being unearthed. You should go see. Anyway, what I was trying to say was that digging up the past is like digging up evidence in a case. You've got to know when to stop using the mechanical digger and use the spade. Then you've got to know when to stop using the spade and use a trowel. It can even come down to fingertips. It's the same in our work, well, your work, not mine anymore. There are always layers going from the obvious to the obscure. Takes time and a lot of careful digging.' He knew his initial petulance had spoilt his analogy.

'Not in that last case.' She was subdued, thinking about it. She couldn't put her finger on it or explain the nasty taste she'd had in her mouth since…since when? Since finding Timothy Bush, she supposed.

Well, there was a lot she could put her finger on. Kay was one thing. Easy. Stuart another. And Jackie Davrot. She just wouldn't go away.

*

The Davrot's short service at the Crematorium had been poorly attended. There didn't seem to be any family. Somewhere, there was a wife of Chas and mother of Jackie but she never showed. Jenkins the Builder was there. She saw his truck in the car park. He was out of his overalls but not in a suit. She was surprised to see him. Couldn't think why he was there. The investigation into the death of Angela Plumitis had included a statement from him, how he thought he'd known the girl, and her mother, years ago, but had been mistaken. But now he was at the Crematorium, for Chas and Jackie. Curious. There had been one hymn, well, *Morning Has Broken*. No idea who chose it. No eulogies. No potted history of life. And then, one after the other, the two coffins had glided away on the conveyor belt and through the curtained door, Chas first, Jackie second. Challis had felt full up for her and she couldn't put her finger on that either!

She was disturbed by the fact that, to put it mildly, the Davrot pair were clearly disturbed. How did they get that way? What was the history? How different and deviant was it? A sickness or a genetic predilection? Jackie so young and female. A unique combination for the crimes committed.

'Sergeant Challis.' The door of her Citroen was open and she was about to get in when the female voice behind her made her turn. The Afro-Caribbean woman approaching her was shorter despite the heeled knee-length boots she was wearing. The fur-edged jacket was open but she was sweatered underneath. A brown leather bag, more like a satchel, swung from her shoulder. She was not chubby but not under nourished.

'Amelia Griffiths. We've spoken on the phone.' She thrust out her right-hand that held her business card but Challis only had eyes for the woman's eyes. It would have been more correct to say that Amelia Griffiths, freelance journalist, had done all the speaking.

Challis made a move to sit down behind the wheel. She expected this woman to pick up where she'd left off and ask about Timothy Bush and Cottel Court.

'I'd like to talk with you, Sergeant, about this case, or cases, that you've been working on. The O'Halloran case. Please, my card.'

Challis snatched it. 'There have been press conferences. You should have attended.' The key went in the ignition. The card got a quick glance before being dumped on the dashboard.

'I have. All of them. But you weren't at any of them. You've had the hardest time of all it seems to me, Melanie. I'd like to hear your side.'

The engine came to life. Challis hated this woman's assumption that familiarity would get her anywhere.

'Look Miss, Mrs, Ms Griffiths, speak to the press office.' She pulled the door towards closed.

'I spoke with Stuart Devlin. In hospital. Poor man. He was only too glad to be interviewed.'

Challis hesitated, trying to look unmoved.

'Stuart...Mr. Devlin...spoke highly of you. Said you go way back.'

A bitter taste curdled on her tongue making her unable to speak.

'I'd also like to know your take on Jacqueline Davrot.' Amelia Griffiths was talking fast, searching for a keyword that would grab Challis's attention. 'Complex character. You knew her, I gather. And her father.'

'I dare say it'll all come out at the coroner's inquest.'

'I doubt that. She's dead, they're both dead. They killed. Nobody cares.'

Probably accurate, Challis thought.

'You'll only get the superficial,' the journalist continued, spotting some hesitancy. 'You care. You want to know.'

It had crossed the detective's mind more than once that the "Davrot Condition" would eventually be written up by some academic. Perhaps this high-speed journalist would be the first one to probe and dissect.

'All anyone wants to know about is O'Halloran,' Griffiths went on. 'I want to know about your part and Jacqueline Davrot's part in his downfall.'

The door slammed.

Impotently Amelia Griffiths shouted an entreaty to call her but the revved up engine and rattling spray of gravel left her words in the cool late afternoon air.

*

She decided to speak what had been on her mind. She was calmer now, as Redland had observed. What she was about to say had made her anxious about this visit.

'You know you can pick up your property when you want to. It's finished with now. It was that that got me transferred. Promotion prospects suspended, like I could have been. Got a severe knuckle rapping instead; removing evidence from a crime scene. O'Halloran got me there, the bastard.'

His lips had been on the cup, preparing to drink. He paused but then went ahead with a long slurp. 'No thanks. They can keep it.'

'I know you never actually opened the dvd case, only the envelope. I asked O'Halloran why he'd had it sent to you but he clammed up.'

She was uncomfortable; his eyes were weighing her up.

He needed to know that he knew her well enough to talk about subjects never even hinted at between them before. He didn't know whether to be cruel or kind. You could find yourself in that position with someone you had known for years, where your relationship had been professional and where trivia and innuendo when slipped into a conversation had always been tempered with the tenor of professionalism, within acceptable bounds, tolerably risqué.

He could have confessed to her that, the day before his heart attack, O'Halloran had let him know in no uncertain terms what Stuart Devlin had told him of the relationship he'd enjoyed with his sergeant six years ago, details that had absorbed and repulsed him as O'Halloran had recounted them with undisguised relish.

But to tell her all that would be cruel, too cruel.

'It's not only the likes of my nephew who have thoughts, desires,' he said with a twist of bitterness. He didn't want to see her in a different light but too many things were out in the open now. 'Look, don't be smug. You get to a certain age and you wouldn't mind having someone around, for all kinds of things, but you're too old, you couldn't be bothered to train somebody up. And I'm not being sexist. It would be the same for you if you're still single at my age and you want a man about the house. You just couldn't be arsed.' He was dead serious. There was clearly a sad belief there. 'O'Halloran…was trying to initiate me if you like. I know that sounds absurd for a man of my age. And anyway I didn't need it. He was always on about it, him and his excursions. Perhaps he thought it would cheer me up. Odd.' He ventured a smile that was wasted on Challis's stony face.

The silence that came then went on so they drank their coffee. There was nothing about Redland's hypothesis that she found uplifting. There were times when you didn't want to realize that a person you'd respected might have feet of clay. You knew nobody was perfect but it was like the first knowing that your parents must have had sex but you would like to believe it was just the once, to create you. As for his assessment of what advancing years promised that was his opinion, not hers.

Challis's cup emptied first.

'I keep seeing him,' she muttered, 'in my house, with his gun at Jackie Davrot's head and then her brains all over my carpet, my mother's…my carpet. I hope they give him life and it means what it says on the tin. I really do. I had him hog-tied, waiting an age for the cavalry to arrive. If Ray hadn't been there I'd have done what little Jackie wanted to do and cut his balls off.'

Redland listened to her, hearing the hatred she had for O'Halloran and sensing the empathy she seemed to have for Jackie Davrot.

Surely not. He mulled it over in another bout of silence.

'How's Stuart?' she asked and he could see how she had leapt to that topic. It had become apparent to everyone that O'Halloran and Stuart Devlin had a long association but it rankled him again, opened up a scabby wound. He had been made privy to the many details that those two men had shared, had wallowed in, about Challis.

'He's…not bad.' He did not want to talk about his nephew. He hated him. She had asked though, about her former fuck buddy, that picture-painting phrase that O'Halloran had repeatedly used as he had described their antics. Since that time it was the only way his brain would allow him to think of the relationship between her and his nephew. 'They managed to save his… his left testicle they think.' He homed in with some malice on the injuries that he thought would be of most concern to her. 'It had retreated up into his groin they fancy. Haven't seen him. Don't know where he is. You lot probably do. Is he in custody?'

Challis took the information in her stride, with amusement. Stuart! Still able to fire on one cylinder. Wonder if Sue's pleased.

'Not sure. He should be, procuring the gun, perhaps accessory, conspiracy. Not my department, as they say. Look, I have to go.' She had an appointment, to find out what Devlin had said to that reporter.

At the front door Redland helped her on with her coat, sad to see her leave, not giving in to the urge to embrace her. She had to turn to face him to see if they were now as they had been before. She couldn't tell.

'Right, Mr. USK-man,' she smiled at his car. 'See you. Look after yourself.'

'Don't forget this.' He gave her his one page report. She took it and planted more kisses, one on each cheek this time. The single sheet of paper represented not only Kay's last case but his as well. Perhaps that was why he'd bothered.

Jared Edwards seemed to be lying in wait for her. He leapt out in full view on his side of the dividing fence. 'It's no better you know,' he started. His red folder was in his hand. 'Look at these photos, just the last month.'

'Ah, Mr. Edwards. I'm not on that anymore. I suggest you contact this officer.' She took out a notebook, scribbled and handed him the torn out page. 'And don't take no for an answer.'

'O, okay.' He read the paper. 'How d'you say this name?'

'Muench. Harry Muench.'

A smile that refreshed them both passed between her and Redland. God, he was going to miss being with her every day.

Sixty-One

There was an eulogy at Timothy Bush's funeral. Barbara Jeffery gave it, part poetry, part prose. It was quite moving, Lockett thought, in a sickly kind of way; very little history of the life of the deceased, more a series of statements about his loss to Miss Jeffery and, by implication, his workmates.

Like the Davrot's it was a simple ceremony at the Crematorium. Many of his TorfGov Software colleagues were there. They sat near the front, with Miss Jeffery appearing to be the chief mourner. James Wheeler sat at the back, Lockett one side of him, an animated Farmer John Gee the other. Gee and Wheeler seemed to have much to say to each other. To Lockett's disappointment James's sister Jennifer was not present.

The service was quick. *Abide With Me* had been chosen by Miss Jeffery. There was no order of service for them to follow. Nobody had taken charge sufficiently to organize the usual protocol.

As they began to file out through the exit it became obvious to Lockett that James Wheeler was keeping up with him. They had spoken a greeting before the service had started - James surprising Lockett by saying he was going to live in his father's house as he'd got himself a job with the NHS in Newport - but had remained silent throughout, neither of them exactly singing out heartily for the hymn. Lockett thought he should offer a condolence.

'Yes, well,' James responded, 'I thought he got a better send-off than he deserved.'

'At least you came, to represent the family. Your sisters not...?'

'Jennifer? No. Elizabeth...not well enough.'

'O I'm sorry.' Lockett maintained eye contact as he wondered if he should ask more. James smiled broadly. He was enjoying Lockett's uncertainty.

Outside, there was a colonnade where mourners would mingle and chat to the bereaved. By the time the two men had shaken the vicar's hand everyone else had gone. Barbara Jeffery had hovered for a minute, thinking she should speak to James but had been whisked away by her manager, keen not to lose more office time. Farmer Gee had hurried off as soon as James had whispered that Lockett was a policeman.

The two men stepped out from the shade and into the sunshine, James taking a huge breath of the cool Spring air. They strolled toward their cars, coats unbuttoned, side by side, in silence. But James was waiting his moment and turned to Lockett as their feet crunched the gravel of the car park. His curvature of the torso angled his face even closer to Lockett's.

'We're a fucking dysfunctional family you see, but yes you probably do see. I'm surprised nobody from the police has come to discuss with us my late father's medical condition.'

Lockett could not help but react but then tried to hide it. 'I'm not sure...'

'He was HIV. It'll come out when the full inquest resumes.'

'You knew.' Lockett remembered the moral argument voiced with feeling by Kay Ruff, that the girls had a right to know.

'My sister Elizabeth has been HIV for a couple of years. She has good days and bad days. Today is a bad day but on the other hand a good day. The bastard is gone.'

Lockett was clearly at a loss.

'Our father had always been a bastard. Ask our mother and why she left him. Eighteen months ago we all discovered who he was and where he was.' He was watching Lockett's face. 'No, when I said I met him by chance when he came to where I work I was lying. I got myself into that demo. I had no right to be there really. Nothing to do with my area of expertise.'

He paused as he tried to decide where to start the longer story. He had rehearsed; he just had to gather his thoughts.

'My sisters have been sexually adventurous for a very long time. Sadly, that's how Elizabeth got infected. She had to curtail her...outings. But Jennifer carried on. Lovely girl, Jennifer. I know you thought so. You probably carried on thinking so even though you knew the kind of things she liked to engage in.'

Lockett coloured up. James smiled.

'Of course you did. Anyway, Jennifer came across father, quite literally, at Cottel Court, about a year ago. He didn't know her of course, except in the biblical sense and to be honest our Jennifer was sorely tempted by the thoughts of incest; always had been...when we were younger...you know.'

Lockett felt a distinct chill throughout his body as he quickly grasped James' drift. 'You and your sisters,' he couldn't help blurting out. 'That's...' There were just too many words damming his brain for him to get a single one out to express his disgust. Besides, bile was rising fast, staunching any verbal flow. James saw his struggle and simply smiled.

'She told us of this close encounter of the unholy kind,' he ploughed on with apparent relish. 'My two sisters hatched a plot and Elizabeth decided she would make a return specifically to go those...extra few inches.'

He paused to make sure it was sinking in. Lockett wanted to turn and run but was rooted, listening. This revelation was taking him down an ancient path long overgrown.

'She infected the old man. He found out he'd got it but didn't know the source and then Jennifer discovered that even though he knew he was still prepared to go partying on a regular basis. A real bastard, yes? God knows who he passed it on to. The girls took a highly moralistic stance fueled by their absolute hatred for the man. They booked another session at Cottel Court, at the end of January, aiming specifically to match with him. They did and they persuaded him to try something new, a bit of restraint. They stripped him and strapped him down. Then they told him who they were. Elizabeth told him what she'd given him and told him he had to stop putting it about. The bastard refused. Jennifer had sneaked in a cut-throat razor and threatened to cut his cock off. You wouldn't believe the vocabulary that can come out of that sweet mouth. She took a few chunks out of it before he swore he'd stop. You wouldn't want to meet her on a dark night, or perhaps you would.'

'She cut him?' Lockett managed to squeak.

'Yup. She said she dropped you a hint, at the morgue, when she was viewing her handiwork.'

He remembered but wanted to distance himself from thoughts of that girl. 'What were the emails about?' he asked, changing tack.

'Just to remind him about the girls and that I obviously knew.'

Lockett was taking deep breaths in pursuit of this train of thought 'But he couldn't live with himself, the fact that he'd...done what he did with his own daughters,' Lockett surmised, almost choking on the words. 'So he killed himself.'

'Hung himself from the gate at Cottel Court,' James seemed to speak from a script. '*The gate that leads to damnation is wide*'. Best place for him, we thought. Nice to talk with you, detective.'

'Wait a minute,' Lockett called, angry now. 'What do you mean, "we thought"?'

James shook his head. 'Shame that woman got him taken down and moved.'

He held out his hand but Lockett didn't see it. James turned his head on his stiff neck, got in his car and drove off leaving Lockett feeling he'd let something nasty slip through his fingers. This was the worst: the worst of the worst.

The car park was filling up with mourners for the next cremation. They brushed past Lockett who was standing fixed to the footpath, his eyes skyward on the smoking chimney of the Crematorium.

Kay's "ugly suicide" had just got much uglier.

Printed in Great Britain
by Amazon.co.uk, Ltd.,
Marston Gate.